World of

by

Tia'Leon Popham

CHAPTER ONE
GRACE

Three days, four nights.

That's how long we have been walking.

We have been lucky to have missed the sandstorms.

Neither of us are prepared to face a sandstorm, we need to reach Tinnstone before another one heads our way.

Sleeping on the sand has been the worst part, using our bags as pillows and our jackets as blankets.

During the long nights, the world is empty, and the moon is cold. Watching the sand blow along the ground is calming but I can't brush off the feeling that we are completely alone in a foreign territory. We have no idea where we are going or what we are doing, and it's terrifying.

I have to tie my jacket around my waist by the arms to save my strength. Carrying all of our items is hard work, adding things will only drag us down.

Myles ran out of water hours ago, and we are stuck in the middle of nowhere. No water in sight. I gave him my bottle, not that there is much in there. We don't have a lot of anything left. I don't think we can go much longer with the rate we are losing water and food.

I am holding the map, but I feel like I'm the reason we are getting lost. I've never learnt to navigate my way through a desert.

Being underground hasn't trained me for this.

The sun is burning my skin, heating up my blood. Sweat drips down my face, matching Myles' wet forehead. Even the wind is warm, a cold breeze seems rare around here. The suns bright rays feel like they're setting my body on fire, killing off the last of my energy. We didn't plan to take this long, we thought we would be near the next city by now.

Small, strange coloured bugs fly around us, but they don't seem to be harmful. They fly near our bags and try to land on our arms or shoulders, but they immediately bounce off us from the way we walk along the sand.

1

My clothes seem to be sticking to my body, hugging me tight as if they are about to fall off.

Rain, I am praying that the sky becomes cloudy and rain starts to cool down the air. I really want to feel the cold wind on my face, just one splash of rain is all I want.

"How much further?" Myles asks again. I've lost count of the amount of times he has asked me that question, today alone. "Are we even going in the right direction?" he stops walking to look around at our surroundings.

I don't know what he expects to find, there is no sight of anything other than sand and sky.

"I... I don't know—"

"You said that last time" he whines.

"Can you try and stay positive... please?" I can't deal with his complaining right now. Myles doesn't continue to walk like I expected him too. He stays in the same spot, turning his body around in every direction visibly possible. "What are you looking for?" I finally question his actions.

I stop walking, watching him huff and puff.

He pulls his bag off his back and throws it onto the sandy ground. "We're lost" he says, sitting down beside his bag and sighing. "It was supposed to take a couple of hours, maybe a day! We have been wandering around like lost puppies for the last three days"

"This is all new to me too! None of this is exactly straight forward" I'm trying to remember everything West had told me; point the map north by using the compass, read the contour lines, but after that is a blur. I think there was one or two more steps.

Five minutes pass of silence, Myles is running his hand through the sand, tracing outlines while I try to figure out the map. I must have gone wrong somewhere, I just don't know where. There is something wrong with the compass, it is turning in different directions, telling me north is in three different directions. This thing must be broke, it wasn't doing this when West was showing me.

"Sit down, it's no use" Myles grabs my hand.

"We can do this—"

"No, we can't" he shakes his head.

The sun is going to go down very soon, we need to keep moving. Training has given us the strength to keep walking and has prepared us for anything strange, but nothing has given us the knowledge to know what to do in a situation like this.

"We should go back" Myles takes me off guard.

I stare and stare and stare. My eyes narrow and my lips twitching. "What?" I almost whisper.

"I think this was a mistake. We're not ready for this... this world is not for us. We have no idea what we are doing and without Hun—"

"No" I cut him off, "My entire life, the only thing I have ever wanted is my freedom, and now I have that—"

He takes a small breath, gathering his thoughts before moving his hand in the air; gesturing to our surroundings. "This is not freedom, and this is not what we deserve" he adds to his previous words.

Something about what he says reminds me of something Hunter had said. *'You deserve someone who is going to love you with their whole heart. A guy who loves you for all of you, your perfections and your flaws'* the words replay in my mind like he was here in person, speaking to me.

"Are you listening to me?" Myles takes me away from my thoughts.

"Yes, sorry— yes, I am" I reply as I get to my feet. "We should keep going" I completely ignore our conversation and look towards the never-ending desert in front of us.

There must be more out there, the map says there are a load of other cities, so we just need to find them. No matter how long it takes or how far away it is. Giving up now would be a waste, like the last couple of weeks was for nothing.

"Grace, you're kidding yourself, we will die out here without the water and food" he says, laying his back against his bag.

"Please, Myles, just a little further" I beg.

A part of him is hesitant, but eventually, he stands up. I steady my feet on the sand as he uses up the last of my water.

We start walking up a large hill while the sun makes it way down to the edge of the world. I'm starting to feel like the nights are lasting longer than the days. "We're going to need to stop again soon" Myles breaks our silence, pointing to the moon behind us.

I nod my head, knowing he's right.

Let's just get over the hill, I keep telling myself.

A steady pace keeps us moving, quick steps push us to the top of the hill. It's taller than it looked, we can see almost everything from up here. The disappointing part of this whole thing is that even from up here, there is no sight of a city.

"It feels like we're walking around in circles" Myles says with a defeated tone. "Come on, let's get ready for night"

I don't say anything as I follow him down the other side of hill. I almost trip, nearly falling down the sand. When we reach the bottom, he places his bag on the sand and he lays his head on the softest part.

My bag drops to the sand, my body falling with it. I sit up beside Myles, my eyes watching the last of the heat bounce over the sandy hills.

"Lay down, you'll never get to sleep sitting up" he tries to encourage me.

"Give me a minute or two" I say before biting the inside of my cheek. The last thing I want to do is sleep. My mind is racing with different ideas of what to do tomorrow, different ways of getting us out of the sand.

"Don't be upset" he says in a soft voice, "You tried, that's more than what others can say"

I tried.

I succussed, is the only thing I want to be able to say.

"Yeah…" I sigh, pulling my knees up slightly to sit in a more comfortable position as he carefully throws his jacket on top of his body. "Goodnight" I whisper, knowing it won't take him long to fall asleep.

"Night" he replies.

While he drifts off to sleep, I sit and think, watching the sand dance in the light wind.

I made the decision to leave just after the war, I left everyone behind in a time of need. That is my only regret. It probably seemed selfish and it was the worst timing, but I saw my opportunity and I took it.

4

I hope West is okay, I hope Lucas and Elijah are getting along, and I hope Hunter isn't being too hard on everyone.

Carter is still on my mind. Wondering if he is still alive or if he is breathing his final breaths is a constant thought replaying on my mind. Wanting to know what he meant by his final words and needing to know who my father is will forever be stuck in the back of my brain.

There are too many unanswered questions.

As the night draws on, I become tired and my eyes slowly become heavy. I lie on my back with my bag as a pillow, staring up at the stars until my eyes close.

Tomorrow is a new day.

Tomorrow is a fresh start.

CHAPTER TWO
GRACE

Today the world has decided to test our limits.

The winds are heavier, the heatwaves are stronger, and the world seems quieter than before, if that's even possible.

But we have reached day four.

Myles has lost all hope at this point, not a single shred of faith is left in him. He keeps complaining about the heat and the waste of energy this is. He never shuts up about his bed and the times we spent in the dining hall with delicious food and drink. Being reminded every five seconds doesn't make this any easier.

"I'm even starting to miss West and Hunter—"

"How about we play the quiet game?" I suggest, more like insist.

He doesn't respond.

As we walk in silence, I start to look around, expecting a change. I feel stupid, like a fool expecting something to appear out of thin air like magic.

"Can I ask you something?" Myles turns his head to the side a little, looking at me in the corner of his eye. "Why didn't you tell me about your… you know"

He is choosing now to ask me this… I guess now is a better time since we have nothing to say to one another.

For some reason, someone was going to kill me. They had planned it for so long, I don't understand why they didn't just attempt to poison my food or suffocate me in my sleep. It never made sense to me, *why kill me when I turn eighteen if I show my ability?*

"I was scared" I try to explain without giving away too much. "The whole system was messed up. I got in trouble for uttering a word to a soldier, I decided it was better if I didn't talk for a—"

"So, what is your ability?" he interrupts my sentence to ask another question.

My mind becomes blank for a second. I'm not entirely sure what I can do. I can control objects; I think I caused the fire to spread around Carter. "I'm not sure" I say, honestly. My training

6

was short, and the battle was too fast for me to keep up with everything.

I don't know if I imagined half of it from the adrenaline.

"You can't—" he begins to speak but stops as an engine can be heard in the distance. We look around to find the source of the noise, but the noise soon fades into the air. Our surroundings become silent once again.

I turn to face Myles as he frantically looks for the engine that was making the noise. "That must mean we are getting close to something, right?" I question.

"Where did it come from?" Myles ignores my question.

"It could have come from anywhere" I reply, uncertain If the dehydration made us imagine it.

Another sound comes from the hills in front of us, and for a split second, I see the top of a car. My body starts to move before I realise, I'm walking. Myles follows beside me, catching up with my sudden fast pace.

In no time at all, I'm sprinting.

Desperation gets the better of me, dragging my body across the sandy terrain as if I was flying. The burn running up and down my legs is no match for my determination. The thought of finding people is beyond any feeling attempting to hold me back. This might be our one chance to find another city before completely losing ourselves in the desert again.

Running up the hill, I dig my shoes into the sand as a way to gather a better grip. Trying to run up a sandy hill doesn't seem to be the easiest thing to do. Every time my shoe makes contact with the sand, some of the sand slips down the hill.

I don't know how much more of this aimless wandering I can take with Myles.

The quicker I can find people, the quicker we can make our way to freedom. Hopefully, the person the engine sound belongs to can help us get back on track to Tinnstone.

"What do you think it is?" Myles shades his eyes from the sun and squints to try and get a look at the car.

"People" I say with a smile as the car comes into view.

The car comes and goes, vanishing on the hills horizon. It is a rusty car with an open back. Brown to match the colour of the sand, blending in with its surroundings. All the windows of the car are rolled down, the warm breeze blowing right the way through the vehicle.

"Keep up" I shout to Myles as he tries to stay as close to me as he can.

We reach the top of the hill. I spot the car doing donuts in the sand below. A blonde-haired girl is sat in the passenger seat, laughing with her hands in the air while another girl is driving the car.

I begin waving my arms in the air as I try to get the girls to notice us. "HEY, OVER HERE" I try to get their attention by shouting over the noise of the engine.

They don't hear me.

Of course they don't hear me.

I glance over to Myles in the corner of my eye and then make my way down the hill. We need to stay close to the car if we want to find the next city. Where there are people, there are buildings.

Thankfully, the girl driving soon spots us, eyes wide as they lock onto mine. I watch her turn the steering wheel, stop the car, and speak to the girl beside her. Shocked expressions stain both their faces when they get out of the car.

Myles and I stop walking as we eventually reach the bottom of the hill. The girls step away from the car, standing opposite us with their eyes burning holes into our faces.

There is a long silence between us all, none of us knowing what to say to one another. The deafening silence grows as the sand around us swirls across the floor. Heat rises up my arms and clams up my skin. The heat causes my cheeks to grow a rosy red colour along with my pale skin turning a bright hot red. In no time at all I can see my once pale skin turning into a sun kissed brown colour.

I part my lips to talk, hoping to break the uncomfortable and awkward silence between us all.

"Who are you?" one girl asks, beating me to it.

"How did you get out here?" the other asks.

Myles and I glance at each other, unsure what to say. When we don't answer them, the first girl steps closer to me. Her long black hair blows behind her shoulders, keeping out the way of her brown eyes. She raises her eyebrows, one holding a long slit in the centre of the brow.

8

"We asked you—"

"Grace Silver" my name slips through my lips.

"And him?" the girl gestures towards Myles.

Myles looks at the girl, staring at her brown eyes as if there was nothing else around him. "It's not your business, we are trying to find Tinnstone, do you know where it is?" he answers her question with another question.

"You're looking for ashes" the other girl laughs. Her long blonde hair moving with her head as she giggles. The brightness of her hair copies mine, but it's a little lighter, matching her light brown eyes. "That city was burnt to the ground months ago" she adds to her statement.

If Tinnstone burnt down months ago, why did Hunter send us on a wild goose chase? He would have clearly known about the city burning down, he could have told us the only thing we were going to find was a pile of dust! Why would he keep this sort of information to himself?

"Asha and I were going to head back soon, a sandstorm will be coming, and you don't want to be caught in it" the blonde girl smiles while the other girl, I'm guessing is called Asha, keeps her lips in a thin straight line.

"Shouldn't you clear this with destiny?" Asha frowns.

"It'll be fine" the blonde nods her head. "Unless… I mean, I don't want to cause an argument—"

"No. You are right; Destiny will be fine with it. Don't panic over this. Besides, we can't just leave them—"

Before Asha can finish her sentence, the blonde girl pulls her away from us. They talk in private, neither me nor Myles can hear a word they say. From the looks of it, neither one of the girls seem happy with what is being sad. The blonde girl crosses her arms and rolls her eyes, the other girl scoffs but that's all I can get from their conversation.

"I don't like them" Myles scowls.

"Give them a chance" I insist. "They are the first sign of life we have seen in days; don't you think it would be a good idea to tag along with them—"

I quickly stop talking as I notice them walking back over to us. "You can hop in the back, don't touch anything" Asha doesn't sound happy to be helping us out, raising her voice a little as she says the last part.

I look past her warning glares. No matter how mean she tries to appear to be, we don't want to be caught in whatever storm is heading our way.

And a ride is a ride after all.

"Thank you" I innocently smile.

I practically drag Myles over to the car. He can be so stubborn lately. He climbs into the back of the vehicle first; I follow behind him while the two girls return to their original seats at the front of the car.

No one says a word.

We all ride away from the sandy hills in silence. The only real sound that can be heard comes from the cars engine.

CHAPTER THREE
GRACE

RoseShire.

I expected a city. Large buildings with crazy monuments, or even just a wall surrounding it. This place, it is nothing like Hunter's city. The small village is in the middle of nothing, I could guess there is only thirty people living here.

We get close to the centre of the town. I can hear the busy streets, loud chatter of people. God, it's good to hear that sound again. Long, boring days of walking around in the sand has drained me; physically and emotionally. Myles didn't talk to me much, and when he did, the conversation was usually the same.

We both had enough of each other by the third day.

"Hide under the blanket" the blonde girl hints towards the thick green cover rolled up behind me.

Myles offers me a questionable side glance and then picks up the blanket. We lay on our stomachs and throw the cover over ourselves, leaning as close to the vehicles floor as possible. *This is weird.* I feel like we're playing hide and seek from when we were younger.

We hide for a while.

I wait for a sign or a word from the girls, but we never get one. Myles easily gets impatient, lifting his head every couple minute to take a short look at our new surroundings. He doesn't seem to trust these people. Neither do I, but they are the best chance we have. I don't feel like walking around in the sand again while there is a storm on its way.

Myles is driving me insane as it is, any longer and I may rip his head off.

The heat begins to rise up my body as the blanket absorbs the sun's rays. I'm melting. My forehead is releasing water that has now started running down to my chin, dripping onto the floor of the car under me. Each time Myles lifts the blanket off our heads, even if it's the tiniest amount, I take a long breath.

I shift, trying to find a more comfortable way to hide under the blanket.

Soon enough, we come to a stop. The engine of the car stops running and I'm left waiting for the signal to get up from the uncomfortable lying position I put myself in. Moving my legs one way and my body the other, I shift myself up onto my knees and then hurl my body over the back of the car. My shoes touch the hot sand once again.

The blanket falls to the floor where I had once laid.

"Stay behind me" one of the girls speaks up, but I don't catch which one says it.

Myles walks in front of me, making sure I'm protected. I smile discreetly as his shoulders tense. His hand slowly reaches behind his back, grabbing onto my hand. The touch alone gives me a sense of relief. For the first time in days, Myles seems like himself. I grip his hand a little tighter, wanting to hold onto his hand forever.

Walking behind the girls, I can't help but allow my eyes to wander around the new place, scooping out the new scenery around us.

Gold coloured paths and archways filled with yellow flowers surround us. The ground is made with sand and grey gravel, the buildings are made from brick, and the cars are camouflaged with their surroundings. Small bugs cling to the flowers, creating their own little homes inside the pistil of the yellow flowers.

This place feels like a golden utopia.

We walk away from the car, making our way through an open archway and taking steps down a staircase. The stairs are built between two buildings, brick walls enclosing the staircase from the rest of the village. I lean my spare hand against the brick wall as a way of steadying my balance.

Once we reach the end of the staircase, we step into a quiet street. The girls lead us over to one of the buildings a three second walk from the stairs. The building isn't big, but it seems large enough to fit a group of people for the night. It's brick walls match the rest of the buildings in the area. One window is built onto the front of the building, but there are curtains on the inside that prevent people from looking in.

"Shake your shoes before coming inside" the blonde girl insists as Asha unlocks the door to the building.

I nod my head and comply, forcing Myles to do the same.

Once we enter the building, the girls spread out into different parts of the room. The door closes behind me as I step inside. The room is open but small. It looks like a living room and a kitchen, both in one. "Please, make yourselves at home, but try not to break anything" the bubbly blonde-haired girl smiles at us.

"AJ are you here?" the dark-haired girl shouts down the hallway. "Nikita has brought some strangers—"

"They would have died in the sandstorm; would you like their lives to be on our hands?" Nikita frowns. Her blonde hair falls onto her shoulders as she turns her head in our direction with her frown swiftly fading into a smile. "I'm Nikita Williams, and that is Asha March" she introduces.

Asha doesn't appear friendly. The constant frown that is attached to her cheery red lips, the slit in her eyebrow, her light brown eyes always narrowing onto us every chance she gets. She doesn't scare me. Her pencil straight black hair falls down the side of her round head. Her sharp eyes compliment the brown nicely, along with her fare skin contrasting the darkness of her features. The only thing that scares me is the disgusted look on her face as she stares me down.

Nikita, on the other hand, has pale skin with long blonde hair and large, light green eyes. Her face is defined with thin eyebrows and a sharp jawline. She has a warm smile which reveals her purely white teeth. She isn't that much taller than me, her eyes almost being level with mine.

Someone walks into the room, entering through the hall with their head turning in every direction. "Who are these new people?" a girl announces herself by asking the obvious.

"Destiny" Nikita grins from ear to ear, running over to her and jumping into the girls' arms. "You told me, you would be gone for a couple days. When did you get back?" she asks.

The girl, they called Destiny, smiles from ear to ear when she sees Nikita. Her earth-coloured skin and sharp features make her light brown eyes pop. She has thick black hair which has been styled into dreadlocks running down from the top of her head and past her elbows.

The hug they share lasts seconds, but they both smile at one another like it was the longest couple of seconds of their entire lives. It's sweet. They pull away, both turning to face the rest of us. "The sandstorm is going to be a bad one, no one is going to be leaving for a while" Destiny explains.

"I guess we're stuck with you for a little longer" Nikita is still smiling.

I can feel Myles pull his hand away from me, using it to move his hair away from his eyes. "Can you tell me who these strangers are?" Destiny repeats her question.

"I am Grace Silver, and this is Myles Colorado. He is... my boyfriend" I gesture from myself to Myles as I talk. Destiny has her arms slowly crossing over her chest, scanning my face with her eyes. I can't decide whether she hates us, or she likes us, her face is too emotionless to tell.

"Destiny Kristian" she smiles at me, walking over to us with her arms open. She engulfs me in a hug, and then does the same to Myles. We are both shocked at the contact. Not many people hug someone when they first meet. "Where are you from?" she asks another question.

Looking from Destiny, who is now standing in front of me, to Myles, I wonder what I am supposed to say. Telling her where we originally come from, they might send us away. I don't want to say the wrong thing.

We need this to work.

Myles steps forward, catching Destiny's attention. "We found ourselves in Soltrix. From there we had to fight a war we knew nothing about, and then left, wandering through the hot desert until you found us" he surprises everyone, including me. I had no idea Hunter's city was called Soltrix. I have been calling it the silver city this entire time.

When my eyes look at the other girls' reactions, Asha is on her feet. She moves around the room, her eyes on Myles with a shimmer of hope. "You left Soltrix?" she seems shocked that we managed to leave the city. "You managed to walk out of Soltrix alive?" she expands her question.

"Does the Supreme know?" Destiny adds a question.

"Why does that matter?" I challenge her.

Giggling to herself, Nikita leans on the dining room table as her eyes remain on mine. "If he knows, then it causes more problems for you" she briefly answers me.

"What is she talking about?" Myles is concerned now.

"You, my friends, are walking targets" Destiny smirks.

My eyes lock onto Myles, as his does the same. The small silence grows larger between us all. I don't know what to say, and neither does Myles. A part of me is thankful when we can hear the main door open, taking the attention off us, even if it only lasts a second or two.

A man, not much taller than Lucas, walks into the silent room. I watch as he drops a bag onto the floor beside the front door, groaning while he swings his arm around to ease some tension from his shoulder. His other hand runs through his messy black hair as his sky-blue eyes glance over at Asha.

The man gradually looks around, mainly staring towards me and Myles. "I left for a minute, and I come back to two strangers in my living room, and a sandstorm about to hit us" he complains with his eyes landing back on Asha. "What's going on?"

"AJ, I can explain" Asha jumps from her spot.

The man, AJ, walks over to the kitchen. He grabs a bag of chips and rips the bag open. "This should be good" he grabs a handful of chips and proceeds to swiftly shove them into his mouth. He looks fed up.

"Nikita saw these people in the desert when we went for a drive. You know what she's like, she's weak. She convinced me to go over to them and bring them back here to keep them out of the storm" Asha rushes to her own defence, putting all the blame onto Nikita.

"It was more your idea than mine" Nikita argues from the other side of the room.

"Right" he nods his head with a mouth full of crisps.

Swallowing the rest of the food in his mouth, AJ looks to Asha. She places her hands on either side of his cheeks, pulling his head down to look her in the eyes. "Please don't be mad, they won't be here long" Asha begs.

He tries to stay strong, his eyes glaring down at her, but eventually he caves in. Carefully nodding his head, he tells her everything she wants to hear without saying a single word.

I feel Myles grab my hand, forcing my body closer to his as he steps forward. I'm standing slightly behind him now, my head poking out from the side. I look like I'm cowering away, which

15

is not the case. Myles is only trying to protect me, which is the only reason I allow him to position us in this way.

"We will stay until the storm passes, and then we are on our way out of here" Myles breaks the attention away from Asha and the new guy.

"Where are you going to go? Tinnstone is in ruins, you are walking into the desert blind" Asha turns her head to us with a frown. "You need a plan"

"Careful, your starting to sound like you care" Nikita has to hold back her laughter as she jokes.

"I don't want their lives on our hands. This is your fault, if you would just leave things alone, we wouldn't be in this sort of situation" Asha complains. "You should learn to leave things alone sometimes"

Nikita furrows her eyebrows.

Destiny clears her throat, concluding the conversation between Asha and Nikita. "Aside from things we can't change, what are we going to do with the outsiders?" she brings us all to the main question. "We don't have any room for them, we barely have enough room for the four of us" she states. She does have a point; this place isn't exactly big.

"Let them sleep on the floor, we have a spare blanket in our room" the man suggests.

"That could work" Destiny agrees.

Myles doesn't seem convinced that it's safe here, but we don't have much of a choice. If I remember anything from the many classes we had as kids, a sandstorm is too dangerous for us to be caught inside. Going out in a storm isn't smart, especially for our kind of people. We have never witnessed a storm before, we don't know what to do or what to expect.

Nikita moves over to the sofa, picking up two pillows and placing them on the floor beside each other. "These are comfy enough to sleep on" she faintly smiles.

"Thank you" I smile back at her.

"Don't thank them" Myles shakes his head.

Asha's jaw drops to the floor, turning her entire body in a harsh spin to face us. "Don't thank us? We are taking care of you when you don't know how to take care of yourselves, be grateful

I don't throw you into the storm and leave you there to die" she snaps at Myles.

I want to tell Myles to back down, but he will only get angrier. "We will stay out of your way" he mumbles, dragging me over to the sofa.

The four people we have just met are now making their way towards the hallway. None of them look happy to have us here, but I can't say I blame them. We are guests, we should be acting thankful and apologies for the inconvenience. We should not be shouting and causing more problems for them.

I don't know what Myles is thinking.

We need to be cosying up to these people to get as much information out of them as we can, not piss them off.

CHAPTER FOUR
GRACE

The lights are turned off. The window blinds are down, and the room is dark. The floor is all tiles. They are cold to the touch, and I am finding it hard to get comfortable. It reminds me of my room while growing up. The floor was always cold, and the bed was never comfortable.

I will never want to go back there.

Myles is stripping, slowly taking his shirt off in front of my eyes. It's nothing new. He had been walking around with his shirt off when we were in the desert, but now that we are under a roof and alone, it feels different.

Outside is howling. Screaming. The sounds of sand and twigs and wind. I can hear everything through the thin walls, I don't know how I'm going to sleep with the wind whistling in my ears all night. Nobody knows how long this sandstorm is going to last, which worries me even more. These people don't appear to like us, if the sandstorm lasts longer than a day or two, we are going to start having problems.

I'm worried, but all I'm focusing on right now is Myles as he reveals his abs to me. He turns around, forcing me to stare at his back as he places his folded shirt on the arm of the sofa, turning back to me straight after. "You're staring" he chuckles with his eyes scanning mine.

A small smile spreads across my lips. "I didn't realise" I innocently lie.

He carefully sits down beside me, pulling the baby blue blanket over his legs. He is leaving his trousers on, making sure he isn't naked encase someone walks in during the night. I'm thankful. I'm not used to sleeping this close to someone, him being naked would be a lot harder for me.

This is going to take some getting used to.

We get settled, sliding onto our backs as we pull the soft blanket over our bodies. I'm cold with my clothes on, Myles must be freezing with his shirt off. "Are you cold?" I ask him, wanting to have some sort of conversation. We haven't talked as much as I would have liked since we left Soltrix.

"I'm good" he cuts his answer short.

"Okay" I sigh.

"Are you okay?" he asks in a bored tone.

"I'm okay… are you—"

"I'm alright" he interrupts me before I can finish.

We find ourselves being consumed by the silence in the room. I want to talk. I've spent so many years staying quiet around Myles, but now that I can talk, he doesn't want too. I don't care what we talk about, even if it's the dumbest thing. I will take anything at this point.

The room lays still. Myles looks up at the ceiling, taking deep breaths. "What is the plan for tomorrow?" he sparks up a different conversation.

"It all depends on the storm" I can't predict when we will be able to leave this house. "The way they made it sound, we won't be leaving for a while" I admit.

Most of the buildings are little huts being held together by bricks, twigs and cement. It will be amazing to me if they are still standing after the sandstorm. They did not look strong enough to survive a storm. Luckily, this house seemed well-built compared to the others, or at least from what I saw. I didn't get a good look at the place from outside.

"I think we should head back" he admits.

"You want to go back to Soltrix..." it feels weird calling it anything other than the silver city.

"Where else are we going to go? Tinnstone is burnt to the ground according to Asha, and we have completely run out of resources. We are very short on options" Myles is giving up on our adventure. He shifts, turning his body on his side to face me. "We should go back… as much as you hate to admit it, Soltrix is our home"

"No" I shake my head.

Disbelief.

Denial.

Disgust. That place was not my home, and it never will be my home. Home is where you feel safe. Home is the place you go when you've had a bad day, a place you want to run to at your

19

darkest moments. Home is not four walls and a roof, but maybe a person or a thing.

Soltrix is not my home. I don't feel safe there, nor will I ever. Spending so much time in that building, I've learnt that if I want something, I have to get it myself. The only person I can depend on, is myself. The whole place is corrupted by a man who is trying to destroy it. The Supreme is looking out for himself, which is something I should have known sooner. More people would have survived if I had seen the signs earlier.

Even if I try my best to deny it…

A part of me didn't want to leave, but it was the best thing for me to do.

"Grace" Myles speaks my name. It used to sound like a melody, but all I can hear now is anger. "We are going to die out here if we don't come up with some sort of a plan" he has a look in his eyes.

A look of worry.

"Myles, I'm not going back" I assure him.

I won't go back.

Now, he is sitting up, staring down at me as my eyes stay glued to his. "Why not?" he whines.

"We have spent years trapped underground. Our entire lives stuck within a system that had done nothing but feed us lies from the day we were born. We finally have the chance to explore and gain the freedom we always wanted… and you want to give that up when things get a little hard?" I frown, my body sitting up like Myles.

He takes a moment to think over my words.

My head lowers, my eyes looking down at the bracelet around my wrist. The red stone surrounded by gold is still as beautiful as the moment Hunter gave it to me. Hunter told me to tap the centre if I ever need anything. What he meant by that, I have no idea, but the thought is nice. It shows he has a heart buried somewhere deep down inside him.

Taking a deep breath, Myles draws my attention away from the bracelet and back onto his face. "We left everyone when they needed us the most. We fought in an attack and then left them high and dry" Myles makes a good point, but it's not good enough for me.

No matter how bad I feel for leaving everyone when we did, it won't make me turn back, it won't stop me from getting the one thing I have been trying so desperately to have. I don't owe the world anything.

"They will be fine without us. Hunter and West are big boys, The Supreme left during the fight, he won't be coming back anytime soon" I stress.

"Your killing me" he groans, standing up from his spot on the floor.

"Myles—"

"Do you know how long I've waited to be close to you, to hear your voice, for you to say my name?" he asks me, but he doesn't wait for an answer. "You have been the girl of my dreams for as long as I can remember. Now that I can finally call you mine, all you want to do is run around, waiting to be killed or drop dead"

I reach my hand out to grab his hand, my fingers gripping onto his. He hesitantly lowers himself back onto the floor, his hand intertwining with mine. The tiniest smile creeps up my face when he allows me to move closer to him. My head leans on Myles' shoulder, my body leaning against his. The silence is calming. It's different from seconds ago.

"I'm sorry" I find myself apologising.

His thumb runs circles around the side of my hand. My hand feels numb, feeling nothing but his skin on mine. I tilt my head up to look at him. He is already looking down at me. His caramel eyes bore into my grey ones.

"It's okay" he whispers.

And then we kiss, for the first time since leaving Soltrix. It is a light kiss, almost like a peck, but his lips linger on mine for a minute longer than I expected. Soft and caring. His gentle lips mould onto mine, again and again. The feeling is familiar to me now. It's not new or unexpected. His lips are a second nature to me, like I've known the feeling of his lips on mine for my entire life. He holds me close to him, his touch too tender.

Like I'm fragile under him.

When we pull away, his frown is taken over by a bright smile. "I needed that" he breathes out. His other arm wraps around my body in an attempt to bring me closer.

21

Myles' eyes lead from my eyes to my lips.

His head leans forward again, planting a long, slow kiss on my lips. We kiss, again and again. The slow kisses are warm and passionate. No rush. No urgency. His pink lips are soft and careful against mine.

And then we pull away all over again.

"We haven't done that in a while" Myles says through a giddy smile.

I smile at his smile.

The wind outside the window gets louder. The sand is whistling, creating its own song. My eyes are diverted from the gorgeous brown eyes gazing down at me, to the window. I've never been in a sandstorm before, I'm worried there are going to be people out there, getting hurt or caught up in the worst of it. Nobody has knowledge of when the storm will clear.

What if people are out there, like me and Myles were, just wandering around in the storm?

"Get some rest" Myles whispers.

"I hope everyone's okay" I sigh.

"I'm sure they're fine" he comforts me.

Something inside me is telling me they're not. I'm sure Hunter and West has everything under control, but as I stare towards the window, listening to the noises being created by the storm, I worry. I worry for Lucas, for Elijah, for West, and for Hunter. I want them all to be okay.

CHAPTER FIVE
HUNTER

I'm losing my fucking mind.

Too many hours of sleep have been lost in the last two or three days. I have been standing in this very spot, not even blinking, for the longest time of my life.

I don't know what day it is.

I have no idea who is around me at this point in time.

All I'm focused on is the screen in front of me.

People call this the monitoring room; I call it hell. I have to stand here and watch as half the city falls into dust. Nobody can do anything but run. I have men rushing out to put the rest of the fire out but rebuilding everything is going to be a huge project. A project I don't have time for. West is going to have to see over everything while I'm busy trying to find the exact location of Todo Poderoso.

My father has tried attacking the city again. It wasn't a long fight. We managed to keep them away from the centre of Soltrix, but they'll come back. Todo's army is growing bigger by the second and mine is depleting quickly.

I don't know how many more attacks we can survive.

I need to come up with a better plan. A real plan. I need something that will help my people overcome the war and in time, rebuild their strength to continue living in the city. A part of me knows the city will fall before Todo gives up but telling the city that will only cause panic and riots. I need to be strong for the city, its people, and for myself.

The doors open behind me, but I don't turn around. I'm keeping my eyes on the gates to Soltrix. Nothing has changed in the last five minutes. Nothing has altered since yesterday or the day before or the day before. "Fuck" I mumble to myself as my frustration grows.

"Don't tell me your still staring at the screen" West's voice comes from the door behind me.

"I'm not staring at the screen" I repeat the exact words he wants to hear me say. He sighs, taking steps towards me. I can

23

see him moving in the reflection of the screens. "What do you want, West?" I frown.

He stops beside me, his arms crossed and his eyes on the same screen as mine. "You haven't left this room since the last attack... I came to check on you" West sounds off. He never checks on me unless he has important information for me. His tone is soft and hesitant. "Are the soldiers alright?" he glances from the screens to my face.

"They're fine, for now" I hum.

"And Grace... have you heard anything from Grace since she left?" he asks.

"No" I respond, bluntly.

"Look, I didn't want to worry you, but there is a storm. It started close to Tinnstone and has now made its way to the small town, RoseShire" West thinks I would worry about a silly little sandstorm. "By the look on your face, it's clear that you haven't checked the tracker on Grace's bracelet"

My head turns to West. "What are you talking about, the tracker is up there" I point to the corner screen, revealing the location of Grace and Myles. It tells us that Grace is located in the centre of RoseShire. "She must have found refuge or some shelter in the town. I don't need to worry about her. She is a strong girl; she can take care of herself"

I know we should go get her.

She has never experienced a storm before, she has no idea what to do or where to go. Myles won't be any help. The boy is as useless as they come.

We should go get her.

I never should have let her go. Soltrix needs her if we are going to win the war. The girl is a hand-full, she takes up too much of my time with her antics. But she is exactly what Soltrix needs. If she dies, I don't know what we will do. Grace should be here, where I know she is safe. I shouldn't have let her go; I should have kept her here.

"She is alone in the storm, probably lost and confused" West continues to push his worries onto me.

Grace will be fine; she will always be fine. West worries too much about her. It was his idea to get her the tracker in the first place, I went along with it due to her being powerful and a big part in my betrayal against my father.

But it's Grace, I should protect her, she has helped me more than she knows. And a part of me does care about her safety, and always will care about her.

"So, you're not worried, at all?" West pushes.

"No" I repeat.

"I am. She shouldn't be allowed out there with Myles. He is an imbecile. He will get them both killed" West has the same feeling as me.

"We can't bring them back without a reason" I remind him of the conversation we had after letting Grace go. As much as I want to bring her back, I need to stick to my word. "Give me a good reason, and I will be the first person on the plane. Until then, keep your mouth shut"

West has a look in his eyes. A smug look. A look I used to hate. He knows something I don't. My eyes peel themselves away from the screens, looking directly at West.

"We have just had news of an attack on RoseShire" he speaks through his smirking lips. For the first time in days, I let out a long sigh of relief. An attack is not good. But that's the best news I've heard in a long time. I would never give West the satisfaction of that though.

I should not be allowing my personal emotions to cloud my judgement.

An attack on a village is bad, I should not be wishing ill upon others. If we can help RoseShire defend themselves against the attack, we should. We will send a handful of our soldiers over to them and hopefully that will bid them a little more time.

But why would someone attack a small village?

What would they gain from attacking a small village such as RoseShire?

"When is this supposed attack?" I ask, shoving my hands into the pockets of my trousers.

West tries to hide his excitement. "They plan to attack during the lantern festival" he practically jumps up and down as he talks.

Nodding my head, I turn back to the screens. "That's not for another four months" I frown.

"Can you think of anything better?" he challenges me.

25

And I can't. I don't know what other option we have. I made a deal, and I will not break it. "Fine. When that happens, we will go and collect her" I declare.

Grace will be back in Soltrix, where she can continue to train and help us.

Four months will give me enough time to rebuild my army and find the whereabouts of Todo Poderoso. I just hope Grace doesn't decide to go venturing further into the desert. She will only come up empty handed.

"And... Myles?" he hesitates to say his name.

Taking a slow inhale of air, I nod my head. "And Myles" I repeat. As much as I hate the guy, we can't leave him alone out there. The city has spent too much money on the PPW to throw him to the sand.

CHAPTER SIX
GRACE

For the first time, I feel independent. I love this feeling, not having to ask anyone for permission to do something or needing to follow orders by someone else.

For once, I feel like a human being.

Myles, on the other hand, hates it. He wants people to give him orders and tell him what to do at all times. He can't think for himself. He needs someone to constantly give him instructions on the most basic things. When to brush his teeth and what to do when he wants to relax.

It scares me how little he can think for himself.

We have been living in Destiny's house for over two days because of the sandstorm. It's supposed to be clearing up any day now. Until then, I'm stuck sleeping on the living room floor beside a whiny Myles. Even when I try my best to have a small conversation with him, he turns everything into a complaint.

He is not the same guy I grew up knowing.

Soltrix has changed him, RoseShire has changed him. He has changed. Myles is finally my boyfriend, and I don't want to ruin that, but I don't know how much of him I can take right now. There is only so much complaining I can handle.

But I'm not about to give up on him.

On us.

My head turns in the direction of the windows, hoping to see a change. Nikita has pulled back the curtains, revealing the harsh wind blowing sand past the house. The sleep here is surprisingly peaceful, but the cold feeling of having no plan when this storm is over has been creeping up on me in my dreams.

Asha and Myles walk into the main room, both laughing at a joke nobody else heard. I look back down at the small bowl of cereal. This tall stool is uncomfortable to sit on. Destiny is strict on only eating food at the kitchen island, so I'm stuck here until I've finished.

They both sit down on the sofa, their laughter gradually dying down. "You need to stop" Asha giggles. I didn't see her as the laughing type. She was moody and very head-strong yesterday. Asha seemed to hate us and now she is laughing along with Myles like they are old friends.

My eyes are glued to the bowl in front of me. Destiny and Nikita walk around the kitchen island, stopping opposite me as they eye up Asha and Myles. "I can't remember the last time I watched her laugh… do you think he's hypnotised her?" Nikita jokes but I don't find it funny.

"Where is AJ?" Destiny looks around the room.

"In his room" Nikita shrugs, most likely guessing.

I use my spoon to finish off the last of the cereal in the bowl and then move off the stool. I walk over to the sink, placing the bowl down and turning around to the girls. "Are AJ and Asha a couple?" I don't know why I'm asking.

The girls look at one another with a smirk. Nikita holds back a large grin as she clears her throat. "They're married" I hear her speak but the words she says don't make sense. "AJ and Asha got married a year ago, soon after they found refuge here" she adds.

"H- How…" I feel awkward. "How old were they?" I find a way around the question. Neither of them look older than eighteen, twenty at most.

"Asha is twenty, AJ is twenty-two" Destiny answers, her eyes glancing over to Myles and Asha as she talks. "They are the reason we are able to stay here. Without them, we would be on the streets"

I never would have said they were older than nineteen, but here they are, married in their twenties. "What do you mean by them finding refuge here?" I ask another question.

"They both grew up in Tinnstone" Nikita frowns. "When the place went up in flames, everyone ran. Luckily, our small town isn't too far away from Tinnstone, a lot of people came here looking for shelter" she explains, her light green eyes slowly landing on mine.

For the first time since arriving, I can't hear the loud howls caused by the wind. Has the stormed stopped? The girls have the same idea. We all make our way over to the window with an urgency in our steps. Destiny opens the window, only for it to be slammed shut by the forceful wind.

"Great" Destiny mumbles.

We slowly make our way to the kitchen, standing around the island again.

"It's a good sign if you think about it. The wind didn't blow off the window. That must mean it is calming down" Nikita tries to see the positive side.

A large shadow hovers over Destiny. "What are you talking about?" AJ surprises us with his presence.

I jump a little when I notice AJ standing in the kitchen. He was so quiet walking in here, if he had stayed quiet, I wouldn't have realised he was standing around us. "Just telling Grace about Tinnstone. And checking on the strong winds" Nikita answers for us.

"Ah" he offers a sound for a response.

My eyes wander back over to Myles. I haven't made him laugh like that… ever. He tilts his head back against the sofa and laughs to his heart's content. I wish he would laugh that way with me. He is filled with joy and Asha the same. AJ seems to notice this too. As soon as he hears Asha's laughter, his head drops with his eyes forced onto the floor.

Nikita and Destiny spot something in the window. They make a move over to the curtains, pulling them back further to get a good view of the outside. I look over my shoulder as the girls watch the sand stop swirling around in the air. "The storm is definitely calming down" Destiny points out.

My eyes look from Destiny to AJ; he looks hopeful. "Is it safe to go outside?" AJ asks, glancing from Asha and Myles to the window.

I turn around, noticing a kid running around with a small kit, hoping for it will fly. The kit drags behind the kids' feet, jumping over every bump on the ground. Gradually, the wind pushes the kit into the air. The small kid keeps looking back at the kit, a big smile growing as he runs around.

"The kid seems fine" Destiny shrugs.

"Let's test it" Nikita smiles as she walks from the window towards a pair of shoes next to the front door.

I make a move from the kitchen, following Nikita as she begins putting on the shoes and opening the front door. A little bit of sand gets blown into the house but nothing major. I grab my only pair of shoes and walk into the open air.

29

"Finally" I sigh quietly.

Being confined to a house for a couple days felt like I was back in the hell hole I was forced to live in. It was like they had locked me up again in that small room. One bed, one desk, one window. The door was locked to prevent me from leaving. It felt like I was sucked back down into the rabbit hole.

Never again.

I'm pulled out of my thoughts by Nikita's high-pitched voice calling me. "Come over here" she drags me away from the house. Nikita is giggling and jumping as we run towards the open sand hills. The same sandy hills Myles and I were found by Nikita and Asha. "You are going to love this" she assures me.

Step after step, we make our way through the town of RoseShire. We are running. Nikita and Destiny can't contain their excitement.

As we reach the end of the town, I see it.

Trucks; big monster looking trucks.

They're going around in circles, forming donut shapes into the sand. There is a crowd of people cheering, clapping their hands and shouting for the trucks to go faster. The sand gets sucked under the trucks wheels and tossed up into the air. Everyone has come out of their homes to witness these machines driving along the sand.

A smile creeps up onto my lips. For once, there is no bad emotions. No fighting, no crying, no death. There is only happy smiles and loud expressions of joy. This is amazing.

"I thought you'd like it" Nikita looks at me.

"Why are they driving in circles?" I question.

"They're called donuts" she giggles. "They do this every time we survive a storm. It brings the town together"

"That's…" I have never witnessed something as joyful as this before. Hunter's city would never celebrate. Especially in this sort of way. "That's amazing"

CHAPTER SEVEN
GRACE

Days went by.

Weeks went by.

Before I realised the date, Myles and I had already been living in RoseShire for longer than we planned.

The town is actually amazing. Everyone is welcoming and helpful. We are still living in Destiny's living room, but we have moved a bed against the wall and have added a couple little decorations to make it our own.

Myles doesn't seem to mind living here now. It took him a while to settle in, but Asha has helped him ease into this new lifestyle. He isn't relying on anyone as much anymore. He has found a job to keep him busy during the days. Him and AJ are guards that take shifts on the outskirts of RoseShire. I have no idea what they are guarding, but it's nice to know we have people looking after us.

I'm just happy Myles has found a purpose.

He claims the job is only temporary, a way of gathering some money for our travels. And I want to believe him. For now, we are using the money as a way of paying Destiny rent as we live with her until we find the next place to go.

But his temporary job has lasted at least a month, maybe even longer than that.

I have been doing my own thing.

Most of the time, I'm talking to people about the wars and the other places nearby. As much as I like this town, I need to keep moving, I want to explore more. The best part about this town is having no time limit. I can take my time, there is no reason to rush.

After talking to some of the town's people, some have mentioned a place called FrostMount. They won't go into a lot of detail about the city, but they said its known for being the home of the devil. People have searched for the city for years and come up with nothing.

They say it should stay that way.

I don't push them any further than that. I don't want to upset anyone.

I've spent too many nights replaying certain moments in my head and thinking over my plan. A plan I no longer have. I need to find my father, I need to stop Todo Poderoso before he attacks Soltrix again, and I want to find a way to live without the feeling of regret. It doesn't sound like a lot, but to me, it is the difference between living and existing, and surviving.

I refuse to only exist.

And I refuse to spend my life only surviving.

I am going to live.

I choose to live.

"Me too" Nikita agrees with me, giggling to herself with her eyes focused on the sand ahead of us.

"Sorry… I was thinking out loud" I apologise, assuming I said my thoughts instead of thinking them.

She turns the steering wheel right, driving us back to the town. "It's okay, I do that too sometimes" she smiles. "Are you okay though? You seem stuck in your own world these last few days" she asks.

The two of us are heading back to RoseShire. We went on a drive to get out of the house. AJ and Myles are currently on a shift, Asha is cooking food and Destiny is at her job. She writes the local newspaper. She is really good at it too.

With everyone busy doing their own thing, we thought we would get out for a little.

"I'm okay" I offer her a faint smile.

She nods her head, holding the steering wheel with one hand and the gear stick with the other. We both bounce a little as we drive over lumps in the sand. "Do you… Can I ask you something?" she glances over to me. When I take too long to answer, she takes the silence as a yes. "What was it like… you know, in Soltrix?" she questions.

I am the wrong person to ask.

I only know what I saw and the people I met.

Most of my time in Soltrix was being locked up in the training room with West, or my room. The other times was a war and running through the city with soldiers chasing after me with loaded guns.

She is asking the wrong person.

"It's a city" I shrug.

"But what is it like? Nobody goes in and comes out alive, when you told us you were from there, we were shocked to say the least. Is it scary there? How did you escape?" she bursts out with multiple question.

I take a deep breath before answering. "The city is big when you're standing in the middle of it" I'm trying to find the words to describe it. "Most of the buildings are silver and the boarder is too big to climb. There is a shield around the outside of the city, stopping anyone from attacking the centre" I explain with a foggy memory of the nice things.

She turns the steering wheel again. "How did you get out?" she pushes for an answer.

I think back to my final goodbyes at the gate, and then I look down to the bracelet around my wrist. "I made some friends" a small, sad smile creeps up my face.

The sand dunes are hard to drive over. Driving down is the easy part but up is a struggle. Nikita is much better than me. In my defence, she has had more practice. I tried driving around a week ago, but I kept stalling the truck to the point that Destiny got fed up with me trying.

Now that I think about it, I don't know how long ago the storm was, or when we came outside, or when Myles and I had decided we would leave RoseShire. "Do you know how long we have been staying with you?" I ask.

I don't plan to stay much longer.

"Three months, roughly" she guesses.

My eyes are wide.

Time has flown so quickly; three months has felt like one week. There is no way we have wasted three whole months here. "I didn't mean to stay that long…" I mumble to myself. I can't spend a lot more time here if that's the case.

We need to get moving again.

"Are you going to leave soon…?" Nikita's smile turns to a frown.

"I didn't plan to stay as long as we have" I admit. "But I don't think Myles wants to leave"

33

There are so many more places to explore and discover, we can't keep staying in one place. So much of the world we have yet to see. All the people we have yet to meet.

I am ready for more.

Nikita debates her words before clearing her throat and parting her lips to speak. "That may have something to do with Asha" she suggests.

"What do you mean?" I don't get what she is saying.

"I think something is going on between them" she warns me, and the tone in her voice tells me she is being truthful.

"Myles wouldn't do that, we are dating. I mean, I am his girlfriend, not Asha" I remind her.

She isn't buying it.

"Grace, boyfriends cheat" she informs me.

"Cheat?" I repeat.

I push my hair out of my face. "They go after other girls. Kiss, date, have… you get the point" she explains.

We drive up another large hill and then we can see RoseShire in the distance. "He wouldn't do that to me" I trust Myles. He wouldn't go behind my back like that. We care about each other too much for that to happen.

"Just be careful" she advices.

As we drive down the sand hill, I see people preparing for something when we reach the town. I see a range of people decorating pieces of fabric and placing different candles in the middle of the fabric. What are they creating?

"What are they doing?" I question, my curiosity growing stronger the more I watch them.

She slowly looks from me to the town. "Lantern fest. It's a yearly festival where we send lanterns into the sky to thank all the soldiers who have died or are fighting in the war" she answers softly.

They are doing this for the soldiers. "You celebrate the soldiers?" the thought brings my heart to life.

Nikita nods her head. "Most of our men have been dragged to fight. Some have gone to Soltrix, some went to Tinnstone" she adds. "This is our way of saying thank you"

"The soldiers would really appreciate what you guys are doing" I gesture to the lanterns.

Her lips twitch. "It doesn't bring them back to us, but we can show how much we appreciate them"

In my mind, I can picture West's eyes lighting up as he sees all the lanterns entering the sky. He would love it. The fact that people are going out of their way to make the effort of saying thank you to the soldiers would put a smile on his face.

I wish Lucas and Elijah could see it.

I wish they could come and watch it with me.

The sad part is the soldiers have no idea they are being celebrated. I wish they knew. I really wish they could come and watch the lanterns.

CHAPTER EIGHT
GRACE

Destiny and Nikita have been keeping me company for the last couple of hours.

I wanted to bake, but I have never made a single piece of food in my life. I don't think I am even capable of making toast if I tried. That's what eighteen years of isolation does.

Destiny was very helpful; she was the one who came up with the idea to bake a cake for everyone. She thought of the idea to give it to the men who are on guard duty today. Nikita wanted to help us, buying all the ingredients we didn't already have. They both worked together to teach me how to make the chocolate base of the cake and the icing.

"Here, try this" Nikita giggles, handing me the spoon she had just used to mix the ingredients together.

I take the spoon out of her hands and taste the mixture attached. It tastes like heaven. "What is it?" I ask, wanting to have some more.

"It is the chocolate mixture; we always have a taste just before we put the mixture in to bake" she smiles. "Why are you looking like that?" she has to hold back the fear in her eyes as she looks at the expression on my face. I have no idea what she is referring to.

"What do you mean?" I narrow my eyes.

"You look as if you have never had chocolate before" she announces the truth.

I hesitate slightly. "That's because I have never had chocolate before" I nod my head, agreeing with her. I feel like I have said something wrong. Is this not normal? "Is everything okay?"

"Nikita, not everyone is privileged to have chocolate. It is not available everywhere" Destiny defends me.

A breath of relief passes through my lips. I don't know how I was going to explain that one. Nikita would push until she got an answer she was satisfied with, and I feel like I would say the wrong thing.

Nobody can find out about the PPW.

"Something smells good" Myles chuckles as he enters the house, swinging open the front door to reveal himself and Asha. "What are you cooking?" he looks over to the kitchen as he takes off his work shoes and leaves them on the left side of the door.

"We're baking" Nikita corrects him.

"We are baking chocolate cake for the guards on duty tonight" Destiny answers the question.

Myles puts on a frown. He looks from Destiny to me, his caramel eyes locking onto mine. "Damn. I should have taken the night shift instead of AJ" he chuckles at his own joke, his eyes creating small wrinkles.

"They will appreciate that" Asha adds.

Myles and Asha move away from the front door as Asha closes it. They walk over to the kitchen island, both staying as close together as they can.

I don't pay attention to them, instead, I look over to the girls as they finish scooping the chocolate mixture into one of the large silver tins. I walk over and pick up the tin, placing it into the oven and allowing Destiny to set the heat. Nikita slowly closes the oven door and the orange light turns on.

"Now, we wait" Destiny smiles.

"What do we wait for?" I ask another question.

"The mixture will rise, and then we will hear the oven make a ringing sound. That's when it will be finished, and all we will need to do then is decorate the top of the cake" Nikita sounds more excited than any of us.

Asha shakes her head. "You two are going to run out of money the way you keep baking things" she makes a judgment as she moves around the kitchen island.

"This was Grace's idea" Destiny offers a half lie. "We only wanted to help, seeing as she has never baked a single thing in her entire life"

Myles chuckles as he looks my way again.

This is the most he has looked at me since we got here.

"Did you girls see people setting up for some sort of lantern festival?" Myles reminds me of the towns people me and Nikita had seen earlier today.

Before I get the chance to respond, somebody else beats me to it. "We passed it on the way back from the dunes" Nikita answers for me, skipping past the most important part. The fact that the lantern festival is for all the soldiers fighting in the war as we speak.

Myles smiles to himself. "Apparently you have done this kind of thing every year" he makes a guessed statement from something he must have heard earlier today.

"It's for the soldiers" I rush to say before someone else jumps to talk.

Myles and I look at one another again.

"That's nice" he nods his head. "It is about time people appreciated the soldiers, and it will be nice to see the lanterns fill the sky. It must be a pretty view" Myles rests his elbows on the kitchen island as he talks.

"Come with me" Asha speaks to Myles.

"Where are we going?" He asks her.

"I will show you where you can get the best view of the lanterns" she says with excitement in her voice.

Myles allows her to drag him out of the kitchen and into the hallway. Nobody tries to stop them from leaving. All three of us just watch in silence as they disappear from the room.

I don't bother trying to say something in an attempt to keep them from leaving.

It would be a waste of breath.

Both Nikita and Destiny feel the same.

They both look from one another, and then towards me with a frown on their lips. I don't want them to say anything. I want them to continue baking, continue laughing, continue to smile like nothing is wrong.

Nothing is wrong.

CHAPTER NINE
ELIJAH

The warm air rests on my skin.

Sand sticks to the bottoms of my shoes as I stand in the hot night. I swat my arm as a small bug tries to rest on my bicep. The air feels heavy on my lungs as I stand in front of a building, a small house.

My eyes watch the window built into the front of the house as it allows me to see straight into the building.

This place, it is not what I had pictured.

The ground is mostly gravel with small piles of sand that has gathered over time from people's shoes. The buildings don't look smooth or well-built. Majority of them seem to be made from red brick and cement.

Flowers and ivy grow up the walls of the buildings, taking over the bricks.

There is no grass in sight, no trees or animals. There are only flowers that appear to be growing around here, and even they seem to be growing out of nowhere. My hand pulls at the flower petals, holding two or three in the palm of my hand. The petals are soft and delicate.

A muffled rustling sound comes from the window, bringing my attention away from the flower petals. I drop the petals, leaving them to float to the ground in a slow and graceful manner.

Through the window, I spot Grace.

She is sleeping on mattress close to the window. She is alone and might be having a bad dream from the way she is moving around. Why is she sleeping alone? I would have assumed Myles would be asleep next to her. He would be helping her with her nightmares.

Yet, he is nowhere to be seen.

I shut my eyes, focus my breathing, and imagine myself being beside Grace.

When my eyes open, I am inside the building,

The warmth from the night air sticks to my skin as the heat from the room suffocates my face. This whole place is like an

39

oven. I don't know how anyone can sleep in this heat. Standing here is enough for my skin to want to sweat.

Grace tosses and turns under the blanket, pulling half of her leg out of the blanket. Her forehead forms small wrinkles as she breaths heavily.

My head turns in all directions, making sure no one is around us as I lower to my knees. I shuffle over to her, quietly, trying my best not to wake her up. The last thing I want to do is scare her when she's having a nightmare. My joggers allow me to stay silent as I move across the floor towards her.

"Shhh" I hum close to her ear.

I use my fingers to carefully move a strand of hair out of her face and behind her ear.

She stops tossing and turning.

I trace circles on the temple of her forehead with my thumb as I smile down at her. Her heavy breathing becomes quiet, dying down as her nightmare eases.

"Your safe" I whisper to her. "I'm here now"

And then I start to hear movement from the hallway close to the kitchen.

I shut my eyes and breath.

"Shit" I curse as I open my eyes.

My surrounding become familiar again. I am back in Soltrix with West staring at me, a smile plastered on his face.

I steady my balance as I look around the room. Myles' bed is still neatly made from when he left. My bed is only half-made from this morning. Lucas and West are stood close to the door, awaiting my arrival. I stare at them both as I walk over to the desk on Myles side of the room, leaning against it.

A part of me wanted to stay with Grace, keeping her calm as her nightmare tried to take over.

"How did it go? Did you find her?" West questions. He is too impatient to wait for me to explain. "Was it the right place or do we need to try again?" he doesn't let me get a word in before he pushes more questions my way.

40

"Let the guy talk" Lucas laughs.

"Sorry. I just want to know how she is" West huffs.

I gather myself. "Grace is fine. Myles… I couldn't see him anywhere, but she was asleep. They are staying in the living room of someone else's house. Whose house, I don't know" I try to give West the answers he wants.

"That is better than nothing" West nods.

"If they have found somewhere safe and are happy, why are we disturbing them?" Lucas asks.

It is a valid point.

What reason do we have for spying on them?

"There is going to be an attack on the village they have taken refuge in. I have made Hunter aware, and we are going to help the village when it happens. While helping, we will grab Grace and Myles, bringing them back here" West explains, and for the first time in a while, I agree with his plan.

Bringing Grace back to Soltrix will ensure that she is safe and being watched. It will allow us to know there is no danger around her and that she is alive.

But she will fight against it.

I know Grace, I know she is stubborn. Once she has an idea or plan in her head, she won't let anyone get in the way. There is no chance she will want to return to Soltrix willingly. Coming back here means no freedom, no more exploring, no more being her own person. She will be confined to the building again, only listening to Hunter's demands.

"She won't want that" I confess.

"I know. But Hunter wants her back" West sighs loudly for us to hear. "And so do I…"

"That is selfish" I argue. "That girl did everything she could to save our asses during the attack. She didn't have to fight; she didn't even need to leave her room. Grace could have watched from the window, not having to put her own life at stake, but she did. She risked her life for us. And in return, all she wanted was her freedom" I continue, getting angrier and angrier. "How dare you suggest we take that away from her"

Grace deserves the life she has always wanted.

She has been to hell and back, with no help from me or any other person in her life.

After everything the world did to her, what we all have done to her, after everything I have done to her. The least we can do is give her the life she wants.

"He's right. Don't bring her back. Not when she is so happy exploring the world" Lucas sides with me.

West lowers his head. "When you put it like that— well it doesn't matter now. Hunter has already put a plan in motion. If I tried to change his mind now, I think he would simply shoot me on the spot" West stares at the floor as he talks. "Shit. Why did you have to make me see reason? I was perfectly happy until you said all that" he groans.

Lucas sits down on Myles' bed, resting his feet. "Although, I don't think we will win the war without her" he glances over to me as he talks.

"Me neither" West agrees.

"We can try—"

"Hunter won't listen. He is determined to win the war, and he knows he has a better chance with Grace. He won't let it go, no matter how badly you try to change his mind" West shakes his head. "She will be fine. Once the war is over, Hunter will let her go, she will have her freedom eventually"

I don't like it.

"I want to be there when you collect her" I demand.

"I don't think Hunter—"

"I don't personally care what Hunter thinks or wants. I will join you" I cut West off.

CHAPTER TEN
GRACE

The bed feels cold and empty. My mind is struggling to switch off. Maybe it is the thought of Soltrix, maybe it is the worry and regret of leaving everyone behind. I fear it is guilt finally getting the best of me.

The warm air is swirling around the living room, my body starting to sweat, my arms, my back, my forehead. I would like to have thought I would have been used to the heat by now.

I roll over to find Myles, hoping to cuddle up next to him to for comfort, but he isn't there. Instead, I am met with only his pillow and half the blanket pushed over to my side of the bed, like he has only just left.

Where has he gone?

He isn't working a night shift, AJ is.

My body sits up. My eyes look around the room. I'm all alone in the living room. Moonlight is shining its way through the window. The lights are all off, and I can barely make out anything through the darkness, but I would know if there was someone else in the room. My eyes are furiously darting around the room in hope of finding Myles.

Something is wrong, I can feel it.

I push the blanket completely off my body and move over to the edge of the mattress. My feet slowly touch the hot floor as I try to stay quiet. As I stand up straight, Myles' long black shirt dangles down to my thighs.

There is a rustling sound coming from the hallway. My head immediately turns in the direction and then I hear a voice speaking. "Be quiet" someone whispers. "Someone is going to hear you and wake up" they continue. I can only make out half the words they say, but it is enough to make me begin walking.

It's too late for anyone to be up, so who is talking?

The voice sounded male, but AJ isn't here. At least, he shouldn't be. The only other person I can think of is Myles, but he may have just stepped out for some air.

My legs continue to walk closer and closer to the small hallway until I'm standing outside one of the bedrooms. Asha and AJ's bedroom. The lights are off, but the door is half open with the sound of movement coming from inside. I step even closer until I'm looking through the open door.

Myles is hovering over Asha's naked body. "What time is AJ home?" Myles asks her, planting kisses up and down her neck. His words are muffled, but I hear them.

Loud and clear.

His lips connect with hers, and all I see is red. "Not for another couple hours" Asha responds between kisses.

Tears build up in my eyes as I watch them.

"I wish we could stay here forever" Myles mutters.

"Me too" she agrees, slowly running her fingers through his soft brown hair.

"Don't tempt me" he chuckles and then goes back to kissing her lips.

I shouldn't be watching this, but I can't look away. I am frozen in place. I am unable to move from my statue. Nothing in this moment hurts more than the pain in my heart and the sudden feeling of losing my best friend and my boyfriend in one. I'm losing Myles to a random girl he just met.

Years and years of friendship, gone.

Red clouds my vision as the ground shakes under me. I have to hold back a sob as their bodies press together. My lips are shaking. My eyes close and my feet slowly move, finally backing away from the door.

One step.

Two steps.

Three steps.

And I'm back in the living room, rushing to my pillow to scream. I want to let all my anger out, but I'm scared of what I would cause if I did. I don't want any conflict. Maybe I do in this moment, but I'm not thinking straight.

I need to contain my emotions.

My body crashes onto the mattress, the weight of my tears holding me down. They roll onto my pillow, causing a wet and damp patch on Myles' pillowcase.

If Myles wants to stay here, then he can stay.

I will not force him to come with me when I leave. I will not drag him away with me if that is not what he wants.

At least there is one thing I can get out of this. Now I can put a date on the day I leave. I will leave after the lantern fest has ended. As soon as everyone goes to sleep, I will leave.

My leaving will be quick and easy.

Leaving Myles will be hard, but it's what he wants.

CHAPTER ELEVEN
GRACE

Today is the festival.

Destiny thought it would be a good idea if we all helped out with the preparations. She even bought extra lanterns for anyone who may not have been able to afford them. The town is all coming together now, anyone and everyone helping in any way they can.

I place a small yellow candle inside the fabric and then move on to the next one. We are repeating the same process over and over until they are all complete. We still have a lot to do, but it will be worth it in the end.

People have placed tables around the street, allowing us a place to work. We are gathered around the tables, different items on different surfaces. Our table has candles while the table beside us has pens and lanterns. My eyes wander around the street at the people working hard to make tonight special.

The other people around us are drawing patterns onto the fabric, creating pretty designs for when they are lit later on tonight. "This will probably be the biggest lantern fest we have had" Nikita cheers.

"It's nice how everyone is coming together" I add.

"Makes a change" Asha brings the mood down.

I thought the town was nice. The people are lovely, and everyone makes sure everyone is okay. Unless me and Asha are living in different towns, I don't know why she said that. I am not the only one who is confused by her statement as Nikita and Destiny look at one another.

My eyes stay on the candles. I can't look at Asha, and I will not look at her for the rest of my time here.

"We need more lanterns" someone speaks from one of the tables opposite us.

"We can grab some" Destiny assures the woman, and then turns to Asha. "Would you—"

"Yep" Asha cuts her off. "Hand me some money to go buy them" she holds out her hand in front of Destiny, waiting for

46

money to be place on the palm of her hand. Destiny gives her some of the money from her pocket. "Thank you" Asha fakes a smile and then wanders down the street.

I would look to rip the frown from her lips.

She is ruining two people's lives, without regret or any sort of remorse. Asha is a cruel human being. I have been picked on and bullied, beaten black and blue, yet no one has disrespected and treated me with such cruelty in all my life. She doesn't seem to care who she hurts; she just takes what she wants.

She has taken away my best friend and my boyfriend, she is destroying her marriage.

But she can't even smile for a second.

She still isn't satisfied.

The girls watch as she walks away before they both turn to me. "What is her problem?" they ask almost at the same time as the other.

I finally look up from the candles to look over to Nikita and Destiny. "I don't know" I admit. She was happy last night and the night before that and the night before that. She has been moody all morning and I have no idea why. She woke up on the wrong side of the bed or something.

That's the expression the girls used.

"Are you okay?" Nikita asks me.

Debating what to say, I decide to come clean to them about my plan. "I'm leaving after the festival" I confess, hoping to say goodbye.

"What!" Nikita gasps.

"You are four months late, but who's counting" Destiny jokes as she covers up her sadness. Nikita slaps her arm and then Destiny nods her head, her dreadlocks bouncing along with her head. "Sorry. I mean, we will miss you" she sighs.

"Please, don't tell the others, especially Myles" I plead.

"Myles isn't going with you?" Destiny sounds shocked.

My brain is thinking of a way to say the right words without making them think there is another reason. "He doesn't want too" he said so himself.

Nikita looks into my eyes, into my soul, and reads me like a book. Her eyes flicker as pity fills them. Her head lowers a little

47

as she understands what I said. She knows what I am thinking from only my eyes.

"You know" she guesses.

"I know" I agree.

There is a slight pause before any of us says anything to each other.

"Know what?" Destiny is clueless.

Me nor Nikita know what to say.

My mouth stays closed. I don't want to say it out loud. If I say it out loud that makes it real. And even after I watched it happen, I don't want it to be true. "Myles and Asha are… well they are cheating" Nikita spells it out for her.

She says what I couldn't.

Destiny's eyes flash from Nikita to me, from me to Nikita, and then become consumed by anger. "THAT BITCH" Destiny snaps. Some of the people around us stop to look at us. They look disgusted and confused. "Sorry" she quickly apologises as their eyes land on her. They go back to their work as her anger bottles up. She seems angrier than me about this.

"Are you—"

"AJ and you deserve so much better than that" Destiny is shaking her head. "How dare they" she is outraged.

It's weird to think about. When Myles and Asha first met one another, they didn't seem to like each other. Now they are kissing and telling each other how much they adore being in each other's company, not wanting to be apart.

Up until now, I assumed they had found common ground and somehow become good friends.

I didn't want to believe it was anything more.

"Do you think AJ knows?" Nikita asks.

I shake my head. "I don't think so" I guess, none of us really know, but I'm assuming he doesn't know considering the fact that they are still married. "I doubt he knows"

"Someone should tell him" Destiny is quick to respond.

"I don't know…" I don't want to be the one to tell him.

"You should tell him" Destiny demands.

"She is leaving tonight" Nikita reminds her.

"Tell him tonight" Destiny is not letting this go.

48

Asha walks back over to the table with a bag filled to the top with lanterns. Her lips are tightly knitted together in a thin line as she approaches us. It is clear to everyone around that she is in a mood. "Where should I put these?" she asks as she stops in front of the table.

One small silence later, and someone speaks up. "Just put them on that table" Nikita points to the table with lanterns sitting on beside us.

We all look from her to each other as she slowly walks to the other table. "Tell him tonight" Destiny tries to keep a low and quiet voice, so Asha won't hear her. "He deserves to know the truth about what's going on. It might be hard, but you are going to tell him before you leave" She begs.

"You don't have too. Take your time, you deal with this in your own way" Nikita comforts me.

Asha places the lanterns on the table, pouring the bag out in front of the people working on the patterns. "Will this be enough?" she asks them.

I watch her, cautiously.

"Thank you" they nod their heads.

Soon, Asha makes her way back to the table to continue her work on the candles. The feeling between us is awkward to say the least. The situation isn't great but it's nice to have friends who understand and can comfort me.

I've never had girlfriends before.

My time has been spent surrounded by boys for so long, I forgot what a girls company was like. Leaving tonight is going to be a lot harder than I thought.

Nikita takes a deep breath as she finishes another candle and places it on one side of the table. "We need to find a good place to watch the lanterns tonight" Nikita tries to make the atmosphere between us all less awkward. "Any suggestions?"

"The sand dunes" Asha suggests.

"We did that last year" Nikita sighs.

They get back to thinking as we work. I would pitch in with an idea if I knew any spots around here. I can't think of a single place in town we would have a good view of the lanterns floating. Now that I think about it, the sand dunes does sound like a good place to watch them being let go.

49

"Will AJ be coming tonight?" Destiny bursts out with her question.

Nikita freezes as the question is asked.

My body tenses.

A huff comes from Asha. "Yes" she frowns. "Everyone is going tonight. All the guards have tonight off" she explains, sounding fed up. "We already talked about this yesterday"

I don't know where to look. My eyes lock onto Nikita's as Destiny nods her head. "I was just making sure" she smirks to herself.

Luckily, Asha doesn't notice.

I feel bad. I don't want to tell AJ. I haven't even processed it all yet. Telling AJ is only going to be worse now than in a day or two. He needs to know, but I also have to get the idea of Myles and Asha being together in my head. Someone else, like Nikita, would be better to tell him.

She is closer to him.

Nikita would know what to say and how to say it without him getting to upset.

He deserves a real explanation.

CHAPTER TWELVE
GRACE

The sky is growing darker by the minute.

With every blink, there is a new star in the sky.

It is truly beautiful.

The boys ended up deciding where we would go to watch the lanterns. We are sitting on the top of the large hill me, and Nikita had driven down a couple days ago. The same hill Myles and I had run down to grab the girl's attention when we first arrived before the sandstorm.

Behind us lays the never-ending sand dunes. It's a nice view when watching the sunset but trying to survive out there in the day is another story. During the night is the best time to travel in the dunes.

We learnt that the hard way.

A lantern is sitting on my lap, ready to float in the air at any given moment. We each have one. There is a lighter ready for when we need to light the lanterns. All we are waiting for now is a sign to light them up.

With time, Myles quickly becomes impatient. "When do we let these go?" Myles asks, looking over at the others for an answer.

"When I tell you so" AJ huffs.

"Fine" Myles grunts.

Destiny is expecting me to tell AJ tonight. I don't know how or when because Asha is sitting next to him. Myles is sat beside me, putting his arm around me. I feel uncomfortable more than anything. Knowing his hands have been on her and not me.

Sadly, that's the only thing I can think about when his hands are on me.

As the moon reveals itself, peeking out from behind a dark cloud no one can see. The cloud is camouflaged by the dark stary sky. The moon shines down on us, and only then, does AJ speak again.

"Now" he shouts.

All together, we light the small candles and the fabric blows up. We let go of the lanterns in front of us, allowing them to float up into the sky.

My lantern is for Soltrix.

It is for Lucas,

It is for West,

It is for Hunter,

And it is for Elijah.

The town lets go of its lanterns, releasing them into the open air. It looks like a sea of flickering stars from the sand dunes.

An ocean of light.

Our eyes are glued to the sky, watching the lanterns float up into the atmosphere, high enough for everyone to see. The soldiers would be happy to know we are celebrating them. We are using lanterns to show hope. It is a sign of faith that the soldier will be okay, and hope that the war will end soon.

"It's beautiful" I say out loud.

"It is" Myles agrees with me, but he doesn't look at me, his eyes are focused on the sky… and Asha.

Destiny and Nikita have made sure to sit in between them, wanting to put as much space between AJ and Myles as much as they physically can. The more space the better. But even the small space doesn't stop Asha. She looks over at Myles and smiles, and he does the same.

He hasn't bothered to look my way since he came out here. I didn't notice this much before, but now it is all I see.

AJ looks clueless.

If only he knew the truth.

As we watch the lanterns, there is a loud noise coming from behind us. Everyone seems to be too focused on the sky to notice the strange noise. The noise reminds me of a plane, although there is something slightly off about it. But maybe I am concentrating on the wrong thing. I should be watching the lanterns the same as everyone else.

A sweet, yet ugly sound erupts from Myles. He is trying his best to hold back his uncontrollable laughter. Asha covers her mouth to avoid us watching as she joins in on the loud and obnoxious laughing.

I can already taste my bitterness on the tip of my tongue.

I turn my attention onto the lanterns.

There is an unusual sharp pain in my chest. It is fresh and painful. My heart pounds hard enough to cause a crack. It is caused by my own thoughts and my own feelings, yet I want to blame Myles. I want to blame RoseShire. I want to blame Asha. I want to blame everyone but myself.

Suddenly, the same trucks that were doing donuts after the storm are now doing donuts as the lanterns rise higher and higher into the air.

Nikita is on her feet, jumping for joy at the sight of the trucks spinning around in circles.

People walk out of town and towards the sand to watch the trucks. The crowd gets bigger and bigger until the entire town is watching. "I want to join in" Nikita says to AJ as she watches the trucks in awe.

"I bet you do" AJ chuckles.

"Let's go join them" Destiny says, pushing off the sand as she stands up. She wraps an arm around Nikita's shoulders and plants a kiss on her left cheek.

I smile at them.

One by one, we all stand up from our sitting positions. I follow beside AJ as we make our way down to the crowd.

Nikita is running down to the trucks, the lanterns still in the night sky. The lanterns grow higher the lower we get down the large sand hill.

Once we reach the bottom, Nikita stands in front of AJ with a hopeful grin. "Let me borrow the truck" she begs AJ.

"Absolutely not. Last time you 'borrowed the truck' you picked up two strangers" AJ protests.

"Come on, we will ask Derek" Destiny drags Nikita over to one of the guys watching the trucks close by.

While Nikita and Destiny try to talk to someone about borrowing their truck, AJ moves over to me, standing next to me as Asha and Myles laugh at one another's secret jokes. AJ and I keep looking at the trucks, wanting to avoid looking at Myles and Asha as much as possible.

I keep looking at the trucks as the wheels push the sand up into the air. The wind is strong, blowing the sand up into our faces and into our eyes. I rub my eyes, trying to get the sand out, while

53

my hair blows behind my shoulders. I feel like I'm about to be blown away by how harsh the winds are.

"AJ" I say his name, hoping to grab his attention.

He looks down at me.

"Grace" he smiles, unsure of what I am about to say.

"I need to tell you something…" I try to come up with the best way to explain it. I don't want to upset him, but I need to tell him before I leave tonight. "I'm really sorry to say this… but Asha and Myles have been—"

And then I hear it again.

An explosion.

The kind of explosion that takes everyone by surprise.

One of the only tall buildings crumbles and then another building and another until fire is the only thing we see. The ground beneath us begins to shake. My eyes look in all directions. Three big silver machines fly in the sky above our heads. They look familiar. Too familiar. One comes down to land, and then the rest follow behind.

"RUN" someone shouts from the crowd.

"They're back!" another shouts.

Chaos brings the peaceful show to an abrupt end, quickly replacing the happy cheers with frightened screams. I'm looking around for an explanation, an answer. I'm lost and confused and dreading the worst. "What's going on?" I question.

Destiny runs over to us, patting my shoulder as her head spins around. "They're attacking again. We need to run before they see us standing here" Destiny rambles on until she is running as fast as her legs will take her.

Gunshots.

Lots and lots of gunshots.

"We need to hide, like now" Nikita demands, gripping onto my arm as she drags me with her.

Left foot.

Right foot.

Left foot.

Right foot.

I'm keeping up with their fast-paced run, almost falling onto my face as the ground becomes hard to run on.

AJ and Destiny are speeding ahead of us, making sure the coast is clear before we head back into town. There is no way of knowing if we are safe or out of danger until we find a place to hide. But Destiny seems to take the lead, directing us past the burning houses and towards one of the back streets.

"Someone tell me what is going on?" Myles shouts over the gunshots as we turn into one of the back streets.

"RoseShire is on fire" Destiny states the obvious, not giving him a real answer.

Everything is happening so fast.

We run down the back street, pushing past people with no intention to stop moving. The gravel walkways are now piling up with bricks and wood. Curtains are burning and large pictures on walls are fading away.

Homes are being destroyed and all we can do is run.

The main street is taken over by an army. The army looks familiar. Soldiers marching in rhythm, not one of them misses a step. They wear red-coloured helmets and black gloves with thick black boots. The same uniform we fought against in the attack against Soltrix.

But then we hear another set of gunshots. Soldiers rush towards the other soldiers. They are fighting each other. The other soldiers are wearing grass-coloured helmets, thick black boots and black gloves. The soldiers are Hunter's. The same army I fought beside to save the silver city.

Soltrix.

My head catches up with everything in front of me.

We are running faster than before, our feet hitting the ground harder and harder.

We are losing speed, gaining breaths, forgetting to remain aware of the army storming through the streets. We are about to be trapped if we don't get out of the street and into a quieter part of town.

AJ turns, Destiny turns, and then we all turn.

A group of soldiers stand in the centre of the street. They watch as innocent people run for safety. This isn't right. Why are they invading this town? What is the purpose of all this? I can't make sense of anything right now.

I turn my head, avoiding eye contact with a soldier. AJ is too slow to look the other way. A loud gunshot is close enough to shake our eardrums.

AJ falls.

His blood pours onto the ground as his limp body stays completely still. A bullet shaped hole burns into his heart. He is dead. He died right in front of us. No scream, no suffering. It was quick and easy.

"AJ!" Nikita gasps.

"Quickly, grab him" Destiny gives her orders.

"He's dead…" Asha doesn't blink. "AJ is dead…"

"He would be dead weight to try and carry his body along with us" Myles shocks us all. Another gunshot flies past us. "We need to move"

The soldier that fired at us starts making their way towards us with their gun aiming.

"He's right…" I sadly agree with Myles.

Another gun shot is fired, but it misses.

Asha looks from Myles to AJ. A flicker of pain washes over her eyes. She slips off a ring from her finger, and places it on the top of AJ's chest. A tear falls from her eye as she stands up, straightening her back.

The soldier smirks as he aims the gun towards Asha. My hand rises and my eyes narrow. I make a swatting gesture with my hand, pouring all my focus into the small motion.

The soldier is blown to the side, his body colliding with a tall cobblestone wall.

"Let's go" Asha sighs, unaware of what just happened.

Destiny holds back her hesitation as she nods her head and begins running again.

I'm quick to copy what the others do. We duck under a fallen log of wood and push our way into one of the buildings closest to us. There is no fire but a lot of damage. We head towards the back of the building where we crouch behind large wooden crates, staying out of sight.

The building is too dark to see anything else. Most of the room has crumbled from the explosions outside. There is glass shattered across the floor, random chairs scattered around as one table lays flipped on its side. If it wasn't for the moonlight breaking its way through the small cracks of the walls, we would be sitting in complete darkness.

"Everyone stays quiet and out of sight, got it?" I hear Destiny order.

"Got it" Nikita nods her head.

"We're just going to wait here until… what? Someone finds us?" I frown.

Asha's quiet sobs fill the silent gaps between our hushed conversation.

"Until they leave" Destiny gives a brief explanation.

I take a deep breath.

Everything is numb. The only thing I can feel is Myles crouching down beside me. My heart is about to fail me as my mind tries to stay calm.

Shadows pass the door, soldiers marching with guns in hand ready to fire.

My eyes close and all I hear are footsteps.

Soldiers.

Two big soldiers walk into my room. They grab me by my arms and drag me down the never-ending hallway. I kick and scream and beg for them to let me go. They never do. I'm thrown into a dark room until the world becomes nothing but a faraway fantasy.

I feel my body shake as the silence through the room becomes deafening. I lean my body against the wall, focusing on my breathing. My eyes open, and I'm back in the dark room with Myles putting his arm around me, pulling me into his lap.

His soft fingers run through my hair and trace the outline of my face.

As much as I can't stand the thought of being close to him right now, his touch is easing the loud noises. It's taking my mind away from everything.

The marching gets louder.

A door breaks on one side of the room. Time stops. No movement or sound. Nothing.

And then it all comes rushing back.

Soldiers burst through the door with their guns raised in front of them. "Nobody moves" one shouts. And we don't. We stay as still as humanly possible. I don't know what the plan is or if there is a plan, but nobody moves a muscle.

"We need to get out of here" Myles demands in a quiet whisper. "This was a terrible idea"

"Shut up" Destiny whispers back.

The soldiers spot us immediately.

As if they have x-ray vison.

They can see us in the dark.

Flashlights are pointing at us, making us stand out in the darkness. "Hands in the air" a soldier's voice booms through the building. Nikita raises her hands, then Asha, then Destiny and Myles. "Stand-up" the soldier orders.

All guns are pointing at our heads.

How did they find us so quickly?

We stand up from our crouched positions, forming a thin line for the soldiers. Our hands are above our heads and our hearts are beating out of our chests.

My eyes squint as a flashlight blinds me. A soldier points the light into my eyes and then nods his head to one of the other soldiers. "We found her" he yells to someone outside.

A gun presses against my back.

Hard.

"Walk" they order.

We walk in a line, one after the other, out of the building and towards the street. The moonlight hits us again. My eyes are narrowing. The army from Soltrix are slowly getting into a formation, all gathering in the main street.

I try to stop walking to look around, but the gun pushing into my back keeps me moving.

By the time I realise how far we have walked, the gun is removed from my back and a hand pushes me to the floor. I land on my knees, my head staring at the ground beneath me.

We kneel down in the middle of a burning street. The buildings around us fall to the ground as the road beneath my knees harshly rubs against my skin. The soldiers who are not aiming their guns our way have their backs to us as they watch for anyone trying to fight back.

My hands rise again, following the orders of the soldiers as Myles and the others do the same. My palms open into a surrender position. All eyes are on us as we kneel on the floor in the centre of every soldier in sight.

Someone steps forward, and my head lifts.

Hunter.

He steps in front of me with his hands behind his back and eyes burning down onto me.

Behind him, stands West and…

Elijah.

My eyes meet Elijah's. A smile threatens to pull at his lips as he looks down at me. Slowly, very slowly, my hands begin to fall. "You…"

"Hello, love" Hunter greets me, crouching down to my level, removing his hands from behind his back. My eyes look back at Hunter. I didn't expect to see Hunter this soon. "I see you managed to find RoseShire" he meets my eyeline as he pushes a strand of hair behind my ear.

I must ignore his touch, moving my face to the side for his hand to fall from my face. "We had a deal" I remind him. I can feel the other eyes on me, but my eyes are continuing to remain on his.

On Hunter.

"Plans have changed" he shrugs my statement off.

His ocean blue eyes are the only thing my eyes will allow themselves to see.

It takes everything in me to avoid Elijah's glare.

I decide to push myself off my knees and stand up. My anger boils, hearing the screams from innocent people as they continue to run and hide. RoseShire didn't deserve this. They didn't deserve their homes to be destroyed.

"What are you doing?" Nikita tries to pull me back down.

"She's insane" I hear Destiny mumble.

The soldiers aim their guns at me, all ready to shoot. My legs keep moving, regardless of the guns and open threats and deadly look in everyone's eyes. They won't shoot me. And if they were going to shoot me, they should get it over with now instead of dragging it out.

"NOBODY SHOOTS HER!" Elijah shouts.

Hunter glances over his shoulder, looking at Elijah with a curious frown.

West turns his head to the side, staring at the side of Elijah's head. Elijah looks over at West. I see West shape the words 'What was that?', but Elijah simply ignores it, continuing to keep his unshaken gaze on me.

I step closer and closer to Hunter until I can smell his coconut scent. He tilts his head down to me. Neither one of us breaks eye contact. My blood is boiling, my hands are shaking, my head is spinning. "You promised me I could leave. I could explore the world and gain my freedom—"

Hunter shakes his head, a smirk staining his lips. "I never promised" his tone sounds confident. "Do you remember the last conversation we had before you left?" he takes me by surprise.

I remember most of it.

We were standing in his room. I told him Myles had asked me to be his girlfriend. Hunter wasn't happy. He told me Myles didn't deserve me.

What does that conversation have to do with anything?

"Do you remember what I told you?" he gets closer to me, closer than I thought possible.

I shake my head.

So much was said, so much has happened since.

He leans down, his breath fanning my neck. "The world can only offer you so much" he whispers into my ear.

"I'm confused" I admit.

"I meant every word" he continues, ignoring what I had just said.

And then a cloth is placed over my mouth.

My eyes are open, staring at Hunter as he smiles. He has his hands behind his back again, watching me struggle like it was nothing.

I struggle against the cloth over my mouth. The hand holding the cloth keeps me trapped in my place as I reluctantly inhale whatever substance has been coated on the cloth. My eyes are already heavy by the time I take another short breath.

Slowly, I look from Hunter's ocean blue eyes to West. I then find myself looking over to Elijah.

West looks far from happy, and Elijah has an unreadable look in his eyes. He is covering all his thoughts with a blank mask. I expected him to enjoy this. To enjoy seeing me struggle.

I don't know what to do.

I can't do anything.

All I can do is wait for the substance on the cloth to work its magic and trap me under Hunter's control.

My eyes gradually close and all I feel is my body crumbling into strong arms.

Hunter's arms.

CHAPTER THIRTEEN
GRACE

I'm awake.

The bedroom I have spent most nights in. The room next to Hunters. The same large windows and large bed. I'm awake in this room again. I sit up almost immediately, my breathing becoming extremely violent.

They have dragged me back here.

My last memory is Hunter showing up during the lantern festival. He destroyed RoseShire with his army. He had blown the place to pieces and then surrounded me and Myles like we were under arrest.

I push the bedsheets off my body, running over to the large windows. Sunrise is upon the city, rising just above the city's walls, reflecting off some of the buildings glass windows.

The silver city.

Soltrix.

I'm back.

A part of me feels like crumbling and crying. But that is the old me. The old me who wouldn't talk. Now all I can feel is anger and hatred. I want to strangle Hunter until he takes me back to the boarder or invents a time machine that will erase everything he has just done.

He killed AJ...

I march my way out of my room, not bothering to close the door behind me. I march down the hallway until Hunter's bedroom door is in front of me. It's locked, no surprise. I bang on the door as hard as I can, making as much noise as I can. I don't care if he is sleeping or working, he is opening this door and explaining himself to me.

He is not getting away with this.

Both my fists bang on the bedroom door until I can hear movement. "OPEN THE DOOR" I shout. "I SWEAR TO GOD I'M GOING TO MURDER YOU" I shout again.

The door opens. Hunter is shirtless, confused and a little worried. He stands in the doorway, breathing heavily like he had just ran to the door.

"Grace, what's wrong?" he sounds startled. When he looks up and down the hallway to find we are alone, his lips turn into a frown. "What are you doing banging on my door like that? I thought you were in danger" he isn't happy.

"You're about to be in danger" I warn him.

I burst into his room, barging past him. "It's three in the morning" he points out as he closes the door. "You should be resting. You have had a long couple—"

"You lied to me. You destroyed RoseShire. You hurt people who were only trying to help. You shot AJ. You drugged me. And you drag me back to this hell!" I am ragging.

"That's one way to look at it" he nods his head.

The room falls silent. I'm taken back by his words. "Are you serious?" I cross my arms, standing in the middle of the room while he sits himself down on the edge of his bed.

"I saved you" he lifts his head to look my way.

"Saved me? Oh please, you are the reason we were almost caught in the middle of a sandstorm" I scoff.

"I didn't know about a sandstorm" he sounds sincere.

"You knew Tinnstone was a pile of dust" I remind him of his lie. "You sent us out there, knowing we would get lost. You probably hoped we would come back thinking we couldn't handle the real world, when all along you knew we were only looking for ghosts"

There is a long silence. A silence so long, I don't expect Hunter to speak.

"You are right" he admits.

I'm shocked to say the least.

Hunter brings his eyes onto mine, letting me know he is sincere. "I knew Myles wasn't capable of keeping you safe. I couldn't stop you, but I came up with a plan that would hopefully bring you back" he explains.

The day we left, I thought Hunter wanted me to go out and explore. I stupidly thought he wanted me to be happy and free. But all this time, he wanted me to fail. "If that was your plan, why did you send an army to RoseShire?" I ask.

If he wanted to bring me back, he didn't need to blow up the town and everyone's homes.

There was no need for gunfire.

"There was an attack. My army was only trying to help the civilians. I travelled there to get you out before they killed you" he gets up from the bed and walks over to the windows.

"Who would attack…" I don't need to finish my sentence; I already know the answer. "Todo Poderoso" I say his name.

It would explain why I saw soldiers wearing red.

Slowly, I walk myself over to the window, stopping in front of the glass as Hunter stands beside me. We both stare out towards the large wall, guarded by many soldiers. The barrier that prevents us from leaving. The wall that protects and traps the people of Soltrix.

I can't find a silver lining for coming back.

"How was your little adventure?" Hunter questions.

My eyes stay fixated on the window. "I loved it. The first three days were hard. Myles had drunk all the water and we were low on supplies. We got lucky when we found Nikita and Asha. They gave us refuge before the sandstorm had hit. We stayed with them for a little" I take a breath. "But then you showed up…"

"I'm sorry" he apologises.

"No you're not" I sigh.

More and more silence. I have nothing more to say. My anger will get the best of me. I will say stuff I will most likely regret tomorrow. I knew the day I left I would see Hunter again; I just hoped it to be in the furthest future.

"You should go get some rest" he breaks the silence with a hushed whisper.

"I don't want to be here" It's taking everything in me to keep the tears back. I don't want to cry. I want to get out of here. I feel like I am back in the same position as before, trying to get out of here at any cost, back when no one would tell me anything. Back when I thought I was going to be killed.

"I know" he exhales.

I make my way over to the bedroom door, opening it before I hear him talk to himself. "But you will thank me one day" he mumbles. I hesitate, but I slowly close the door behind me as I leave the room.

CHAPTER FOURTEEN
GRACE

Black leggings and a sports bra.

I'm back in my training clothes, as if I never left.

A soldier woke me up for breakfast, which I didn't take too kindly. The only reason I'm obeying to Hunter's orders today, is to see West and the others. I want to see them all to make sure they're okay.

The fireplace is in the same place on the opposite wall to the door, but there are no flames. The chandelier is hanging in the centre of the room, all the lights switched on. All of the paintings on the walls, the high ceilings, and the long dining table in the centre of the room.

Nothing has changed.

When I walk into the room, everyone is already waiting around the table. Most of them seem to be wearing trousers the soldiers would wear. They're matching. Heads turn in the direction of the door when I walk inside, West is already on his feet as he tries to hide his smile. Myles also has a smile on his face when he turns to meet my eye.

West is walking over to me before anyone else, his eyes wide with excitement. "There she is" West greets me first. "My favourite freak" he picks me up and spins me around.

I giggle as the room spins. "Freak? Is that what you call me now?" I joke as he slowly puts me back on my feet, his eyes looking down into mine.

As I step to the side of West, my eyes take a quick glance around the room until they land on Lucas. His bright red hair, pale white skin and multiple freckles catch my eye. He looks almost tired. He flashes his light blue eyes at me while the skin around his eyes crinkles up as he grins. He is wearing a grey turtleneck jumper and a pair of army trousers.

That's a change for him.

He parts his lips to talk, but someone beats him to it. "I'm surprised you didn't die out there alone" I hear Elijah speak from the other side of the table.

"It's nice to see you too" I gush.

"I didn't say I was happy your back" he challenges, and I know he isn't joking. "I was hoping you would stay gone"

Elijah always has to try and ruin my mood.

He adjusts the collar to his white button up shirt. He has left the top button undone, allowing the collar to show his neck.

"Be nice" Myles huffs as he sends a warning glare over to Elijah.

"I am" Elijah snarls.

My stomach quietly growls as the smell of food floats in front of my nose. I hold onto my stomach, hoping no one can hear it growling. Elijah runs a hand through his dark hair. His light blue eyes watching my every move. I catch him, and he forces his eyes away from me.

"Well I missed you" Lucas confesses with a smile, taking away the awkwardness between everyone. "It's been boring around here without you"

"That may be because everyone has been sticking to the rules" West corrects him.

"I'm not that bad" I huff.

"Sure, Cupcake" West sarcastically agrees with me.

Hunter walks into the room. I wonder where he has been looking like that. He is wearing a black suit with a gun strapped to his waistband. his top button undone. His hair slicked back, and his hands are shoved into the pockets of his trousers. He looks too good for this time of the morning.

His eyes wander around the room. "Are you all done wasting time?" Hunter speaks up, raising his voice slightly.

Without hesitation, we all sit down, allowing the women from the kitchen to serve breakfast. Hunter sits at the head of the table like always. A plate of waffles is placed in the centre of the table and West is immediately excited. His face lights up with joy at the sight of waffles. Slowly, we dig into our food, grabbing different types of food and putting them onto our plates.

"Tell us, what's the outside like?" Lucas is quick to ask.

"Horrible" Myles jumps to answer. "Most of the walking was in sand. We ran out of supplies after a couple days and by the time we knew what was going on, there was a storm" he sounds like he hated leaving.

My head lowers.

"I bet you were glad to come back" West chuckles.

"Blowing up RoseShire was a bit dramatic, but yes" he says, honestly.

I stay focused on eating the food on my plate. Myles was the one who didn't want to leave RoseShire. He wanted to stay with Asha. No matter how much he lies about hating being on the outside, he wanted to stay with Asha.

"Grace" West turns his attention onto me. "What did you think?" he draws everyone to me.

My eyes rise from my plate. "I…" I hesitate as everyone looks at me. "I loved it" I answer, knowing Myles is disagreeing with me in his head. "The long journey to RoseShire was exhausting and tiring, but when we got there and managed to survive the storm, it was amazing"

Hunter is trying to hide the small smile on his face as he watches me express my enjoyment. I can see him in the corner of my eye. He isn't fooling me with his forced frown.

A huff and a puff comes from opposite me. "Sure" Myles doesn't sound convinced, and all I want to do is shout at him for everything he has done. The things I could say to him.

I feel nothing but anger and betrayal.

"Since you are back, we need to discuss—"

"No" I protest against Hunter.

"No?" he repeats. "You think you have a choice?" Hunter raises an eyebrow.

"We all have a choice" I challenge.

I don't know where to look. "You haven't seen the things that have been happening around here recently" Lucas speaks up with his fork lowering to the plate in front of him. "The war is getting worse. Almost everyone has died, and we are yet to stop the army from attacking the barrier"

Shock rushes through me.

Horror runs my blood cold.

The war is still going on and they are still fighting. More soldiers are dying. "They're still attacking?" Myles speaks the words on my mind as his eyes widen.

"More than ever" Lucas sighs and then shoves his fork into his mouth.

Hunter and West quickly flash each other a look from across the table. They talk without saying anything. It looks like they are reading each other's minds. Knowing what one is thinking and what the other is feeling. And then they look over to Elijah as he parts his lips to say something.

"They won't give up" Elijah adds.

As if ignoring what Elijah just said, Hunter looks over to Myles and then stares in my direction. "You two will be back in training immediately" Hunter states, bringing his glass filled with orange juice up to his lips. "We cannot waste any time"

"Four months too late" Elijah mutters under his breath.

"Four months?" I repeat.

We were gone for four months.

"It felt longer" Myles scoffs loud enough for the whole room to hear.

He is lying through his teeth.

My eyes glance from Myles to my plate. The scrabbled egg decreases from my plate with each bite. I stab the egg with my fork, again and again. There is barely any food left in the middle of the table when I raise my head.

West has already eaten all the waffles.

As I stare at the food, I think back to yesterday.

What happened to Nikita? Destiny? Asha? Nobody has mentioned them. Myles hasn't asked. He doesn't even seem to care. There was so much gunfire, did they survive?

I want to know they are safe.

"What happened to the others?" I ask, looking at Hunter for answers.

Hunter doesn't react. "Who?" he continues to eat.

"Nikita, Destiny… and Asha" I remind him. "What did you do to them? Are they safe?"

"They are safe" Hunter doesn't look up from his plate.

"What does that mean?" I don't believe him.

Nobody is looking at me now. Lucas and Elijah seem to be clueless about who I'm talking about. Hunter isn't bothered by my questions, and West is nervous. Am I the only one who cares about them? Myles is too busy shoving his face with food to acknowledge the conversation.

I'm frustrated.

68

They took care of us when we needed them, now I need to return the favour and make sure they are safe.

"We took care of them" Hunter gives a vague answer.

Knowing what Hunter is like with people, anything could have happened to them.

My eyes narrow onto him. "Where are they?" I question him, hoping Hunter will give me a real answer this time. "I want to know they are okay" I plead.

Hunter needs to tell me they are safe.

"Grace—"

"They didn't hurt them" Myles assures me.

I don't say anything.

I wait and I wait for someone to explain. Not one person wants to tell me. The silence is killing me. "What aren't you telling me?" I know something is off.

"We brought them here" West finally speaks up, getting tired of the same questions.

And I'm enraged.

"You… why?" I give Hunter my full attention.

Hunter's blue eyes slowly look up from his plate, landing on mine. He doesn't say anything to me. He keeps his lips stitched together as he stares into my eyes.

I forcefully slam my hands on the table and stand up from my chair. "They are good people. They should not be here. They should be back home living their normal lives. You need to take them back to RoseShire and leave them alone" I demand.

"I will do no such thing" he shakes his head.

"They were only trying to help us" I exclaim.

My blood boils as I watch him. He runs a hand through his hair. "I don't care" he shows no emotion.

"I do" I challenge him.

They will not rot away here like we do.

I refuse to allow Hunter to make them part of our fight, they are good people after all. Nikita should be back home, driving the car around in the sun dunes. Destiny should be going to work at the local newspaper. Asha… she should be as far away from me as possible.

And AJ should be alive.

There is no chance of me allowing Hunter to keep them here.

My feet begin moving, the chair scrapping on the floor as I move it out of my way. I walk around the chair and towards the door. Two more chairs scrap against the floor behind me but I ignore them. I'm going to find where the others are being held and I'm going to let them go home.

After all they did for us, they don't deserve to be stuck here, in Soltrix, with us.

"Oh, she's off again" Myles mutters from the table.

"Shut it" Elijah shuts Myles up.

It takes a lot for me to keep walking, instead of turning around and punching Myles in the face.

CHAPTER FIFTEEN
GRACE

The hallway is empty.

The hallway is lonely.

I walk fast and steady, making my way down the long hall as quick as I can. Bright white lights and freshly painted walls surround me as I begin jogging. My walk becomes a fast-paced run by the time I reach the first corner.

There are no soldiers in sight.

I turn a corner and then another. I run past doors and other hallways. After all this time, I should have some way of knowing where to go. I should know the place better. Yet, I still have a lot to learn about the building. In my opinion, they should put a map somewhere. It would make running away so much easier.

No soul is in sight when I reach the elevators. My finger pushes the button multiple times, hoping the doors will open quicker. Why won't the doors just open!

"Stop her!" Hunter shouts from behind me.

My head turns to look down the hallway, finding Hunter and West walking towards me. They are not running. They are walking. As if they know I won't get very far. But this time, I'm not trying to escape the building. I'm trying to find Nikita and the others.

Soldiers appear out of nowhere.

They were not here moments ago.

The elevator doors open, and I try to rush inside before the soldiers can reach me. I'm not quick enough. Two soldiers grab my arms, holding me in place. "Put me down" I shake my arms to try and release myself from their grip.

My legs dangle in the air as they hold me off the ground, making sure I can't run away. Their grip is too strong. My arms are hurting from their tight hold on me.

Hunter and West stop walking. West crosses his arms as he watches me struggle. I relax slightly, giving up against the strong men holding me. "I won't run" again.

"You and I both know that is a lie" Hunter frowns.

He stops walking in front of me, standing in my direct eyeline. "Are you going to put me to asleep again?" I ask.

"If I have to" he nods his head. I look away from him as he fills the space between us. He gets closer and closer to me until his breath is fanning my face. Coconut fills my nostrils. "Is it too much to ask for you to stay still?" he examines my face for a response.

A tight thin line spreads across my lips. "Are you going to stop kidnapping people?" I glare at him.

He looks taken back by my question, shocked almost. "I don't kidnap innocent people" he corrects me, but he doesn't convince me.

All I can do is stare.

Neither of us move as the silence between us grows to a point where one of us is about to snap. He then looks from me to the soldiers. "You can put her down now" he orders, and they immediately oblige.

My feet touch the floor, gently. The elevator doors open, and I see my opportunity. I move swiftly towards the doors as the small window of opportunity closes. Someone's hand grips my elbow, stopping me from going any further as the doors slowly close shut. My hair falls past my shoulders as my head wipes around to face Hunter again.

"I want to see them" I plead.

"Let the girl see them—"

"Stay out of this, West" Hunter snarls, but he doesn't remove his eyes from mine.

I struggle against Hunter. "No, go on, let him talk" I rip my elbow from his hand. "He was agreeing with me"

Hunter grabs my arm, pulling me against his chest. My head lifts until my eyes are back on his, glaring up at him. "You need to stop resisting me" he sighs. "I am only trying to do what is best for you"

The grip on my arms tightens. "You're hurting me" I try to grab his attention.

He doesn't listen to me.

"I have been waiting for you to come back. Four months you were gone. Four months of standing in front of a screen waiting for you to come back" Hunter confesses.

My eyes widen with each word that escapes his lips.

"Hunter…" West tries to help me.

Hunter looks from West back to me, realisation hitting him like a stack of bricks. He clears his throat and straightens his back. "You are to go to your room" he commands. "I will see you tonight for dinner"

"What about—"

"This conversation is over" he cuts me off. "Goodnight, Ms Silver"

With that, the two soldiers grab my arms and force me away from Hunter. They walk me into the elevator and press the button for my bedroom.

CHAPTER SIXTEEN
GRACE

The room is quiet as the world spins. I can feel the fresh air brushing against my bare legs as the blanket wraps around the bed. I'm too warm to be snuggling under the covers. The bed is too big for my small body to fit perfectly.

My head lays flat on the pillow, my eyes watching as the ceiling falls fast asleep. I left the balcony doors open, hoping for the room to cool down. The night is always cold here. I have had enough of the heat, I'm ready to feel snow on my skin. I have prepared myself for the winter.

Hunter's soldiers have locked me in my room all day.

I refused to come out for dinner. He wanted to lock me in my room, so I will stay in my room. Breakfast filled me up enough for the day anyways. After all these years, I have survived a lot longer periods of time without food.

Listening to Hunter's demands is the last thing I will do right now. Not until he tells me where Nikita and the others are being held in the building. He cannot get away with doing whatever he wants and receiving no consequence. I will stay in this room for the next week if it means he sees to my demand.

The wind blows into the room, creating a whistling sound with each gust. I sit up, pushing my body off the bed and onto my feet. I make my way towards the balcony, wanting to feel the cold air on my face. This room is feeling more like an oven with each breath I take.

My eyes glance over to Hunter's balcony. A small part of me wanting him to be standing there, looking and waiting for me to join him. But he is not. He is probably fast asleep while the rest of the world struggles.

Behind me, I can hear movement in the dark.

From one corner to the next, each shadow having a mind of its own, there is movement. My entire body spins on my heels to see who is there. Who is exploring my room. Who is daring enough to try and sneak up on me.

74

But there is no one there.

The entire room is nothing but one big darkness. Not a single light is on. "Is someone there?" I ask the darkness, but I don't get a response.

Something falls onto the floor from the desk, and I know there is someone inside the room. "I can hear you" I confess.

I feel insane. Talking to the darkness. I haven't done that since I left the PPW. "Whoever you are, I am not afraid to fire at you" I shout, pretending to hold a gun in my hands. I pull my hands up and clasp them together with two of my fingers pointing into the space in front of me.

Now, I just feel stupid.

"With what? Your fake guns?" a deep voice speaks from the darkness, and slowly Carter emerges from the darkest shadows of the room.

My eyes widen as I stare and stare and stare until the image of Carter feels real. "C- Carter…" I say his name, wanting to wake up from my dream. He can't be here. I thought he was gone. He disappeared. He was badly hurt.

Now he is standing in my room, without a scratch.

"Why are… How are you here?" I ask.

Too many questions spring to mind as I analyse his body through the darkness. "Did you intend to kill me?" he asks a different question, changing the topic away from his sudden appearance.

"What?" my blood runs cold.

"During our fight" he reminds me. "Did you want to kill me?" he then repeats his question.

I become silent.

I don't know what to say. "Carter…" I can only reply with his name.

He sees right through me, reading me like a book. "It's okay. I knew you would try" he nods his head. His back straightens as he brushes his top. "Dad was furious. You're lucky he sees potential in you" and again, I don't understand what he is telling me. He keeps repeating the word 'dad' but there is only denial running through my mind.

"What are you talking about?" I become more confused with each word he speaks. "Who is dad?"

"You'll know soon enough" he assures me.

I walk off the balcony, getting closer to Carter. His bright blonde hair waves in the wind. It's messy and unlike him to be in this state. His emerald, green eyes are searching the room, he is barely looking at me.

"That is not an answer" I snap.

He knows he needs to give me better answers than the ones I'm getting. "There is going to be a war. A war to end all wars. We want you to fight with us. Help us put an end to all the madness" he puts his hand out between us. "Join us. With you on our side, we can finally stop the war"

"Join who?" I question.

Carter is missing a very important piece of information.

"Me and dad" he smiles, innocently.

"We are not related" I deny, shaking my head.

"I was hoping you would find out differently, but it is never a good time to tell you" He moves his hand away from me, scratching the back of his neck.

My brain is beginning to feel like the scrambled eggs from this morning. "I don't have a family" I continue to deny and deny and deny. "I don't have a father and I definitely do not have a brother. You are nothing but a liar—"

He shakes his head. "I promise you, I'm not the one lying to you"

I can remember the first day I met Carter. "You were in the PPW" I remind him of the day he showed up in Mrs Penticon's classroom.

"I remember" he agrees with me.

"You sat beside me" I continue.

"I know, I was there" he nods.

Now that I think back to the moments I was around Carter, I always wondered how he was brought here after he wasn't picked by Hunter. He never showed his ability. He never had his name called out. If I think back, I don't remember him being in the room at all.

He shoves one hand into the pocket of his black joggers and his other hand stays behind his back. "Dad had this plan for me to kill you. I couldn't. I did try, trust me. I got close to it too. But in the end, you are my sister... I can't kill you"

"You were trying to kill me…?" I force the words out of my scratchy throat.

"Multiple times. But something in me wouldn't allow you to die" he sighs. He moves over to my bed, sitting down on the end. "It may have something to do with our blood. That's what dad tried explaining to me"

"You tried to kill me" that piece of information sticks to me like hot glue.

"Call us even" Carter waves his hand in the air. "That is in the past. Now we need to focus on getting you out of this building" he claps his hands together.

"And go where, exactly?" I raise my eyebrows.

"FrostMount" he smirks.

FrostMount sounds familiar. The people of RoseShire had spoken about that place. They told me it was known for being the home of the devil. What that means, I still have no idea. "Is that where you have been?" I guess.

The wind pushes me further into the room. I stop when I am standing directly opposite Carter. He looks up from his lap to meet my eye. "Yes. Zara managed to pull me away from the fight before you hurt me too badly. Lucky me, I guess" he scoffs as he rolls his eyes.

"Zara?" I repeat the name.

Who is Zara?

His eyes move away from me, wandering behind me as he scans over the chest of draws and then the wardrobe. He is looking for something. He came here for a reason. "What are you doing here?" I ask another question.

"I came here to get you" he lies.

I catch his eyes wandering around the room, he is looking around for something specific. As if he is certain that I have something he needs. "You're looking for something" I make a judgement. And he doesn't deny it. "What is it?" I frown.

He shakes his head as he brings his eyes back onto my annoyed face. "Nothing you need to worry about" Carter shuts my question down.

Carter stands up from the bed, walking past me towards the chest of draws. And then my desk. And then the bed-side tables. He searches every inch of the room, only to come up empty handed. I want to know what he is looking for. What he thinks I have. What is so important he has travelled all the way here to retrieve?

The room looks a mess for once. The draws are left open, and the desk is left in the centre of the room. "Are you really working for Todo Poderoso?" I ask another question as I try to get as much information out of him as I can.

He doesn't bother to give me an answer.

Instead, he continues to search.

"Are you trying to take over the city?" I ask a different question as he continues to ignore me.

"Your always so serious. Lighten up. Learn to relax every once in a while" he complains.

There is a light flickering behind me. I can see it through my shadow. Through the moons reflection. There is something behind me, I can feel it through the shiver running down my spine. I turn around, only to find a girl standing on the balcony with her wavy black hair blowing in the wind.

She appeared out of thin air.

Like magic.

Her wavy black hair stops before her shoulders. She runs her hands around her shoulders, a shudder of pain hidden behind her tight frown. Her fair skin and freckled face. The girl shields her eyes from my sight. As if she doesn't want me to know her. Like she wants to stay unknown. I can't make out where she has come from or how she got up here.

"Carter" she calls out to him.

My eyes are back on Carter.

"It was nice seeing you again sis" Carter pats my shoulder as he walks past me.

My frown grows.

Following him with my eyes, my head turns. He continues to walk towards the girl. Towards Zara. He cannot leave yet. I need to know more.

"Where are you going?" I ask, trying to keep him here as long as possible.

Carter stops beside the girl, turning back around to face me one last time. "Back to FrostMount" he answers. "You don't have what I need… but I'll see you again soon, unless you want to come with me?"

"And what if I don't?" I cross my arms.

"No pressure. We will come to collect you soon enough" he assures me.

And I don't doubt him for a second.

I cross my arms as Carter waits for my response. "Right, I will take that as a no" he smugly grins and then looks to the other girl. She hasn't taken her eyes off me. Watching me intensely, making sure I don't try anything stupid. Like she doesn't trust me. Not that I blame her. I don't trust her either.

But before I can ask any more questions, they disappear into a bright purple light, blinding enough to throw me off my balance. They are gone, and I'm left confused and alone, all over again.

CHAPTER SEVENTEEN
GRACE

Hunter is making me train.

I am standing against the back wall, watching West struggle to find a piece of information in a small file. His fingers flick the page back and forth, my eyes analysing the page. He looks concerned and confused and concentrated. My eyes watch him curiously. Intensely. I want to know what he is looking for.

Why are we standing around doing nothing?

"What are you looking for?" I ask, getting impatient.

"I spent most of the night researching, only to come up with nothing" he says with frustration, throwing the file to the wall and slouching his shoulders slightly. "Never mind. We should probably start training before I get called incompetent"

The writing catches my attention.

My feet feel heavy as I walk over to the file, picking it up with one hand. The brown file is open, revealing all the secrets hidden in the letters on the pages. I read and read, scanning my eyes over the small page. My name was written all through the file. The information was about me and my life. My birth, my whole childhood spent in the PPW, my parents…

Within seconds, I am infuriated. "What the hell is this?" I look up from the file as West crosses his arms.

He looks at the file, and then me. "I was trying to find information about your ability" he admits.

"Where did you get this?" I ask another question.

He hesitates. "Our private records"

It says my family is unknown, my ability is classified. All they know about me in this record is my name. My name is the only piece of information they can tell me about myself. "This is useless" I huff.

"Your telling me" He agrees.

I read the paper again, looking over the words. One word keeps catching my eye. "What does classified mean?" I have to ask, wanting to know more.

His eyes stay on me. "It means only important people can know" he explains. "I'm guessing Hunter will know... or the Supreme" West shakes his head. "It doesn't matter. It doesn't help. We will have to figure it out on our own"

The room feels small. I feel smaller. "I'm not using my ability" I protest.

"You need to train" West commands.

"I... West I don't want too. Please..." I sigh, lowering the file to my side.

"Why not?" he furrows his eyebrows.

I'm scared. Petrified even. Last time I used my ability to a large extent, it did something to me. I lost control. I became an entirely different person. I can't control myself.

"I just don't want too" I repeat.

I begin walking to the door, hoping to escape. West grabs my arm and stops me in my tracks. He slowly parts his lips to talk again. "Can you tell me about Carter?" I change the topic before he pushes me into setting the room on fire.

"Don't change the—"

"Did you think he was working with the Supreme?" I continue with my question.

He lets go of my arm, allowing it to drop to my side as he takes a short but deep breath. He contemplates the question in his head, staring into my eyes as he thinks. "I didn't" West sounds ashamed. "I should have known but I was too busy thinking and worrying about the war to notice"

"No one knew" I sigh, trying to reassure him that it wasn't his fault. "His betrayal was a shock to us all"

My words take West off guard. "Why are you asking about Carter?" he asks me a question.

I want to know more but nobody except Carter can give me the answers I want. A part of me wants to travel to Carter and chain him up until he tells me everything I want to know without any more lies. "No reason" I shrug it off as curiosity.

There is a pause.

A long enough pause for me to count the many passing seconds in my head.

"Let's get back to training" he tries to stir away from the conversation again.

81

"I have already told—"

He puts his hand up to stop me from speaking. "We will stick to fist combat today and try another time. But it will be soon" he warns me.

Maybe I can't hold it off forever, but the longer I protest, the better it will be. The sheer thought of using my ability has my body trembling. I hurt people, too many people, the last time I tried to use my ability. I don't want anyone else to suffer at the hands of me.

My arms fall to my sides. "Put your right foot forward. I then need you to place your weight on the back foot" he gives me his orders, standing beside me with his hands ready to correct my position. "Hands ready to attack" he states, as if he is expecting me to know what he means.

"What?" I ask.

"Like this" he says, moving to stand opposite me.

West stands in the position he wants me to copy, and then waits for me to mirror his stance. I put my right foot in front of the other, my hands curled into tight fists, my fists up in front of my face. We both look as if we are about to fight one another to the death.

My eyes watch and wait for him to make the first move.

When he doesn't move, I get impatient. "What are you waiting for?" I ask.

"You are going to make the first move" he claims.

Before giving him another second to wait, I make my first move towards him. One step, two step, three step. My right fist hurls towards his face. I wait for impact. I expect there to be impact. But instead, all I get is his hand wrapping around mine and my back pressing against the cold concrete floor.

"Ouchhh" I groan.

He shakes his head. "You need to be quicker"

West stretches his hand out between us, allowing me to grab onto it. He pulls me back to my feet. "Thanks" I speak as I brush myself off. My skin-tight leggings are sticking to my legs as my long white top swings when I move.

"Again" he demands.

We get into the same position. This time, I move quicker than before. My fist connects with West's arm, completely and utterly missing his face. He grips my waist, spins me around to the point of my body stumbling into his chest. I take a deep breath as he steps backwards.

Once again, we get into the position. "Tell me about your favourite person" he asks, confusing me with his question.

I strike, managing to hit him on the shoulder. "Why?" I ask him, moving back to my original spot. "That has nothing to do with training"

This time, West attacks me. I push his arm to the side as his left fist tries to connect with my stomach. "I want to get to know you better. We have been working together for a while and I know very little about your personal life" he admits, his eyes looking from the floor to my position.

My eyes narrow. "The file should tell you everything you want to know" I frown, moving backwards as he tries to throw another fist my way.

He finally manages to lay a punch. His fist makes contact with the side of my stomach, hitting me hard enough to knock the wind out of me for a brief moment. I stumble enough for him to grab my arm and throw me over his body. I'm thrown onto my back, hitting the concrete harder than before.

I groan from the pain he causes me.

"You need to stop doing that" I wince.

He outstretches his hand for me to grab. "We both know the file says nothing" he looks down at me.

"It is as much as I know about my life" I grab onto his hand.

West shakes his head again. "I want to know the interesting stuff. The stuff you can only learn from talking to someone" he explains as he helps me onto my feet for the second time.

West gets back into his fighting stance, so I do the same, my body copying his. I take a deep breath. "Sarah… she was the sweetest person I have ever met. She was the only person who truly understood me… There wasn't a bad bone in her body. She would bring me books to read and tell me stories" I hold back the urge to cry.

One, two, three, and we attack again.

"Hunter's people made sure she didn't get a chance to show the world that" I can see the night replaying in my head.

My arms swing, time after time, until I hit something. I keep swinging after I make contact. I don't stop. My blood is at its highest boiling point. I punch and punch and punch until West is on the floor, shuffling backwards.

I quickly snap from my trance, watching West try his best to get away from me. "That's enough" he stops me encase I try to continue. My body freezes in the same spot.

Red marks are forming all over his face, mainly around his left eye. "I'm sorry" I apologise.

West shakes his head and gets back onto his feet, making a grunting noise as he holds his jaw. "Hunter didn't know—"

"No, you're right. I should be blaming Hunter's dad. The Supreme is to blame for all this. Todo Poderoso is to blame for it. They are trying to rule this world into the ground. They are killing innocent people for the fun of it. They need to pay" my anger rises to the surface.

In the blink of an eye, West tackles me to the ground. He takes me off guard and winds me, once again. I feel myself try to gain the ability to breathe. "You need to snap out of it. That won't change anything. Thinking like that will only bring you more anger" he cautions.

As I straighten myself out, I feel my limbs freeze. All my surroundings become a blur. Nothing is spinning but I can't see a thing. It's all a haze. It's like someone flicked my switch and turned my power button off.

"Woah..." he expresses his shock.

My breathing becomes quick and shallow. "What?"

"Your eyes" he gestures towards my face, his eyes glued to mine. "That's new" There is no mirrors in the room. I'm left shaking and confused. I'm frantically looking for a reflection, but I come up empty handed.

I'm frantic and scared and lost. My hands are shaking violently, and my legs feel like they're going to buckle as I try to balance on my feet. The loud throbbing in my head is repetitive, beating again and again in a familiar rhythm.

I'm shaking.

The whole room feels like it's shaking.

My eyes look down at my hands, finding them covered in blood. The warm thick liquid slipping through my fingers as my pulse quickens. When I look up from my hands, I'm back in my room, surrounded by the same four walls I had hoped to never see again. Sarah's body lies by my feet, her dark blood pouring into a puddle.

I breathe. Closing my eyes and then opening them again, taking my time as the air leaves my lungs. I'm in my room, a pillow is being placed over my face as Carter's eyes stare into mine. A saddened look upon his features. I struggle, kicking and screaming against the pillow.

Blink. Scream. Blink. Scream. I cry and cry. Anything I do won't stop the air escaping my burning lungs. My eyes slam shut, holding back the tears. All I see is red. Red, red, red. The colour is burnt into my brain, clouding my senses. When I open my eyes to get away from the constant changes, I gasp.

Fire and water and earth and then air. They are hovering over their own pedestal, each individual pedestal having a different colour. The four elements are right in front of me, balancing on a thin line between imaginary and reality.

Red.

Red.

Red.

All I can see is red. My skin is dancing with flames. The air feels thicker. Every long second passes with another heat wave hitting me like a sack of sand. My body continues to shake slightly as my legs begin to give up on me.

My reality kicks in. The room is a blur again and West is shaking my shoulders. I can hear the door opening behind me, but I can't turn around.

"Control it!" West snaps.

Control isn't in the cards right now. I can't see, I can't feel a thing, and the world is lit on fire. A trail of fire spreads from my feet to one of the training mats. A bright orange light tries to break through the red, but it doesn't stand a chance.

"Grace—" someone shouts from behind me.

Elijah?

My body caves in on me. I feel myself fall to the ground and all the red dots slowly fade to blackness.

Then I hear rushed footsteps behind me. "What the hell were you doing?" I can hear Myles' voice from behind me.

Someone is kneeing beside me. I can feel their hands pressing against my neck. "She has a pulse" the person beside me speaks.

I'm awake.

I'm conscious.

I just can't see.

The black dots fade and fade, but not enough for me to sit up straight. It feels like my body is leaning against a leg or a crouch or an arm. "Elijah…?" I say his name, watching as he holds me in his arms, waiting for me to wake up. My eyes look up at his as I realise, I've been slumped in his lap this entire time.

"Shh" he whispers in a soothing tone.

He carefully runs his fingers through my messy blonde hair in an attempt to keep me calm. I blink up at him. The motion makes me feel safe. Elijah's touch is comforting. His touch is delicate. It is a mixture between electric and tender.

A part of me doesn't want to leave his embrace.

My eyes stare up at Elijah, waiting for the dream to turn back to reality. In reality, he wouldn't be this close to me, with our breaths almost touching, voluntarily. Elijah can't stand to be nice to me, yet alone keep me comfortable and safe.

But I still find myself buying into the illusion that Elijah is caring and worried. I choose to believe this is real, that what is going on around me is my reality.

"Welcome back" West crouches down in front of me. "How many fingers am I holding?" he then holds up his hand with two fingers up, like a peace sign.

My head is pounding.

"Two" I answer.

Thankfully, I give him the answer he was looking for. The people around us become familiar. Myles and Lucas. They are looking down at me with worry in their eyes and relief in their smiles. I keep my eyes on Myles, only to be returned with a small smile back.

"Good" West sighs with relief.

Elijah's hand falls onto my arm, his skin touching mine for the first time in a long time. For once, it isn't harmful, it is soft and gentle. There is no harsh bitterness involved.

Without realising, my body snuggles up into his slightly, but he notices. Only he notices. Of course, he notices.

The unfamiliar feeling between us makes the pair of us freeze in the moment. I move my eyes up, looking at him as he stares down at me. We are frozen in time, our eyes gazing into each other's with surprise held within our features. His hand remains on my arm. Neither of us want to move.

Nothing has ever felt like home to me, not like this.

This feeling is different.

This is new.

West stands up straight. "Give her to me. I will take her to the medics" he reaches out for me. "While I take her, you guys need to put out the fire" West speaks to Elijah.

Elijah's arms tighten around me, lifting me from his lap and up into the air. My body rejects the movement, my arms pushing me away from Elijah the minute his left hand meets my waist. I stumble. "I'm fine" I lie. Nobody looks convinced and I'm not surprised.

The state of me deceives my lie.

I'm scooped up into West's arms. "Tell your face that" he jokes as he begins carrying me towards the door.

Nobody says anything as I'm carried out of the room and down the hallway.

CHAPTER EIGHTEEN
GRACE

My head feels light, mainly because of all the blood that was taken. The medics are trying to get to the bottom of why I had suddenly collapsed. They have been doing tests, taking many different samples, and made sure to keep me awake.

But all I want to do is sleep.

West has been by my side since the moment I woke up from my own mind. He has been back and forth the medics to make sure everything is running smoothly. I trust him enough to know he won't let anything bad happen to me. I'm lucky he wants answers as much as I do.

Hunter is in the chair beside me. When he heard what had happened, he rushed down to check on me. He hasn't left my side either. As much as I want to stay angry at him for going against his word, the small action of staying with me makes me smile.

My arm is hurting from the bloods, along with every other bone in my body. I take deep breaths as I wait around for the medics to come back with answers.

The images are replaying in my head as I close my eyes for the hundredth time today. Fire, water, earth and air. Carter suffocating me with a pillow. Bodies on bodies. I saw things I would have never imagined before, yet they are now stuck in my head, replaying like a broken record.

I watch as West walks back and forth, his legs moving quicker than his thoughts. He mumbles now and again but no one understands what he is saying. "Drink some of this, it will help with your head" Hunter holds out a cup of water.

My eyes look from Hunter to the plastic cup. "Thank you" I quietly say as I take the cup out of his hands. Slowly, I take small sips of water. It's cold and refreshing, exactly what I needed. I just want the dizziness to disappear.

Finally, West stops pacing. He walks over to the side of my bed and sighs. "It shouldn't be too long before the results are back" West tries to reassure me. But I think he is saying it to calm himself down. "There has to be a real explanation for this"

"Can I go to my room now?" I ask, wanting to get out of this bed. "I can wait for the results in my room—"

"You need to wait here" Hunter shakes his head.

I gently rest my head against the pillow that has been prompted up against the headboard. The cup of water is taken from my hands and placed on the bedside table. "I… I want fresh air" I complain.

"It won't be long" Hunter repeats West's words.

As I look around, Myles is nowhere to be seen. My boyfriend isn't here to make sure I'm okay. I'm not surprised but I'm a little hurt. Being with Myles is not how I imagined it. I saw a long happy life with him. Instead, he has cheated and lied and completely forgotten I exist.

Maybe we moved to fast.

Out of everyone, Myles is the only person I was hoping to walk through the medic doors.

But instead, Elijah walks into the room.

Of course, it would have to be the one person who would make snarky comments towards me instead of comfort. He is probably the last person I want to be around.

"The fire's out" Elijah's voice erupts through the silence filling the room. He enters the room with Lucas walking in behind him, my eyes wandering over the both of them.

Lucas faintly smiles as he meets my eye. He is standing beside Elijah. I look from one to the other. I don't know who to keep my eyes on.

Elijah stands up straight. I find myself looking over every detail of his face, over and over again. His tall structure and dark hair, the light blue eyes that could be mistaken for grey in certain lighting. I can see the frown tugging at his lips. I notice the way his jaw is tensed.

I continue to memories his features like I always do.

"Thank you" West nods his head.

"How are you feeling?" Lucas asks me.

"You look like shit" Elijah claims.

My lips frown at Elijah. That is the last thing I wanted to hear right now. "We are just waiting for the results" I answer Lucas question, my eyes looking everywhere but at Elijah.

Hunter hasn't said a word since they arrived.

89

He is keeping his head down while Lucas steps further into the room. "We should go" Elijah hurries Lucas. "I want to get away from the smell of death"

"Where is Myles?" I manage to get the question out before they leave.

"He was in bed last time I checked" Lucas recalls.

"Oh… okay thanks anyways" my eyes lower.

"I'm sure he's just busy" Lucas tries to make me feel better, a sad sort of smile tugging his lips.

Lucas turns to leave, but Elijah lingers.

Elijah is staring at me with pain in his eyes. He doesn't look away from me. He debates something inside him, hesitating to leave. But to me, it doesn't make sense. If he wanted to stay, why would he make a fuss to leave so quickly.

Eventually, the boys leave the medic ward as fast as they appeared. A part of me was hoping Myles would have come with them, but maybe I'm asking for too much. Myles didn't show any worry when it happened, he was not going to start showing any worry now.

Hunter picks his eyes up from the bed. "I don't know why I ever let my father talk me into bringing people like him into this building" Hunter shakes his head in disappointment.

One of the medics from earlier walks over to my bed while carrying a clipboard in their hands. West jumps at the sight of a medic. He is more excited than I am. The medic stands at the bottom of my bed as their eyes land upon Hunter.

They stare and stare, not taking their eyes off him.

"The tests have come back clear" the medic states. "She shows no sign of a brain injury, her bloods are normal. The only real concern we have is the fact that her body collapsed out of nowhere. Was she dehydrated or feeling nauseous before—"

"No she wasn't" West cuts the medic off. "We already answered these questions"

The medic knits their lips into a thin line, getting more and more uncomfortable the longer West becomes impatient towards them. "There isn't much more we can do. She is free to leave when she is ready" the medic claims.

"That is not acceptable" Hunter quickly frowns, moving his eyes onto me. "Do more tests!" he then demands.

I push the blanket off me. "It's fine. I'm fine" I insist. I'm ready to leave. I would rather go to my room and sleep the rest of the day away. "I'm okay now"

"This is bullshit" West snaps.

"There is nothing more we can do. She is different. The tests don't work on her. The only thing I can think to do is to take her to the PPW and get them to run the tests" the medic tries to suggest.

Almost immediately, I panic.

My head shakes and my eyes widen. "No— no no no. I'm not going back. Never, I will never go back" I protest. The sheer thought of being back in that hell hole turns my blood cold. I never want to be trapped in that place again, I won't let that happen. I've come too far to go back there.

The medic walks away, leaving us in silence.

West and Hunter are looking at each other, reading each other's thoughts. They know what the other is thinking while keeping their mouths shut. My eyes are flickering between the two of them, waiting to be clued in on what they are thinking about. Neither seem to want to talk.

I give up waiting. "What are you both thinking?" I ask.

My words seem to snap them away from their thoughts for a moment. "Nothing. Go back to your room and rest, we can continue training tomorrow when you are better rested and fit to train" West concludes our training for the day.

Nodding my head, I don't waste another second. I stand up from the bed and walk swiftly out of the medical ward.

CHAPTER NINETEEN
GRACE

My face rests against the cold surface.

I am so tired; I could sleep forever.

In class, they had people try to discover their ability, but I got nowhere. I am far behind everyone else. I don't think I have an ability like the rest of the people here.

Maybe I am useless.

"You are not useless" Elijah can hear my thoughts.

I lift my head from the table, looking in front of me to see Elijah shoving his fork into his mouth.

"Was I thinking out loud again?" I ask, sheepishly.

"Yep" he doesn't seem fazed.

"Sorry..." I look down, fidgeting with my fingers as my hands rest on my lap.

Elijah chuckles. "You don't need to apologise. What were you thinking about?" he is still looking at me, watching me. He has a small smile on his pink face.

His messy dark hair slightly falls in front of his light eyes, the kind of eyes you could debate. Light blue? Light grey? I still have no idea. I could stare at his eyes all day and try to figure them out. But I shouldn't. That would be weird. His pink lips tilt into a bigger smile as he watches me study his features.

"I was thinking about class yesterday..." I admit.

"Ah" he nods his head. "Don't think about it, you got a lot of time before you're eighteen. You will figure out what you can do before then" he reassures me.

"Yeah— your right" I agree, but the worry remains.

I look around the dinner hall, looking at the multiple kids eating away at the disgusting food. The taste is like the scraps off a soldiers boot. The soldiers food looks delicious, ours looks like it was created from a garbage bag.

Elijah and I are sitting in the middle of one of the long dinner tables. The people sitting around us are too focused on each other to notice us.

I don't know many people.

I don't want to know many people.

I like sticking to myself.

I only know around three or four people. Elijah, Sarah, Myles… and a girl called daisy, but she hasn't been around for a week or two now.

I tend to stick to Elijah; he makes sure I am not alone in the days and keeps me company in the nights if I have another nightmare.

Myles tends to stick to a different group of people.

He likes to socialise and make friends. I don't think I have had a real conversation with him. We sit together in one of the classes we have, but we don't talk, he is too scared to get in trouble with the teacher to talk.

But he is the only other person I have spent time with around here.

"I met this guy yesterday, his name is Nolan, I think. He seems nice. Have you spoken to him before?" Elijah sparks up a new conversation. I only respond with my head shaking. "I think you'll like him, he likes reading, like you. But he reads the geography books from class. I caught him sneaking one under his top at the end of class" Elijah chuckles at the memory.

"I like reading" I smile.

"I know" he smiles back.

Nolan… I don't recognise the name. He might be in one of my classes, but I have never spoke to him. But if he likes to read, he can't be that bad.

"What is the newest book Sarah has given you?" Elijah questions me. He is the only one here who knows about Sarah giving me books to read.

I trust him.

He is one of my only friends here.

I know he wouldn't do anything to hurt me.

"She gave me Romeo and Juliet" I answer him. "The book is supposed to be about two people who fall in love, but they are not allowed to love each other"

"Sounds like something you would like" he says, finishing the last of the food on his plate.

I nod, pushing my plate into the centre of the table.

CHAPTER TWENTY
GRACE

I snap out of my daze to be met with a room filled with loud scrapping of knives and forks with a hint of talking every now and again. Everyone is eating the rest of the food on their plates, trying to saver every last bite.

My eyes are still staring at Elijah, trying to work him out.

What happened when I collapsed, the feeling between me and him, I cannot remove it from my head. Some part of me wants to feel it again.

I want to reach out and feel his skin on mine. Feel his eyes burning down into mine as his lips try to reject the smile tugging at the corners. I want him to say my name as I nestle my head into his lap one more time.

But over and over again, every time the thought crosses my mind, I need to remind myself.

It is Elijah I am thinking about.

He is the last person I should be having these thoughts about.

As I completely snap from my daydream, I force my eyes away from Elijah.

The rest of the day I've spent in my room lying in bed with my head in my pillow, thinking about everything. I need a day to myself. Thankfully, West allowed me to miss training, and gave me a couple hours of peace. It was nice to take a break from all the stuff happening around me. Going from doing my own thing to training all hours of the day is a big jump.

Now, I have been dragged downstairs for food. I decided to dress up nice since I had enough time on my hands. I am wearing a long green dress with a slit down the right side of my leg. I found it hanging up in the wardrobe.

Sitting around the long table, I have to cross my leg over the other to keep my legs warm. The room is cold. A harsh but subtle breeze is making its way around me, pushing the hairs on my arms up.

My mind focuses on the conversations that are happening around the table.

94

Talk about the war can be heard from Elijah as he slowly eats the rest of the food on his plate. Lucas is discussing peace to Elijah, hoping to bring the topic of war to an end. Myles is keeping to himself, minding his own business with his eyes on the dancing fork he is twirling around.

From under the table, I feel something nudge my knee, startling me. "How are you feeling?" West asks as his eyes turn to meet mine. He looks sincere. A warm smile slowly making its way across his face.

I nod my head in an attempt to respond to his question as I continue to chew the piece of food in my mouth. When I finish chewing, I realise he is still waiting for an answer from me. "I'm okay" I offer him a faint smile.

"What happened?" Myles asks me, lowering his fork from his mouth. "Why did you collapse?"

"Don't be insensitive" Lucas glares at Myles.

Myles only rolls his eyes.

The sensitive boy I used to know is no longer the same boy sitting on the other side of the table. It's like he is a whole new person. The complete opposite to the Myles I grew up to know and love.

"We have more important things to discuss" Elijah steers the conversation away from me.

I shift uncomfortably in my chair. For once, I am thankful Elijah has said something. I am glad he has steered everyone off the topic of me, even if it is only for a minute.

"Like what?" Myles frowns.

"Anything other than her" Elijah complains.

I refuse to believe Elijah was the guy on the floor making sure I was still alive and breathing. This cannot be the same guy who held me in his arms, making sure I was comfortable and safe for when I woke up.

There is no way all of that was Elijah.

I can't picture it.

"Once you have finished your food. You may leave the table and go to your rooms" Hunter finally speaks.

Hunter's hair has grown out. It's a lot longer than how I remember it. The blonde highlights at the ends of his hair are almost touching his eyes, restricting his view. His roots seem to be a dark brown, getting darker with each passing day.

"You speak like a dad" Myles scoffs under his breath.

And with that, Lucas and Elijah are on their feet. They are already making their way down to the end of the table, wasting no more time around us. West stands up beside me, his eyes glued to Elijah's back. "We need to have a word before you go" West demands, aiming his order towards Elijah.

Elijah nods, heading out of the room with Lucas and West following behind.

All that is left is Hunter, Myles, and me.

We sit in silence, finishing the remaining food that sits on our plates. Only the sound of scrapping forks and plates being cleaned can be heard. A pin drop could be heard in here. I can hear the lightbulbs losing their energy. The paint getting older with every second that disappears.

The silence is deafening.

As time progresses, I look up from my plate to see what Hunter is thinking. He finished his food a while ago. Hunter will not leave the table until everyone else has, but he seems to be getting impatient. I can see it in his features. Every so often, I can see him checking the gold watch attached to his wrist.

My eyes remain on the watch, trying to work out what the current time is. That's when I hear the sound of Myles, he pushes his chair back, causing a loud noise to echo through the room and then begins to storm out.

I want to talk to him. It feels like forever since I even said a word to him. Not since I saw him with Asha… "Myles" I shock myself when I call out his name. I guess now is a good time to talk to him.

He doesn't turn back to look at me. The dining room door opens, and he leaves the room. I take a deep breath and stand up from my chair. Looks like I am going to have to run after him if I want to have a conversation with him.

My feet start moving when Hunter begins to clear his throat, the sounding bouncing off the walls. "I need to—"

"I will come back" I cut Hunter off before he even gets his sentence out. He is going to tell me he needs to talk, but right now, all I care about is talking to Myles.

I head out of the room, entering the hallway as I try my best to catch up to Myles. "Myles!" I try to grab his attention, again. He should be the one chasing me after what he has been doing, not the other way around. "Myles, can we just talk for five minutes?"

My words just about reach him. His footsteps sound like elephants charging, echoing through the hall. "I don't have anything to say to you" he says, not bothering to stop walking or turn around.

"Please…" I plead.

He finally turns around. "What do you want?" he raises his voice. "I have nothing to say to you" he repeats.

"We haven't talked… in a long time" I sigh, relief washing over me that he finally stopped walking away from me. "I can't remember the last time we had a real conversation, and you are supposed to be my boyfriend!"

"I don't want to be here" he snaps. "I was starting to like the life I had— We had in RoseShire"

~~You liked being with Asha.~~

"Me too— You think I wanted to come back here?" I am quickly becoming angry.

"You didn't stop them" he is angry too.

I'm taken back.

After everything, Myles expected me to fight against the soldiers. There was nothing I could do. There were guns from every direction being pointed at us. He wanted me to fight against Hunter. Against West. Against Elijah…

He didn't even put up a fight, Myles got on his knees and allowed Hunter's men to bring him back. He cannot put all the blame on me.

"W- What?" I stutter.

"You clearly had the power to stop them, and you did nothing" he raises one arm in an angry manner. "You let them bring us back"

My head is furiously shaking. "Hunter—"

"Yeah… Hunter, again. It always seems to be Hunter this and Hunter that. Do you even remember me?" I can't tell if Myles is hurt or angry anymore. I should be the one hurting, he was the one to cheat on me. "I preferred it when you didn't talk" he confesses.

"You don't mean that" I sob.

"I do" he argues.

"No—"

"I am done. I can't keep acting like we are the same people we were last year. You've changed for the worse" Myles says through his frowns. I am speechless. I can't think of a single word I can say in response. A long second passes before I hear him talk again. "I'll see you later" he doesn't look at me, saying his final words and then continuing to walk down the hallway.

My skin has run cold. I feel like an icicle melting in the summer heat. My blood heats the world, keeping the lava at its rightful temperature. My blood is defrosting the cold glaze of my skin, but my skin is fighting back.

I feels like I am at war with myself.

And then my head begins to spin. I slowly walk back into the dining room, hoping to find a glass of water waiting for me on the table. Yet, when I walk through the doors, all I am met with is Hunter. He hasn't moved from his chair. He is sitting at the end of the table.

The room feels like it is dancing on flames. The heating must be on full blast. The chicken could have cooked itself on the table. The sun could survive in these conditions. I have no idea how Hunter can sit there without breaking a sweat.

Hunter's hands are clasped together on the table with his clean plate pushed forward slightly in front of him. He has rolled his white sleeves up and neatly folded them past his elbows to look more presentable. "I didn't think you would be coming back" Hunter looks up from the table.

"Well I'm back" I sigh.

"Good. Now, we can talk" he gestures towards the chair beside him. I walk over to the table, pulling out the chair and sitting down beside Hunter. My hands rest upon my lap as my eyes settle on the empty glass in front of me. "I want to take a walk with you" he innocently smiles.

"Why?" I ask, wanting to know his altera motive.

"I have not had a chance to talk to you. Not since you left. I want to hear about it" he claims.

"There isn't much to say" I shrug.

He doesn't seem to believe me. "You have been away for four months, there must have been something interesting that happened" Hunter encourages me to talk to him about my time in RoseShire.

Staring down at the gold bracelet around my wrist, I run my fingers over the red stone in the centre. My brain begins to scramble for a memory. "I met these people... Nikita and Destiny, AJ and Asha. They all helped us stay out of the sandstorm. They allowed us to stay with them while we got on our feet. They were nice people" I frown at the thought of not knowing how they are now. "Where are they now?" I ask.

"I would not know—"

"You held them at gun point and I'm pretty sure you were about to handcuff them. You should know if they are safe. Where in the building are they?" I question him.

"Listen, love, they are safe. We can leave it at that" he tries to shut the topic of conversation down.

"Where are they?" I repeat.

He doesn't speak.

His eyes are on me as his lips tie themselves together until it becomes impossible for him to speak. He will tell me. One way or another. I know Hunter is hiding something. The look in his eyes tells me everything. He doesn't want me to know something. He should know by now, there is no point trying to hide anything from me because I find out.

My back leans into the chair. I will sit here all day; I have nothing else to do. He can take all day to answer me if that's what he wants to do. "I am keeping them safe" he answers too vaguely for my liking.

Again, I get nowhere.

I move a strand of hair out of my face. Nothing about what he says is straight forward when it comes to giving me the answers to my questions. I hold back the frustration in my tone. "What do you mean by that?" my eyebrows furrow.

My hands start to feel clammy, waiting for him to explain anything feels like waiting for paint to dry. "Let me take you on a walk—"

"Stop" I cut him off. "Answer my questions" I demand.

He lowers his eyes and stands up. "If you allow me to take you on a walk, I will answer your questions" he bargains.

"How do I know you're not just saying that" I challenge him.

"Trust me" he reaches his hand out for me to grab.

I look from his eyes to his outstretched hand. Debating my options, I decide to place my hand in his. The chair moves back as I stand up, copying Hunter. He smiles lightly, watching our hands connect. I have to hold back the urge to pull my hand away from his.

The slightest touch from him is making me blush.

He leads me around the dining table, gently dragging me by my hand out of the room.

CHAPTER TWENTY-ONE
GRACE

Hunter has walked me down to the ground floor. We are walking the long halls of the building, each footstep getting heavier. My arms wrap around my body as the dress clinging to my skin keeps me from freezing to death.

There is a cold draft down here.

The walls are speaking to one another, becoming closer the further down they go. They are hugging one another to keep warm. A thick coat of dark grey paint has splashed the hall, the colour creating a darker atmosphere. There doesn't seem to be anyone down here. No soldiers in sight and no sign of life.

A dryness spreads throughout my throat as we get closer to the end of the hallway. There is something sinister about this place. I just can't put my finger on it. Maybe it is the lack of plants or the little lighting or the empty feeling, but there is something not right about this hallway.

Where are we going?

Hunter is walking with his head up and his eyes focused on the door ahead of us. He keeps his back straight as he walks with a purpose. I don't know who he is trying to impress, but it certainly isn't me.

Once we reach the end of the hallway, we are outside a large black metal door with multiple locks. I count six locks. It is heavily guarded for a reason, only someone with all the keys to the locks could get inside, and even then it looks like a lot of work. Although, there is no soldiers to stop us from getting inside if we do have the keys.

We stand in silence.

I'm waiting for something to happen, yet we continue to stand and wait for nothing. We don't make a move to open the door, Hunter seems to be waiting for someone else to do it for him. The anticipation is killing me.

Slowly, Hunter looks down at me. "Don't touch anything, don't speak to anyone unless I say you can, and DO NOT under any circumstances, wander off" he demands.

He is treating me like a child, I am capable of taking care of myself. I roll my eyes but nod my head. Hunter knocks the door. One, two, three, four, five. Suddenly, I hear movement from the inside. There is someone on the other side of the door.

Hunter reaches into his pocket, pulling out a chain of keys.

I watch with curiosity as he begins unlocking the locks with a different key each time. A small key for the first lock, a long key for the second, a large key for the third.

On the other side of the door, there sounds like more locks as someone begins doing the same process as Hunter.

As Hunter reaches for the final lock, my hands shake. I don't know what to expect. I want to know what is beyond a door with so many locks and keys. What could be so important that they need to lock a door this many times? The thought of wanting to know is killing me.

"Remember what I just said?" Hunter reminds me.

I nod my head.

A soldier pulls the door open from the inside, allowing us entrance into the room.

I feel Hunter's arm snake its way around my waist. "What are you doing?" I ask him, looking down at his arm.

"Don't you dare leave my side" he warns me.

I listen to him. I have no idea what Hunter is about to walk me into, listening to him is the only thing I can do. I can't mess this up if I want Hunter to tell me what he has done with Destiny and Nikita. He needs to be able to see that I am being cooperative and following his wishes.

We walk into the dark room; the sound of groaning can be heard from every direction. Rattling and screaming, crying and shouting. There has to be hundreds of people in here. I just can't see any of them. All of them are hidden inside the darkness.

"What is in here—"

My words get cut off before I can finish my question by Hunter covering my mouth with his big hand. My eyes widen as I stare up into Hunter's eyes. I can smell the coconut scent on his hand. Like a lotion he recently used.

"Not a word" he warns me again. He carefully removes his hand from my mouth, watching my face as he waits for my acceptance. "This way" he walks me through the darkness.

102

I gradually become familiar with the dark atmosphere, my eyes adjusting to the point where I can see cages and people. Too many people to count. There is no light in here whatsoever, not a single lightbulb. This is a different kind of torture. This is the type of torture that would drive anyone crazy. The people in this room must be criminals.

That's the only explanation for keeping people in here.

The foul taste of rotten fish is dancing along the tip of my tongue. The smell of death filling the room. If I could see what is further in front of me right now, I imagine the sight would keep me awake at night.

"Grace!" someone shouts, the sound of someone hitting metal can be heard from my right. "Get me out of here!" they continue to shout. "Grace!" they repeat.

My head spins in circles as I try to see where the voice is coming from. To my right, there is nothing but darkness. To my left, there is nothing but darkness. I can't see a single thing all over again. I step forward, again and again, straining my eyes to look beyond the black void.

That's when I see them.

Nikita. Destiny. And Asha. All of them are trapped in separate cages. There are no chains attached to them, but the cages look impossible to escape. I freeze in disbelief. They are trapped down here, hidden away from the rest of the world.

"What the hell Hunter" I gasp, rushing over to the cages as my hands reach out to grab the bars. "Have they been here this whole time?"

Hunter holds me back before I get too close. "This is for your own protection" he explains, restraining me.

I struggle against his strong grip, pushing and shoving to try and escape his grasp. "My protection" I repeat his words out loud. "You're insane. Get them out of there"

"I can't do that" he denies my demand. "They know who you are. If word gets out about you, Soltrix will be another target for more cities. I won't allow it"

"So you're going to keep them locked up like animals?" I am enraged.

"I don't have much of a choice, love. If the world knows about you, I won't be able to keep you safe" he claims.

"You mean, you won't be able to use me to win the war" I scoff as he grips me tighter. A part of me knows that all he really cares about is winning the war against his father. I am just a pawn in his game. An easy weapon that can bring him victory. "This is not fair" I continue.

"You know that isn't true" he denies.

"They don't deserve this" I ignore him.

"Maybe—"

"They are good people" I hold back a sob.

I feel my energy draining. My body stops struggling against him. My back slowly rests against his chest as I feel the energy vanish from me. I'm still a little weak from what happened during training. I don't have enough strength to fight against Hunter right now. He holds me in place, making sure I can't get close to the cages bars.

Destiny is on the floor, sitting up against the cage as she rests her body. She looks tired and hurt. Nikita tries to reach out for me. I can't tell whether she looks pale, or it is just the lack of lighting. As for Asha, she looks shocked more than anything. All three of them seem drained.

Physically and emotionally.

"Grace… you're working with him?" Destiny's voice can be heard above the groaning.

"No" I answer too quick. "He brought us away from the attack in RoseShire. He was trying to help"

"I don't believe it. He is the bad guy here, he only cares about himself" Asha spits. "Look what he has done to us"

My body builds enough strength to push Hunter off of me and he lets me. Hunter allows me to step forward a little. Only slightly. I'm still not permitted to get too close to the cages. I can't even get close enough to get a good view of them.

"He was trying to help you" Destiny's voice is raspy.

"GET ME OUT OF HERE" Nikita shouts, shaking the bars.

"Don't bother, we are going to die in here before they decide to let us go" Asha huffs.

"I will get you out of there" I promise.

Taking one large step, I try to get closer to Nikita's cage again. She is reaching through the cages bars for me, trying to grab onto me. I slowly reach my hand out in an attempt to grab her hand. Hunter stops me, again. "You know the rules, love. Stay away from the cages" he reminds me.

Someone clears their throat. I just about make out the image of Asha smirking to herself. She is looking straight at me through the darkness. God I hate her. She knows exactly what she is doing. "Where's your boyfriend? I bet he wouldn't be happy to know your down here with him" she gestures towards Hunter.

Something takes over me. She angers me. "I am your only hope of getting out of here. If I were you, I would stay on my good side" I shock myself. Thankfully its dark down here, otherwise it would be clear to everyone that I am just as surprised as the expression on my face. "Hunter, let them go"

"I told you—"

My words quickly cut him off. "I don't care what you told me. You are going to let them go back to RoseShire" I demand.

Sweat builds up along the palm of my hands. My skin is feeling clammy the longer I stand here. I am waiting for Hunter to unlock the cages, but at this rate, I feel like I am going to be waiting forever. He is showing no sign of letting them go.

"This is over" he grabs my arm.

I'm pulled backwards.

"What—"

I shove his hands off me, only to be met by his hands on my wrists. He pushes my hands behind my back and begins pushing me away from the cages and towards the door. If only I continued to train when I was in RoseShire. Maybe I would have a little more strength against Hunter to put up a fight.

The sound of my heels hitting the concrete floor can be heard echoing through the dark abyss. My feet are shuffling as Hunter pushes me. He isn't wasting anymore time in this dark space. "Get your hands off me" I protest.

"You are playing a dangerous game" he warns me.

"I don't care" I have lost all care.

I want him to let them go. A life in those cages is no life at all. He will never let them out at this rate. I can't go on living my life knowing Hunter has forever locked good people like Nikita and Destiny up.

"You don't care?" he repeats.

"No. I don't care anymore" I huff.

"Fine. This is on you" he says, and then removes his hands from me.

One gunshot.

Two gunshots.

Three gunshots.

All at once, I fear the worst has happened. Hunter has just shot them. Murdered in cold blood. I don't move. I can't move. I continue to fear the worst.

"Their deaths are on your hands. I hope this teaches you to let things go when I tell you to" Hunter uses a demanding tone when he talks to me. He talks down to me like a child. As if I can't control my own actions.

I turn back, running to the cages.

Nikita, Destiny, Asha.

Their bodies are limp, lying on the floor of their cages as the blood once swirling around their bodies now creates pools on the floor around them.

My hands grip the bars to Nikita's cage.

How could Hunter do that?

The urge to cry and mourn their deaths is strong, but I hold back all my tears.

Crying won't bring them back.

CHAPTER TWENTY-TWO
HUNTER

West is watching the screens, again.

As I walk into the control room, West spots me from the reflection of the screen. He doesn't turn to look my way. Instead, he waves the soldier standing on his left to leave the room, leaving us completely alone.

My eyes scan the room. All the screens have different rooms in the building, revealing what everyone is doing. On the screen West is staring at, in one corner is Grace sleeping in her room, in another corner, there is Myles staring at the ceiling and Elijah reading a book. At the bottom of the screen, there is one large image. It is the reception part of the building.

A soldier is talking to one of the receptionists, from what I can hear coming from the speakers, it is about a file.

West's eyes are switching between the screens.

Grace looks peaceful sleeping.

Her hair is spread across the right pillow as her head lays on the left one. Her body looks curled up into a ball as she hugs the blanket for warmth. There is only the sound of her slow breaths that can be heard coming from her side of the screen, she is silently asleep.

I'm glad she isn't causing any problems tonight.

"You killed them" West shakes his head.

"She didn't give me much of a choice. Grace was never going to let something like that go" I offer my excuse.

"Don't blame their deaths on Grace" West defends her.

"Drop it" I don't entertain the conversation.

On the other camera angle, my eyes narrow, focusing on the receptionist. She is typing away on the computer as a soldier stands opposite her desk, watching her. His lips are moving, his words repeating again and again.

Why is one of my soldiers asking about a file?

The blonde woman looks uncomfortable and on edge as her shaking hands type on the keyboard. She glances up at the soldier numerous times, hoping he continues to stay patient with her. The soldier leans his hands on the desk with a long sigh erupting from his throat. As I watch the situation unfold, I hold back the urge to question West.

Slowly, the blonde woman stops typing. West zooms in on the soldier, making sure he doesn't get any closer than he already is to the receptionist. "I'm looking for file 01" the soldier asks, pushing off the desk to cross his arms.

The receptionists face says everything she can't. "I am terribly sorry, but that file does not exist" she apologises, the lie being evident on her features.

"Look again" he demands.

"I already told you—"

"I said, look again" he repeats.

West spins around on his chair, turning to face me with a worried look in his eyes. "The soldier is snooping" he frowns and then turns back to the screen.

"Do you think he is a spy?" I question, looking closer at the screen.

"Did you really ask that? If they walk like a spy and talk like a spy. Guess what idiot? They're a spy" West glances over his shoulder. "I don't trust anyone around here" he has made that crystal clear from the day he got here.

My eyes scan the room for a chair. "What is the update with the PPW?" I say as I pull up a chair beside West, sitting down next to him.

His eyes fluctuate between me and the screens. He tries to search his brain for an explanation. "I decided to go with Elijah. People seemed to listen to him. If he was to go in and scoop out the good ones, he would be more help than Myles or Lucas" he explains himself.

I nod my head.

Elijah has the popularity with the people down there, as hard as it may be to believe. His insight could be more help than our files. The last time I flew over to the PPW, most of the abilities were useless or too weak to use in a fight. Elijah will be able to find the best for me as he will know what they are capable of during the training sessions.

"Take Grace with you" I decide.

West leans his arm on the back of the chair, making it easier for himself to turn his body to face me. "Grace? That is a good joke and all, but this is supposed to be a serious conversation we are having" he furrows his eyebrows.

"It might be helpful. The medic mentioned her going to the PPW for testing. I agree with the idea—"

"She won't like it" West rejects the idea.

I let out a breath. "A soldier is asking for her file. File 01 is Grace's file. Someone is trying to find information on her, if there is a spy here, I want her as far away as possible until we find them" I try to make him see logic. "Sending her there makes more sense than keeping her here"

"You think sending her back there will do anything?" he doesn't sound convinced.

"I think she will be safer out of the building until we figure out who the spy is working for and what information they want. Grace will be under your supervision" I summarise.

"Mmhh" he hums. My eyes watch him. "If that is what you believe to be best" West scratches the back of his neck.

"What does that look on your face mean?" I worry.

He stretches over to one the tables beside him to pick up a letter, straightening the envelope before handing it to me. It is handwritten, but not signed. The words written on the small piece of paper makes my mind run wild.

My head slowly rises from the letter. "The war to end all wars is coming" I repeat the words written on the paper.

A knock at the door interrupts our conversation. All our movement stops, my hands lowering to my lap to hide the letter from the person standing on the other side of the door. I offer a nod towards West. "Come in" he shouts, giving the person behind the door the chance to walk inside.

The door swings open, revealing Elijah Haul. He was the last person I expected to walk into the room. His smirking lips and slicked back hair along with him wearing the same clothes from dinner tells me he hasn't been to sleep.

Moments ago, I saw him reading a book in his room.

His teleporting must be improving.

"Elijah, what is it?" I ask him, wanting to know his reason for coming up here.

The prodigies are not supposed to be this far up the building, apart from Grace. The monitoring room is off limits to anyone who doesn't have access. I'm a little amazed Elijah knew how to get up here.

"I have information on Carter" he surprises me.

Elijah makes sure to close the door, waiting for one of us to speak up. "Don't just stand there, tell us" I quickly become impatient.

"Grace... she was talking to him in her room. I saw them together" Elijah informs us.

West hums. "What was discussed?" he tries to get as much information from Elijah as he can.

West doesn't want to believe him. His body language is closed off to Elijah, his eyes watching me for my reactions. It is clear West is close to Grace, and It's not something I want to believe either, but Elijah would not make up a story. There has to be a reason for him telling me.

"All I heard was them talking about a dad and a place called FrostMount" he gives us a vague answer.

"Where was this?" West asks as he folds his arms.

Elijah keeps a cold expression on his face. "I saw them in her room" he admits.

Now I'm angry.

Deep breaths fill my lungs as I calm myself down. Why is he in Grace's bedroom? She knows no one is supposed to go into her room, especially at night. Me and West are the only people permitted to enter her room, and now Myles seeing as they are dating. But Elijah should not be anywhere near her room, and she knows it.

"What are you doing in Grace's room?" West has to ask the question for me.

"I was practicing teleportation..." he shrugs.

A part of me doesn't believe him. Something in me has a feeling he is lying. But I want him to leave the room before I run out of breaths to take. "Thank you for informing us" I grip the paper in my hands as I continue to hide the letter.

When nothing more is said, Elijah leaves the room at the same pace he entered. I hope he is lying, just wanting to cause a

110

problem for the fun of it. He seems like the type of guy to enjoy causing trouble.

I remove my hands from my lap and place the letter on the table beside West. "Check over the cameras in Grace's room over the last couple nights" I order. "I want to know what was discussed and I want to see if Elijah is telling the truth"

"I don't trust him" I scowl.

"I will get on it" West frown.

West slowly moves his chair around and turns to face the large screens again. He begins looking through all the camera footage to find any sighting of Carter. If Elijah is telling the truth, Grace has a lot of explaining to do.

CHAPTER TWENTY-THREE
GRACE

West is pushing me harder today.

The training feels like he wants me to hurt. He is pushing me to the point of my body breaking in half. We have been stuck on warmups for the last hour. Every set we complete, and I think we are about to start the real training, I get disappointed all over again. This all feels intense.

Maybe I would feel better if I had more sleep.

West appears to be on edge today. He hasn't cracked a single joke yet and the cold expression staining his face makes me think the worst. He doesn't seem like himself today, but I don't know what has changed.

Even during breakfast, he was quiet and distant.

My arms shake as I push myself to complete another one of West's demands. Thirty push ups. I am currently on ten. My body refuses to take any more of this. He has gone crazy to think I can finish thirty push ups. I've already done sit-ups, squats, lunges, planks. He never makes the warmups this hard, he usually eases me into training.

"Can we take a break now?" I beg.

"No" he shakes his head. "Go again"

I do another push up.

"West—"

"Again" he demands.

I do another, and another.

I am exhausted. My legs are shaking, and my arms are about to give way. I push myself to complete another push up as we come to the end of the warmup. I have now counted a total of fifteen push ups, and that is the most my body is capable of doing today. There is no more strength in my muscles to keep going.

Using all the force my body is willing to take, I push my body off the ground using my arms and then lower myself back onto my stomach. Sixteen. Seventeen. Eighteen. And then the energy escapes me.

"West—"

The door opens to reveal Hunter and two soldiers. He doesn't look happy. His hair is slicked back, held in the same style with gel like always. The arms of his clean white shirt have been rolled up to his elbows, the top button of his shirt has been left undone.

His signature look.

As he stalks through the training room, the two soldiers follow behind him, standing beside each other. Stone-cold and heartless. That is what they look like. The same look all soldiers hold when they are on the job. Soldiers are not allowed to show emotion when they are in their uniform, especially when they are around Hunter.

I sit up from my current position on the floor, my eyes shifting from Hunter to West. West looks ashamed. He doesn't want to turn his head to face me, avoiding eye contact.

What is going on?

The room becomes still, giving Hunter the appropriate time to scan his eyes around the space, his attention landing on me almost immediately. His hands clasp together behind his back. His head continues to be held high. Hunter refuses to show any form of emotion.

"Sit her down" Hunter orders his soldiers.

My eyes widen as the soldiers make their way over to me with a chair dragging behind them. One soldier places the chair in the centre of the training room while the other grips my arm tightly, pulling me towards the chair. I don't fight against the soldier as his sharp nails dig into my skin.

I don't believe this is happening.

The pain of the soldiers nail cutting deep into the skin on my arm keeps me tied down to reality. If it wasn't for Hunter's darkened eyes, I would laugh at the situation. Hunter would never let the soldiers treat me in such… bitterness. Nobody would hurt me around him.

Now, Hunter seems to be turning a blind eye as I wince from the soldiers grip. I am seated on the chair with two strong hands holding me down by my shoulders. Switching from one to another, I stare at both West and Hunter, expecting some sort of an explanation from them. There is something going on that I don't know about.

Hunter crosses his arms against his chest, his eyes steady on mine. The long, drawn-out breath he takes before parting his lips tells me this isn't going to be good. "Tell me everything you know about Carter" he demands.

I have to hold back my laugh. "Hunter, you are talking to me like you are interrogating me" I keep my eyes on him.

"Answer the question, Grace" West continues to hold an ashamed look as he talks to me.

They're being serious. The looks on their faces tells me this isn't a joke. "The last thing Carter said to me... our dad... I think we share the same father" I confess. "Why are you asking about Carter?"

"Have you seen him after the war?" Hunter continues to ask his questions.

"What kind of a question—"

"Grace" West cuts me off, shaking his head for me to stop protesting the questions.

Suddenly, this all starts to make sense to me. They know Carter is alive. Hunter and West must have figured out where he has been hiding since we fought. Unless they know Carter was in my room a couple nights ago, and they somehow heard our conversation. Maybe they know where to find him...

"Yes" I nod my head slowly. "It was brief, but I found him looking through my things"

"Why didn't you say something?" Hunter raises a brow.

"It felt like a weird dream more than anything... I don't think I believed it really happened" I respond, honestly.

Hunter steps forward slightly, gradually closing the gap between us. "Are you and Carter related?" he pushes another question. His eyes stare down at me with uncertainty, he can't decide what to do with my answers.

"I don't know..." I lower my head.

Two boots come into my eyeline. Soldier boots. I shift my shoulders but the soldier behind me gives me little to no space to move under his grasp. I carefully lift my eyes to meet the other soldier as he stands in front of me. He smirks as he makes a fist with his right hand. One punch to the stomach throws me further into the back of the chair. I groan from the pain as I look up to meet the soldiers eye.

114

"Is Carter your brother?" Hunter changes the words of his question.

"Maybe… I do- don't believe him" I hold my stomach.

The soldier throws another punch at my face, causing my head to turn to the side. I close my eyes, holding back the urge to show my pain. Inhale, exhale. I open my eyes and turn my attention back onto Hunter.

"I don't believe you" he spits.

"Hunter—"

Another punch to the face cuts me off. The punches are starting to get harder and harder. This soldier is enjoying this more than he should be. He doesn't try to hide the smirk of excitement he has when I don't answer the way Hunter wants me to answer.

"What about the war to end all wars. What do you know about that?" Hunter isn't giving up.

"I don't know anything about that—"

Another punch.

"The soldier will continue to hurt you if you don't answer my questions" Hunter explains. He crouches down in front of me for our eyes to meet on the same level. "Let's try this again. I want you to answer honestly. What do you know about the war to end all wars?"

I haven't seen this side of Hunter.

I hate it.

"Nothing" I spit back.

Hunter shakes his head as he stands up straight. "I know you discussed it with him" he confesses. How does he know that? The conversation was in my room. The only people there at the time was me, Carter, and the girl who showed up to take Carter back to FrostMount.

Unless there are camera's hidden somewhere.

"Do you have a camera in my room?" I gape.

"Stop avoiding the question" West speaks up.

I take a short breath. If I could give him more information about this, I would. "He didn't tell me anything about it" I say the truth. Carter never gave me information about the war. As much as I would love to tell Hunter everything I know, what I know is nothing.

115

The soldier takes his opportunity to throw yet another punch my way. And then another and another until I let out a gasp from the pain. Blood is running from my lip, the taste of metal clear on my tongue.

"Stop" Hunter finally demands.

The soldier doesn't stop. He keeps punching me, his fist continuously making contact with any part of my body it can find. The soldier holding me in my place hasn't let go of my shoulders yet, he is waiting instructions from Hunter. I try my best to fight against the soldier, but I don't get far.

"Soldier, that's enough" he grabs the soldier's fist before it can make contact with my face.

"Sir" the soldier doesn't apologise.

"Go" Hunter gestures for the soldier to leave.

The soldier stands in his place, stunned. Storming away from Hunter, the soldier makes his way to the door and leaves the training room. Hunter doesn't look at me, his eyes remain on West as the other soldier finally lets go of my shoulders.

"Go to your room. Training is over" West still won't look at me, but I know he is talking to me.

I don't know what to say.

Carefully, I shrug my shoulders to try and release some of the tension created from the grip of the soldier. One arm wraps around my stomach, holding it to calm down the rough vibration. It feels like my heart has fallen from my chest and has started to beat inside my gut. The pulsating rhythm of my pain creates a song in my chest.

I wince from the pain as I gradually begin to stand up from the chair. The soldier watches me, warily, preparing for any sudden movements I may make. Hunter turns to face the door, walking out of the room without turning back to check if I am hurting. The soldier follows behind him like a little dog on a lead trying to catch up to its owner.

Hunter has put his job before me.

He has chosen to treat me like an enemy, hurting me for information. He looked at me like a stranger, someone he has no memory of.

Like I was nothing to him.

116

I part my lips to speak, but no words seem to want to come out. Being alone with West has never felt this awkward.

We are both standing in the unknown, becoming guests to the silence.

West doesn't want to look my way, and I don't want to look anywhere other than his face. I scan and scan and try to understand the purpose of all this. The hurt, the questions, the real reason Hunter would put me through his interrogation.

Slowly, my eyes move. They stare down at the chair as my mind replays the situation over again in an attempt to understand Hunter's reasons.

Holding my stomach, I turn my attention back to West. I can only see the back of his head. He has made the decision to face the wall, refusing to look in my direction. "West… what is going on?" I ask him.

Do they really have cameras in my room? I want to know how they found out Carter paid me a visit the other night. The night he was in my room, no one else was around, there is no way Hunter could have found out about the conversation we shared unless someone told him, or he has hidden cameras. I need to check the room when I finish here.

West doesn't respond to my question. His head hangs low as his eyes worriedly scan over my beaten features. The thick red blood running from my lip causes concern for him, along with the harsh bruise forming on my left eye.

Not wasting another second, West walks towards the door. His footsteps echo throughout the training room. I watch every step he takes until he leaves the space, the door slowly closing itself behind him. The floor shakes under my feet as the door slams shut.

Finally, I allow myself to breathe.

A long, drawn-out breath escapes my lips. I sit back down in the chair as I catch up with my thoughts. I have never seen that side to Hunter before, and I never want to see it again.

I thought Hunter would never hurt me.

I was wrong.

CHAPTER TWENTY-FOUR
GRACE

Standing up from the chair again, I force the door open and walk out of the room and into the open area that leads from my training room into the other boys training rooms. The open space is empty. Not a soldier in sight. They must have followed Hunter when he had stormed off earlier.

My head glances from one side of the space to the other as my hand holds onto the cold wall. One door opposite me makes a quiet scrapping sound as it opens. I look over to find Elijah walking out of the room with his trainer. They are both laughing with one another.

Elijah's laughter is contagious.

It is something I never thought I would truly hear.

But I am hearing it. Loud and Clear. Like a song with the sweetest melody.

The happy sound quickly comes to a halt when he sees me alone outside my training room. He mumbles something to the guy beside him and then they share a look. The trainer nods his head, walking away from Elijah. I watch the guy leave us alone together.

My eyes lower to the ground as Elijah slowly makes his way over to me, his footsteps letting me know how close he is before stopping in front of me.

By the time I lift my eyes to see what Elijah is doing, I find his light blue eyes scanning over my face. They eventually work their way down to the arm wrapped around my stomach as I try to stop the throbbing pain.

A glimpse of worry or horror or guilt flashes across his features before he masks it with a cold front. A sudden shiver runs down my spine as he gets closer to me. I wrap my other arm around my body, both arms holding my stomach as our bodies almost press up against each other.

The empty space now feels small.

As if the emptiness never existed.

His frosty exterior melts for a moment or two as our eyes do all the talking. Light blue. I would like to imagine a clear blue sky would look as beautiful as his eyes. But I don't think even the clearest sky could compare.

"Who did this to you?" he finally talks.

"Elijah… not now" I sigh, wanting to go up to my room and lie down. I don't want to talk about it. Talking about it will only make it real. And I don't want it to be real.

I try to walk away from him, taking small steps as I separate from the closeness between our bodies. Elijah is too quick. He grabs my arm and pulls me back. I stumble until I am back in my original spot. "Your bleeding" he states the obvious, his eyes glued onto mine.

My head nods as I struggle to free my arm from his tight grasp. He uses his other hand to push my waist, causing me to walk backwards until my back hits a wall. A gasp threatens to leave my lips. "Elijah—"

"Don't make me repeat myself" he warns.

He waits and waits for an answer. Time could pass us by without a second thought. He would wait a lifetime for me to answer his question. Elijah shows no sign in moving away from me, his hand remaining on my waist. His other hand removes itself off my arm and rests against the wall.

Looking from his arm beside my head to his eyes, I give in to his question. "Hunter" I answer him.

I can't determine the exact emotion that keeps flashing through him, but whatever it is, he doesn't want me to know about it. "Hunter wouldn't hurt you" Elijah shakes his head.

"Hunter gave his soldiers instructions to hurt me" I have to speak through my frown.

"He wouldn't do that" he doesn't believe me.

"He did…" the words come out as I exhale.

Something different washes over his features. He alters slightly. Takes a step back, shifts his weight from one foot to the other. He folds his arms over each other across his chest. I watch as his chest rises and falls with each breath he takes. He finally gives me enough room to breathe.

One door opens and then another, the familiar sound filling my ears. Two fresh footsteps enter the space. Elijah's head turns before mine, scanning the area to find the owners of the footsteps.

"Isn't this a surprise" Myles speaks with sarcasm.

Myles and Lucas have walked out of their training rooms, both standing in the centre of the space, watching as Elijah and I create a good distance between us. Lucas offers me a small smile while Myles becomes consumed by anger.

"Is everything okay?" Lucas asks me before he gets a good look at my face. "My god... what happened—"

"Did you do that to her?" Myles puts the blame on Elijah.

"No" Elijah snaps.

"You did, didn't you. Just like before" he scoffs. "Nothing has changed. You are still the same guy, beating her up and bullying her to feel better about yourself" Myles speaks with each step he takes, getting closer to Elijah.

Lucas's breathing increases.

He looks as if he is about to have a panic attack. His skin has run pale, his cheeks have turned red, his lips have dried up like the desert. His chest is rising and falling at a fast pace with his heart beating out of his body.

Elijah towers over Myles. "You don't know what you're talking about" Elijah keeps calm.

I stand back, pushing my back against the wall again, staying clear of the boys. "I know exactly what I'm talking about" Myles challenges.

"Guys—" Lucas tries to intervene.

Myles cuts him off before he can get a real sentence out of his mouth. "She used to silently cry herself to sleep at night because of you and Nolan. She would let you pick on her and tease her" he points his finger in the air. "You are the reason she had all those trips to the nurse"

"She was weak" Elijah shrugs.

"She was alone" Myles shouts. "She had nobody"

Elijah stays quiet for a moment. "She had you"

And then Myles becomes still. He doesn't move. He doesn't blink. Everything becomes unimportant to him. Elijah takes a step back, giving Myles enough room to leave. Neither of them want to exchange any more words.

120

"That's enough" Lucas says through a breath.

"Get him out of here" Elijah demands.

Lucas nods his head in agreement. The tension between us all could kill. It would suffocate like a pillow. I would love to cut the tension with a dagger. The intense frowns on the boys faces tells me to stay quiet through all this. If I talk, I feel like I will only make matters work.

"You're an asshole" Myles yells.

"Thank you" Elijah fakes a smile.

Lucas hustles Myles away from us, trying his best to get away from the space as fast as possible. Myles shuffles into the hallway and up the stairs with Lucas following behind him, leaving Elijah and I alone once again.

"I don't know what you see in him" Elijah shakes his head in disapproval.

Everyone keeps saying that.

After seeing him and Asha together, I don't know what I'm doing. He doesn't love me. He doesn't want to be with me like before. We have both changed. The people we used to be are long gone. As much as I would like to claw onto the person I used to call my best friend, he isn't that guy anymore.

I am clinging to a memory.

"He cheated on me…" I confess, quiet.

So quiet I don't expect him to hear it.

"What?" he wants me to repeat myself. My head lowers as I remember the night I saw him. When I don't say anything, he clears his throat. "That piece of shit—"

"Doesn't matter now…" I interrupt him.

It is weird, saying it out loud.

He debates his next words very carefully. "Aren't you still with him?" he asks.

"Yeah— but he doesn't—"

"You really are stupid" he scowls.

His response shocks me. "What?" I express my surprise as my eyes glare up at his. No comfort or remorse. But this is Elijah I am talking to; I shouldn't expect anything of the sort from him.

"You heard me" he raises an eyebrow. "You are dating some guy who treats you like crap and goes off with other women" he says, bluntly. I can only stare. How do I respond to something like that? "You deserve better than him"

I've heard that before.

"And you know what I deserve" I argue back. "You are the bully I had to put up with throughout my life. The reason I would be stuck with the nurse for hours each day with bruises and cuts and tears. You made my life a living hell and now you stand there telling me what you think I deserve"

"You are a lot stronger for it" he tries to justify his actions.

Every day I spent around him and Nolan, I learnt how to keep my mouth shut. They would kick me, pull my hair, punch me, and go out of their way to make fun of me. They would try to find a new way to torture me each day. It appeared to be their favourite hobby. Something to pass time. They enjoyed causing me pain on a daily basis.

"I pity you" I hiss at him.

"You always have" he reminds me.

The cold wall on my back cools down the inferno growing inside me.

"Just... leave me alone, Elijah" I lower my voice.

"Oh, cause you have so many people around to help you right now. You are in pain, yet you still rather tell me to leave you here alone than admit you want my help" he snaps.

"I don't want you help—"

"Whose help do you want then? Myles?" he raises a brow.

I lift my eyes, looking through my eyelashes up at Elijah as he steps closer. "Myles is my boyfriend. He is my best friend! I would rather him than you" I spit the words out.

Elijah's hand meets my waist again. He pushes his body up against mine as my back presses further against the wall. His light blue eyes stare down at me, his tall structure towering over me like it normally does. His shadow covers mine, merging into one as the lights from behind Elijah become blocked off to me.

Everything he wants to say is on the tip of his tongue, but just like every other time, he says nothing.

He continues to stare down at me, his eyes glancing between my eyes and my lips. It is as if he cannot decide where to settle his eyes. My lips, or my eyes. I find myself watching his eyes. I wonder to myself what is going through his head.

122

"Do you hate me?" he asks.

My features become blank.

What sort of a question is that?

"Grace, do you hate me?" he asks again, impatient.

"Y- Yes… I hate you" I give him the answer he wants.

He nods his head. "Good. Hate me, Grace. I want you to hate me like no one has hated me before"

My eyes narrow.

"You want me to hate you?" I am confused.

He takes a step back, removing his hands from my waist. "Go and rest" he commands, gesturing to the stairs.

I roll my eyes. I won't get anything more out of him. I am done with the conversation. I wrap both arms around my stomach again. My head is bouncing, and my stomach is crying. The soldier was a lot stronger than I had hoped. His punches felt like a brick was being swung in my direction. Not just someone's fist.

Hunter really does train everyone to be weapons.

That guy would be lethal in a one-to-one fist fight.

Instead of trying to think of another comment to make towards Elijah, I slowly turn my body and begin walking away from him. He doesn't stop me this time.

"Put some ice on your lip" he suggests.

Building up all the anger I have gained in the last hour, I turn around and walk straight up to Elijah. My hand turns to a fist and flies through the air before I have the chance to stop it. My fist makes direct contact with Elijah's face.

Bullseye.

"Now, we are matching" I smirk up at him.

And then I walk into the hallway, towards the stairs.

CHAPTER TWENTY-FIVE
GRACE

Looking through the wardrobe feels like a chore.

I had a good night of rest, apart from the sharp pain in my stomach. I struggled to sleep on my left, so I ended up on my right side, which was surprisingly more comfortable. It was one of the best nights of sleep I have had in a while.

Rummaging through my wardrobe, I find a pair of black leggings. Breakfast is something I wish I could avoid. Walking down to the dining room to sit beside West and Hunter seems like a nightmare to me. I don't want to see them. Even if that means avoiding training.

My lip is still busted up from yesterday. The throbbing in my stomach has thankfully stopped, but the obvious bruising around my eyes has formed clear enough to show everyone this wasn't just a training accident.

Looking in the mirror this morning was a reminder to me of how quickly people can change. How easy it is for them to flip a switch and treat you differently. The look in Hunter's eyes is something I may never be able to forget. There was no concern or emotion at all towards me.

The door creaks open slowly, shuffling across the carpet as it swings open. I don't turn around to face the person, allowing them to enter the room. The sound of the door being pushed makes my ears alert. We are alone. The door closes shut, all I can see is the wall and the wardrobe. I wait for the person to talk before facing them.

"Grace, oh, there you are" West speaks as if he only just noticed my presence. I don't speak a word to him. "How are you feeling?" he has the nerve to ask.

Again, I don't speak.

I have gotten pretty good at biting my tongue over the years. Placing the black leggings on the top of the wardrobe to hang, I begin looking for a long t-shirt. Any colour would do for me. I'm not picky when it comes to fashion. I never used to have a choice of clothing, being picky isn't in my nature.

You get what your given.

I think I still have that mindset sometimes.

I'm not used to having food just handed to me and fresh clothes neatly folded in draws for me. No matter how long I have been here, I still can't get used to the feeling. It feels like it could all be taken away from me in a heartbeat. The clothes and the food and the warm bed.

Even in RoseShire I had those things.

I just don't want to wake up one day and find myself back in the hell hole. Waking up to find all of this was just one long dream. To find that none of this was real. Looking around to see the same four walls that kept me trapped.

"Grace, can you hear me?" he tries to get my attention by walking over to me. He softly places his hand on one of my shoulders, but I shrug it off immediately. "Ah… you're ignoring me" he gets the hint. He takes a deep breath. "Look, I'm sorry, you need to understand… we felt betrayed and— and I didn't get to have a say in what the soldier did to you. That was all Hunter's doing" he apologises.

Slowly, I turn around to face West. "You should both know I would never betray you" I remind him.

"The situation is bad" he admits. "You were talking to the traitor. You need to understand how bad that looks"

"I understand it means Hunter ordering soldiers to hurt me for information" I narrow my eyes onto him.

"Don't be like that—"

I interrupt him. "You could have asked me… not beaten me for the answers. If that was you, would you stand there and listen to my crappy attempt at an apology?" I try to put West in my shoes.

"No…" he huffs. I nod my head and walk over to the bed, placing the leggings and the long white t-shirt on the quilt. "Do you need some ice for—"

"I'm fine" I cut him off. "I don't need anything"

West takes an exhausted breath. "Okay" he moves over to the bed, getting closer to me. "I need to give you some bad news" his body straightens.

The bad news will have to wait for another day. I don't want to hear anything negative. "No" I protest, wanting him to keep the bad news away from me. "I don't want to hear any of it. I don't want to hear any bad news today. Keep it to yourself until tomorrow"

West's eyebrows furrow. "I'm afraid I can't do that. You need to hear this" he sounds serious. He takes a moment to think about the correct way to put the news. This must be serious if West is acting like this. "Hunter has decided it would be safer if you join me. We leave first thing this morning after breakfast" he doesn't allow me to protest the arrangement.

"We are leaving the city?" a small smile spreads across my face as my eyes light up.

"Yes" he can see my excitement. "Don't get too excited"

"Why not? Let's go now! We can skip breakfast" I am almost jumping with happiness. "How is this bad news?"

"We are going to the PPW" he says the three letters I dread most of all.

My happiness crashes.

It falls deep into the pit of my stomach, swallowed by the acid bubbling around my body.

He wants to take me back to that place. I hoped to never return there. That place still gives me nightmares. It still pulls me back to the poisoned memories of my childhood. Nothing will give me back the life I was robbed of down there, and no one can change the past.

"W— What?..." I stutter.

West can see the horror writing itself on my features, my eyes burning into his. He needs to explain himself. "I know, it's the last place you want to go. But it is the safest option for you right now" he isn't telling me the full story. There is something he is keeping from me.

"Safest?" I want him to elaborate.

"We don't need to get into that now" he pushes the question aside.

"You think it is a safer option for me to be in the PPW than here?" I don't believe him. This must be a joke. Hunter honestly believes the one place I have never felt safe, is currently the safest place for me. It just doesn't make sense. There has to be something else. Is this Hunter's way of trying to punish me some more? "Are you trying to get rid of me?"

"No—"

"THEN EXPLAIN WHAT THE HELL IS GOING ON" I shout, loud enough for the rest of the building to hear.

He takes a step back. "I found a soldier trying to look at your file. He was searching for you. They could be a spy. They may want to hurt you. Hunter and I need to get you out of here for the time being, just until Hunter finds out what the soldier wants" he elucidates.

A soldiers, maybe a spy, was looking for my file. There is someone trying to look into my background, my past, for some unknown reason. There is nothing in the file. West and I know that for a fact. A soldier would have no reason to be looking for it. Unless the guy wasn't a soldier, but someone disguised as one.

"Describe the soldier to me" I demand.

"Nothing to describe" he shrugs. "All I could see was the back of the guys helmet and the soldier uniform"

"It could have been Carter" I guess.

He shakes his head. "Doubt it. He wouldn't be able to just walk into the building undetected" West assures me.

"He got into my room without a problem" I scoff.

Carter is working with someone. A girl. I think her name was Zara. He was able to walk into my room undetected and left without a trace. If I didn't wake up, I wouldn't have known he was in my room.

"Cupcake, you need to understand, we only care about your safety" he claims.

"You only care about the truth, and you will do anything to get it" I put one hand on my hip.

"Sounds familiar" he uses his head to gesture at me. "I do remember a certain girl doing anything and everything she could to get the answers she wanted"

"I don't hurt the people I care about to get them" I frown.

West walks over to the door, opening it slightly for a soldier to enter through the gap. The soldier is smaller than him. The soldier is holding fabric in one hand, and a pair of plain white shoes in the other. The shoes look like trainers I would usually wear down to training.

"You will need to wear this" he instructs me.

127

The soldier stretches out his arm to give me the freshly washed fabric. White shorts. Long white t-shirt. Shoes small enough to fit my feet. It is the same outfit I used to wear day in and day out.

It takes everything inside me to force myself to take the items off the soldier. "Can you leave for me to change?" I ask.

"Yes, I will be waiting outside" he nods his head. "I will be escorting you to breakfast today" he adds.

West and the soldier exchange a look between each other and then make their way back to the door. They give me the privacy I need in order to change. If I wanted to, I could use this time to find an escape. Do everything in my power to keep away from the PPW.

But I will listen to West.

If someone is trying to hurt me, leaving is the best thing for me right now.

I trust West.

CHAPTER TWENTY-SIX
GRACE

The plane looks smaller than before.

The white frame looks as clean as the day it was built. It could blend in with the clouds. I don't remember the wings of the plane being bigger than the plane itself. They look huge as I walk under them. My small figure looks like an ant compared to the planes outstretched wings.

With each step I take, I find myself dreading the worst. I don't want to go back. I fear I will be trapped down there for the rest of my life. The same image replays in my head. Hunter planning to take me back to get rid of me, to leave me there to rot for all eternity.

I walk up the steps. Each step weighing me down a little more. The door is already open, waiting for me to walk onto the plane. One step and I can already count four soldiers, all sitting on different sides of the plane. A row in the centre of the plane separates the seats. I take a couple more steps to make room for anyone behind me.

I feel like a lost puppy without West.

The amount of white surfaces on the plane is enough to blind someone. The only object on the plane that doesn't seem to consist of anything white is the dark blue seats. The seats on the right are mainly empty. On the left of the plane is where most of the soldiers are now sitting. The people who are working on the plane have also chosen seats for when the plane decides to take off.

Someone behind me clears their throat, startling me a little. I move out of their way and stand closer to the toilet that is located near the front of the plane. I make sure to keep out of everyone's way. Causing troubles isn't on my mind. All I am worried about is when the plane lands.

I look around for West, but I don't see him anywhere. He has wandered off somewhere. That doesn't fill me with a whole lot of confidence, nor does it make me feel any better. Having West close to me was giving me some ease on the matter, but now he is gone. I may be mad at him for what happened yesterday, but I can't do this without him.

I can't go through with this if he isn't by my side.

To no surprise, Hunter isn't on the plane either.

Another couple of steps. I hold onto the top of one of the seats as I look around for the best place to sit. Someone stands from the back, messy dark hair rising above the heads of the seats until I recognise exactly who it is.

Elijah Haul.

When his eyes lock onto mine, he looks furious.

His light blue eyes daring to move away from mine. A tight white t-shirt and white joggers. He is wearing the same outfit he was wearing when he showed his ability to Hunter. The only difference is the shoes. We never wore shoes. I assume they will make us take the shoes off before going back down there.

I make small steps until I am standing in the middle of the aisle. His light eyes look me up and down as if he cannot believe his eyes. I move a strand of hair out of my face as he frowns.

"What are you doing here?" Elijah takes me by surprise.

"I could ask you the same thing" I cross my arms.

He walks through the aisle, stopping with only a one seat gap between us. "You are not meant to be here" he rejects the idea of me joining West.

"I'm here, aren't I?" I shrug, not knowing what to say.

I don't know why I am entertaining the conversation.

The last time Elijah spoke to me, he told me he wanted me to hate him. He would rather me hate him than make an attempt to become his friend.

"You know where we are going, right?" he is acting like I have just stumbled onto the plane with no idea what is really going on. "We are going—"

I quickly interrupt him. "I know where we are going. I'm not stupid. What are you doing here? West never mentioned you tagging along with us" I question him. What purpose will Elijah have coming with us? Now that I think about it, I don't know why West was going in the first place.

"Hunter needs me to do something for him" he doesn't give me any information.

"Like what?" I ask, wanting more details.

130

"Ask West" he avoids the question.

"I'm asking you" I fake a smile.

Elijah rolls his eyes and makes his way to the back of the plane, returning to his original seat. He completely ignores the question I had asked. He really hates answering me. I think he has made it a new hobby to look over any question I ask him.

As the plane becomes busier, I decide to find a seat and sit down somewhere in the centre. The seat I choose happens to be next to the window. I slump down into the seat, my eyes set on the scene outside the window. The sky is clear, not a cloud in sight. I miss the clouds. Clouds always give the sky a different picture to paint.

My seat has another two seats facing opposite, and one seat beside me. Luckily, no one on the plane has decided to sit with me, giving me the space I need to take a breath. The soldiers around the plane are giving me looks that could kill. I ignore them the best I can, pretending to be too fascinated with the world outside the window.

The seat beside me becomes filled with someone. My head turns to face the person who has decided to make the brave decision to sit beside me, only to find West. "How are you feeling?" he smiles as he sits comfortably beside me, one of his hands clutching a load of papers.

He needs to stop asking me that question.

"Not great" I respond, honestly.

West nods his head. "You'll be okay. I will be there. You won't leave my sight" he tries to comfort me.

"No offense, but I don't believe you" I admit.

My words don't seem to affect him. "I know this is hard for you. It's for the best right now" he offers me a small, warm smile. "I promise, I won't leave you there. You will never be trapped in that hole again"

A part of me hopes he keeps that promise.

"I will hold that promise to your grave" I lightly warn him, offering a small smile back at him.

"Good" he chuckles.

The plane starts moving backwards, causing my heart to jump out of my chest and begin running for the ground. The feeling is horrible. It makes me want to throw up. The motion of moving backwards and the loud noise the plane makes as the engines turn on.

My hands grip onto the seat, praying the seatbelt is tight enough to keep me strapped down onto the seat for the whole duration of the flight. I don't want to get up until we are back on the ground and the engines have been stopped. Until then, I am happy to stay seated.

I hope this isn't a long flight.

I don't think my stomach can do too many summersaults today without bringing up my entire breakfast.

As the plane takes off, my blood runs cold. My ears make a popping sound and then everything becomes a blur to my eardrums. Like the whole world turns to muffle. I close my eyes and hope for the jerky feeling to stop. The plane lifts off the ground and begins its journey into the air, flying into the endless void of blue.

Eventually, the plane levels out, and the seatbelt sign turns off. West looks from the light to the other people seated around the plane. I hold onto the seat a little longer, making sure it's safe before resting my hands on my lap.

"I'm going to check on the pilot. Do you want a drink or maybe a snack?" West asks me.

"I'm good" I shake my head.

"Alright, don't move" he unbuckles his seatbelt and makes his way down the aisle towards the front of the plane.

I watch him walk away before finding something else to place my focus on. I rest my elbow on my thigh and stare out the window to watch the sky. It is an ocean of colour and an empty void of blue. I look for birds. A pigeon, or maybe a small black bird. Any kind of bird.

But sadly, to no surprise, there isn't a bird in sight.

"You won't see any birds" Elijah's voice brings my eyes away from the window.

I huff, my eyes landing on Elijah. He has found the seat opposite me, making himself comfortable. "I never do" I sigh with disappointment. In the corner of my eye, I see different people make their way up and down the plane. "Didn't like sitting alone, did you?" I raise an eyebrow.

"You looked like you were about to cry, thought I'd save everyone on the plane the trouble" he leans back into the seat and turns his head to face the window.

Of course he says something like that. He will take any chance he can get to make a snarky comment towards me. "I'm not about to cry so you can go back to your seat and stop bothering me" I glower.

He ignores my statement. His lips turn into a tight smirk as he watches the sky. "How's the black eye?"

"I've had worse" I recall the many times Elijah gave me a black eye or busted lip.

Elijah holds a smug look on his face and then he slowly replaces it with something sad. His lips form a tight thin line as his eyes lower to his lap. "I didn't think there would come a day we would return to the hell hole" he admits.

"Me neither…" I don't want to think about it.

"I bet the boys are missing me" he chuckles.

"Nolan is probably lost without you" I scoff.

"Probably" he agrees.

"I don't want to go back" I confess, grabbing his attention from the window. He only stares at me, waiting for me to talk again. "I hoped to never see this place again, and now we are going back, and I don't know how long we are going to be stuck down there…" I stop myself.

A low groan comes from Elijah. He doesn't look at me, but I can tell he is frustrated. "Don't be such a cry baby" he has a sour look on his features.

Once again, he is being an ass.

"You don't have to be a jerk about—"

"I'm being honest" he corrects me.

I don't want to be near him. He should go back to his seat in the back of the plane. "Go sit somewhere else" I snap.

"No" he snaps back, bluntly.

"No?" I repeat.

"If you want me to leave, I'm staying" he explains, telling me everything I need to know. He wants to annoy me. He wants to get under my skin the same way he always does.

I shouldn't let him get to me the way he does. I used to be good at keeping silent around him. Staying silent was the one thing I was good at. It was my talent. Some people had the power to move things with their minds, some could create a ball of fire in their hand, or control electricity. My superpower was staying quiet at all times.

Now I can't even do that.

"You were right before... we will never be friends. Not in this lifetime" I narrow my eyes onto his face.

He looks happy about my claim. "Finally, you've come to your senses" he rests his elbow on the armrest beside him. He holds a happy smile on his lips.

As much as I try to be nice, I can't keep pretending to be someone interested in being his friend. We are both beyond the point of friendship. It is best if we keep our distance from one another. That way, nobody hurts each other, and we don't have to deal with the constant arguing. "I am done trying to be nice to you" I give up.

A quiet sigh of relief passes through his mouth. "The whole nice girl act never suited you anyways. I like it better when you hate me" he grins.

He still wants me to hate him.

"You are sick" I glare.

A little bit of shaking from the plane makes my skin turn green. My hands reach out to grab anything, hoping for something to keep me grounded. I shut my eyes as my hands grip the first thing they can reach.

And then the plane steadies itself again.

I keep my eyes shut as I wait for a sign that everything around me has returned to its normal self. But I never get a sign. I only receive an annoyed groan from in front of me.

"Grace" Elijah calls my name. "Grace, get your hands off me" he demands.

I open my eyes slightly, finding my hands gripping his knees in an attempt to calm myself down. In my head, I was holding onto my seat, or the two armrests beside me. Or even the seat beside Elijah. But not his knees out of everything. My hands rise from his knees and land back on my lap.

"Sorry…" I apologise.

West walks back over to our seats, stopping in the middle of the aisle to stare at Elijah. His eyes switch between the two of us, settling on Elijah again with concern. I can't begin to imagine the thoughts running wild in his mind. Me and Elijah willingly sitting together isn't something you see every day.

He places his hand on the head of one of the seats. "Is everything okay here?" West asks us both.

Elijah stands up from the seat. "Everything's fine" the familiar cold expression returns to his face. Elijah pushes past West and makes his way to the back of the plane, sitting down in the seat he came from.

That was weird.

Even for Elijah.

West sits back down next to me, his eyes scanning the plane to seek out a handful of people. I sit in silence, counting down the minutes, the hours, until we land.

CHAPTER TWENTY-SEVEN
GRACE

We had to leave our shoes on the plane. We need to look like we haven't left. Blend in with everyone like before. Like nothing has changed since the last time we were here.

West has given us specific rules to keep us in line and to keep everyone from finding out the truth about the time we have spent above ground.

Don't talk about the outside world.
Don't mention Myles, Lucas, or Carter.
Don't bring up Hunter.
Don't tell anyone how or why you came back.

Elijah knows what he needs to do, and I know what I have to do. Neither of us need to cross paths while we are here. I just hope I can go back to being the nobody. The quiet girl who most people would stay away from. And I hope Nolan leaves me alone while I'm here.

The familiar pale walls, ceilings, floors. The same horrid soldiers walking the halls. Nothing has changed. Nothing at all by the looks of it. I can still feel the shiver running up and down my spine, caused by the cold flooring. I have missed nothing about this place. There is only bad memories surrounding this place. My mind is consumed by bitterness.

West is wearing a soldiers uniform. A small PPW is pinned to his uniform, matching all the other soldiers around us. He looks exactly like the night he picked me up from my room and dragged me into the outside world. I remember it like it was last night. I can still remember my first time seeing him when we reached the skylight.

Even his buzz cut hairstyle is the same.

I imagine a clock ticking with each step we take down the hallway. Tick. Tock. Tick. Tock. The clock chimes twelve when we reach the dinner hall doors. I keep my feet firmly planted on the ground as the weight of my worries hugs my torso and leans on my shoulders.

Elijah keeps his hands behind his back, his head held high with anticipation. I can't decide whether or not he is genuinely excited, or he is putting on an act.

"Remember, you are looking for the most powerful people to bring back with us" West speaks to Elijah in a whisper, and then turns to me. "Keep to yourself. I am here if you need me" he tries to comfort me the best he can. "I will catch up with you both later on tonight" he assures us.

One nod to the soldiers, and the dinner hall doors open to reveal us to everyone. All eyes are already on us before we enter the room. This is far from comforting. Everybody has stopped eating to look our way. They would rather try and find out what is going on here than eat the small amount of food they are given a day. This might be their only time to eat, and yet they would rather spend it looking at us.

I hate this.

"Stay away from me" I whisper to Elijah as he begins to walk away from me.

Elijah turns his head to look at me as he stops, hearing my quiet demand. We both stare for a moment. A second too long. Thankfully, he breaks eye-contact first. He shakes his head and makes his way over to his old friends, sitting down at the table beside Nolan.

I have to pry my eyes away from them, looking around the hall for an empty seat. People are still staring at me. They know something is going on. They must do. I just want to find somewhere to sit alone. I don't want to communicate with any of these people. They will ask question I can't answer, and I can only see it ending badly.

Maybe a table with the fewest people around it.

Continuing to look around, I spot the old seats Myles and I used to sit in. All of the seats around them are empty, which is perfect for me. I make my way over to the seat and sit down with a small smile on my lips.

Myles and I would sit here together; he would talk, and I would listen. He could tell these amazing stories about his thoughts on what the world was really like outside. He would go into detail about all his theories. It used to be one of the highlights of my day. I remember waking up to his smile and looking forward to coming in here and listening to him talk.

I miss that side of him.

He was always so sweet and innocent. Myles would do anything to make me smile. The amount of times he would sit in the seat beside me and tell me how we could one day leave this place, how the soldiers would let us go outside for the first time and run free. How we could finally be free together.

That story came true…

But it lasted for nothing longer than a blink.

The Myles I am dating, and the Myles who used to sit in the seat beside me are two very different people. I am so sick of comparing them. The guy I knew is gone. At some point, I will need to accept that. Even if I don't want too.

"Grace Silver" someone says my name.

My head lifts from staring down at the table. Allowing my eyes to wander around the room, I find three people settling down in the seats around me. Two guys and one girl. They look at me with curiosity. I try to get a good look at them all, but I can't say I know any of them that well.

I only recognise one of them. I think we had a training session together once. The other two are completely new to me. The three of them must be friends.

Wandering eyes cause my head to lower in an attempt to stay out of people's eyeline and keep to myself.

When I realise the group around me still keep their eyes on me as I stare at the table, I decide to take a good look at who they are. I scan over each of them individually.

The boy I recognise, I can't remember his name. He has thick, curly black hair with dark brown eyes. The left eye has a small black dot. It looks like a freckle. One little black dot which separates him from the others. The last memory I have of him, I think I remember him being Italian. He had a thick accent that stood out above the crowd.

The guy seated beside me; I have no idea who he is. He could be anyone. His fluffy brown hair bounces on top of his head as he sits down. A pair of pale green eyes stare into mine, watching with thrill dancing along his pupils. He looks far too eager to be sitting here.

And then there is a girl. She is sitting opposite me; beside the boy I recognise. She has her elbows on the table and her head rested on her hands. Long strands of light blonde hair falls down the side of her rounded face. The dirty white t-shirt clinging to her body makes her bright blonde hair look silver.

"It's— uhh— It's Ben" the boy I recognise stutters as he begins to introduce himself. "Do you remember me?" he tries to get me to remember. My head shakes in response to him. "Ben Aquino. We had a couple training sessions together"

"I don't… sorry" I apologise.

All of their eyes widen at the sound of my voice. I take them off guard. They quickly look from me to one another, showing each other their surprise. "You talk" the smiley girl announces. I nod my head. "Everyone was wondering when the day would come where you would talk" she continues.

"I'm Kane, Kane Rick. I don't think we ever properly met; I probably know more about you than you do of me" the other guy introduces himself. "This is Ben's girlfriend, Iris"

"Nice to meet you…" I try to be nice.

"Kane saw you sitting alone and thought you may want some company" Ben explains their action.

"I'm happy to be alone—"

"Nonsense" the girl, Iris, waves her hand. "Tell us, where have you been?" Instead of answering her question, I have to stay silent. West made it clear; we can't tell anyone where we have been. Most people will know Elijah left with Hunter, but nobody will know I went with him. "Too soon?" she notices me shift uncomfortable.

"Too soon" Ben repeats in agreement.

Looking around the dinner hall, I catch most eyes looking over at Elijah. Even I find myself glancing over to him every so often. He was popular before we left, feared more than liked, but leaving this place doesn't seem to have changed the fact that people still want to be around him.

Although, I'm curious as to where everyone has gone.

The room doesn't seem to be filled like it used. "Where is everyone?" I find myself asking. The dinner hall isn't half as full as I remember. Most of the seats are now empty.

"Not sure" Kane says, moving his head to look around the room. "Some people just disappear. You know how it goes around here. We don't tend to pay that much attention to it anymore"

People didn't used to disappear this quickly.

In the amount of time I have been gone, there is half the people here now. It would usually be one or two people every four months. By the looks of the place, it has been one or two people every week.

"They are probably somewhere nice" Ben sighs. "Better than this hell"

"Don't be so negative" Iris swats his arm.

"I'm just saying" he defends himself. "Living the same day over and over again can get boring"

"I bet Elijah loved leaving with the Supremes' son. He saw more of the world than any of us combined" Kane has a curious look in his eyes. He wants to ask a million questions but is holding himself back. "Why do you think he has been brought back?"

"Maybe he wasn't good enough" Ben shrugs.

"Or maybe he was too good for them" Elijah talks in the third person. He jumps into the seat beside me, wrapping an arm around my shoulders.

Nolan sits down beside Iris, a large grin staining his small lips. He looks happy to see me. "Leave us, will you? We have a lot of catching up to do" Nolan speaks through his teeth.

Kane and Ben exchange a saddened look before standing up from their seats, encouraging Iris to do the same. She nods her head to unspoken words and leaves the table with them. I am left alone with Elijah and Nolan.

Great.

"I saw you talking" Nolan raises both eyebrows. "I bet you have the ugliest voice; we always knew you would. Isn't that right Elijah?"

Elijah only nods.

"What made her talk?" Nolan asks Elijah as if I'm not sitting directly in front of him.

"No idea" Elijah huffs.

"After all this time, the mute has a voice" Nolan cheers.

140

Nolan is someone I hoped to never see again. His voice alone makes me want to stick pins into my heart. I make a move to stand up, but Elijah uses the arm wrapped around my shoulders to hold me down.

"Where are you going? Nolan has some more catching up to do" he keeps the conversation going.

"He can ask you whatever is on his little brain" I say as I shove his arm off my shoulders.

A shock washes through Nolan but he quickly recovers as he rests his arms on the table in front of him. He clears his throat and directs his eyes onto me. "I want to know how you managed to sneak out of here without being caught" he gets to the point.

My eyes stare into Elijah's. I don't know what to say to Nolan. Elijah could have already given him an entire made-up story on where he has been and why he has come back. If I lie and then contradict what he has said, we are both going to be caught out before we even last an hour here.

"Like I said… ask Elijah" I want to get away from them.

I manage to stand up, stepping away from the table. A soldier looks my way and stands from their chair. The soldier walks over to me with a stern look on his face. They never look happy. "Sit down" the soldier orders.

Hesitating at his demand, I frantically look around for an excuse to leave. "I'm finished eating" I lie, knowing I haven't even gotten myself food. I don't know what's worse, the clear fact that I'm lying or the smug chuckle erupting from Nolan behind me.

"Sit down" he repeats.

Glaring up at the soldier, I sit back down. I return to the seat beside Elijah, frowning as he watches me sit down. I will always hate the soldiers down here. Nolan doesn't hide the amusement writing itself over his face, his shoulders rising and falling as he laughs.

"You should know the rules by now" Nolan laughs. I don't acknowledge Nolan or Elijah. My eyes try to find the closest exit. West is nowhere to be seen. He must have somewhere else he needs to be. "I bet your excited for training later" He continues to push a conversation onto me.

"She isn't listening to you" Elijah states the obvious. He grips my hand and holds it down on the table. "Come back into the real world" he demands.

I hate the smug look on his face. The eyes of the devil, that is how I would describe the eyes staring into my soul. He will never stop enjoying the pain he causes me. I have no idea how I thought Elijah could ever be a good guy. He will always be the same. I am delusional for believing he could change.

I am an idiot.

"Tell me about your adventure" Nolan grins.

"Myles Colorado is officially her boyfriend" Elijah gossips like a thirteen-year-old girl.

"We all knew it was going to happen. I'm surprised it took them this long" Nolan doesn't sound impressed. "Where is Myles now?"

Elijah and I exchange a look. A knowing look that we need to lie. We need to say anything other than the truth. I'm staying quiet, Elijah can do all the talking. I don't owe Nolan an explanation, nor do I owe him my words. He shouldn't expect anything more than my silence.

"He was still with the Supremes' son last time I saw him, must be one of the favourites" Elijah doesn't completely lie.

"Myles was always a teacher's pet" Nolan rolls his eyes.

"He is almost as pathetic as her" Elijah gestures towards me with his thumb.

"You guys are so original" sarcasm laces my tone.

Nolan reveals a shocked look every time I speak. I find it pretty entertaining, at least I'm finding the positives in the situation. But I'm counting down the seconds in my head until we can leave this horrible dinner hall. I have spent less than half an hour in here and I'm ready to pack my bags and leave.

"Ouch… that one hurt" Nolan laughs again.

He sounds like a dying sealion.

"Good—"

"I liked you better when you didn't speak" Nolan tries to hurt my feelings. "Although, you are funnier now" he chuckles.

Like I thought before, they use me as a source of poor entertainment. "Grace and funny in the same sentence sounds wrong" Elijah shakes his head.

Both boys are looking at me.

"More like a clown kind of funny. We laugh at her, not with her" Nolan explains himself.

My lucky break finally arrives as the dinner hall doors open wide. All heads turn to face the doors with some people already on their feet getting prepared to leave. Nobody wants to stick around any longer. The soldiers can't keep up with how fast everyone is trying to leave the dinner hall.

Taking the opportunity, I leave the table.

"Where do you think you're going?" Nolan reaches out to grab me, trying to bring me back to them. As if he hasn't had enough of my presence already.

"Leave her go" I hear Elijah speak as he stops Nolan from following me. "She won't get very far"

As my legs pick up the pace, I manage to slip past the two dinner hall doors and back into the main hallway. The never-ending hallway I had always wanted to see to the end. It's not as big as I remember it. It feels smaller. Even the group of teenagers walking in a straight line looks half the size it used to be.

This place feels empty.

CHAPTER TWENTY-EIGHT
GRACE

Thankfully, I was only forced to spend a small amount of time around people today. By the time we arrived and slipped back into the routine of everything, it was time to go to our rooms and sleep.

West demanded he would be the one to escort me to my room. He doesn't seem to trust the other soldiers down here, giving them the dirtiest looks as we pass them by. West won't even crack a single smile around these people. The soldier uniform he is wearing brings out a different side to him.

Walking through the hallway, I take deep breaths. I have to remind myself to breathe. The process isn't programmed into my system. If I don't remind my body to take oxygen into my lungs, I will forget. There is too much on my mind to think about basic things like breathing.

The air down here tastes different. It's not fresh or cold or light. The air is heavy and man-made. Everything down here feels unnatural. The food, the people, the time. Everything is moving at a different pace to the world above ground.

A year ago, I wouldn't know any different.

Now that I have been outside, tasted the world that was kept from me for so long, I know the amount of lies that once swirled around my head. All of the rubbish they filled my mind with, all of the countless hours I had spent learning about a world that never existed. My entire life spent in this one room was for nothing.

I will never be able to get the years back. The nights of constant nightmares, the days of sitting in a classroom filled up with teenagers who would enjoy making my life hell as we listen to a teacher lie to our faces.

A part of me always knew there was something off about this place. I always knew something wasn't right about the way they would tell us stories of The Supreme and how he saved us from death and destruction.

Meeting the man himself, I know for a fact that story is far from the truth. The Supreme was power hungry and not a man of his word. He lied his way to the top and betrayed the nation for more money and power. He was arrogant and far from generous. He is no leader in my eyes, and he never will be as long as I live.

Hunter is ten times the man he will ever be.

I force my arms by my sides as West walks beside me with a thick gun strapped across his chest. The gun is long with a sharp trigger ready to be pulled at any given moment. The thought of West having to use the gun scares me, especially somewhere like down here. The space is small, a bullet would kill someone if the gun were used.

The cold exterior West is keeping up worries me. I prefer the West who would make jokes and laugh. This West is like a robot, emotionless and heartless. He needs to smile. Show me West is still somewhere inside that soldier disguise.

His left-hand rests upon my lower back as he guides me through the hallway. He doesn't leave my side, making sure no other soldier tries to pull any stunts. My eyes glance at each soldier that passes us, watching their facial expressions change from the slightest sight of me.

I wonder if they remember me.

The look on their faces tell me they do.

Keeping my head down, I allow West to guide me down to my old room. I can still picture the room in my head, a vivid image of the place I once lived. Now, the room is more of a distant memory. A memory I place at the furthers depths of my mind, almost completely unreachable.

As we continue walking, my eyes catch a glimpse of light blonde hair and eyes that have become familiar to me. But not the good kind of familiar. I try to look closer, believing my eyes are trying to deceive me. As I manage to get a clear view, my breath gets caught and I cough.

When I find my breath again, I lift my eyes to try and see the blonde boy again. Only to lose him. I could have sworn that was Carter. He was standing in the hallway. He was right ahead of us. I saw him. I must have seen him.

"Keep walking" West orders.

Eventually, we reach my old room. We stop outside the door while West unlocks it. I take one deep breath, and then a second, and then a third, and then I lose count. Am I about to over breath? Is that possible? My lungs feel like they are on fire as I stare at the door slowly opening.

Freezing cold steel walls with nothing but a bed, a desk, and a small chair. The familiar scent of nothing takes over my senses as it floats into the air around me. I spot the same long window that allows anyone and everyone to look into the room, giving me little to no privacy. This room brings back all the memories I want to forget.

It brings back everything I hate about myself.

West nudges me into the room. He doesn't give me time to process. I stumble into the room with West following close behind. He closes the door behind him, allowing us a space to talk without people hearing.

I sit down on the creaky bed, feeling the hard mattress through the thin grey blanket. The room is exactly the same, as if it hasn't been touched since I left. Like they were waiting for me to come back. The thought creeps me out. I can't begin to imagine how long they have been waiting for me to return.

"How was it?" West asks me about dinner.

I manage to catch my breath as I look only at West's face, trying to ignore my surroundings. "Horrible" I don't sugar coat it. "Elijah is rude and mean and a complete ass"

"That does sounds like him" West agrees with me.

The thought of West being in the room with me gives me some comfort. He is staying while I find my bearings. West is making sure I'm okay. I appreciate that. He is sticking to his promise. "I just don't understand him" I shake my head.

"I need to talk to him tomorrow night about his decision, he is going to drive me up the wall if I have to talk to him for more than a minute" he complains.

"Decision on what?" I question him.

"Hunter will fill you in when we get back" West waves the question off.

He reminds me of a different question. A question that has been stuck on my mind all day. "When do we leave?" I ask. It has been less than a day and I want to leave. If we stay any longer than one night, I don't think my sanity will be intact by the time we leave.

If we leave at all.

The question makes him look away from me. He makes his way across the small room. "Three days" he mumbles as he takes a seat on the desk chair.

"You can't expect me to survive three days here" I gasp.

"Think of it this way, you coming here will allow you and Hunter time to cool off" he makes a good point. I don't want to be around Hunter, not after what he did to me. Maybe it is best if we stay away from each other for a while, it will do us both some good for the time being.

But not down here.

Not in this place.

"He shouldn't have ordered the soldier to hurt me for information" I state, glancing over to the large window that allows people to see into my room. "But your right, we need time away from one another"

"I'm glad you agree" he smiles.

I nod my head as my eyes scan over his outfit. The dust-coloured pants and jacket from the shoulders down. West is wearing the brown boots that are somewhat covered in sand like the other soldiers. He has taken the helmet off, placing it on the desk behind him as he turns the chair to face me. He looks like every other soldier, and it scares me.

"Do you have to wear the uniform the entire duration of our stay here?" I hope he says no.

"I need to look the part, but women always love a man in uniform" he winks.

"What women" I laugh.

"Hot women" he grins.

"Let me know when you see any" I continue to quietly laugh at his statements.

His grin slowly fades as my laughter dies down. "But on a serious note, how are you?" he asks. His eyes are on me, looking at me. He is really looking at me. Like he knows how I am really feeling.

I don't bother lying to West. "This place. This room. The people. All of it, it's something I will always hate. I want to burn

147

this whole place to the ground and watch it with a smile. I never want to see this hell hole ever again" I answer with harsh honesty. I don't hold anything back from him.

"As long as I'm there to help" he smiles with his hands clasping together.

"Really?" I announce my surprise with wide eyes.

"I hate this hell hole too. I've been telling Hunter to get rid of it for years" he explains. "When you decide to follow through with that plan, give me a call"

"I will" I giggle.

"Good" he beams a smile at my giggle.

If it wasn't for West, I wouldn't be able to handle being back here. He is keeping me from pulling all of my hair out of my scalp and running around like a wild animal. He is the reason I am still sitting in this room. I feel comfortable around him.

The room fills with silence. My mind fills with images of what Myles might be doing right now. He probably hasn't even noticed I'm gone yet. Myles would be sitting in bed, reading a book about poetry or a superhero. He is probably forgetting all about me. That's what he does when I'm around, what's the different now that I'm gone.

We haven't been the same for a while.

I haven't been able to get the thought off my mind.

"Do you think Myles is a good boyfriend?" I blurt the question out before I can stop myself.

West looks taken off guard as much as I am. "Where did that come from?" he asks, startled.

"I don't know… forget I asked" I ramble.

"No. No. You can't take the question back" he won't let this go now. "Tell me, is there trouble in paradise?"

"We are fine—"

"That question suggests differently" he crosses his arms and leans back into the desk chair. I keep my mouth shut, wanting us both to forget I ever asked the question. "Ugh fine, he could be better, but hell, most guys don't know what the difference between a rose and a sunflower is so how should I know if he is a good boyfriend or not. Only you can know that"

148

I don't know how to tell him. How do I explain to West about Myles cheating on me with another girl? Words can't describe how I feel about it. "I think he cheated on me" I claim.

West jumps, almost on the edge of his seat. "What?" he wants me to repeat myself.

"Myles… I think he cheated on me" I repeat.

"You think?" he doesn't seem to understand. "You either know or you don't"

Cheating is being dishonest and unfaithful. I know what cheating is. But in my head, I don't want to place that label on Myles. I don't want to call him a cheater. But after the way he has treated me for the last couple months, maybe I should stop pretending he will change.

"He was kissing Asha… I have replayed the moment over and over and I don't know if I'm being dramatic" I admit.

"Asha? One of the girls from RoseShire?" he tries to put a face to the name. "Wow he must be really desperate to get off with a girl from that dump—" he cuts himself off as my head lowers. "Sorry, but he seriously decided to go off with another girl behind your back?"

Nodding my head, I look back on the night I saw him kissing Asha. His hands were all over her while she clung to his body, wanting to be closer to him. "I caught them one night; he doesn't know I saw him"

"I swear you are still dating… oh Grace" the look of pity fills his eyes as he looks at me.

"I don't know what to do" I confess.

"You break up with him" he gives me the same answer I already have in my head.

Elijah has told me to break up with him, now West is saying the same thing. I know they are right. Breaking up with Myles is the only answer at this point. He betrayed my trust and showed me the amount of loyalty he has for me.

But I have been dreaming about dating Myles for years, giving that all away just seems… wrong. It feels like I would be giving up on him too easy. Maybe it was a one-time thing, he might regret it. The whole thing may have been a mistake.

But even after coming away from RoseShire, he didn't go back to being the Myles before Asha.

149

He showed no sign of regret.

"Myles doesn't deserve you as it is, but that just proves it to you" he continues.

"You don't know the Myles I know" I defend him. "He was sweet, and kind and he would do anything to see me smile, even when I didn't speak to him. I never said a word to him, but he treated me like a human being"

He shakes his head. "That was before he was exposed to the real world" West reminds me.

"Yeah..." I agree.

"Best advice I can give... get rid of him" he shrugs.

West gives me the honest truth. He's right. I need to end the relationship between Myles and I for good. Elijah has said the same thing more or less. I just need to find the right time to talk to Myles about everything. Maybe he will explain what was happening so I can stop overthinking it.

"Elijah said the same thing, give or take" I sigh.

"You asked Elijah about this?" West looks surprised.

"Not really... the conversation, well it just kind of... happened" I don't explain it very well.

Two soldiers walk past the window, looking through the window. They glance over at me and then their eyes land on West. Neither of them know what to do, they turn their heads and face forward again, pretending they didn't see anything.

"What's the crack with you and Elijah anyways?" he asks.

"What do you mean—"

"You know what I mean" he raises both eyebrows.

I glance from West to the window and back to West. He is looking at me, waiting for an explanation. "Elijah enjoys making me feel small. He has always hated me, and he always will" I shrug my shoulders.

"He doesn't hate you" West disagrees.

"What? Of course he does" I laugh at him. "He has made it clear to me the amount of hatred he has towards me"

He shakes his head. "I spoke to him last night, there wasn't a single piece of hatred inside his bones when you came up" West doesn't make any sense.

"What are you talking about?" I have to ask.

I need him to give me more details.

"Shit" West scratches the back of his neck. "I shouldn't be saying anything" he retracts.

"I want to know" I encourage him to continue.

He only nods his head. "Elijah saw what the soldiers did to you. It was after training. He was furious at the fact that Hunter gave the orders to hurt you that badly, and he made a big fuss about not giving us any more information" he explains but I still have more questions.

My mind runs wild with different questions to ask him, but only one escapes the tip of my tongue. "What information did he give you?" I push another question.

"He was the one who told us about you and Carter" his words cut through me. How did Elijah know about that? "Once he told us, we searched the cameras and watched the whole thing back, watching your conversation with Carter until he disappeared"

"Elijah wasn't there…" I mutter under my breath.

West hears the words I whisper to myself. "That's the part that confused me too" he admits with a puzzled look growing on his face. "His excuse was pathetic, he said he was practicing teleporting but neither Hunter nor I believed it"

I'm more confused than ever.

"That's weird" I put it nicely.

Elijah hasn't been in my room before. I would never let him past the door if he even tried. For him to teleport into my room is odd. He has no reason to be in my room, and he has no reason to come near me without someone ordering him. If that was his excuse, he is definitely lying.

But I want to know the truth.

What's the real reason he was in my room that night, and how didn't I see him?

"Hunter doesn't like him" West chuckles.

"He needs to join the line" I joke.

"It's a very long line" he jokes back.

We both laugh. Hunter and Elijah aren't liked by a lot of people. For different reasons. I'm surprised they manage to get from one place to another without someone trying to start a fight with them. Neither of them have people manners. Hunter is too blunt and doesn't care what people think of him, and Elijah just doesn't think of anyone but himself.

They could use with learning how to be polite.

"Look, I should probably go before any of the soldiers start thinking I'm not doing my job. I'll be patrolling the hall for the next couple of nights. If you need me, I'll be around" he offers me a small smile.

I nod my head. I don't really want him to leave me alone in this room, but I can't keep him from doing his job. He needs to blend in here. The soldiers probably already know who he is because West is close with the Supremes' son, but he needs everyone else to think he is a normal soldier.

He stands up from the desk chair, straightening himself out and taking large steps to the door. He places the helmet back onto his head and then he opens the door but turns his head before stepping out of the room.

"I'm sorry again for what we did to you..." he apologises again, his eyes looking at my busted lip and black eye.

I only offer him a small smile as a response.

He holds the gun tightly in one hand and quickly leaves the room. The door slowly closes behind him with the all too familiar sound of the door locking echoing through the room.

I'm alone in this room...

CHAPTER TWENTY-NINE
GRACE

The training room is filled with floating objects and large obstacles. Five people have already made their way onto the running machines.

That was always Myles' favourite thing.

He would look forward to going on them.

Boring old white walls surround me. Every wall in this hell hole is the same. There are bright white lights fitted into the ceiling, lighting up the entire room. Exactly like the room I'm forced to sleep in, there is a window running from one end of the training room to the other. Anyone who walks through the hallway can see into the training room.

My eyes scan the training room, looking for somewhere to go instead of standing near the door. I am standing alone to the side of the room, keeping a close distance to the door. My body leans against the wall as I watch the running machines. I can still remember the long hours I spent on those.

The three people from yesterday's dinner are talking to one another in the corner of the room. They seemed like a nice group. I still don't understand why they sat with me. I don't think they ever spoke to me before I left. They probably only sat with me to try and get information on where I have been and why I'm back.

I hold onto my wrist, only to find that the bracelet Hunter had given me is gone. I forgot I took it off. It must still be in my room in Soltrix.

Although, I did like the bracelet.

My wrist feels naked without it.

Keeping my head facing the running machines, I notice two or three soldiers in the corner of my right eye. They are watching everyone through the window. They mainly focus on the people using their abilities, making sure they stay in line and follow the rules.

One step out of line and the soldiers are ready to storm into the room to put that person in their place. I wouldn't be surprised if they still used the dark rooms as a way of giving people punishments for breaking the rules. The dark rooms seemed to be their favourite thing.

"You look lost" the girl from yesterday giggles as she stands beside me. Iris, I believe her name was. Her long, light blonde hair has been pulled back into a high ponytail.

"I'm just getting used to it all" I say, keeping my eyes on the running machines.

"It must be weird… coming back here" she sympathises with me. I can't tell whether she is trying to get information out of me or if she is just being nice.

"It is…" I sigh.

"What's it like?" she turns to face me. "Outside of the hallway?" she is fishing for answers. I had a feeling she was only talking to me for information, but this proves it. "I know you didn't want to answer yesterday but I have to know. My entire life has been spent down here; I just want to know there is more to life than this. There has to be, right? I'm begging you to tell me something… anything"

She sounds like me a year ago.

Only I didn't announce my curiosity. I kept my thoughts and questions to myself. That is until I met Hunter. He was the only person I found myself asking questions around, speaking like it was first nature. I can't fathom how I felt so comfortable around him to talk so openly, but I did.

"I don't remember it" I lie.

"You don't remember?" she sounds disappointed.

I hold back my breath, hoping she believes me. "They must have wiped my memory" I say the quickest thing that comes to my mind.

"Elijah said the same thing" she nods her head. A sigh of relief passes through my lips. "He was lucky to be selected to leave… the Supremes' son has Myles and Lucas. I wonder if they are okay" she worries about nothing.

I know Lucas and Myles are fine. Lucas is enjoying his time in Soltrix, and Myles is getting used to being back in the main building again. Anything is better than being stuck down here. They are loving life compared to this. I bet they don't even think twice about this place, forgetting about this hell like it never happened.

"Have you girls decided what you may want to start training on?" Kane asks as he walks over to us with Ben.

Both boys stop walking in front of Iris, causing us to create a small square between the four of us. Ben and Iris exchange a slight smile as he stops walking. "I think I'm going straight onto the mats" Iris decides.

"Me too" Ben grins.

"What about you?" Kane gestures to me.

"Me?... Oh, I'm not sure" I answer him as my eyes scan over the room.

There isn't a machine I want to go on. Most of them are full anyways. I am happy to stand here and watch everyone else train, but I know the soldiers will have something to say if they catch me slacking. They refuse to let people sit around. I need to blend in, pretend like I am following the rules.

"Grace, come onto the mats with us. We can help each other out" Iris smiles.

Training on the mats could mean two things. We are either trying hand to hand combat, or we are using our abilities on one another. If it's the first option, my training with West may pay off after all. If it's the second option, count me out of it. My ability is best kept unused.

I can't control myself when it comes to my ability. Using it down here could become a problem. Anything could happen with it. I need to learn to control myself before I decide to start practicing it around other people.

"I'll watch you guys from the side-lines" I try to stay out of training with them.

At least this way, I'm not alone.

"Ben and I will go first, me and you can go up against one another when we're done. If you want" Iris jumps with joy.

Following behind Kane, we make our way to one of the empty training mats on the left side of the room. The blue mat has been stained with blood. Red blotches are scattered across the mat, telling everyone how much use this mat has really had in the last month. No matter how many times the piece of equipment is washed, if it's washed, the remanence of blood will forever remain.

155

My back rests against the wall while the others get the mat ready for Ben and Iris to begin. Kane drags the mat out of the way of everyone else, giving Iris enough space to stretch her body and make sure her ponytail is tight before stepping onto the training mat.

"First one to go down has to go up against Kane" Iris smirks before they start.

"Sounds good to me" Kane nods.

Ben and Iris step onto the mat. They walk around in a circle, trying to sike each other out. Kane and I watch intensely as we anticipate the first person to make a move. Kane steps backwards until he is standing beside me, resting his body up against the wall, comfortably.

Iris makes the first move, shooting water out of the palm of her hand, heading straight for Ben.

He ducks his head in an attempt to dodge her sudden attack against him. The water disappears as it jarringly hits the wall behind him. I'm thankful we are standing against a different wall, or we could have been hit with that attack.

Ben quickly lifts his head in shock, turning to glance at the disappearing water. He chuckles and quickly decides to make the next move of attack. Behind Iris, a water bottle sits on a metal bench. Ben lifts his hand, placing all his focus on the large bottle of water. Swiftly, the bottle lifts off the bench.

Iris doesn't seem to notice his quick movement because when the water bottle hurtles towards her head, she doesn't move out of the way.

The bottle hits the back of her head, causing her to fall forward onto her face. She groans, taking a moment or two before using her hands to push herself up from the mat. She sits up and looks around at me and Kane.

"I think that means I win" Ben gloats as he crouches down to Iris' level. He gently grabs both her hands and helps her to her feet. "Did I hurt you?" he checks if she's okay, using one hand to hold the back of her head.

"I'm okay" she smiles up at him. Ben kisses her forehead and helps her off the mat. "Kane, you're up next. Knock him dead for me" Iris winks at Ben.

"My pleasure" Kane smirks evilly.

Kane steps onto the mat with Ben.

Iris stands in the same spot Kane had previously stood in, leaning her back against the wall like me. Kane runs a hand through his fluffy brown hair and then throws his hands to his sides, revealing the long metal claws that grow from his nails.

That one's new.

"Awe, that's cute" Elijah and Nolan bless us with their presence.

"Has Grace shown you what she is cable of yet?" Elijah is only looking at me when he talks. He holds a smug look on his face as he holds eye contact. "She is amazing, you have to see her in action... show them Grace"

"I'm good" I refuse.

Elijah isn't going to give up. I know him too well by now to know he won't take my no for a real answer. He will keep going until he is satisfied. "Come on, show them what you're really capable of" he pushes me to reveal myself.

"I said no" I protest.

"Stop being boring" Nolan complains.

Kane and Ben stop fighting, stepping off the mat and making their way over to us.

"She clearly doesn't want to" Kane tries to help.

"Stay out of this" Nolan warns.

"Come on" Elijah insists, stepping closer to me. He leans down and before I know what is happening, he throws me over his shoulder. He begins walking away from the wall and towards the training mat. "You'll be fine. I promise I won't hurt you" he says with a low voice, almost like a whisper, as if he is only talking to me.

No one else hears him.

He places me down on the mat, my feet touching the mat as his body takes four steps back.

We stare at one another, both of us standing on either ends of the mat. He stands in a position ready to fight. I don't want to copy his stance. I don't want to fight. My eyes glance from Elijah to the others watching us.

"I don't want to—"

"Stop being such a cry baby" Nolan groans.

Elijah shakes his head. "Keep your eyes on me. Not him. I want your eyes on me, and only me" he demands.

And I listen.

My eyes remain on Elijah, watching and waiting for him to make the first move to attack. I don't look anywhere other than his light blue eyes.

He doesn't move.

"Are you going to make a move?" I encourage him, wanting to get this over with quickly.

He smirks. "Do you want me to make a move?" his question is laced with a cocky tone. The kind of tone that implies there is a second meaning behind his words.

I roll my eyes.

Instead of waiting around, I take it upon myself to move. My feet move forward, and as I get closer to him, I swing a fist in his direction, hoping to hit him. My fist flies through the air, but that is all it does. No contact is ever made. Elijah disappears before my fist can reach him.

My body spins around.

Elijah is standing in my original spot. "You're going to have to be quicker than that" he chuckles.

I want to smack the cocky smile off his lips.

"It would be easier if you would stand still" I huff.

"That is too easy. I want to give you some sort of a challenge, make you earn it" he confesses.

I make a move to throw another punch, but he grabs my wrist before my hand manages to hit him. He uses his strong grip on my wrist to grab my other wrist. My body is pulled closer to his until his minty breath fans my face.

My eyes look up through my eyelashes.

He looks down at me, my body pressed against his chest. My throat finds it hard to swallow. Elijah is close. I can feel his skin is on mine, and I don't hate it.

I try to hate it.

It takes everything in me to reject the temptation to relax under his touch.

His leg swings and knocks my feet off the ground, taking me off guard. My body falls to the floor with Elijah following. His grip on my wrists doesn't faulter, holding them both above my head as we land on the floor.

Elijah's body hovers over mine, my wrists held above my head and our chests rising and falling in sync with one another's.

One of his hands holds both my wrists, the other is holding himself up, preventing him from completely lying on top of my body. My eyes don't leave his. There is a long silence between the two of us, neither of us knowing what to do. I watch his eyes intensely as they work their way down my face, stopping on my lips. I find myself doing the same, leading my eyes down to his lips, and lingering.

And then I realise where we are.

I wriggle my hand under his grip until I manage to focus all my energy on pushing him off me. I move my hand in one small swatting gesture. One move, and he is thrown off the mat by the air itself. He lands on the concrete floor, creating a slight sound that sounds like a painful groan.

I help myself onto my feet and make my way off the mat.

"Fair play" Kane claps his hands.

My eyes watch Elijah get back onto his feet.

I catch him smiling to himself, his head shaking as he looks at the floor. He brushes his shirt off as he begins to straighten himself out. When he faces everyone again, he has a frown plastered onto his lips. The smile is quickly replaced as if it was never there.

I hear someone huff.

"You really are just a bitch" Nolan snaps.

As I turn to see what has twisted Nolan's anger, he is already marching towards me.

His fist makes contact with my face, knocking me to onto the floor without warning. He watches me lift my head as I try to get to grips with what has made him angry all of a sudden. Nolan moves his foot, pushing it onto my right wrist.

The concrete feels cold on my skin as his foot applies more pressure to my wrist. "I'll personally make sure you never use your ability again" Nolan shouts in anger.

I start to bite the inside of my cheek while my lips purse together. As his foot becomes heavier on my wrist, I find it harder to stay quiet. I reluctantly let out a gasp as the pain gradually

159

becomes unbearable. Somebody needs to get him away from me before something snaps.

By now, the whole room is watching, but nobody tries to stop him. Nolan always enjoyed a crowd. He enjoyed putting on a show for the people. Slowly, he applies even more pressure to my wrist.

Shooting pains spread up and down my arm, coursing through my veins.

"I get it... stop!" I plead.

No one makes a move to help.

"This'll teach you to stay in your place" he says, looking at me with an evil smile.

"Aye, Nolan, that is enough" Elijah steps in.

Nolan turns his head but doesn't remove his foot. "She needs to learn where her place is. Because she went away, she has clearly forgotten" Nolan tries to encourage Elijah to get on board with his anger.

My eyes find Elijah's again.

Tears build up as Nolan's foot applies the most pressure my wrist has ever felt.

"You are going to break my wrist!" I shout.

"Alright, cut it out" Elijah takes a step forward.

I let out a scream of pain. Tears stream down the sides of my face, running from the ends of my eyes.

Elijah looks down at me, watching the pain spread across my face. Something unreadable flashes inside his eyes, something new, and in the blink of an eye, he is rushing towards Nolan. He forcefully pushes Nolan away from me. "I said, that's enough" Elijah growls.

I curl over, holding my wrist as a throbbing pain spreads up and down my right arm.

Out of everyone in the room, Elijah is the one to step in and put a stop to Nolan.

Nolan lands on the concrete floor, followed by a loud thud as his body connects with the ground. Elijah begins to climb on top of Nolan. Everyone in the room is watching them. Nolan tries to fight back against Elijah, but Elijah is too strong for him.

My eyes close shut as I try to block out the world around me for a second. I don't want to speak, I don't want to move, I don't want to listen. All I want is to do is stay in a ball until the pain disappears.

I hate Nolan.

I hate the people here.

I hate this place.

Footsteps stop beside me, hearing movement of two or three people. I continue to sob as quietly as I can. I don't want to draw any more attention to myself. My mind no longer has the thought of the crowd watching over me.

My eyes slowly open to find Ben knelt down beside me while Kane and Iris stand with their bodies leaning over his head. They are all looking down at me with pity. None of them really know what to do in this situation. All looking at each other for a solution.

The sound of the training room doors opening erupts in my ears. Five, maybe six, maybe even seven soldiers walk into the room. I'm too focused on my wrist to count. I don't turn my body to check. "Everyone back to training" West's voice fills the room, sending a shock wave through everybody.

West, the only person I want to see.

He will help me; he will know what to do. Hopefully he will know how to stop the shooting pain.

Feet shuffling across the floor muffles the voices of the crowd who had just witnessed my assault. Nobody down here likes to get involved with Elijah and Nolan, especially when it comes to situations such as this. But I wish someone would try to help the way Myles used to.

Myles would try his best to keep me away from the boys, no matter the situation.

Soldiers escort Nolan and Elijah out of the room. The crowd watches as they leave, waiting until the doors close to go back to training.

Elijah surprised me.

He helped me this time. He stopped Nolan from causing any serious damage. Normally, Elijah would find the whole thing funny and amusing, but this time he is looking at me with something new.

The same unreadable look he has been giving me lately.

"Can you move your wrist?" Kane asks me.

161

I don't bother trying.

My eyes find Ben as he tries to figure out a way to help. He has no idea what to do.

"Get her up" West's voice barks orders, charging over to us with a soldier following right behind him. "Two of you can take her to the nurses office"

"We can" Kane and Ben volunteer.

"Good" West responds, bluntly.

I don't think I have cried this much in a long time.

The boys grab my arms, one on either side of me as they lift me onto my feet. Kane is on my left; Ben is on my right. My wrist is sending alarm bells to my head, and I want it to stop before I snap. My body has lasted this long without losing control, let's not give up now.

CHAPTER THIRTY
GRACE

The nurse held an ice pack on the swelling for a while and has now wrapped a bandage around my wrist. The fabric is tight on my skin, holding everything together. She is a different nurse to the one I used to see on a daily basis. The other woman must be off sick… or something much worse, but I don't want to think about it.

As the nurses door opens, I can see the back of Kane and Ben's heads. They are both sitting on the floor with their backs pressed up against the wall. Kane and Ben sit either side of the nurses door, waiting for me to finish.

I didn't expect them to wait for me.

The quiet sound of the door opening sends the boys heads spinning in my direction. Ben sees me first; his eyes sink down to my wrist almost immediately. He examines the tightly wrapped bandage and frowns. "Is your wrist okay?" he asks as soon as his eyes finish looking over every inch of the fabric.

Using the wall as a support, the boys lift themselves up off the floor. The white joggers they are forced to wear has marks running down the backs of their legs from where they have been sitting. It looks similar to sand marks, probably from the soldier's large shoes.

The pure white tank tops are still somehow untouched.

I hold onto my wrist as I watch the boys. "Just sprained… thankfully" I let out a tired breath.

Kane brushes himself off. "You got off easy, that could have easily broken" Kane puts my injury into perspective. He has a point. If Elijah didn't stop Nolan when he did, my wrist could have broken.

"Your right" I agree.

My eyes glance beyond Ben's thick curly hair, noticing the hallway is empty. Not a soldier in sight. That is weird for down here. There is normally a soldier everywhere I look. No wonder the boys were allowed to stay out of training. There must be something going on.

"Where are all the soldiers?" I ask, looking up and down the hallway for a sign of movement.

"Not sure" Ben shrugs.

"Something must be happening; I saw them all heading down the right" Kane guesses.

"That's weird" I narrow my eyes.

Wait... could that mean the plane has come early to take us back to Soltrix? Maybe that's where all the soldiers have disappeared too, they have gone to greet the plane.

I think my hope is getting the best of me, but I allow it.

My head turns to the right.

The right side of the hallway was the way out if I remember correctly. It has the stairwell which leads to the top, and also to the other floors above this one. I wonder what else is down here.

I keep looking down the hallway.

Sadly, still no movement.

"Before one of us forgets, a soldier told us to take you back to your room" Kane recites.

I can only think of one soldier who would make that kind of order. "Was it a male, black buzz cut, about this tall" I raise my hand to gesture West's height.

"Yeah, how did you—"

"Lucky guess" I giggle.

"He was trying to ask us what happened, we told him everything. I hope that's okay" Ben explains.

"It's fine" I would have told West anyways; they have just beaten me to it.

Ben shakes his hair, the black curls bouncing on the top of his head. "It gives us an excuse to miss training" he smiles as he nudges Kane with his elbow.

"You'll do anything to miss training" Kane playfully rolls his eyes at Ben.

"It's a waste of time" Ben scoffs. "Seriously, what are we training for?"

I have to stop myself from laughing at his statement. It reminds me of what I used to think. Every day, I would wonder what was the purpose of training. "Trust me, you'll be thankful for it one day" I challenge his claim.

Potentially powerful weapons.

Knowing what this place is really for puts everything into perspective for me now. I know they are only training us to eventually use our abilities for war. They want to build us up to be the perfect weapons. Guns are no match for what some of the people in this hell hole are capable of.

Gradually, the three of us begin walking through the hall side by side with one another. "You must hate being forced to come back here... for whatever reason that is. I'm sure the life you had outside this hallway was far better" Kane tries to spark a conversation between us.

I wish I could tell them the truth.

They deserve to know. Everyone here has a right to know the reality of their world. If people knew the truth, maybe they would come together to overtake this place. The soldiers guns can only do so much damage. The soldiers wouldn't be able to contain us all at once, especially if we use our abilities. There is no match for someone up against all of us.

"Sorry about my girlfriend... she has always wanted to see beyond the hallway" Ben apologises on Iris' behalf. "I know her timing could be a little better, but she means well"

"No doubt she was pushing questions onto you earlier before we came to your rescue" Kane chuckles. "No need to thank us by the way"

As we continue walking, a noise bounces from one wall to the next. The noise takes us by surprise. Ben and Kane glance at each other for an answer they don't have. I find myself rapidly turning around to search for the cause of the loud sound. By the time my eyes finally see something in the distance, I feel myself stepping forward, wanting to get a clearer view.

My eyes squint.

A group of soldiers march through the hallway, heading straight for us. They march like robots. I can't see where they have come from. The hallway is too long to see exactly which door they have emerged from. At least we know where the soldiers disappeared too.

Slowly, my eyes begin to spot someone in the centre of the group of soldiers. The group of soldiers carefully surround the person in the centre, leaving no gaps for people to slip into their formation. Nobody can get past them.

The person in the middle must be important.

Looking through the large group of soldiers, I manage to direct my focus on the person in the centre. I can only see bits and piece as they walk. A long black coat blows behind their legs, stopping at the back of their knees. They are wearing a matching pair of black trousers to the long coat, which has the same stripped-like pattern running up and down the legs, along with a short-sleeved top tucked into the waistband.

My eyes rise a little further, trying to see the owner of the half-dressed suit. They are tall, at least six foot two. They have a jawline sharp enough to cut through metal itself, and ocean blue eyes that would send anyone crazy. Their brown hair with blonde highlights on the ends has been pushed back with some sort of hair product.

Hunter.

My walking comes to a sudden halt as my eyes catch a small glimpse of Hunter. He has arrived. Hunter has flown down here from Soltrix. Why didn't West tell me Hunter was already on his way? I thought we had more time trapped down here. If he was supposed to come down here, he is far too early.

This was meant to be my time away from him.

But I can't express how happy I am to see him.

Kane grabs my arm to pull me to the side of the hallway, pressing our backs against the closest wall as we give room for the soldiers to walk past. The hallway isn't wide enough for the soldiers to slip past us, we have to force ourselves as close to the walls as we can.

Hunter knows I'm watching him. I can see it written over his features. He is looking at me in the corner of his eye, making sure I am out of the way of the soldiers. Him just being here makes me feel a little better, knowing it's not just West looking out for me around here. I'm not alone down here.

I will never be alone down here as long as I have them.

"Isn't that the Supremes' son?" Ben gestures to Hunter.

"Hunter" I say his name out loud.

A smile creeps its way across Kane's lips. "Do you think he is here to take more people?" he gets excited.

"Don't get your hopes up" Ben frowns.

"This time might be different" Kane stays positive.

166

I'm far too focused on Hunter to try and join the boys conversation. I keep my eyes on his as he does the same. He doesn't break eye contact until he is too far past us to turn his head any further.

"Whatever the reason, it can't be that important" Ben makes a guess. "If it was important, the Supreme would be here himself"

"You never know" Kane continues to smile.

"Only time will tell" Ben shrugs.

I finally turn my head to the boys. Neither of them know what to think of Hunter's arrival.

Hope may ruin them.

If only the boys knew how much of a traitor the Supreme was…

CHAPTER THIRTY-ONE
ELIJAH

Four soldiers had to separate me and Nolan.

It took two soldiers to throw me into my room.

There was no chance in hell I was going to allow Nolan to get away with what he did to Grace.

He had no reason to hurt her like that. She had done nothing but prove to me and everyone in that room that she is stronger than before. She has grown guts. Grace can take me in a fight and win, which is more than what she could do before we left. Nolan took her strength as a threat.

Nolan felt threatened.

I know him better than anyone, I can see when he is scared or feels threatened.

But that is no excuse.

No matter how many years I spent tormenting and bullying Grace, I will never let anyone else hurt her. Nobody is allowed to hurt her apart from me.

"What the hell was that?" West's voice causes me to turn on my heels. He is standing by the door, arms crossed, and eyebrows raised so high they could touch the ceiling. "I told you to stay of trouble, yet you find it suitable to start fights and beat up a guy on your first real day back"

"Nolan had it coming" I scoff.

I turn, sitting down on the end of the bed.

"I was told what happened" West huffs, walking further into the small room. He leaves the door slightly open. I watch him as my elbows rest on the tops of my thighs. "You attacked Nolan in order to protect Grace"

"No" I lie, rolling my eyes. "I was just tired of hearing her screams and pathetic crying"

West takes a deep breath.

"The only person you are fooling here, is yourself" West sees right through me. "Me and you both know, deep down, you care about Grace a hell of a lot more than you let on. What I can't seem to understand, is why you pretend to hate her. Why put her through so much when you—"

"Shut it, will you" I groan.

I stand up from the bed, moving towards the door and closing it completely.

"I'm right, aren't I?" West smirks with wide eyes.

"You know absolutely nothing" I deny. "Grace and I were friends long before Nolan or Myles came into the picture. I was the one who knew all her secrets, I was the person she would tell everything. Even in our darkest days, we had each other" I admit, my words becoming louder.

West doesn't say anything.

"When she stopped talking, I didn't know what to do with myself. I blamed myself every single day, and I still continue to blame myself. Nolan and I became closer, and he seemed to find it funny whenever she cried. I was a kid, an extremely stupid kid, and bought into the idea that picking on her would make her a stronger person" I continue. "Years went by, and she still didn't say a word to anyone. At first, I thought she was only talking to Myles. I hated him for it. I thought he had put it in her head that I was the bad guy. But I quickly learned she hadn't spoken to him at all…" my words trail off.

"You hurt her—"

"Don't you think I know that?" I snap, running a hand through my messy hair. "God, I—" I can't seem to find the right words. "She was the best thing in my life. When that was ripped away from me, I didn't know what to do with myself. I won't admit that to her. It got to a point where no matter what happened, it was too late for me to stop. Nolan was set on ruining her life as part of his… his entertainment, and I had already ruined any chance of me and her—" I cut myself off.

"Shit… Man, I thought this was just some— well, I didn't realise you loved her" he announces his surprise.

"I do not love her" I deny, again.

"You are a shit liar" he shakes his head.

"You've got what you wanted… you are the only one who knows— I haven't told anyone that before" I sigh.

West becomes quiet.

169

He racks his brain for words, for something to break the small silence quickly growing throughout the room. He lifts his head as his lips begin to twitch.

"Does this make us friends?" West smiles.

I groan. "Don't make this weird"

"Elijah and West, becoming friends, who would have ever thought?" he makes it weird.

"You make me regret—"

West pats my shoulder. "Don't worry, I won't say anything to her" he assures me.

I nod my head, knowing I can trust him.

"You are aware you are going to have to sit in the dinner hall and do your best to keep your cool, right? I mean, you need to stay away from causing any more fights, which might mean you apologise to Nolan" he reminds me.

Shit.

"I'm not saying sorry for something I am not sorry about" I refuse. "He was about to break her wrist; I will not apologise for preventing that from happening"

"It is for the time being" he makes his way towards the door as his hand reaches for the handle. "Hunter has arrived and the last thing you need is for him to hear about this" he warns, and I know he is right. I cannot be bothered to deal with Hunter and his annoying breath down my neck.

The dinner hall is empty.

I am one of the first people to enter, scoping the place out to find the best area to take a seat.

Walking past the tables, I sit myself down around the table at the back of the room. In lines, people enter the room. It doesn't take long before the doors close, and they start serving the usual plates of uneatable food to everyone in sight.

Nolan decides to sit down opposite me.

I can't tell whether he is pissed off with me or pretending like the whole situation in the training room never happened. A part

170

of me wouldn't put it past him for trying to pretend the fight never happened, he has done it before.

Once Grace was escorted out of the training room, Nolan and I went at it, shouting anything and everything at one another until the soldiers could finally get a hold of us. Neither one of us was ready to surrender to the soldiers. The soldiers are supposed to be strong, yet it took them a lot longer than I expected to get a handle on the situation.

We sit in silence.

The people around us talk about what happened as if we are deaf. We receive stares and unapproving looks every now and again, but I ignore them. I can't remember a time when I didn't receive these sorts of looks from everyone.

I begin to eat the food, wishing I was back in Soltrix where I was fed food that didn't look like it came out of a sewer.

Every once in a while, I notice Nolan look at me, expecting me to say something. What he is expecting me to say, I have no idea. I continue to stay silent as the room fills with loud eating and constant chatter.

"So… are we going to sit in silence this whole time?" Nolan finally speaks.

I look up from my plate.

"You tell me" I say through a frown.

"You haven't said a word since you sat down" he complains with his fork still jabbing away at his food.

"Neither have you" I point out.

He has no argument, no leg to stand on.

His eyes lower back down to his plate. "Is this the part where you tell what the hell that was during training?" Nolan angrily stares at his plate as he talks.

"There was no need to attack her for winning a fight. It made me look weak" I make up something on the spot. "Hurting her for beating me in a fight gives off the impression to everyone else that I need you to fight my battles for me" I am hoping he buys into my words.

"Mmhh, well next time, don't attack me for it" he hums.

I nod my head, but I know I would do it again in a heartbeat if given the chance.

Nolan's head suddenly lifts like a meerkat, turning from one direction to the next. "Where is Grace now, anyways?" he asks, looking around the room in hopes of finding her sat alone. "She should be around here somewhere"

My eyes start to scan the room in an attempt to find her before he does. But she isn't here. There is no sign of Grace. She must be in her room, sleeping off the pain from her wrist. "Maybe she is in her room?" I assume, trying to get Nolan off the topic of Grace for a little.

"Getting special treatment again" Nolan scoffs loud enough for me to hear as his eyes roll. "Princess treatment" I hear him mutter under his breath.

The way Nolan says 'princess treatment' reminds me of the nickname I used to give Grace. I would call her Princess Mute like it was a bad thing. Maybe I didn't like the way Hunter would give Grace princess treatment when we first arrived in Soltrix. Call me jealous. I always assumed he had an altera motive behind his actions towards her.

"We're good, right?" Nolan asks.

"Sure" I agree.

I'm more worried about if Grace is alright.

All I want to do right now is hold her in my arms and tell her how sorry I am…

CHAPTER THIRTY-TWO
GRACE

Hours trapped in a box.

These four walls make the building in Soltrix feel like a heaven. Sitting in this room, being back to square one, it's one of the worst feelings. It's as if the last year of my life never happened. Like putting down your favourite book and looking around to find the world you had in your head was only your imagination.

If Destiny was here, she would probably be sat in this very spot, coming up with a million ways she would break out. Nikita would go along with anything Destiny said, and AJ would be thinking about all the places he could find food on the way out.

They deserved better than death.

I don't know what Asha would do. I don't know her as well as the others. I didn't want to know her.

I was always too busy avoiding her to get to know her.

Being trapped with only my thoughts, I have time to look over everything. I know in my heart there is only one way I can be free. Be truly free. Not looking over my shoulder all the time for Hunter or the Supreme or Carter. There is one solution to everyone's problems.

Someone needs to kill Todo Poderoso.

I need to kill him.

The war to end all wars. That's something Carter had said to me when I found him snooping through my room. It's also something Hunter had asked me about when he had me beat up for information. It must mean something. And my best guess is nothing good. The war to end all wars sounds like they have something big planned.

Someone needs to stop him before that happens. The worst part is not knowing. It could mean anything. It could be his way of distracting us while he plans something much worse to destroy us with. My fear is not knowing what he is going to do next. Not being able to predict him.

And I think Hunter feels the same.

A knock on the window takes me off guard. The hair on my arms stands up straight as my heart jumps. Elijah is in the hallway looking into the small cage they call a room. He must think he is really funny, scaring me like that.

Elijah takes a couple steps forward, carefully opening the door. He pokes his head through the small gap in the door. "Is this a bad time?" he looks to me for approval to enter.

I thought the door was locked.

I turn my body away from him, my back facing the door as I cross my legs. The bed gives me the capability to turn my body all the way around, facing the wall if necessary. "What do you want, Elijah?" I ask with an annoyed tone, keeping my back to him. I'm hoping he gets the obvious hint that I don't want to talk to him.

"How's the wrist?" he sounds genuinely worried.

"Fine… thanks to you" I sigh.

I glance over to him in the corner of my eye.

He parts his lips to talk again but doesn't let the words come out. He keeps his thoughts to himself as he takes a step or two into the room. Elijah gently closes the door behind him, giving us privacy we don't need. He isn't getting the hint. I want him to leave, I don't want to be alone with him.

I feel the mattress dip beside me.

When I look up from my lap again, I see Elijah. "Let me see it" he demands. I keep my eyes on the wall, keeping my mouth shut. I attempt to move my hand before he reaches out to grab it, but I'm too slow. He grabs my hand, pulling it in front of him for his eyes to examine my bandaged wrist. "I'm sorry, I am, I didn't expect him to hurt you" he takes me by surprise with his apology.

"I just want to be left alone" I pull my hand away from him.

Elijah helped me, I know he did, but I don't want to be near him right now. When he is around people, he is a different person to when it is just me and him. I don't have the energy to deal with him tonight.

"Can't you see I'm trying to be nice" he frowns.

"Yeah. It's weird. Stop it" I snap.

He takes a long-frustrated breath. "What do you want from me?" he snaps.

"What—"

"I'm horrible to you, and you are constantly nice to me. I try to be nice to you, and you shut me out! Tell me how I'm supposed to act" his voice raises.

"I gave up trying to be your friend" I huff. "All I got in return was bruises and lies. You told me yourself; you want me to hate you. You should have expected me to give up eventually"

"Grace, give up? I didn't think the term was even in her vocabulary" that sounds like a compliment.

The thought of him complimenting me makes me want to smile. But knowing Elijah, it probably wasn't meant to come out as a compliment. I shake the warm feeling off and think back to where the conversation was going.

"Turns out you're not just a bully, but also a stalker" I get back on track, steering the conversation back on the road.

"I am not a stalker" he challenges me.

"Oh really? So tell me, what were you doing in my room when Carter showed up?" I interrogate him.

"How do you—"

"That doesn't sound like an answer" I cut his question off as I turn my body around on the bed to face him.

Elijah debates something in his mind, contemplates the same thing in his eyes. I watch as they dance, twirling to the rhythm of his thoughts. He hesitates to answer the question like it was the biggest secret he has ever owned. There is a part of the question he really doesn't want to answer.

It only makes me want to know more.

"Fine… The truth" He clears his throat. "During the first couple weeks of being forced to sleep in a room with your boyfriend, I found myself driven crazy by his obnoxious snoring. He is the epitome of a loud sleeper. I needed to get out of the room until it calmed down… so one night I decided to try teleporting away from him…"

The long pause he creates sends my mind into overdrive with the possible ways this could go. Elijah has never been up to my room with me, how could he possibly know where to teleport himself to? "You don't know where my room is, how could you teleport there?" I try to get him to continue.

"Right…" he scratches the back of his neck. "I had gotten used to seeing you all the time, I think I missed the familiarity of

175

it. I ended up teleporting outside your balcony the first time I tried it. Turns out, my ability works with people as well as places I have seen. I think of the person I want to see, and before I know it, there they are" he smiles to himself. "I've gotten pretty good at it now"

"Elijah" I want him to stop going off topic.

"After the first night, I did it again. Not often. But it brings me comfort… seeing you" he confesses with his head lifting from his lap to look at me. When he sees the glimmer of hope in my eyes, his lips twitch.

"So, let me get this right… you have been showing up outside my balcony every couple of nights to… what? Watch me sleep?" I summarise.

"When you put it like that it sounds creepy" he cringes.

"What way do you want me to put it?" I ask. He doesn't respond to me. He has no response to give. "I can't believe I didn't know this—"

He straightens his back and runs a hand through his hair as he rushes to explain. "I haven't done it in a while. The night you and Carter were talking in your room was the first time I had done it since you arrived back" he defends himself. "I'm guessing Hunter was the one who told you—"

"West, actually" I correct him.

"Yeah, I was the one who told Hunter about you and Carter. I didn't expect him to hurt you. I wouldn't have said anything if I knew he was going to do that to you" Elijah explains himself.

He almost sounds like he cares about what had happened to me. "Careful… your starting to sound like you care" I warn him.

I wait for him to deny it.

I feel like I wait for an eternity for him to answer me with a snarky comment. He places his hands on his knees as his feet rest on the floor. Again, I wait for one of his rude remark like he would normally make. "No one is allowed to hurt you. Not while I am around" he claims.

"What?... only your allowed to hurt me?" I raise a brow.

"Yes" he nods.

The room falls silent. My brain is scrambling for some sort of explanation. I don't know what to say to that. Elijah is up and down like a rollercoaster. I can't tell whether he is being serious or if he is trying to mess with my head. "Do you want a thank you for that?" my eyebrows furrow.

"Far from it" he mumbles.

The way he is talking is making my brain feel like mashed potatoes. This isn't the Elijah I know. At least, it's not the same guy I've hated for the entirety of my teenage years. He is not being his usual cocky self. This isn't the guy who has tormented me and bullied me for the duration of my life on earth.

This is the guy I was friends with, before he met Nolan.

He is different. He is a mixture between harsh and soft, sweet but bitter, comfortable but nervous.

Like his old personality is trying to break out.

He is playing tricks on my mind.

From the way he is acting, he is switching, alternating in and out of the old him and a completely new version of him. I can't seem to predict which one I'm talking to. He has been acting weirdly lately. Whether that is because we have spent more time together recently, or he is hiding something.

But he is different.

As much as he tries, he isn't the same guy he was when we spent our days down here. He has become soft. The hard exterior he held up has dropped ever so slightly. I think he has shown that today. He lowered his mask and showed his true colours when he stopped Nolan.

"Thank you… for helping me today" I don't look at him, I feel obligated to look at the floor. "If you didn't stop Nolan, my wrist may have broken—"

"Don't do that" he shakes his head.

"Do what?" I'm confused.

"Thank me like it wasn't my fault" he says, ashamed. "It was my idea for the two of us to fight. Nolan thought he was helping me by hurting you— Don't thank me for that"

"But you stopped it—"

He interrupts me. "I stopped it because you had that look in your eyes" he snaps. "That same fucking look I used to look away from. I needed to look away to finish what I started. I got good at it, looking away. But I couldn't do that today" his tone lowers ever so slightly. "What the hell have you done to me? You've turned me into a—"

"Elijah—"

"Those eyes are burnt into my brain, reminding me every single waking day how badly I treat you. How much I have hurt you. And recently, I feel like all I see is you! Like a constant reminder that I'm an asshole to you" he rants.

"You're an asshole to everyone" I challenge him.

I hope my weak attempt to try and lighten the mood in the room works, but reading his face, I know it doesn't.

I swing my legs off the bed, my feet touching the cold concrete floor. He stands up from his spot on the bed. He moves around the room until he is turned around and facing me with anger bubbling up inside him. I can't tell whether he is anger at me or himself.

"I have no reason to be one towards you. Hunter is too proud of himself and gives little to no thought about anyone below him. Myles is too stupid for his own good. West… don't get me started on him" he explains his reasons for being an ass to everyone. "I think Lucas is the only good guy out of them all" his words become quiet.

I sit on the edge of the bed in silence, allowing Elijah to get everything off his chest. It seems like he has been holding all this in for a while. Maybe this will do him some good. By letting him get everything off his mind, spilling all his thoughts and feelings to me like I'm his personal diary, it may ease the anger he unleashes on everyone. I'll do anything to get him to calm down right now.

"But you… I don't have a reason" he continues.

"So why act the way you do?" I question him.

Again, he hesitates. "I don't know"

"You must know" I push.

Elijah rests his back against the wall as he allows his eyes to wander over to the window. Nobody has passed in a very long time. The soldiers must be with Hunter. I follow Elijah's eyes until I'm staring at the empty hallway. I don't like it when it's quiet like this.

The sound of Elijah breathing brings my eyes and attention away from the window. "I don't" he mumbles, hiding his true expression with a bored tone.

178

Today I have seen a completely new side to Elijah. A side I didn't know he had, something I never thought I'd see. He has shown me he is capable of caring about something other than himself and I know he can be a somewhat good guy if he tried hard enough.

Today has proven that.

But for some unknown reason, he continues to try and put up a wall between himself and the rest of the world. He has a wall of defence surrounding him, keeping him from ever getting hurt. Nobody can get close enough to care for him and he doesn't get close enough to feel anything. That can only lead to a sad and lonely life.

This is the first time I feel like I am seeing the real Elijah.

"I shouldn't have come—" he snaps out of his thoughts.

"What—"

I stand up from the bed.

"This was a mistake" he continues, ignoring me. "I will see you in the—"

"Your leaving?" my eyebrows raise higher than before.

He doesn't answer me. He pushes himself away from the wall and makes his way towards the door. Suddenly, I find myself reaching out, grabbing his arm in an attempt to stop him from opening the door.

"Elijah" I say his name out loud.

He stops moving, his head lowering for his eyes to look down at my hand gripping his arm.

"I still have questions—"

"Just let it go" he shakes me off.

I can't let it go. "You are acting strange. I cannot keep up with you. One minute you want to hurt me, the next you can't stand the thought of me having a bruise" I summarise. "You confuse me"

Elijah grabs onto my arm, spinning us around until I am standing in his previous spot, my back pressed up against the wall he leaned on. My eyes are glued to his as he stares down at me with something dark inside his eyes. His body is close to mine. Too close. Close enough for my skin to feel his breath.

My breath is caught.

My body is frozen.

179

I am trapped between Elijah and the wall.

He holds me in my place, one hand tightly gripping each of my arms. I force myself to blink. I breath him in. He smells like a field of fresh roses. The air between us is hot as his scent floats its way up into my nostrils.

His eyes are searching for something. He is looking at me, really looking at me. My lips, eyes, nose. He looks everywhere on my face before settling back on my eyes. His right hand leaves my arm. My head lowers, watching his movements. He runs his fingertips up the side of my arm, taking his time as he slides his fingers over my shoulder and collarbone.

He stops under my chin.

Gently, he tilts my head until my eyes are back on his.

I feel his body getting ever so closer against mine. The world around us fades away. It is only me and him. Nothing else matters in this moment. Elijah is my sole focus. He engulfs my thoughts and my feelings.

I want to know what he is doing. Why is he touching me like this? Elijah is close to me, being gentle with me, as if he thinks I am fragile. As if his touch could completely destroy me if he didn't hold back.

And in this moment, I would let him.

His fingers hook themselves behind my ear, closing the rest of the gap between our bodies.

My lips part as a gasp threatens to escape when Elijah presses his body against mine again. The silence grows heavier but the burning tension between the two of us grows quicker.

His breathing increases at the same pace as mine. I feel my heart beating out of my chest. His eyes alone are the reason I feel butterflies fluttering around my stomach. He shuts his eyes for a second too long, long enough for me to miss the blue. When his eyes open again, they return to staring into my soul.

"Please don't hate me for this" he breathes out.

And then he consumes me.

He's kissing me and kissing me and kissing me. He kisses me with everything inside him. Urgency runs through him as our lips merge together. They mould as if they were designed for one another. Fitted for perfection.

My hands find his chest as my eyes close. I lean further into the kiss, running one of my hands up his body until it stops on his shoulder. This only drives him to deepen the kiss.

All of a sudden, he's kissing me harder, deeper, and the urgency has turned to desperation. Without the ability to gasp at the change in pace, I grip onto his bicep while he devours my mouth like it was his dying wish. The same arm I am holding onto moves down, his hand pushing at my waist in an attempt to keep me against the wall.

The movement causes me to realise I was leaning into his body, wanting more and more of him.

We explore the taste of each other.

But as quickly as the kissing started, it stops.

Elijah pulls away from me, moving his entire body off of me and taking steps backwards. He creates a good enough distance to reveal how badly his body is shaking. His heavy breathing causes his chest to rise and fall at a rapid pace. Mine copies.

The room is anything but silent.

Instead, it is surrounded by the sound of heartbeats and panting. It feels like we were drowning in gasoline and have now lit the spark that has set us aflame.

Elijah just kissed me.

I lift my eyes from the floor as I watch him. He straightens his tank top before running a hand through his hair. Neither of us speak. We don't know what to say. He doesn't look at me. I wait for him to say or do something, but he can't even bring himself to glance at me.

As I part my lips to talk, Elijah opens the door. He keeps his eyes down as he makes his way out of the room and into the hallway. He makes sure the door is tightly closed before walking down the hallway. He leaves me standing alone in confusion.

CHAPTER THIRTY-THREE
GRACE

My body jolts up into a sitting position.

Tears stream down my cold cheeks as reality fades back into my eyes. The nightmares that haunted my sleepless nights for so long, have finally returned to me.

They have come back to taunt me.

A part of me can still feel the soft embrace of Sarah's gentle arms. Her delicate smile that felt like a warm blanket covering all the horrible things I experienced throughout the days. It was the worlds way of showing me, giving me hope, that there were nice people. A small handful of people. The amount of people you could count on one hand.

I shift on the bed, moving my body to sit along the edge of the mattress. My legs dangle, my feet pressing against the cold surface of the concrete floor. The blanket wraps around my small shoulders as it tries to keep away the cold air.

The stiff air is something I never missed.

My mind drifts in and out of the thought of Sarah. Even with the slightest image of her clouding my eyes, I feel the need to push the memory away.

I still remember her tucking me in at night – when I was a young girl. The way she checked up on me the one day I was sick. Sarah protected me against everything bad around here, and she made sure I was never alone as long as she lived.

A hundred candlelit memories flash before my eyes as the thought of Sarah grows stronger.

Careful breaths make me feel trapped. My lungs can be heard screaming from inside me, telling me to get real air. To get out of here. The air is crushing me, pushing on my chest as it pumps through the long hallway. I feel the room becoming smaller and smaller.

I'm going to suffocate.

Rushing to my feet, I throw myself towards the door. I wrap my hands around the door handle. I push and pull and kick and hit. Nothing works. The heavy door really doesn't want to open for me. Someone has locked the door from the outside, stopping me from getting out.

This is stupid.

My hands press against the door again. I keep pushing on the handle, hoping it opens. In my head, I believe the door is stuck. I refuse to believe it is locked. I will break the window if I have too. I need to get out of this room.

All of my rage and panic comes out in one big storm. A hurricane. A world wind of hysteria. I feel everything inside of me, flowing from my fingertips. The pain and the fear and all the madness in-between.

Get me out of this room.

Get me out of this room.

I keep repeating to myself, over and over again as the world around me becomes a blur.

And then the door opens.

The door bursts open, swinging inwards as my body slumps to the side.

Luckily, the hallway appears to be empty. Not that I am paying a lot of attention to it. My legs collapse on me, and I hit the floor, landing on my bruised knees. The gust of wind caused by the door hits my face, kicking my lungs into over-drive.

I find myself crawling through the door as my body feels like it can breathe again.

I crawl out from the door using the palm of my hands and around to the wall next to me. My back leans against the steel wall as I catch my breath. I hold my hand on my chest to slow my breathing, taking short breaths.

The walls felt like they were caving in on me. I couldn't do anything to stop them.

"Grace?" Hunter says my name.

My eyes shift from the floor.

Hunter and West are by my side in a heartbeat, checking if my pulse was steady. Hunter is crouching down in front of me while West kneels down on my left. Both of them look at me with concern. I look away from them, focusing my eyes on the floor in front of me.

"Grace, you shouldn't be out of your room, especially at this time" West reminds me.

I ignore him, trying to stop my body from shaking. I have never experienced anything like this before. My nightmares don't usually make me act like this. I have no explanation for my body to react in this manner.

"Hey… you're okay" Hunter comforts me.

A hand is placed on top of mine. I stare down at my hand as it lays on top of my thigh, covered by Hunter's large but gentle hand. My eyes follow his arm until they land on his ocean blue eyes. He tilts his head slightly.

His small gesture sends a wave of relief through my tired mind. As I look over towards West, I notice him and Hunter exchange a look. They both look as if they know something I don't. Both are communicating telepathically, hiding their true words from me.

Their eyes do all the talking.

"Tell us what happened" Hunter encourages me to talk to them.

I take a long breath before parting my lips to talk. "The room… it was getting smaller" I take small breaths as I talk. "I couldn't breathe in there"

"Are you claustrophobic?" West ask me a question with an unfamiliar word.

"What?" I ask, confused.

"Small spaces, love. He means, do you get scared of small spaces?" Hunter explains.

"No… I have lived in that room my entire life. That hasn't happened before" I answer West's previous question.

The hallway is empty for the first time. Abandoned by its men. Forgotten by its people. I can't remember the last time the hallway was silent. No soldiers, no doctors, no teenagers, and no scientists. As if everyone has hidden away, hibernating for the long night.

"You are lucky we found you out here before someone else did" West shakes his head.

"I'm fine" I sigh.

Suddenly, the thought of Sarah comes back to me. She is back in my brain. Her memory still haunts me. Her face stains my vision, consumes my thoughts. There is nothing else in my brain but her. She is stuck in my brain all over again, like an old record

184

player, damaged and broken. The gunshot, the blood, the scream. It replays like a jammed record, playing over the same malign memory.

Even when I close my eyes, the vision remains. It stains my eyes and ravages my thoughts. Daydreaming has never felt this wrong. This isn't me. I am not the one thinking of these memories. No matter what I do, the image of Sarah refuses to leave my mind.

"Someone is putting thoughts in my head" I blurt out.

"What?" Hunter becomes alert.

I don't know how to explain my statement without my words sounding crazy. "Sarah... I see Sarah" I confess. People would talk about seeing things during training, years ago, and they got ignored by everyone. After a couple of months, the soldiers found a girl who had the ability to manipulate others thoughts and control what they see.

The sound of West standing up from beside me fills my ears, taking a couple of steps to the left and then a couple to the right. I think he looks up and down the hallway, checking every crack in the wall. Counting the heartbeats in my head, it takes him fifty-three seconds to scan his eyes anywhere and everywhere. He makes sure not to leave a single spot of dust left unchecked.

"See anyone?" Hunter asks West.

"Nothing" West answers.

I wish I could see what was going on. My eyes are fighting to see the truth, to see what is happening in front of me. The world is nothing but a fantasy when vision is taken away. My senses become heightened as my eyes become dishonest to me.

They are lying to me.

"Let's move you out of the hallway" Hunter gestures towards the room I just crawled out from.

"I am telling you. It's not me. I'm not doing this. Someone is in my head" I struggle to get the right words to come out. "I can't explain it—"

"Stop right there!" I hear West demand but I can't see who he is talking too. I can't see anything, only the repeating memory of Sarah. "I said stop" he repeats.

A gunshot.

That is all it takes for the vision to disappear.

The image of Sarah vanishes from my eyes, replaced by nothing but a white wall ahead of me. For once, I am thankful Sarah fades into the back of my mind, bringing me back to reality. I have lived that moment for what feels like a lifetime.

I refuse to live in the past any longer.

As I get a sense of my surroundings, I see blood. A girl, blonde bobbed hair with icy blue eyes, lies in the centre of the hallway. Dead. A pool of blood surrounding her lifeless body. I see dark blue powder on her fingertips and a large electric collar around her thin neck.

"You killed her" I gasp, rushing to sit up. My head stays facing the body but as my eyes get a real grip of the world around me, I carefully allow them to make their way from the gun to the person's face. I quickly realise it wasn't West who shot the girl... it was Hunter. "Why did you kill her?" I say before using one of my hands to cover my mouth.

Hunter slowly lowers the gun. "Her eyes were glowing purple" he doesn't answer my question.

"She was inside your head" West continues Hunter's explanation. "Like you said. But damn, I can't remember the last person who could do that. Get into people's minds like that. It is some freaky shit" he says with shock. He probably has no idea what happened to the last girl who could do that.

The girl gradually lost her mind. She became absorbed by everyone else's thoughts and memories; she lost the ability to separate her own mind from the rest of ours. It was sad to sit around and watch. From the short time that I knew her as a young girl, she tried to hide herself from everyone, keeping out of the soldiers radar.

But even she couldn't escape her fate.

"Why was she trying to get inside my head?" I ask, confused, and dazed.

"That is something I am going to find out" Hunter assures me with confidence.

"Do you think—"

"Let's get you back to your room" Hunter repeats his suggestion from before, cutting West off before he can finish his question. I wonder what he was trying to ask. "It is safer if you

186

stay low. Until we know more about this girl, I want you to stay out of the way and keep to yourself"

I have always been good at that.

"Okay" I agree, trying to get to my feet.

I force myself to balance as I hold the wall. The girl really did a number on me. My mind feels all fuzzy. Everything is muddled. The last ten minutes is all a hazed blur to me. The girl must have had a reason to play mind games with me, but now I will never get to ask her why.

Hunter keeps the door open for me while I step back into the cold room. West stands guard encase there are any more surprises waiting for us around the hallway. He has his hand over the gun in his waistband for anything that jumps out at him, ready to attack and defend.

As I walk back into the room, I sit down on the bed I had previously slept on. "Get some rest" Hunter offers me a small smile, holding back all the other words he wants to say.

"Will you stay with me?... just until I fall asleep" I ask.

I don't want to be alone.

"I can't" he looks pained to answer. "I need to go back to the office to plan for the next couple of days"

Back in Soltrix, he stayed up with me while I cried about the war. He made sure I was better before heading back to his own room. Now, he is too busy to stay with me. Hunter has higher priorities. But I understand. I have too. He is running an entire city and trying to maintain this building on top of that. He has a lot to do for someone with only twenty-four hours in a day.

I just wish I had some time with him.

"Sorry for asking" I apologise.

"Don't apologise" he shakes his head. "I will see you in a couple of hours"

I don't know what he means by that, but I look forward to seeing him. I nod my head and smile faintly. He closes the door behind him as West begins to walk down the hallway.

I am left alone, in this room, with nothing but my foggy thoughts for company, all over again.

CHAPTER THIRTY-FOUR
GRACE

Sunlight can do a lot to a person.

It can bring joy, happiness, and excitement. The sun is a sign of brighter days and hope.

The sunlight represents life and clarity, and purity and positivity. Hope is the part of the sun that people cling too. I cling too. Nothing beats hope. I cling to the sun because it gives me hope of better times. Something to keep me going every day in this hell.

Down here, we are deprived of the sunlight.

Nothing but false light being spread across the hallway.

Breakfast this morning has made me miss the sunlight even more than normal. Two days down here has made me feel like the last year was nothing but a long dream. A false sense of hope. A dream I would revisit in a heartbeat if I had the chance.

My skin is growing paler by the minute.

Thankfully, with West roaming the hall, I am reminded that the year was real.

It truly happened.

And after this is done, I get to return to the world.

Unlike the poor people stuck here, who may never get the chance to see the true light of day. Some people are stuck to believe all the lies they are fed, doomed to an eternity of false beliefs.

Looking around the room, I feel sorry for everyone.

They have no idea what it is truly like to be outside of this hallway. They don't know the extent of the world. They may never get to live their lives to their full potential if they spend the rest of it locked down here, kept hidden.

They are spending their time, sitting around talking to one another about pointless things that mean nothing to no one. They rot away down here, patiently waiting for some big shift in the long pattern. A waste of life. A waste of time. A waste of perfectly good people.

Endless days and never-ending nights.

Nothing upon nothing.

I use my fork to stab the mash potato, not bothering to pick up any of the food on the plate. I'm not hungry. The food looks nothing more than a decoration on the table to me. The tasteless flavour of water is still fresh in my mouth, giving me enough hydration to reject the food in front of me.

Watching the different groups of teenagers is the only thing keeping me busy. I am seated alone at the end of a long dark grey table. The cold metal on my skin sends me a familiar feeling I hoped to forget. My white shorts don't cover my thighs, giving the metal a chance to keep my legs cold.

Not a single part of this place is heated.

Not that I am aware of.

The dinner hall is quieter than before.

A timer is clicking in my heart, curiosity getting the best of me. I want to know where everyone is disappearing to. This was never the normal around here, not on a scale this big. It makes my nerves crawl to think about all the kids that didn't make it to the end of the year.

The ones who have vanished.

I hope they are somewhere better than here.

Footsteps lead from one table to the next. Someone is walking over to the table, and it's not a soldier. My eyes look to my right, watching as Elijah approaches me. He is alone. I look around to find Nolan but I come up empty handed.

Elijah is alone.

All I can picture is his lips on mine when I look at him.

He stops walking in front of the table, looking down at me with his usual smug grin and his amused eyes. My eyes lead up his sharp jawline, relaxing onto his light blue orbs. His arms are crossed over each other, tensing his biceps. Elijah's dark hair has grown long enough to fall in front of his eyes, which it does. He doesn't bother to try and move it.

His arms drop, his hands leaning on the table.

I flinch, expecting a different action from him.

"You are pathetic, you know that?" Elijah speaks from beside me, towering over me. "You need to get some friends"

"I have friends" I challenge his statement.

"Friends that are alive" he argues.

189

"What is that supposed to mean" I narrow my eyes onto his smug face.

A soldier notices Elijah standing. They gesture with their head for Elijah to sit down. Elijah nods his head, sitting down in the seat opposite me with his elbows leaning on the table. He keeps his eyes on me, watching carefully.

"Sarah" he says her name out loud.

My features become flushed with shock.

"Don't—"

"I remember her. You never spoke after she was moved to another floor. I tried putting the pieces together but never did. Figured you missed her and it caused you to forget how to talk to people" he guesses. "Or maybe you lost faith. Which does explain why you kept to yourself a lot"

"You have no idea…" I trail off. He doesn't know what really happened to her. They covered up her murder with the only thing they are truly good at around here, lying. "She was killed… right in front of me… and it was my fault" I choke out.

He is silent for a moment.

Another moment.

He is silent until the world does a full turn.

"Shit—"

"I don't want to talk about her…" I look away from him.

Elijah places his hand on top of mine, sending a shock wave through my veins. My eyes shoot up from the table as they scan his features for an answer.

Relief washes over me as his hand rests on mine.

I am glancing from his eyes to his hand until I finally settle on his face. The small contact feels like the heat bouncing off RoseShire's sands.

He is being nice.

Why is he being nice?

"Is that why you stopped talking?" he asks me. I shake my head, causing him to search for a different question. "Then why…" he stops himself. "Why did you stop talking if it wasn't because of Sarah?" he asks another question.

His words bring my senses to their knees. His words bring all my logic crumbling to its demise. "I don't want to talk about it here" I shut the conversation down almost immediately.

Elijah is the last person I want to discuss this with.

"Okay" for once, he doesn't push.

This doesn't feel like the Elijah I know. He seems to have reconstructed himself overnight, taking away his usual self and replacing it with a more advanced model. Maybe he just hit his head, causing him to become confused and delusional. There is not a chance on planet earth that Elijah would be nice to me for even a split second without someone forcing him or having an altera motive.

I pull my hand away from his.

The warm feeling of his hand on mine slowly fades, replaced with the cold bitterness of the false air pushed around the room. He retracts his hand from the table, placing it on his lap. The fret in his eyes causes me concern for him.

Why is he looking at me like that?

The silence only makes the tension between us more apparent and awkward. "Are we going to talk about what happened?" I question his intentions as I keep my eyes away from his.

As he parts his lips to answer, something or someone catches his attention. I follow his eyes until I find my head turning in the direction of the main door of the dinner hall. The doors are held open by soldiers, waiting for someone to enter the room. We wait and wait, watching and anticipating the person who is about to walk through the doors.

West enters the room, followed by Hunter.

When eyes land upon Hunter, all havoc breaks loose. The room erupts into chaos as the sight of Hunter brings back the memory of us cramped into the large room where he stood tall on the balcony, overlooking everyone. The people down here probably remember that day as if it happened yesterday.

That was a big day for everyone.

It was the day that changed my life forever. I wouldn't be able to forget it. I wouldn't want to forget it. That memory will be stored in my brain for eternity, remembered as one of the best days of my life. Without that day, I would have never got the chance to experience the world the way I have.

Even with all the negative stuff, I managed to see more of the world than anyone else in this room.

The world isn't perfect, I know that, and with the weight of the world constantly on my shoulders— I still count my blessings for that day. I count my blessings for Hunter. I count my blessings for West. Sometimes… I even count my blessing for Myles and Lucas.

Because of them, I am alive today.

"Silence" West raises his voice. Hunter stands in front of the soldier's dinner table, his hands clasped together behind his back the same way he always stands. His back straight and head held high. West stands beside him with his body tense. The room is too chaotic to listen to West. "SILENCE" he shouts.

The room turns to silence, listening to West's loud order as everyone keeps their eyes on Hunter. "I am sure you all remember me" Hunter begins his speech. "Since my previous visit, things have changed. The world has changed. I need a handful of you… the best of the best… to help me in something that could be life changing"

Everyone is closely watching Hunter, giving him their full attention. My eyes wander over all the joyful eyes until I make the decision to keep my eyes trained on my plate in front of me, wanting to block out the half-truths he is about to say.

A girl, almost the same age as me, stands from her seat at the table. I don't know her. I don't recognise her. She has dark brown hair that matches the colour of her angry eyes. Her pale but yellow skin shines in the light. She holds her hand out in front of her as she points one of her fingers towards Hunter as anger takes over her.

"You liar!" she shouts.

All focus is on the girl. She is drawing attention to herself when she should stay quiet and pick her moment correctly. I pity what is about to happen to her. Death or isolation. There is no alternative option. But I think she already knows that. The girl already knows her fate.

"Sit down" a soldier demands.

"We have been trapped down here our entire lives, the world outside is supposed to be destroyed… but I think you're lying to us" she takes a stand. "I think you know the people in this room are too powerful for the real world, so you trap us down here and treat us like we are below you. But we all know you are just scared of us... we know we could kill you in a second if we really wanted to"

Hunter's interest spikes.

"What's your name?" he asks her.

His question throws her off. She cocks her eyebrow and tilts her head slightly. The girl was not expecting this to be his response. "Evie" she stands her ground, keeping her posture perfectly straight when answering Hunter's question.

Hunter nods his head. "I like your enthusiasm, Evie" he offers her a small smile.

In the blink of an eye, Hunter is holding a gun. He aims it towards Evie and pulls the trigger. Another blink of an eye, the girl is on the floor with blood surrounding her body. She is dead. Murdered in cold blood.

She should have expected this to be the result.

Everyone knows how this place works.

To expect something different is insanity.

Hunter puts his gun away and turns back to the rest of the people in the room. "In training, you will be put up against each other, using your abilities against one another" Hunter continues his speech. "Show us who has the real power. Those who are chosen, will leave first thing tomorrow morning"

And then, all at once, the whole room turns into uproar.

My eyes widen as I finally realise what is happening. The whole reason Elijah has been sent down here. Elijah is looking for the best people to take into the war. It makes sense. Elijah was always popular, he knows everyone, making him the best choice to find the people with the best abilities.

The thought brings a small smile to my lips. Before I left to explore, I tried telling Hunter and West to bring people like Lucas and Myles out from here and allow them to help us in the next attack. It was clear we will not win with only guns. If we wanted to win, we needed more of us.

We need to fight fire with fire.

I am happy to know Hunter is listening to the words I had spoken all those months ago. He listened to my idea and is using it. He knows I am right. If he continued to try and fight with nothing but guns and bombs, they would get nowhere. It is like taking a sword to a gun fight. It is never going to work out for the person with a sword.

"If you are not interested, let one of the soldiers know, and I will personally make sure to keep you locked in your rooms for the next week" Hunter doesn't give anyone much of a choice in accepting his offer. "Good luck" he finishes, taking a final breath before gliding back through the room towards the open doors.

West glances over to me and Elijah before following Hunter out of the room. The two soldiers holding the doors open slowly close the doors behind West, leaving everyone to ponder on the thought of getting a second chance.

The room breaks into a loud chatter again.

Everyone has become hyper and joyful, ignoring the dead girl who is now being cleared up by a handful of soldiers and scientists. Evie was fighting for what she believed. She was attempting to do the same thing I had thought about for so many years, but the difference between me and her.

I knew the risks and did nothing.

She knew the risks and still tried.

"I remember feeling like that" Elijah brings me out of my thoughts. He gestures to the excited teenagers around. "They have no idea" he shakes his head.

"It's cruel" I sigh.

The excitement in the room reminds me of Myles. He was bouncing to get out of here, he didn't consider any of the problems with what was going on and it landed him in a world of delusion and denial. He knew nothing of the truth and he continued to believe everything was perfect... until it was too late for him. Until he was standing in the middle of someone else's war and had to fight regardless of what he wanted.

"If I had the chance" he stops himself, looking around to make sure no one is listening to him. "I would shoot Hunter in the back of the head, and I would do it with a smile"

I can only stare.

No matter what he wants to think, this whole building was the Supremes' idea, not Hunter's. The Supreme is the man to blame for all of this. "Hunter isn't the problem here" I state.

"He isn't the solution, either" Elijah challenges.

I agree, for once.

Hunter isn't the solution; he will not be the one to throw the final punch. Hunter can't do the things we can. But he is in charge of Soltrix, and he holds all of the power when it comes to the people. This whole situation is personal for him, it was his father that betrayed him, and it is his father that holds all of the knowledge we need in order to finally take down the man to blame for the war.

Todo Poderoso.

No matter when or where, no matter why or how, we need to bring him down to his knees. This war is no longer just Soltrix's war. It is everyone's war, because if the Supreme and Todo Poderoso go down, then maybe there is a chance for us all to live in a world where we don't have to hide anymore.

There is a chance for us to escape forever.

CHAPTER THIRTY-FIVE
GRACE

Soldiers hold strength.

They are the reason things get moved around here. It could be a person, an object, a wall. Whatever is in the way, it will be moved if needed. The soldiers hold no weakness. They need to stay strong if they value their job. A weak soldier is not a soldier worth keeping around.

As I watch the soldiers move around the room, I make sure to stay out of the way. They move around the different equipment as the space in the centre of the room is cleared for the specific training session we are about to endure.

The atmosphere is hot and sweaty and humid because of all the body heat in such a small area. I could smell the body odours as soon as I entered the training room. There is a mix between body odours and cleaning supplies.

I don't know how, but the area still manages to hold a small hint of a cleanliness smell as I walk around, maybe it is due to the cleaning supplies they make us use after every training session. We are required to wash down all the equipment at the end of each session and if we don't comply, the soldiers ensure we go through some sort of punishment.

Each piece of machinery and equipment is modern and looks brand new, you wouldn't think this stuff has been down here for eighteen years.

All the equipment has been pushed to the walls, making room for the two people in the centre to use their abilities to their full potential.

Nolan stands on the other side of the room, watching and waiting for something to happen. Ben and Kane stand to my left, keeping their backs close to the wall. Neither of them are talking, instead, they are looking towards the soldiers. The girl who is normally with Ben and Kane is nowhere to be seen in the room.

I assume she is with other friends.

My arms wrap around my stomach as the soldiers slowly complete their task of moving the equipment. I am surprised they

196

didn't force us to move everything, that is something they would normally do. Maybe it has something to do with Hunter being here. The soldiers probably don't want to risk getting on the wrong side of him.

Kane and Ben move closer to me as the soldiers finish moving the last of the machines. Teenagers have gathered in a circle, leaving space in the centre of the room for the people who are about to go up against each other. The soldiers have somehow managed to cramp all of the teenagers from the dinner hall into this one tiny training room.

Keeping everyone in this one training room a year ago would be impossible, but with the numbers decreasing, this is now possible.

Two girls step into the middle of the room.

The first girl, she goes by the name, Jules. I remember her from a couple years back. She had long silver hair when I knew her. She has cut it off since then. Now she has a skin fade with a platinum blonde colour. She has the ability to change the wind and create storms.

She manipulates the air.

I don't know the other girl. She doesn't look familiar to me in the slightest. Her jet-black hair runs past her thighs, bringing out the light blue in her eyes. She is a lot taller than Jules. The girl has to be at least five foot eight.

Both girls look smug and confident.

I wish both of them the best of luck.

We all watch in anticipation. "Who will win?" Ben asks the question on everyone's mind. We are all standing around, trying to guess in our heads who will walk away from the fight unharmed.

A guy overhears the boys talking, stepping closer to them as he joins their conversation. "My bets on Jules" the guy, who now stands beside Ben, answers before Kane can get his words out from his mouth.

"Nah, we all know Beth can take her down" Kane stands up for the other girl.

"You clearly haven't seen what Jules can do lately" one of the girls around them perks up.

The guy only shakes his head.

197

"Care to put money where your mouth is" Ben grins like a Cheshire cat.

Kane clears his throat. "Alright, Jay, what do we get if you are wrong?" he speaks as he crosses his arms, his left eyebrow cocking slightly.

Jay ponders on the question for a moment. "You have to sneak me onto the top floor" he smirks.

"Nice try" Ben laughs.

"We can't do that" Kane denies his request.

"No, you can't. But I know she can" the guy, Jay, gestures towards me with his thumb.

My eyes widen slightly as I realise the guys are all turning to look my way. "Keep me out of whatever games you guys are playing" I insist, wanting no part in whatever they are doing. I don't want to get caught up in their foolish betting.

Jay frowns and turns his back to the boys.

Kane and Ben take their eyes off me, looking back at the two girls as they begin to fight.

I can feel someone's breath fanning the side of my neck, heating up my face. "They are children" Elijah startles me as he whispers into my ear, standing behind me.

I keep my head facing forward, watching the girls in the centre of the room. "Coming from you" I challenge him.

"Ouch" he pretends to be offended.

The feeling of his body behind mine is enough to put me on edge. Elijah is unpredictable. He could do anything behind me, and he knows he would get away with it down here. That information alone is enough to alert all my senses.

His breath on my shoulder and neck drives me crazy. I can feel him leaning over my right shoulder, watching the girls from over my head. He knows how much power he has over me and he uses it to his advantage.

"What do you want?" I ask him.

He takes a long, drawn-out breath. "I came over here to comment on your inability to fight someone without losing control, but luckily for you, I don't have the energy" I can hear his smirk through his words.

I don't want to be around him. "Nolan looks lost without you" I gesture over to Nolan as he stands alone, hoping Elijah will get the hint to walk away.

He doesn't get the hint.

"He'll survive" Elijah shrugs my statement off. "What will you do if they ask you to go up against someone?" he brings up a good question. I didn't think that far ahead. Surely, they won't ask me to fight. They would be stupid to think I would.

"I want to talk to Hunter" I admit. "I should be able to sneak out before they get the chance to ask me"

"You won't get very far" he argues.

I try to turn my body around to face Elijah, but he quickly stops me. I feel his hands grip my waist, forcing me to face the girls as they finish the fight. He holds me in place, pressing my back against his hard chest. My hands subtly grab onto his but my efforts are wasted. He doesn't remove his hands. He has a better grip on me than I do on him.

Elijah has the advantage.

Giving up, I watch the girls intensely. They are both on their last couple of minutes. Jules is brewing up a storm, ready to finish the fight and become the first champion. The other girl looks terrified. She is trying to mask her fear, covering the scared emotion with a confident façade.

I have faith that Jules will take the girl down.

The smirk on her face tells me all I need to know.

"You won't make it down the hallway, yet alone up to the top floor" Elijah continues.

"What do you mean?" I ask, looking into the top corner of my eyes to try and get a glimpse of Elijah.

"Come on, Grace, we haven't been gone that long. You should know there are soldiers everywhere. We are supposed to be staying under the radar. You can't be seen wandering the hall alone, especially to go somewhere you shouldn't be" he makes a good point.

I wish he was right.

My hands try to push at his again, hoping to get his hands off my waist. It doesn't get me anywhere. He tightens his grip on my body and presses my back harder into his chest. The closeness takes me back to last night. To the kiss. To his hands all over me and his breath fanning my face.

He was so close to me.

And neither one of us protested it.

'Please don't hate me for this'

His words make me doubt everything I have believed for all these years.

What happened last night, was something I had never in my life imagined happening. Elijah kissed me. He kissed me and I kissed back. No matter how much I think about it, it continues to confuse and twist my mind.

It will only worsen if I don't speak about it.

But there is never a good time.

"Grace—"

"Hunter wouldn't let them do anything to me" I say with fake confidence, getting back to the conversation. I thought saying it out-loud would reassure me, but even that didn't work. "I can just sneak past the soldiers and find the end of the hallway—"

"Sure, give that a try" his tongue is lacing with sarcasm.

He really knows how to push my buttons. "I don't hear you coming up with any brilliant ideas" I roll my eyes.

My words don't faze him. "Just stay behind me" Elijah spins me around to face him. I lift my head, looking up into his light blue orbs as they gaze down into mine. "They won't get the chance to ask you if you are with me"

I believe him.

I believe every word he tells me. How he can stop any of the soldiers who dare to make me compete against someone, how he could shield me from revealing myself to all the people in the room. My heart skips a beat at the thought of hiding from the world behind him.

The feeling makes me want to rip my heart out from my chest and throw it against the closest concrete wall.

My body is rejecting my thoughts. It's Elijah. I shouldn't feel protected and safe around him. I shouldn't trust him. He is the same guy who bullied me for all those years after everything that had happened. He hasn't changed. Nothing has changed. I refuse to let myself fall into his trap.

His hands remain on my waist. "Careful... you sound like your trying to help me" I joke, trying to laugh my way out of his stare. The world around us fades, and I am left watching his lips move without letting out a single word. He speaks under his breath. I wish I heard him, but the words are so quiet, I miss them completely. "If you cause a distraction, I can sneak out through the door—"

"Why would I do that?" he cocks an eyebrow.

"Well... someone has to distract the soldiers" I lower my voice to prevent the soldiers from hearing.

"I'm not helping you get out of here. It is asking for trouble, and you could get hurt" he refuses. "Stay here"

Hunter is in the building. He might have gained some new information over the last two days. There may be news about the Supreme. I feel like I have missed too much spending my time down here. My instincts are telling me to find Hunter.

I want to find Hunter.

I try to push Elijah's hands off me again. "Fine, I don't need your help" I look away from him. I have never needed his help and I never will. "I'll manage on my own"

I don't know why I bothered asking.

"Grace—"

"Elijah, let go" I demand, cutting off his words.

The strong grip on my body vanishes. Elijah frowns as he drops his hands from my waist. He doesn't look amused. The emotion in his eyes is unreadable, but I don't stare at him long enough to try and understand. "Don't come crying to me when your crappy plan fails" he warns me.

His words don't affect me.

Not once have I run crying into Elijah's arms. I have never cried to him about anything. He used to be the reason for my tears. Day after day, week after week, he was the cause of my bruises and pain. I will never run to him when I need a shoulder to cry on.

Never.

I don't bother responding to his remark. My body turns to face the doors, watching and waiting for the soldiers to make a move for the girls. Two, three, four soldiers I count standing around the training room doors.

A gust of wind pushes my hair behind my shoulders. My eyes look over my shoulder, watching as the girls finally bring the fight to an end. Jules is trying her best to win. She wants to come out on top, set the bar high for the rest of us. Jules is doing anything and everything to stay on her feet. She refuses to give up the fight.

But the other girl is winning. She is stronger and faster and better. She raises her hands as she shields her face from the harsh wind. Bubbles surround Jules ankles, pulling her feet from under her. Jules falls to the ground, causing the wind to disappear as she loses focus of her ability.

Jules slams her fist on the ground as she admits defeat.

Everyone in the room claps their hands, all except the soldiers. I glance from soldier to soldier. One by one, they walk from the doors over to the girls. Two soldiers grab Jules, two soldiers grab the winning girl. The winner is escorted over to the back of the room while Jules is taken off to the side.

As the soldiers move the girls around the room, I take the opportunity to slip through the doors.

The doors silently close behind me, allowing me a chance to walk down the hallway without them suspecting anyone has left the room. I duck my head down to pass the training room windows, keeping low to stay out of sight. Luckily for me, the hallway is completely empty.

Now, I just need to make it down the hallway.

I need to do the one thing I had always wanted to do as a child. The one thing I had longed to achieve. The same thing that kept me up scheming till early hours of the morning.

I need to make it to the end of the never-ending hallway without being caught.

CHAPTER THIRTY-SIX
GRACE

Each step brings me closer to the end.

Each step brings me closer to the impossible.

The soldiers are scattered across the building. They are too busy on higher priorities to notice my absence. To notice me walking around freely. Hunter's unexpected arrival has caused the adults to scatter with fear. Everyone is making sure everything is perfect for him. Running errands for him like he is the king and they are his loyal slaves.

Pitter. Patter. Pitter. Patter.

The sound of my feet hitting the floor gets louder as it echo's from wall to wall. My pace becomes quicker with each heartbeat that I skip. Thud. Thud. I want to get out of sight as soon as possible. The longer I spend walking past the windows, the less chance I have of reaching the end.

Reaching the near end of the hallway, my hand stretches out to grab the door handle.

I make it.

I make it to the end.

The stairwell is exactly how I remember it, apart from the extra set of stairs spiralling downwards. Maybe it was too dark for me to notice. Everything was happening too fast; I probably didn't bother to look that way. I was too busy looking up. It was a lot to take in at the time. My small brain couldn't comprehend all that was going on around me.

One step. Two steps. Three steps. Four steps. Five steps and then I lose count. I don't waste any time. My left hand grips the railing, helping me rush up the stairs. It takes all fibres of my being to keep myself going. I can't stop to look around, I can't hesitate for a second to catch a glimpse of the new and unfamiliar surrounding I have put myself in the centre of.

Keep going.

Just a little further.

One level. Two levels. Three levels. The third floor is where I stop. It is the last floor before I reach the sand. Before I reach

203

freedom. My hand stretches out from the railing, gently wrapping around the cold handle of the door that connects the stairwell to a brand-new hallway.

My emotions cloud my judgment. They prevent me from doing what needs to be done. Just open the door and venture down the hallway, that is all I need to do. My body hesitates to move as the last set of stairs stand in the corner of my eye.

Stop hesitating.

I talk to myself as time passes quicker than normal. I can feel the minutes slipping past me.

My old self would run as fast as I could to get to the top and escape. She would do anything and everything to open the door and breathe the fresh air. She would not be standing here debating her options. A part of me will always be her, wanting the life I always dreamed of. But the world isn't the way I expected it. I have seen the reality of it all.

If I don't help Hunter and stop Todo Poderoso, there won't be a world to explore.

The thought of running away from everything, getting out while I still can. It is holding me back. I force my eyes shut, diverting them away from the last set of stairs. I push the door open, waiting for soldiers to be on the other side.

I wait for the worst.

But the worst never comes.

The hallway is no longer one long hallway. The soldiers are not where they are supposed to be. The entirety of the third floor is one single hallway on the side and a large open area with a ceiling held up with tall quartz pillars. The open area has seats and doors with separate rooms – I'm guessing offices or rooms for the soldiers to sleep.

A step forward, and I realise how empty the third floor really is. There is not a single person in sight. A part of me is starting to worry. Where is everyone? I was able to come up here way too easily. This all feels too easy.

With a loud bang, the door shuts behind me. I jump, my head spinning to face the door. A quiet squeak threatens to escape my lips. I am one of the first teenagers to have made it to this floor alive. This whole situation feels wrong. In the back of my head,

I know this isn't right. There is something very wrong around here, and I want to know what.

But I need to stay focused on finding Hunter right now, I can't get side-tracked.

It was always rumoured that the Supreme was on the top floor of the building, so I am guessing the same logic would apply for Hunter. But it is only a guess. I could be very wrong – too wrong.

This could be a big mistake.

My eyes scan over the room. I look for any sign of life or movement. The place looks abandoned. Walking over to the centre of the open area, I look over all the scattered papers. It appears that whoever was up here left in a hurry, or they were forced out of here.

I pick up one of the pieces of paper that has been left on the floor. The paper is brown and looks fairly old. My fingertip traces over the writing on the top of the paper. They look like coordinates. A map lays in the middle of the paper. It is a map to somewhere I have never seen.

An adept artist has designed this map.

Running my fingers over the detailed map, my hand slowly turns the paper to glimpse at the back. Words, forming a sentence, have been written in a rush.

Three planes, six groups, on way to

And then the sentence stops. They must have run out of time before they could finish writing. This information was clearly important enough for someone to feel the need to write it down in a state of urgency.

My attention to the writing is forced away when I hear a door opening from the small hallway. I lower my hands, the paper along with them, as my head spikes up. I am no longer alone in here. There is someone else on this floor. The soldiers must have left someone behind. Someone to ensure nobody disturbs all the secrets hidden within the walls.

Panic washes through me. I find myself throwing myself behind one of the eight pillars holding up the ceiling, gripping the paper to my chest.

I fear the worst.

Talking to a soldier cost me two weeks of my life. I have no idea how much time I would lose, how much suffering they would put me through, for coming up here. Maybe Hunter would stop them from putting me in isolation, or maybe he might just let them get away with it.

"Whoever you are, hiding behind that pillar. I can see you. Come out with your hands above your head" Hunter's voice echoes through the hallway. Air gets trapped in my lungs as my throat closes up.

It's Hunter.

Slowly, very carefully, I step out from behind the pillar. I hold back a breath as his eyes lock onto mine. "Grace" he breathes out my name.

"Hunter—" I cut myself off, trying to gather an idea of what to say to him. "I can explain—"

He doesn't let me explain anything. "You should not be up here. Grace! The soldiers will come back at any moment and catch you" he frantically shifts his head from left to right as he takes quick steps towards me.

"What's going on?" I ask him as he drags me away from the open area.

The grip around my wrist tightens as my body is dragged towards a tall brown door. "Most of the soldiers are having a meeting with West, talking strategy. I was supposed to be continuing with the plans for tomorrow" he explains.

Hunter throws me into his office. I try to grab my balance as I stumble. I catch myself on the desk, my hands gripping onto the edges. The door closes as Hunter turns to face me. I can see the rage in his eyes. He isn't happy to see me. My lips part as I am about to ask another question, but he beats me to it. "Did you not hear the part where West told you to stay off the radar?"

"I did" I answer his rhetorical question.

He holds back all the words he wants to say to me. "Why come up here?" he asks me. "Why risk yourself being caught and held in isolation"

"I needed to… I wanted to see you" I admit.

My answer was not good enough for him. "That is not an excuse" he shakes his head, walking around the room until he reaches the chair behind the desk. He pulls the chair out from under the desk but doesn't sit down. "You of all people should know better"

I look anywhere other than his face. I look at the books neatly stacked on the bookcase. I look at the grey radiator on the left side of the wall, heating up the cold space. I look over to the random chair placed in the corner of the room. Even the small piles of dust collecting between each bottom corner of the desk catches my attention before Hunter does.

This room is an office.

Hunter's office.

The room seems to lock from the inside, preventing any and all from entering when Hunter is working. As I take a closer look around the desk, I see a name. The Supreme. The name is written on a small display stand. This was the Supremes' office before he left.

I slowly sit down in the chair opposite Hunter, shifting uncomfortably as my confusion becomes more recognisable while the time ticks on. My eyes scan the rest of the desk. "This was my father's office" Hunter confirms my thoughts.

I look up to meet Hunter's eyes. "How are you feeling since your dad left? I haven't had a chance to ask—"

"Life goes on" he interrupts my question. "He betrayed us all, that man is nothing but a waste to me" I can see the hurt behind Hunter's eyes he is trying so hard to disguise.

"He is still your dad—"

"He is not my father anymore" he snaps, slamming his hand on the surface of the desk.

His eyes snatch away from mine. His reaction delays, the realisation of what he said writing itself onto his face. His hand wraps around the white mug which is placed in front of him on the desk. A single sip, short and quick, and he places the mug back in its original place.

When Hunter doesn't say anything else, I find the cogs in my head turning over themselves to try and change the topic of conversation. "When are we leaving? Tomorrow? Next week? I can't stick it here anymore" I question him, ignoring his previous statement.

"In the morning" he answers as he sits down.

207

There is not enough space for everyone here to move to Soltrix. Hunter is going to need a bigger building if he plans to take everyone with him. "Where are you thinking to put everyone?" I push another question.

"Not everyone will be coming" he confesses.

"What?" my eyes widen.

Hunter takes a deep breath before shifting his eyes to the door behind me. "Only the people with abilities worth keeping are coming with us" he explains. "The rest... they will stay here until we find a use for them" Hunter continues.

"No" I frown. "No. It's not right" I refuse to leave anybody else behind. It's not fair. If they don't have a use now, they will never be of use to Hunter. "You cannot leave them down here to rot away like walking corpse"

"Life isn't fair sometimes" he says bluntly.

Not only is he blunt, but he shows no remorse for leaving the rest of the people down here to slowly die. Hunter doesn't care about the teenagers; his only concern is what they are capable of doing. As long as it benefits Soltrix. All he seems to care about these days is the city.

Nothing more and nothing less.

"How many?" I ask.

His eyes look up from the desk. "Twenty-five, if we are lucky" he answers, but he knows before the words leave his tongue, I am not happy with it.

"That's it?" I gasp.

"That is all we can handle" he claims. My frown has completely overtaken my lips. There is no hope for a smile. He notices me shift in my spot, watching my features as he parts his lips to talk again. "I am sorry you have been down here longer than you may have liked. I tried to make this quick for you" he apologises.

"This was to 'Keep me safe' if I remember correctly. I am no use to you being here apart from keeping out of your way while you deal with a spy" I gesture quotation marks when I talk, reminding Hunter of the true purpose he brought me back to my hell. "Did you find the spy?"

Hunter nods his head but doesn't reveal any information to me. "Myles and Lucas are on their way as we speak. They will help keep everyone in line while we begin transport" he changes the topic, again.

A part of me is shocked Myles is coming. I never thought Myles would willingly come back. I expected he would have tried to protest with everything in him to keep away from this place. After I left this place, I never wanted to return. I guess I assumed Myles felt the same.

But I came back, I didn't put up a big fight or a dramatic scene. He most-likely reacted the same.

"Are they okay?" I ask.

Before he can get his words out, there is a knock on the office door. A loud knock, letting anyone and everyone in the room know someone is waiting outside. "They're fine" Hunter sighs, rushing to answer my question before the person enters the room. He gracefully stands from his chair as his focus shifts from me to the door. "Come in" he demands to the person on the other side of the door.

Three soldiers walk into the room.

"Sir" the soldiers say in unison.

"What is it soldiers?" Hunter turns to a cold machine.

One of the soldiers acknowledges my presence with an astonished look in his wide eyes. "How did she get up here? There should have been a soldier on patrol" the soldier makes his shock known to the room.

Hunter's hands grip the top of his chair. His jaw tenses and his nostrils flare. I knew he would be uptight about the soldiers finding me up here. "No point dwelling on the matter now. Take her back to the training room" He waves me off.

Two of the three soldiers take steps towards me, each grabbing one of my arms. I don't protest. I don't make a fuss like I usually would. I don't make an effort to struggle out from their grip. For once, I have no reason to struggle against the soldiers. I have what I came for.

But I do wish I could have had more time with Hunter. I feel as though I never spend time with him anymore, not like we used to before I left.

But I now know we are leaving this hell tomorrow.

I am removed from the seat, tenderly dragged towards the office door. They are only being gentle because Hunter is standing in front of them. If Hunter wasn't in the room, I would be treated differently. I am thankful he is here, but I know as soon as we leave the room, they will treat me a lot rougher.

"Don't lose her" Hunter warns them. "If I find one strand of hair missing from her head, I will personally make sure the next thing you see is a gun between your eyes"

His threat is far from empty.

Suddenly, the atmosphere turns cold. A shiver threatens to run down my spine. Hunter's hard stare adds to the sour taste on everyone's tongues. Nobody makes a move to leave, nor do they make a move to talk. The room falls to complete silence while someone finds the courage to speak.

Finally, someone takes a breath. "Yes Sir" the soldiers nod with understanding.

"Leave" Hunter orders.

They blink, quick enough to almost miss it, and then they escort me out of the office.

CHAPTER THIRTY-SEVEN
GRACE

I am escorted back through the large area that was once empty, but now filled with soldiers. Everyone stops what they are doing to look my way. They don't hide their surprise. Eyes settle on me. Confused expressions stain the faces of those watching.

Nobody had anticipated my presence waiting for them as they returned from the meeting. The shock on their faces is most likely from my ability to reach the end of the hallway without getting caught. I am the first person to do it and be alive to tell the story.

I will probably be the last.

I consider myself lucky.

The grip on my arms tighten the further we walk from Hunter. Each breath, each step, each glance towards the door, I find myself preparing for yelling. Even with Hunter's direct orders, the soldiers may still yell at me. When Hunter is not around, they can say and do whatever they wish, as long as they don't get caught.

We leave the large area. The soldiers escort me down the stairwell. Step after step. I am forced to walk at the same slow pace as the soldiers. They are taking their time, wanting to treat this walk as a leisurely stroll.

The sound of the door from the third floor finally closing causes both soldiers to share a glance over at one another. It is clear they both have been keeping their words until they knew they were alone. The soldier on my left takes a long and deep breath as his strong grip becomes even tighter around my sore arm. "Matthew was supposed to be on patrol" the soldier on my left breaks the silence first.

"I haven't heard from him" the soldier on my right responds with a shrug.

Their conversation isn't worth listening to. My ears tune out, waiting for their pace to quicken. We gradually pass the second floor, eventually reaching the first floor. I wait and wait and wait for one of the soldiers to open the door that leads into the never-ending hallway.

But they don't.

We continue walking.

Now, I have no idea where we are going. The new set of stairs stands before me, giving me access to a floor I have never known about. The soldiers are taking me down into unfamiliar territory. Within a matter of seconds, my curiosity gains the best of me, and I find myself speaking. "Where are we going?" I ask them, almost immediately regretting my decision to ask a question.

"Don't speak" the soldier to my right grips me tighter.

I do as I am told. Knowing from experience, I won't win the argument. The last thing I want to do is to cause any more problems for Hunter. He has a lot to do before tomorrow, I am the last thing he should be concerned with. All I need to do is stay under the radar until tomorrow morning.

We walk down the final set of stairs, reaching the bottom floor of the PPW. No more stairs. This is it. We have reached the lowest point of the PPW. All that is down here is a steel door opposite the last step. The door has no window, letting nothing past. The only way through the door, is by knocking a total of five times.

One.

Two.

Three.

Four.

Five.

Not even a blink later, and the door is opened by a woman in a long white doctors coat. The woman has sun kissed skin that brings out her caramel brown eyes. Long dark brown hair that runs down her back and stops just above her waist. She has made the decision to tie her hair back into a high ponytail, keeping it out of her way.

A metal clipboard is held against her chest. Diagrams and small notes are scattered across the sheet of paper attached to the clipboard, allowing the woman to write things down if needed. I catch a glimpse of the name 'Dr Lopez' written on a small pin clinging to the right of her long white coat.

My eyes glance from the soldiers and then settle on the woman. She offers me a small smile as her eyes examine every little feature of my face. She tries to read me like a book, her eyes flicking the pages of my mind. Thankfully, she doesn't try for long. The woman slowly turns her head to begin walking, leading us through the large room.

I am forced forward.

The soldiers stay one step behind me in an attempt to keep me from running away. Their hands leave my arms, allowing me a little freedom to roam. In the corner of my eye, I can still see their hands ready to grab me again. I take the small opportunity to scan over the room, looking in every nook and cranny.

Nothing about this place feels good, but I can't find it in me to look away. This is all new to me. Even after eighteen years of living down here, this floor was never available for me to explore. No one has any idea the extent of this place. They hide this part of the building from us for some reason, a very big reason. I intend to find out that exact reason.

Exploring this floor may give me something productive to do until we leave tomorrow.

But the soldiers brought me down here without Hunter knowing, which doesn't look like a good sign. This is something the soldiers are doing without orders. They don't want Hunter to know for a reason.

I have a terrible feeling about this.

The soldier's refuse to stay too far away from me in fear that I will escape. They remain a single step behind me. The small gesture comforts them. The soldiers believe they can keep me inline by staying close to me.

"Put her over there" the woman points to a chair placed in the centre of the room.

The soldiers do as they are told. Their hands find my arms again, gripping onto me as hard as they can. The harsh grip on my skin is going to leave a nasty mark. Nobody is taking any risks with me. For some reason, they are treating me as if I am ready to run at any given moment.

"What's going on?" I question them both. My eyes look up at one soldier and then the next. Neither of them want to look at me. "You are supposed to take me back to training" I remind them, wanting to get away from the possibility of these people trying anything they shouldn't.

The soldiers walk me over to the chair, stopping directly in front of the metal contraption. Again, I look from the soldier on my left to the soldier on my right. They are waiting for me to sit in the chair.

They wait for what feels like hours.

I carefully contemplate my very little options in my head, eventually coming to the conclusion to willingly sit in the metal chair. I won't win against their strong hands, not unless I use my ability.

I would only win if I used my ability, and I refuse to do that down here.

"Sit still and be quiet" one of the soldier's responds, but I don't catch which one.

"The girl can talk" the woman challenges the soldier. "I want to know all about her" the woman places the clipboard down on one of the many desks around us. "Grace Silver, isn't it?" she asks, but it is obvious she already knows the answer.

"Yes" I reply with eyes of steel.

A cold, sharp metal straps over both my wrists. It clicks into place, holding me down onto the chair. The soldiers make sure everything is tight enough to hold me in place. They don't want to take any chances with me. They take a couple steps away from the chair and stand off to the side, allowing the rest of the people around them to do their jobs.

"My name is Dr Lopez" she offers me her name, although I already know it. She is trying to be nice, trying to show me she isn't the bad guy here.

I don't say anything.

I don't know where to start.

She looks at me. Waits for me. She expects me to force a conversation between us, push questions and give over any and all information about myself.

"You know my name. Why do you know my name?" I ask her, glancing around the large room.

This place reminds me of a science lab. The test tubes, the multiple computers scattered around on desks. Everyone wearing the same lab coats, protecting themselves from the chemicals they work with.

I find the sharp tools laid out across the closest desk. The hair on my arm spikes as I feel my skin begin to crawl. I feel like a frog in a test tube. As if they are about to dissect me like a science class project. They would cut me up and pull out my organs like a fish.

Slowly, the woman turns to the soldiers. "Hunter doesn't know she is down here?" Dr Lopez says the statement as if it was a question.

The two soldier take another two steps away from me.

"No. He has no idea" one of the soldiers answers.

"Good. Let's keep it that way" she subtly warns them. Dr Lopez then turns to face me again. Her caramel eyes are filled with excitement. She tries her best to contain her elation, trying to maintain professional. "Tell me, what does Hunter see in you? There must be something"

My mind becomes blank. "I don't understand—"

"Alik Hunter. He seems fond of you, and I want to know why" she narrows her eyes onto me. "I want to know what is special about you"

Alik Hunter.

That is the only piece of information I pick out from her statement. Alik Hunter is his full name. I am shocked. Hunter was never his first name. This entire time, I assumed it was his name. I never once questioned it.

I wonder why he never mentioned his real name.

"I don't know" I answer honestly.

"Think harder. There must be something about you, a reason for his interest" she pushes me to think about him.

We are friends. Good friends. He is the reason I am still alive today. Without Hunter, I would have been killed. I owe Hunter a lot. I would never tell him that, but I am very grateful for him in my life. He is someone I have grown to like; someone I wouldn't want to live without.

But there is no good answer to her question.

"I read your file" the woman innocently smiles. "I know what you are capable of… to some extent"

I have a feeling this has something to do with the spy.

215

West told me a spy was looking for my file. They were searching the building for it. The spy put their life in danger for a small brown file with nonsense information held inside. If Dr Lopez has read my file, I have a gut feeling she either knows about the spy or is the reason for the spy being in Soltrix.

"What is this?" I ask, looking down at the metal on my wrists and then up into the corner of my eyes to try and get a glimpse of the lights above me.

"We designed the chair to hold people like you still. It comes in handy when we test out your ability" she explains with a wicked glimmer in her features. "For years we have been curious about you, like an itch we could never scratch, but now we have a short window of opportunity to explore our questions" Dr Lopez continues. "Trust me, we will explore *every* question we have"

"Hunter won't like this when he finds out—"

"He won't find out" she assures me.

What scares me, is that I believe her.

This whole place has cameras in every corner. There is no way this woman will get away with this without Hunter or West knowing about it.

Four people in lab coats appear beside me. Two on each side of the chair. They begin to place something on both of my temples. I can't see what they are doing. From my view, it looks like wires are coming from the brain. When the wires are attached to my head, it feels like glue.

"What is this?" I ask.

My eyes are trying to see what they are doing to me, but there is no way of me seeing. My head cannot turn, I can't see anything behind or above me.

As the scientists continue to adjust the wires, Dr Lopez watches me. "You are going to use your ability, and we will record the data on this computer. After each push, you will be given a small jolt. Don't worry too much about the jolts, they are meant to push you into channelling more power" she begins to explain the process to me.

"No" I protest.

I wriggle in the chair, trying to struggle against them. The effort I put into fighting is low, but it brings me a small sort of comfort. I know I can't fight back against them in the position I am in, but I can try. And I do. I use my energy to swing my head from side to side in an attempt to make it difficult for the scientists to attach things to my head.

"You don't have a choice" Dr Lopez holds her smile. "You may as well make it easier for yourself and comply with my demands"

"I won't do it" I refuse.

"You will" she says, confidently.

Dr Lopez turns to one of the scientists seated in front of the computer. She places a hand on the back of the man's seat as she stares down at the computer. She examines the small writing on the screen. All the graphs and the diagrams. She scans over it all.

"Everything is ready" the scientist nods their head.

"Good" she hums. "The Supreme will be grateful for this information. Make sure there are no mistakes"

The scientist nods his head again in agreement. "I won't let you down" he begins tapping away at the keyboard of the computer.

Dr Lopez turns back around to face me. The clipboard has disappeared from her grasp. I look around to try and see where she may have put it, but I can't seem to see it. My mind is all over the place. I can't remember if I saw her put it down, or if I missed it completely. "Are you ready?" she asks me. Her eyes stead on me, but I make sure to look away from her fixated gaze.

"I won't do it" I repeat.

"If I have to find motivation, I will" she warns me. I want to know what she means, but I don't want to hear it. "We have your friend, Elijah Haul, ready if we need him"

"Elijah is not my friend" I almost laugh.

Elijah probably had a shiver run down his spine as Dr Lopez said the word friend. He would have a lot more to say about the woman's statement if he was here.

"Are you sure?" she smirks.

She acts as if she knows something I don't. Like a secret she is holding back from me until she can use it as a high level of leverage. I want to know what it is. What could she possibly have over me? She thinks she has control over the situation, control

217

over me. The smirk staining her lips tells me Dr Lopez thinks she is winning, which she is.

But she is wrong.

She can't actually believe hurting Elijah is her leverage to get me to co-operate.

"We saw the security footage. We know he snuck into your room on your second day" Dr Lopez crosses her arms. "I know you guys are friends. Why else would he risk being caught by our soldiers to check on you?"

"Elijah is an idiot" I give her a half-hearted answer.

"Maybe" she mumbles.

Dr Lopez is driving me crazy with her questions. "I don't understand why you are… uhh… well why do you care about Elijah and I's— relationship?" I have to question her reason for pushing the conversation.

For the first time, the thought of having the words 'Elijah' and 'relationship' in the same sentence doesn't make me want to burst out with laughter.

Her smirk falls almost flat. "I want some straight answers from you" she is becoming impatient with me.

"I don't trust you" I respond, honestly.

My sentence strikes a nerve in Dr Lopez. She glances over her shoulder to the soldiers; a sour look on her nose. "Go get the boy" she orders. My eyes try to widen themselves but I force them to stay completely still.

When the soldiers start to walk, I panic.

"You won't hurt Elijah—"

"I will do what is necessary" she cuts me off.

"He is no one to me" I rush to speak.

My panic is clear to her. She is smirking at me like she has won, she has gotten exactly what she wanted.

"There is no point lying to me" she shakes her head.

I take a deep breath.

I continue to watch the soldiers walk away. "Okay. Okay, wait!" I break. "No, just wait" both the soldier's stop walking at the sound of my voice. Dr Lopez can't bring Elijah from the training room. I don't want him to get hurt… "If you drag Elijah from the training room, it will cause Hunter to suspect something is going on" I try to reason with her.

Why am I protecting Elijah?

I know he wouldn't do the same for me.

"I am not worried about him" she doesn't batter an eyelid as she talks. "Unless you are going to comply with my wishes, I will bring him down here and make you comply" she raises her eyebrows. I blink. Once, maybe twice. I can't read her. I don't know if she is lying. "I want to hear you say it"

"Yes" I cave in.

Defeat washes over me, filling me with the instant regret and worry for what is to come.

"Smart choice" her smirk returns. "let's begin, shall we?"

Dr Lopez picks up the metal clipboard from one of the desks she had placed it on. I watch her carefully. "What do you want me to do?" I speak through my frown.

"We will start slow. You will channel a small amount of your energy. Only a little spark maybe" she grins from ear to ear as she describes the instruction.

They want me to use my ability. I don't want to hurt any of the people around me. If I use my ability, I don't know how far I can go without losing control over myself. Dr Lopez has no idea what she is asking me to do. She has no idea how little control I have over my own ability.

"Are you sure—"

"Yes. Now begin" Dr Lopez doesn't give me a second to hesitate.

I don't say a word.

Closing my eyes, I focus on the thought of fear and anger and rage. I picture every time I was forced to go into a silent cage of my mind with nothing but my thoughts for company and my breathing as a grounding for my reality.

I can't become too angry. I only want to use a small sliver of my ability. Using a small amount won't hurt. I used to twirl small objects for fun, to keep my mind calm. A spoon. A pen. Maybe I can focus on something small to keep control.

My eyes focus on an empty chair beside the soldiers. The idea is to slightly lift the chair, allowing them to see what I can do without causing harm. Training with West is the reason I can levitate objects without breaking anything.

I feel like an idiot for helping these people.

"Watch the cameras for Hunter" Dr Lopez demands one of the women sitting on my right.

The woman taps away at the mouse, opening different images on the screen. She brings up the live camera feed from the cameras around Hunter's office. All I can see are soldiers walking in and out of different rooms. "He is located on the fourth floor" the woman responds to Dr Lopez's demand with a thin line forming on her bright red lips. They must consider the floor with Hunter's office as the fourth floor. "No sign of movement yet"

Dr Lopez takes a deep breath of relief. "Alright, Grace, are you ready?" she clasps her hands together.

I keep my focus on the chair.

Again, I don't respond.

CHAPTER THIRTY-EIGHT
HUNTER

Stacks and stacks of papers have been left on top of this desk, waiting for me to return. Most of the information on the paper has no relevance to me. It is my father's papers. Now that he is gone, all his work has been left to me.

My soldiers returned from their meeting with West, scattering across the floor as they try to complete the many tasks I have set. It keeps them busy while the trials are taking place downstairs. I don't want to be pestered by the soldiers while I am trying to work, I have had enough distractions.

Grace being a huge distraction.

She needs to stay in line.

She knew she needed to stay under the radar, but instead she escaped the training room and ventured up the stairwell. I should have seen it coming. I should have known she was going to try and explore. She was struggling after a day here, keeping her down here is most likely causing her mind to go temporarily insane.

But she should know to listen to me by now.

She cannot afford to take risks.

As I look over the desk, glancing over to the seat Grace was previously seated in, I see a map left on the chair. The map is unfamiliar to me. It does not belong to me. Grace must have left it when she was escorted out.

Reaching over the desk, I manage to pick up the map off the chair.

The map is of FrostMount.

The only people who would have this sort of thing just lying around would be my soldiers. FrostMount, Nightridge, Ashbay, Moonond. All the cities and villages scattered across the country have maps drawn out for people who intend to visit. I hold a map for every city, village, town. I have them to ensure if anything happens, I know where they are and what to expect.

But why is FrostMount's map lying around?

My mind tries to picture where Grace could have found this map. Maybe it was lying around in the main area? Grace must have found it when she was snooping around. She tends to do that a lot.

Sometimes I think I should just leave the girl on a leash and let her drive herself crazy. Maybe that would teach her to obey the rules like everyone else around here.

I turn to paper over, looking at the writing on the back.

Three planes, six groups, on way to

The words don't mean much to me. I don't know why my soldiers would feel the need to write these words down, and they look like they were written in a rush. The words must be important if the soldiers felt the need to write them down.

I turn the map back around. My eyes scan over the area marked by a thick black pen.

"This asshole" West swears as he bursts through the office door, his eyes dark and angry. "He had one job" he doesn't hold back his rage.

My head rises as he crosses his arms in a huff. Someone has caused him to become enraged. I can see the blood boiling inside of him as he tries to stand still. "What has happened?" I ask, my eyes daring to look anywhere but his face.

Rage is dancing along his pupils. "Elijah, the sonofabitch, he lost her" his tongue is lacing with anger.

I place the map on the desk. I push the sleeves of my white shirt up, resting my elbows on the desk for comfort. "I already sorted Grace out. She was snooping around. I caught her and sent her back to the training room" I try to assure him, but he doesn't look convinced.

West merely laughs at my claim. "Bring him in" he shouts to the soldiers outside the office door.

Two soldiers walk behind Elijah, making sure he doesn't make any fast movements to leave. Neither one of the soldiers look towards West, keeping their eyes on me. They don't dare to look anywhere else. It has been an unspoken rule between the soldiers to look at me if I am in the room, nobody else, only me.

I never made the rule, but it shows respect.

"Where is she?" Elijah looks around the room.

"Why is he up here?" I direct my question to West.

"He lost Grace" West repeats his statement. "I swear to god if she is hurt, I will kill—"

I shake my head. "Nobody here will hurt her, especially while I am around" I assure West.

Elijah huffs. "Tell that to the two soldiers you ordered to escort her back" he pushes my buttons.

He is wrong. *I hope he is wrong.* "My soldiers wouldn't go behind my back" I deny his accusations. The soldiers know better than to defy me. If what Elijah says is true, the soldiers will pay greatly.

"Okay, tell me where she is! Where is she?" he proves his point, once again.

I become silent.

"I checked the training room, the hallways, all the other floors. I can't find her anywhere" West lists, holding his hands behind his back. "The only place I haven't checked is the first floor, but she would have no need to go down there"

My blood boils the more time goes by. I don't want to believe the soldiers are behind this. "I sent two soldiers with her… They had a responsibility to make sure she got back safely" I say, pushing the palm of my hands against the desk as I rise to my feet. "Check the cameras" I demand.

West turns to the soldiers. "You may go" he orders.

Both soldiers turn and leave the room. Neither one of them say a word. It's for the best. I don't want to look at another soldier until I know Grace is safe. West walks over to the door, closing it swiftly. He knows time is precious to us. We have too much to do around here before tomorrow, we can't afford to waste anymore seconds.

Especially if Grace is somewhere she shouldn't be.

"Use my computer" I insist, moving out of the way of the desk for West to use my computer to check the cameras.

West moves almost right away, rushing around the desk and over to the computer. He turns it on and moves the mouse to open the cameras up on the screen. One by one, the cameras show us a live feed of each floor, each hallway, and the stairwell.

By now, there are soldiers everywhere.

Quickly, West opens the one of the camera feeds from half an hour ago. One by one, the cameras located in the stairwell reveal the soldiers walking Grace down to the first floor. She looks as confused as I am. What reason do they have to take her down that far? They are not following my orders.

My eyes darken when West opens up the camera inside the lab. It shows us exactly who is behind this.

Dr Lopez.

She has placed Grace in the chair they use to test the rest of the teenagers for their abilities. They have placed the wired hat to tap into Grace's mind, being able to have control over her temperature and keep her stable as she follows their evil and selfish wishes.

I would love nothing more than to shoot Dr Lopez in the head, the heart, and the stomach. I would take my time to hurt her. I would watch as the blood poured from her body and she begged me to stop. She would regret ever going behind my back to complete her little science projects.

All because she defied me.

"I am going to rip their heads off" West lets his anger get the best of him. "I will skin them alive if they hurt her"

He takes the words right out of my mouth, but I know better than to say my thoughts aloud.

Before I can get another word out, there is a knock on the office door. This better not be one of my soldiers. "Come in" I demand the person on the other side of the door.

The office door slowly opens. Lucas and Myles are on the other side of the door, staring at the three of us. Both boys don't know what to do, where to look, what to say. They look at the three of us individually, trying to assess the situation in front of them.

"You are late" I frown.

My statement only causes more frowns to copy mine. I hold my stare on them.

One of them clears their throat as they try to think of what to say. "The plane was low on fuel" Myles huffs as he places a hand in the front pocket of his trousers.

"That is not good enough" I snap.

Lucas flinches.

Myles doesn't like my response. "Don't blame us, we weren't flying the damn thing" he rolls his eyes.

He has grown a backbone. First time I met Myles, I was assured he was a quiet boy who followed the rules. Which he was, for a while at least. He never spoke above me if he could help it. He wouldn't dare try. I liked him that way. He was a lot easier to tolerate.

After coming back from his little adventure with Grace, I fear he has turned cold and distant and bitter. Myles has become a different person.

I have to take a deep breath, stopping myself from saying anything else out of anger. "West, take Lucas and Myles to their room for the night. I want them to stay out of sight until the morning" I order.

"What about Grace—"

"I will deal with her" I cut West off.

"What has happened with Grace?" Lucas asks, worry held within his eyes.

West and I exchange a quick look of concern. We both know better than to tell them what is going on. It is not a big problem; it can be solved. There is no need to cause concern between the boys. They need to stay focused on getting some rest and being up early for tomorrow.

No words are shared. West knows what to do. He leads the boys out of the office and back into the main area.

"What are we doing—"

"There is no *we*" I interrupt Elijah, emphasising the word 'we' as I talk. I was hoping he would have left with the others, but instead he has chosen to pester me. "I am going to go get her. You need to go back to the training room and continue to find the right people for the war"

"I am coming with you" he goes against my orders.

"No, you are not—"

"I don't remember asking for your approval" he cuts me off for the first time. "This is Grace we are talking about"

Elijah is the last person I expected to care. A month ago, he would look at me and I'd expect him to laugh if I expressed any concern for Grace being in danger. He is standing in front of me with the same anger that I have, maybe more.

Elijah could punch a hole through the steel walls if he had the chance.

I dare ask what has changed.

My head nods, but I want to protest. "Fine. Stay behind me. Do not say a word" I groan, walking around the desk as I begin to make my way towards the door.

A gun is strapped into the waistband of my trousers, making me feel a little more relaxed than I was five minutes ago.

A gun always calms me down.

Nothing more is said.

Elijah complies, following behind me as I leave the office.

CHAPTER THIRTY-NINE
GRACE

My energy feels like it is being sucked out of my body.

The more I try to push myself, the harder it gets for my eyes to stay open. Adrenaline is fighting against me. My heart is yelling at me to stop. I know my limits, my body knows my limits, yet I am still trying to help this woman.

Even the scientists around us are looking worried as they watch me try to continue.

This is wrong.

It is all wrong.

Dr Lopez steps by the side of me, watching me intensely as I levitate the chair opposite me. I focus my eyes on the chair as she stares into my soul. I can't concentrate with Dr Lopez standing there. "We need you to work at full capacity, Ms Silver" Dr Lopez encourages me to keep going.

I want to shake my head and scream, but I can't.

I can't move an ounce of my body.

My eyes grow heavy, my heart grows quiet. I can barely feel my hands. I have never tried to channel my ability for this much amount of time before.

My body isn't used to this feeling.

Someone clears their throat. The sound of a scrapping chair comes from beside me. I can't turn my head to look but it feels like someone has pushed their chair back to get a better look at something. "Her heart is weakening" someone breaks the silence in the room. "Stop her. If she goes any further, she may lose consciousness"

"Don't make her lose focus" Dr Lopez ignores the person talking. She doesn't want anything stopping me from giving her the data she wants. Dr Lopez seems like she will stop at nothing to get her way.

"Dr... she cannot keep going" the person continues. "You won't get the results you need for the Supreme if her body decides to gives up. Give her a rest, we can try again in an hour or so" they try to reason with Dr Lopez.

My eyes spring open.

"Your… this is for the— Supreme" I force the words out of my mouth.

I heard them mention the Supreme earlier, but I didn't think anything of it…

"Don't speak" Dr Lopez orders.

This has gone too far. I should never have given into her demands. I could have stopped her from hurting Elijah if she stuck to her word about using him for leverage. I should have been smarter. I should have stood my ground. Now, Dr Lopez is going to get exactly what she wants.

I try to stop myself from using any more of my ability, but something stops me. Something inside my body refuses to give me control. "Why can't I— stop?" I ask, shutting my eyes to let out a breath.

This is not good.

"Thanks to new technology, we attached a device that allows us to keep a constant magnetic flow running through you when you activate your ability. This prevents you from stopping" she explains.

My lips part to gasp, but no air escapes.

Pain has never felt so harsh. My blood is running cold, I can feel it coursing through my body. It has become sharp like icicles, cold like steel. My fingers have grown numb, and my head has grown foggy. The machine clinging to my head is the reason my soul is being sucked out of my body.

"The more you restrain, the more it will hurt" Dr Lopez tries to explain but I ignore her.

I rattle my wrists against the metal holding me down into the chair. I refuse to be her little lab rat any longer. Whatever research they are trying to conduct here, I will not be any part of it. The woman will not get what she wants out of me.

I will make sure of it.

Even if it hurts.

"Ms Silver—"

"I will not help you. Not anymore" I scream as I fight against the pull on my strength. "The Supreme will not get what he wants… not this time. Not out of me"

Ouch.

Another jolt shoots through me.

"The jolts will get worse the more you fight" she assures me as she watches me struggle.

Before I can protest anymore, a door opens.

The loud noise of the door slamming against the wall brings everything and everyone to a stop. I focus my eyes ahead, trying my best to see anything other than the floating chair in front of me, but I can't even do that.

As my eyes zoom in and out of focus, I manage to see who has caused the sudden panic in everyone.

Hunter and Elijah.

"Stop the machine" Hunter's voice bounces from wall to wall. I have never heard a voice so loud.

Even with the clear demand, nobody moves.

"Did you hear me?" his nostrils flare as his eyes continue to darken. "I said, turn it off" he repeats himself.

Dr Lopez steps forward, stopping directly in front of my eyeline. She causes me to lose my focus on Hunter, and I have to close my eyes to stop myself from screaming. I bite my inner cheek, wanting the pain to stop. Resisting against the machine is making the shooting pains worse.

She is right.

I am the reason the pain is getting stronger.

"I cannot do that, sir" Dr Lopez challenges Hunter. "We are very close to finding out exactly what Ms Silver is truly capable of. Turning off the machine will only delay our findings"

"He said, turn it off" Elijah repeats Hunter's words.

I can make out Elijah's blurred silhouette. He is standing to the side of Hunter. As I force myself to focus on him, I notice him looking back. I have to blink, once, twice. His eyes don't leave mine.

"Men, handle them" Dr Lopez orders the soldiers.

The soldiers don't hesitate.

They approach the boys, both soldiers curling their fists up into balls. Neither of them go for their guns. They are ready for a fist fight. They are prepared for blood shed.

The soldier on the right throws the first punch, aiming to hit Hunter. His punch appears strong, but Hunter is too quick for him. Hunter catches the guys fist as if it was a feather. The look of disgust on Hunter's face is enough to know this is only going to end badly for the soldier.

As for the other soldier, he goes for Elijah.

Elijah strikes first. He throws his fist towards the soldier, throwing his entire body into the punch. It is hard enough to cause the soldier to stumble back slightly. Elijah breathes like a weight has been lifted from his shoulders. He looks as if he has been waiting his whole life to do that.

They both fight like their life depends on it. They hit and hit and hit. The soldiers don't hold a chance against the two of them together. The boys fighting side by side, they seem to hold more power, more control.

Nobody could stop them.

One punch, two punches, three punches.

One soldier is on the ground, but one of the scientists tries to fight. The small scientist stands in the soldiers place, throwing their fists at Hunter any chance they get.

As the boys fight, I try to wriggle out of the chair. This is my chance to find a way out of this contraption and help them against the soldiers. Not that they need my help. They seem to be doing fine on their own. But I want to get out of this chair before my body collapses on me.

Before I faint.

"Not so fast" Dr Lopez takes me by surprise. She holds a knife tightly in her grip with a deadly look held within her crazy eyes. "You are going to focus on that chair and give me enough data for the Supreme. Am I making myself clear?" she then holds the knife against my neck.

It presses against my flesh.

It pierces my skin.

"DO IT" Dr Lopez snaps.

I have to hold back wet tears as my body screams for it all to stop. "I would rather... die" I breathe out the words. The knife cuts a little deeper into the side of my neck. "You don't need to— The Supreme will only kill you once he gets what he... what he wants" I try to reason with her.

"The Supreme is a good man" she is deluded. "He has done nothing but try to help you. Don't you see that? I suggest you do the same and help him"

230

The sound of another person hitting the ground brings my eyes from Dr Lopez to Hunter. His dark eyes scare me as he straddles one of the soldiers bodies, continuing to punch their body. Scientists have decided to join the fight. They attack the boys with everything they have.

Which isn't a lot.

The scientists grab anything they can find and use it as a weapon against Hunter and Elijah.

Elijah is hard to keep track of. One minute he is throwing someone against a desk, the next, he is on the other side of the room punching a man to the ground. And then, all over again, Elijah is nowhere to be seen.

Bang.

Crash.

Loud groans of pain.

Scientists are being thrown around like rag dolls. Desks are being broken and tipped over, computers and test tubes are being smashed.

Glass has scattered across the floor. The boys are making a mess of everything they have done down here. Everything has been spilled into piles of nothing. All the hard work and dedication the workers have put into this place, has been destroyed in a matter of seconds.

I look at Dr Lopez again. "Whatever the Supreme has promised you… I can tell you it is a lie" I assure her.

Something inside her clicks, and she removes the knife from my neck. My thick red blood drips from the tip of the sharp object. Her arm stretches out as she points at the chair with her knife, moving her head back and forth between my eyes and the chair. She can't decide where to look.

There is something sinister inside her.

I can't pull my mind away from the pain long enough to think straight.

When I don't comply to Dr Lopez demands, she takes a deep breath and smirks. "Fine. I will do it for you" she begins walking over to one of the computers. Her fingers tap away at the keyboard. "Let's see how long you last"

231

The chair which has been floating in the same spot for over five minutes, has now began to rise. "What— What are you doing?" I ask, my eyes filling with worry and confusion.

I make an effort to stretch my hands, feeling the power escaping my fingertips. The ability to keep my eyes open has been taken from me, replaced with darkness. I see nothing, I feel everything.

The darkness creates a bubble, keeping me from all the fighting around me.

"I wouldn't do that if I were you" Hunter speaks over the sound of Dr Lopez tapping away on the keyboard.

A gun being loaded can be heard in the same direction as Dr Lopez. The typing sound stops and is replaced with the fighting coming from behind me.

"You are making a mistake" Dr Lopez cackles.

"You will turn off the machine now" Hunter ignores her statement.

I begin to see red.

The same kind of red that appears before I lose control and something bad happens.

I fear the worst.

Almost instantly, I see the elements again, the same vision I saw the last time I used my ability.

Earth, fire, water, and air float on individual pedestals as a dark red cloud surrounds the background. All corners of my mind are engulfed in a haze. Blood, running like a river, gushing all around me.

Like the last time, a light orange begins to appear in the back of my mind. Fire. A bright flame sparking in front of my closed eyes with no intention of stopping.

"She is close. So close. I cannot turn the machine off before she pushes herself to her full potential. The data will be enough. She just needs to complete the data" Dr Lopez refuses to comply with Hunter. "You will have to kill me"

There is no hesitation.

A gunshot creates a ripple through the air. I can hear a computer smash from beside me. The smell of smoke from the gun fills my nostrils as the room falls into a chaotic silence.

The red disappears.

The fire and the blood and the elements are gone, replaced with a dark nothingness covering my eyes.

I rest my head upon the back of the chair as the pull on my soul slowly fades away. My eyes remain closed. I have to build my energy up before I can consider moving any part of my body, including my eyes. I need to rest. I need to sleep. I need water. I need a lot, but all I want is to get out of this chair.

In a half-hearted attempt to pull my arms from the metal wrapped around my wrists, I force my body slightly further into the chair. The movement is weak and pointless. It was never going to work. But I had to try.

Suddenly, I can feel someone pull at the metal holding down my wrists. The wires are removed from my head, giving me enough control to drop the chair that was once floating onto the floor. I hear it crash on the ground as the legs of the chair smash apart, breaking away from the base of the chair.

My body relaxes for the first time.

I gradually open my eyes, only enough to see who is in front of me. Only enough to squint up at the person trying to free me from the chair.

Elijah is looking at the metal.

He isn't paying enough attention to my eyes to notice I am looking back at him. He is too focused on getting me out of the chair to see the faint smile tugging at my lips.

"Elijah…" I breathe out his name.

He freezes.

His entire body tenses up. He doesn't move. He doesn't respond to me. Elijah takes a second to gather his thoughts. I notice him take a short breath. He then shakes his head and continues to figure out a way to free me.

One wrist becomes free to move around, allowing me to lift it up slightly to move a strand of hair from my face. The small movement forces me to take another moment as pain rushes through my veins.

"Don't expect this to be a regular thing. This is the last time I save your ass" Elijah says as my other wrist becomes free.

"Yeah…" I try to laugh but I don't have it in me.

233

He crosses his arms as he examines my eyes. He watches as my eyes flutter open and closed. He doesn't take his eyes off mine. "Where does it hurt?" he asks me.

"How did you—"

"I know when you're hurt" he answers before I can get the question past my lips. "Tell me where it hurts" he repeats.

"I don't… feel good" I admit.

It wasn't the answer he wanted, but it is as good as it is going to be for now. "Come here" he sighs, gently wrapping his arms under me and pulling me out from the chair.

I am carefully lifted out of the metal chair, and into Elijah's strong arms.

His touch is gentle.

So gentle.

I carelessly rest my head against his bicep as he holds one arm under my knees, and the other arm around my body. He is careful not to hurt me. He doesn't make any sudden moves as he carries me over to the desk Dr Lopez once stood.

I glance up at Elijah's emotionless face with my hands resting on my chest.

"I— I can walk" I lie.

"No you can't" Elijah sees right through me.

He looks down at me, staring at me like I am the only person in the room.

Elijah's light blue eyes are the only thing my eyes manage to stay centred on. Everything around me is blurry. The world has disappeared from my eyeline, replaced with only a mirror image of what I can picture from memory.

I don't even miss it.

My tired eyes could remain on Elijah's for an eternity if I allowed them.

"You don't have… to carry me—"

"Yes I do" he disagrees with me, again.

"Elijah—"

"Will you stop being stubborn?" he groans. "Accept the help for once"

He lifts his eyes away from mine, looking forward. And I miss his eyes immediately. I want him to look at me again, keep my mind away from the mess around me. I find myself following his eyes. I look in the same direction his eyes are looking. He is looking at Dr Lopez.

Dr Lopez is dead.

The back of her head has a single bullet hole. Her blood is smeared across the desk, her head lodged into the centre of the smashed computer screen.

I have learnt very quickly that some people deserve to die in this cruel world.

No matter how badly you want someone to be a good person, some people are pure evil. They will never change. The only option for them is death.

Some people deserve to die, and she was one of them.

"Are you okay, Love?" Hunter asks me.

I nod my head lightly.

"What is all this?" Elijah asks the question I have been thinking about.

Hunter slowly looks from me to Elijah. "It is a lab for testing new abilities. We use blood samples and sometimes extract certain abilities to find cures. Just last year, we found the cure for cancer" he says, proudly. "This place was for good. We were helping a lot of people" he takes a minute. "It is a shame Dr Lopez turned out this way, but it is for the best. I cannot have a traitor working for me"

This is the place people used to fear.

People would spread rumours about a lab. A place you would never return from. Myles would have nightmares about the sheer thought of being taken away to the lab.

"What happens now?" Elijah ask.

"I will find someone else to take her place" Hunter does not waste time.

Hunter is already thinking about the next step for the lab, he has not stopped to even consider the blatant fact that he just killed another human being. I doubt he has even given it a second thought.

I don't want to stay in here any longer.

"Can we— can we get out of here?" I ask.

Hunter and Elijah look down at me. They look from my face to each other. "Yes. You should take her up to her room, and make sure the door is locked" Hunter orders Elijah.

"What are you going to do?" Elijah questions him.

It is weird seeing them both get along. For once, they are both on the same page. They are both talking to one another without shouting or fighting or arguing.

It is nice.

"I need to have a word with West... and my soldiers" he looks annoyed as he says the last part. Hunter is a man who likes respect and honour. I highly doubt he is taking the scientists and soldiers betrayal lightly. "I need to make sure everyone is on my side if we are going to continue fighting together" he finishes his explanation and places his gun in the back of his trousers.

Elijah nods, but no more words are exchanged.

I am carried through the lab of bodies. Hunter watches us as we leave, following shortly behind us.

CHAPTER FORTY
GRACE

My body is still shaking a little.

It has been shaking from the moment Elijah placed me in my bed, to the second I woke up.

I haven't been awake long. Maybe twenty minutes. I kept having the same nightmare, over and over again. No matter how badly I tried to sleep, I kept waking up. My body wants to rest, it doesn't want to be woken up every hour.

But my mind had other ideas.

Instead it wanted me to relive the same dream, forcing me to remember every micro-detail of the ongoing nightmare.

It was weird.

In the dream, I saw the Supreme, Carter, and the girl from my room in Soltrix Carter had disappeared with. The three of them were standing together, with a man in the centre. He was tall and dark, hidden away from my eyes by shadows. If I had to guess, I would say the man in my dream was Todo Poderoso.

It is the only explanation I can come up with.

No matter what I do, I can't seem to stop thinking about him.

He is in the back of my head, constantly, reminding me how much I still don't know.

There is still a huge question mark over his face.

I need to meet him. I need to see him for myself and ask him everything I have been thinking about.

"Grace… are you awake?" Myles whispers as he gently pushes the door open, bringing me out of my own head.

"Yes, I'm awake" I sigh, gradually sitting up on the bed.

I didn't realise Myles had already arrived.

He holds onto the door, keeping it half closed, keeping it half open. "Can we talk?" he asks before fully entering the room. He is waiting for me to give him permission to enter. For the first time in a long time, he is being nice.

I curl my legs up into a loose ball as I rest my back against the wall. My dirty blonde hair falls over my knees. "What time is it?" I ask a question on top of his.

"Five" he responds.

Five in the morning, five in the afternoon. I don't think I will ever know while we are down here. My best guess, it is five in the morning. It would explain the dark circles forming under Myles' dull brown eyes.

"Why are you awake?" I ask another question.

"I couldn't sleep... I needed to see you" he confesses.

My breath hitches. He *needed* to see me. "You haven't spoken to me in a long time. You made it pretty clear you wanted me to leave you alone. Why do you need to see me now?" I narrow my eyes onto him.

He walks over to the bed, letting the door close on its own accord. He sits down on the end of the bed, keeping his distance from me. His eyes scan over the room as a small smile creeps up onto his face.

It is a sad kind of smile. The kind of smile you see when someone is trying to be happy for another while they secretly hold sadness in their heart, or when someone is trying to hide their pain from the world.

I want to ask why he is smiling.

"Do you remember, I would wake you up every morning with a happy attitude about how it was going to be a great day" he almost laughs at the memory. "I would talk to you, keep you company. You would look at me with those bright eyes. Like I was everything to you"

"I remember" I carefully nod my head as the memory floods back to me.

I remember it all like it was yesterday.

"We were happy" he sighs.

That is where our stories differ. We remember certain things differently. Myles was happy. This place was routine and order, nothing was allowed to be out of sync. He was content to follow along with whatever happened, as long as we had each other, he was satisfied.

I, on the other hand, wanted to tear the whole building down until I got out. I was not happy. I was not content to live a life of solitude down here. I was miserable. This place was a prison to me, not a home. Myles and Sarah were the only good thing here and Sarah was taken from me in this very room.

"I was not happy" I retort. He only stares. "You know I wasn't happy here" I remind him.

"Sure you were—"

"This place was a prison— is a prison" I correct myself. "I can never be happy in a place like this. You should know me better than that"

Myles is forgetting how badly I wanted to leave. He is looking over all the times I would sit and hold back tears as he tried to comfort me the best way he could. He would sit with me and talk about his thoughts of what the world could look like while I curled up into a ball.

There was nothing more important to me than leaving this caged hell.

"Your right" he agrees. "I should know you better than that. But I don't. I don't know who you are anymore. You are not the person I grew up with. Soltrix changed you"

"It made me better" I claim.

"It ruined us" he argues.

I lower my knees, moving close to the edge of the bed to let my feet rest on the floor. The cold and bitter concrete on my feet sends a shiver through my body. I place my hands in my lap and take a deep breath.

"I can't apologise for missing the old you" he is being honest with me; I am thankful for that.

"I do miss our friendship" I admit.

"Me too" he agrees. "I liked you… a lot. I'll admit it. But when we became a couple, it didn't feel right to me"

A part of me is glad he said that.

Finally, one of us said it out loud.

"Maybe we are just meant to be friends" I guess.

Something inside is telling me to speak about the kiss between me and Elijah. I feel the need to tell Myles, but there is also something stopping me. I don't know why Elijah and I kissed. Maybe it was just in the moment, something that will never happen again.

I don't know.

But I know I shouldn't speak about it until Elijah and I have talked.

Myles nods his head, but he looks as if he is about to say more. "I slept with Asha" he comes out and says it. No sugar coating. He isn't tiptoeing around it.

"I know…" I respond.

His eyes widen.

"You knew?" he looks taken back by my claim.

My head nods. "I saw you… briefly" I make it clear that I wasn't watching them. I don't want him to think I was spying on them. "I came across you guys, I didn't mean to see you" I don't know why I am trying to justify myself.

I shouldn't have to justify myself for seeing something that was never meant to happen in the first place.

But from my currently position, I cannot argue. Elijah and I kissed, while Myles and I were technically still together. Even if we weren't talking at the time, we were dating. From where I stand, I am just as bad as Myles.

"Oh…" he makes an 'o' shape with his mouth. His head lowers into his lap as his eyes stare at the floor. "Why didn't you say something sooner?"

My eyes lift slightly.

"I had never had a boyfriend. It was all new to me. I didn't know how to handle the situation" I shrug. "And I didn't want to lose you in my life"

He hums.

"The world ruined it for us" Myles blames everything but himself.

He always points the blame onto other things, rather than pointing the finger at himself.

My head shakes. "We only have ourselves to blame" I challenge his claim as he keeps his eyes away from mine. He doesn't respond. He doesn't have anything to respond with. I glance from him to the wall opposite us. "I still want you as a friend" I break the short silence.

Even after everything that happened between us, I don't want to lose him in my life.

His head lifts immediately.

"Really?" he tries to hide his smile.

The smile growing on his face takes me back to every single morning I would wake up.

It would be the first thing I see when my eyes opened.

Before I can say anything more, he jumps from his spot on the bed. He springs over to me and engulfs me in a hug. I fall onto my back as he lays on top of me. I giggle from the foreign movement while he breathes in my scent.

"I'm really sorry, for everything. I am sorry. I am so sorry, Grace" he apologises.

He holds me like it is the first time he has ever held me.

Like it was his last chance to have me in his arms.

I smile against his hair. Maybe there is a chance for us to gain our friendship again. Even after everything.

There is still hope for us.

CHAPTER FORTY-ONE
GRACE

After Myles left, I finally managed to get some sleep. It wasn't long, but it was better than nothing.

I feel much better than I did yesterday.

Eating is also helping. The food the cooks have produced this morning is a lot better than it usually is. They have served scrambled eggs and toast. It is not much to Myles and Lucas, but after living off scraps and pretty much rubbish, it is a nice change around here.

Lucas and Myles are taking their time with their food. I watch them take small bites now and again. Elijah and I, on the other hand, have almost wiped the plate clean.

Iris, Ben, and Kane glance my way every now and then, smiling at me with bright eyes. I have to lean forward to see them, looking down the table. I am seated down the other end of the table, the closest to the dinner hall doors.

I pick up my fork and continue to dig into the scrambled eggs while Lucas and Myles continue to play a silly game. They have been trying to stay occupied, playing an unknown game for the last ten minutes.

It seems to be keeping them entertained.

As kids, everyone would make up silly games to make the time pass quicker. But I haven't heard of this one. The game the boys are playing must be a new one; something they have just come up with.

"Something beginning with S" Lucas states.

"Shorts" Myles guesses.

"No" Lucas shakes his head.

"Umm… spoon" Myles guesses again.

"No" Lucas repeats.

"I'm not sure… uhh— Soldier?" Myles guesses again.

"Yes!" Lucas cheers.

"That one was obvious" I giggle.

Elijah's eyes are staring into Myles' head. He has a look of disbelief staining his features. "That was the dumbest shit I have ever heard" Elijah frowns. He doesn't bother to hide his disappointment. "What a waste of breath"

"It's a game" Myles explains.

"Not a fun game" Elijah scoffs.

"Lighten up" Lucas grins with his teeth.

"I had a long night. It is eight in the morning. The last thing I want to hear is you two idiots playing a silly little game about things you can see around the room" Elijah rants.

Neither of them know what happened yesterday, they don't understand how tired the pair of us truly are. But Elijah needs to be nicer. They are trying to pass the time, and I don't blame them. It can get boring down here. Playing a silly game won't hurt anybody.

"You try it" Lucas encourages him to join in on the game.

Elijah looks over at me. He debates the offer in his head for a moment, and then leans slightly forward with his arms resting on the table. "Something beginning with B" he plays their game.

My eyes widen. Only a little. I did not expect Elijah to join in on their game. I expected him to come up with a snarky comment that sent everyone into an awkward silence.

"Umm—"

"You only get three guesses" Elijah smirks.

Lucas nods his head and laughs, accepting Elijah's new rule to the game. "Boots?" Lucas takes a guess.

Elijah shakes his head.

"Bread?" he takes another guess.

Elijah shakes his head.

Lucas looks around the room, slowly losing any hope of winning the game. "I don't know" Lucas runs a hand through his bright red hair. "Brad?"

"Nope" Elijah chuckles. "Buffoon" he gives Lucas the real answer, gesturing towards Myles without Myles seeing him.

Lucas laughs at the gesture, nodding his head frantically as if he is agreeing with Elijah's claim. I laugh along with them, finding it funnier how Myles hasn't caught on to what we are laughing about. He was too busy looking around the room.

"What?" Myles asks. "What did I miss?"

"Nothing" Elijah wraps an arm around Myles shoulders and messes with his hair. Myles pushes Elijah away and tries to fix himself immediately. He runs both hands through his fluffy brown hair.

I rarely see this side of the boys. No arguing. They are all smiling like old friends. They are getting along. It is nice to see compared to how they used to be. Myles and Elijah used to be at each other's throats, now they are laughing and making jokes at one another.

Lucas has started to come out of his shell a little too.

It's nice.

"You guys are assholes" Myles mumbles.

"You love us" Lucas smiles at him.

Elijah looks back down at his plate as he moves the left-over food around with his fork.

I wonder if any of them have seen West or Hunter this morning. I haven't seen either of them, not since yesterday at least. "Do you guys—"

My words get interrupted abruptly by the room violently shaking. The lights turn off for a split second as plates fall from the tables and the bins tip over at the back of the room. It feels like the earth shakes beneath our feet. And then it all stops as if it never happened.

The lights turn back on, revealing the mess that has now been created.

Everything happened in the blink of an eye.

That was scary.

Everyone looks around at one another, no one knowing what to say or do. I look from Lucas, to Myles, to Elijah. Not a single person here seems to know what is going on. We are all clueless and on edge. "What on earth was that?" Myles says the thing on everyone's mind.

Suddenly, there is a loud explosion from the hallway.

The soldiers rush to the doors. They make the decision to keep one door closed, only opening the left door. One of the soldiers carefully steps into the hallway, inspecting where the commotion is coming from. They take their time, making sure they don't miss anything important.

We all watch in fear.

There is too much uncertainty in the room.

The soldier rushes back into the dinner hall and slams the door shut. Not a breath later, and the doors are locked. We are trapped in here with no explanation. The soldiers are trying to keep out whatever is waiting in the hallway.

"What is going on?" I ask the soldiers, swiftly standing up from my seat.

I am no longer looking at the soldiers. My eyes watch the doors, looking through the thin glass panes in the centre of the two dinner hall doors. I see no movement.

"Sit down" one of the soldiers order.

And then the room erupts into panic.

A soldier bangs on the dinner hall doors. I stay standing, watching the soldier try to claw his way into the room. I blink, once or twice. I count two soldiers now. They are both trying to get into the hall. Neither of them are using guns yet, but I can see large weapons on the waist band of their trousers.

This can't be good.

In a short second, the soldiers have begun to barricade the doors. Nothing is getting in, and nothing is getting out. All I can think about is the fact that there is no other way out of the dinner hall, the only way out is the way in.

I slowly sit down, looking around the room at the scared faces watching the doors. This is new for everyone here. They have not seen war. They have not experienced real fighting. It was all training and pretend duels. It has all been controlled and it was mostly safe up until now.

If this turns ugly, there is no telling what they will see.

"Those are enemy soldiers" Elijah states, pointing to the soldiers trying to break into the room.

All our heads turn to the doors again. The soldiers outside the door are wearing red. I didn't notice before. The colour red is plastered all over their uniform. The same red uniform we had to fight against in the battle against Soltrix.

Red.

They are wearing red.

Shit.

"The Supreme— Todo Poderoso is behind this" I make a quick judgment.

The boys have no idea what to say or do.

245

"We need to get out of here" Myles comes to the same conclusion he always has. He wants to run, like last time. He is only thinking about surviving.

I am done surviving.

"We will have to fight our way out" I think out loud.

"We won't all make it" Lucas gives me the reality of the situation.

The weight of the room is feeling a little heavy on my shoulders. I can feel Elijah's eyes burning holes into the side of my head. He won't take his eyes off me. I feel like I could suffocate under his gaze. "Are you strong enough to fight your way out?" Elijah asks me.

"I'm fine" I try to assure him.

My eyes lock onto Elijah's. He doesn't question me any further. He doesn't believe me. I can see it in his eyes. But he doesn't challenge me.

"Who is going to tell everyone?" Lucas looks from Elijah to me, expecting one of us to talk to the others.

As much as I don't want to do it, I feel like I know exactly what to say. They need to hear the truth if they are going to fight alongside us. I need to tell them exactly what they are about to witness if what we think is true.

If this is a fight, we need to be prepared.

I take a deep breath and begin to climb onto the table, being careful not to step in the food.

"Everyone" I try to grab everyone's attention. They are too busy watching the commotion by the doors to realise I am trying to get their attention. I take another deep breath. "Hey, can I have your attention!" I shout.

They all look my way this time.

"Thank you…" I huff. "This is a bad situation. I know. You guys know nothing about the world that is about to be forced upon you" I take a breath. "It is all a lie. They lied to you all. The world above ground is still alive, it is filled with life" I try to explain everything at a rushed pace.

I take a second to gather my thoughts.

"But it is also filled with war. There is a war going on as we speak, and if you don't all work together, you will be caught up in the centre of it. Trust me… I know"

246

"Why should we trust you?" someone shouts from the crowd of teenagers that have now gathered around the table.

"The boys and I… we had to fight for a city we didn't even know existed a year ago. The boys were forced into a battle against guns and bombs and— They didn't get a choice. They had to fight" I give them the harsh truth. "Now I am giving you a choice. Stay here and end up in the Supremes' hands, or come with us and fight with us"

They only stare at me.

"I can't tell you what is waiting for us on the other side of those doors, but I know we can get out of here if we use our abilities and fight together" I conclude.

The room falls silent, the only sound is now coming from the hallway. Gunshots and loud shouting. Some people keep their eyes on me, wanting to tune out the frightful sounds coming from outside the doors.

Elijah stands up from his seat, followed by Lucas and then Myles. I remain standing on the table, watching the sad horror fill everyone's eyes.

And then it happens.

The soldiers manage to burst through the doors.

Our soldiers pull out their guns to shoot, but they are too slow. The other soldiers are quicker. One by one, in the blink of an eye, they are shot to the ground. The red soldiers are too quick, too prepared.

Ours didn't stand a chance.

A scream or two comes from the back of the room. A few people have started to sprint as far away from the door as possible, wanting to stay away from the soldiers.

I watch as Hunter's soldiers die.

Their bodies lie on the cold floor, unmoving. Pools of red-hot blood pours over the concrete. Lifeless bodies pile up into a stack of nothing. They are kicked to the side by the soldiers in red, as if they are nothing but an inconvenience, something that needs to be disposed of.

The red soldiers raise their guns at us as they enter the room further.

"Everyone in a single line" one of the soldiers order.

Nobody moves.

I look down at the boys, watching as Lucas becomes rigid and anger. His fists clench by his sides as he glares towards the soldier. He doesn't bother to hide his frustration. He looks like he is about to do something he might regret.

And nobody is going to stop him.

"I have had enough of soldiers" Lucas announces his true anger. He begins to run at the red soldiers. He pushes his hand out into the air, the palm of his hand breathing fire into the soldiers faces.

A gasp leaves my lips as I watch the soldiers burn.

"Get down from there" Myles reminds me of my current position. I am still standing on top of the table. I was too busy watching the scene unfold to remember to step down.

I take the chance to step down from the table. My eyes scan over the plates of food still remaining on the table, my feet being careful not to step in anything. I step down onto the seat and then I step down again onto the floor.

To my surprise, I misjudge the drop from the seats to the floor. I trip over the air itself. I don't scream or cry for help. I allow myself to fall. My body falls and falls until I no longer feel the air rushing past my skin.

My eyes flutter open, looking directly into Elijah's light blue orbs. Elijah caught me. His arms have snaked their way around my body, holding me tightly against his chest. My eyes look from his arms back to his eyes. He made sure I didn't hit the hard ground the way gravity intended me too.

"Sorry" I apologise.

"Watch where your stepping" he warns me.

He doesn't loosen his hold on me. I stare at him and he stares at me. I find myself memorising every little detail of his face like I always do. Something clicks inside of me, and I find myself looking at the Elijah I once knew all those years ago.

Before the bullying and torment.

I see the Elijah I was friends with, the Elijah I trusted with anything and everything.

There is something that has changed inside of him lately, whether that is the way he pretends to care, or the way he is looking at me. But it is something. There is something different about him. I want to know the reason for this change.

248

"Guys" Myles brings me back to reality. "Where do you think Hunter and West are?"

This is not the time or the place, but I can't seem to look away from him.

Elijah's arms finally release me from his hold.

I have to remind myself of my surroundings before I can fully understand Myles' question.

"Somewhere safe I hope" I answer him.

Another explosion.

This time it is bigger, and louder, and right in front of our eyes. The explosion is close enough to knock me over. I fall to the floor with Elijah and Myles shortly behind me.

Ringing.

Loud vibrations go off in my ears.

Smoke fills the space around us, clouding my eyes. I rub my forehead with the back of my hand, pushing my hair out of my face. My head is pounding. My eyes are squinting. I look around to make sure no one is hurt. To make sure no one was caught in the explosion itself.

Two hands grip my arms, someone standing on either side of my body. They help me back onto my feet. They steady me. I turn around to find Ben and Iris. They offer me a small smile and then they divert their eyes over to someone who has been crushed by a large part of steel.

Everyone is helping one another. A handful of people have been hurt by the explosion, some worse than others. One girl has been pushed to the ground, held down and trapped by a large piece of steel. Kane and two others are using their strength to pull the heavy object off her body, hoping to get to her before the steel suffocates her.

I pry my eyes away from the coughing girl.

The wall is down. The wall which separates us from the hallway has collapsed, leaving us all unprotected against the soldiers waiting on the other side.

They take the opportunity to fight us. The soldiers begin climbing over the rubble left by parts of the floor that have been torn up by the explosion. The soldiers are carrying guns and heavy weapons. They are ready to fight.

"What the hell was that" Myles coughs out.

249

I stumble over to him, bending down to grab his hands and pull him off the floor. He straightens his back and brushes himself off. "Are you hurt?" I ask him, looking over every inch of his body for blood or red marks.

He shakes his head.

Fire spreads across the room, preventing the red soldiers from getting too close to us.

The flames are high and the heat is creating waves of hot air around the room. I can feel my skin crying. Sweat drips from my forehead, cleaning off the dirt around my face. This feels hotter than the desert itself.

"Anyone got a plan?" Lucas appears beside me, his hands outstretched to keep the fire roaring.

My head turns to the side, facing Lucas.

The soldiers throw water onto the fire in an attempt to put the flames out. Where did they get the buckets of water from? It is as if they were prepared for Lucas. Like they knew he would try to use his ability against them.

Everyone moves swiftly, knowing exactly what they have to do if they want to get out of here alive.

They listen to my words, take on board my claims.

Guns are being fire out into the air. Random objects are being thrown in every direction. Knives are being used in hand-to-hand combat. Fire, water, earth, and air are the elements that are being channelled to fight against the soldiers. Pieces of the floors rubble are propelled forward, knocking some of the soldiers over.

Sparks of purples, blues, yellows, oranges, greens, are flashing in front of our very eyes.

I don't want to use my ability.

I can't.

The last time I tried to use my ability without something keeping it contained, I almost hurt West. I can't risk the same thing happening here. We could be crushed by the building, killed off before we get the chance to get out.

I need to find a different way to help.

A soldier falls to his knees in front of me. His helmet has fallen off, thrown somewhere out of sight. He looks up at me and I look down at him. I lift my leg and slam my foot into his face, hard and fast. His eyes close and his head turns to the side, his body falling flat on the floor.

I crouch down and pull out the soldiers gun from the waistband of their trousers.

The gun is loaded, waiting to be fired.

My fingers wrap around the weighted trigger. I stare at the small gun in my hands. A thick black pistol. Every load gives me six shots.

I crouch down again, searching the soldiers unconscious body for any left-over bullets I can use when I need to reload the gun. The soldier carries two boxes, both filled with fresh bullets waiting for someone to use.

"Out of the way" someone pushes my body to the side, moving me out of their way as they stab a kitchen knife right through a soldier's shoulder.

That looked like it hurt.

"Do you have a plan?" Elijah shouts as he fights his way back to me.

"Not yet—"

"Someone should think of a plan" he suggests. "People are going to die unless someone thinks of something fast" he doesn't seem to have any ideas of his own.

My lips part to talk again, but something stops me.

A soldier runs my way, their gun ready to fire a bullet into my chest. The man looks determined. He is going to kill me. He can already see my quick death in his mind. The soldier wraps his hand tighter around the gun, his fingers lingering on the guns trigger.

I close my eyes, knowing my movements won't be quick enough compared to the soldiers. I won't have enough time to raise my own gun and shoot the soldier down.

Don't move.

Don't shoot.

BANG.

A gun is fired, but it isn't the soldiers.

"You can thank me later" Elijah talks over my shoulder, letting me know I am still alive. I am still breathing. My heart is still beating. Elijah was quicker than the enemy soldier. "Pay attention. This isn't the time to daydream"

251

"Thank you—"

"Don't thank me" he cuts me off.

Elijah is impossible.

I don't bother to respond to him, instead, I hold my gun in the air encase another soldier tries to run my way. I am more prepared this time. I cannot reply on Elijah to watch my back for the entire duration of this fight. He needs to take care of himself, he shouldn't be looking over his shoulder for me.

"We should push through" Myles chimes in.

I can barely hear him.

Myles is pushing soldiers back using his force fields. They don't stand a chance against him. He is running from the back of the room, trying to keep close to us.

"Maybe" I give him a half-hearted response.

"Maybe isn't good enough" Elijah says as he shoots down another soldier heading our way.

"You think of something" I huff.

"Lucas can blow the fire back; it will cause the soldiers to retreat back into the hallway and—" he is interrupted by one of the soldiers walking into his back. Elijah turns around and throws his fist into the soldiers' face, knocking the soldier out. "And it will give us a chance to make a run towards the hallway. Maybe even get to the stairs"

That's not the worst idea.

"Yeah… that could work" I nod, shocked he came up with something so quickly.

My eyes scan the room, keeping my body close to Myles and Elijah. I can't see Lucas anywhere. It is too chaotic to see anyone clearly. There has to be an easier way of finding Lucas in this frantic mess.

"I am going to find Lucas" I shout to the boys.

The dinner hall isn't too big, I am sure I can find him in no time. It's fighting my way through the room I am going to struggle with the most.

"Myles, go with her" I hear Elijah shout as I begin to make my way into the centre of the room. "Make sure she—" Elijah gets cut off by a soldier tackling him to the ground.

I turn around, watching the soldier and Elijah wrestle on the ground. Without a second thought, I raise my gun and fire at the soldier, hitting him in the back. Elijah pushes the man's body off and finds me, staring at the gun in my hand.

Before he can say anything, I spin around and walk into the fight.

Right foot.

Left foot.

Right foot.

Climb over a table.

Left foot.

My eyes catch a glimpse of Ben, kneeling down with long quiet sobs escaping his lips. He holds onto something frail. A hand. A hand so pale it could be mistaken for a ghost.

I look closer, taking small steps towards him. He is beside a body. Iris's body. Her bright blonde hair runs over her limp shoulders and down the front of her body, covering most of the blood spreading across her chest. Two bullets have hit the centre of her heart.

My hand covers my lips, supressing a gasp.

"Shit" Kane mummers. "Shit shit shit" he continues to swear uncontrollably under his breath.

I can see him holding onto his left arm in the corner of my eye. "Are you okay—" I cut myself off when I see the slash across his bicep. Someone has swiped a sharp object across his skin. The object has cut the flesh, opening his arm up for blood to run freely. "Stay there" I order him.

The floor is filling with bodies.

Majority of the bodies are soldiers. Enemy soldiers and our own soldiers.

We won't make it out of here alive at this rate.

Hastily, I lean down and rip a long piece of fabric from one of the dead soldiers' uniforms. The fabric is long enough to wrap around Kane's arm, hopefully applying pressure to slow down his blood loss.

"Stay still" I demand as I grab his arm and wrap the fabric around the open wound.

As I rush to wrap the fabric around his arm, I swiftly notice his hands. More specifically, I notice his fingers. They have turned into claws. Long, sharp silver claws. They look like metal,

253

or steel. He has created a deadly weapon with nothing but his hands. It is the perfect protection.

I finish wrapping the fabric around his arm.

"Thank you" he doesn't smile.

I tie the fabric and clutch my gun again. "Help me get everyone out of here" I get straight to the point.

He nods his head. Fast and rushed. He knows we don't have a lot of time left. The clock is ticking quicker than usual. I can't see us making it out if we don't start moving now. Lucas's fire is spreading, and our window of opportunity is closing.

A soldier smirks as he looks me in the eye, his gun aimed at my head. I close my eyes and pull the trigger of my gun. The bullet doesn't miss, hitting the soldier in the stomach. A groan leaves his mouth as he doubles over, dropping his gun and clutching his stomach.

"Grab Ben" I shout to Kane, gesturing towards Ben as he grieves Iris's death. "We are getting out of here"

He isn't wasting any time.

Kane moves right away, springing down to grab onto Ben's arms. Ben struggles against Kane, trying to stay close to Iris's lifeless body.

I look around the smoky room.

This is a frightening scene to watch.

My hand is gripping the gun tighter as I try to reload the gun with the new bullets.

Slow and steady is not an option.

Everything needs to be fast and rushed if we have any chance of moving out of the gunfire. Nobody has a time to breathe. The soldiers fighting us are making sure to exhaust us, making it even harder to stay strong.

They have planned this perfectly.

We were taken by surprise and cornered into one room. The only thing we have as a weapon is our abilities.

Horror fills my eyes as I watch innocent people die. Killed in cold blood. Some of the people in the room will never see the light of day. They will never get the chance to feel the cold fresh air run laps around their skin. Some of these people will never see the truth behind the lies. The reality of the world.

I need to stay focused.

The fighting around me should stay my main focus. I have to figure out a way to bring everyone out of this building.

"Myles" I shout.

"Lucas" I shout.

"Elijah…" I shout.

I shout and shout as I run through the room. Kane and Ben are following behind me, trying their best to keep up with me. They fight through the many soldiers still left standing, the sound of screams and cries filling our ears as we crawl through the smoke.

But now we have a bigger problem ahead of us.

A problem I didn't want to predict.

The fire has started to weaken.

CHAPTER FORTY-TWO
GRACE

The touch of another human being used to be longed for. It was something people had dreamt about and wished for on their birthdays. To be held and to be kissed. Books upon books were written all over the world about a humans touch and how it brought light to another's life.

In this moment.

The slightest touch from another person brings fear to my mind, and horror to my body.

If someone is close enough to bump my shoulder, I know I am in danger. I know the gun in my shaking hands needs to be up and ready to fire. Ready to kill. Nobody should be close enough to touch me.

Nobody.

"I see Myles" Kane points over to the fire.

Ben doesn't talk. He simply moves across the small space between us and the fire.

A gap in the fire has started to appear, allowing more and more soldiers into the room. This cannot be good for anyone here. If more of the soldiers get through, we may not be able to get out. Not through the broken wall at least.

I follow with Kane, staying close to Ben.

Lucas is slouched up against one of the tables close to the fire, coughing up blood. He doesn't look good. His eyes are half closed and his body is shaking. I can't tell if it's from pain or adrenaline. Or maybe it has something to do with the large arrow sticking out of the side of his chest.

"What happened?" I announce my shock.

Where did someone find an arrow to shoot?

"Someone fired an arrow from the back of the room. He couldn't see it coming. By the time I had taken down one of the soldiers attacking us, he was already on the ground. I tried to help, but I couldn't do anything" Myles answers, holding back tears that threaten to run down his blood covered face.

256

I kneel down to his side. Lucas is going to be okay. He has to be okay. "He is going to… he will be fine— We need to get him up" I frantically try to come up with a new plan.

"He can't get up" Myles informs me. "If we move him, it could aggravate the injury and make it worse"

"Go" Lucas coughs out.

My eyes fall from Myles to Lucas. He doesn't deserve to be left behind. "We can't leave you—"

"I will only… only slow you down" he encourages.

"No. I refuse to leave you here to die. There must be a way to get you out of—"

There is a third explosion. It shakes the ground beneath our feet, causing everyone in sight to stumble. The explosion seems to come from above. Maybe the third floor? I am surprised the ceiling didn't cave in on us all.

"I see another opening" Kane rushes us.

"Go" Lucas repeats.

I look around in a panic, my head moving quicker than my eyes. Myles grabs onto my right arm, pulling me from Lucas in an attempt to keep moving. "I'm sorry, Lucas" I fight back my tears. "I am so sorry" I continuously apologise.

He looks at me, long and hard, a smile tugging at his light red lips. I force a sad smile for him. The kind of smile that kills a piece of my heart. The kind of smile that keeps me glued to the floor. I don't feel it in me to get up and fight, to turn my back on him when he needs me.

But I have to keep moving, for everyone's sake.

As I stand up, I turn my back to Lucas. I can't look him in the eye and walk away. It's too cruel. Too malicious. Watching the life drain from his eyes is something I never want to see.

An arrow flies across the space in front of me, hitting the wall closest to Myles. The arrow was a centimetre or two away from hitting the side of my head. My eyes are wide. That was too close for comfort. Far too close for my mind not to worry the person is going to fire another one.

I can't see where it came from or who shot the arrow.

"This way" Kane points to the opening between the fire.

My eyes stay locked onto the smoky abyss, watching for anyone who tries to attack us from behind.

We step through the gap between the fire, encouraging our people to follow behind us. But as I stand in the hallway, it becomes very clear the fire is going out, growing weaker the quicker Lucas's life fades away.

The fire is being sucked away with Lucas.

The explosions fire, Lucas's personal creation, it is all fading away.

I take deep breaths as smoke escapes my lungs. I hold my hand over my chest as I cough, hoping to ease the sharp pain in my ribs. My eyes close and open, again and again as I cough out the bad air. When my eyes open for the ninth time, I look over at the boys.

Ben. Kane. Myles. Elijah—

Elijah.

"Where is Elijah?" I snap back into reality.

"I lost him…" Myles sighs.

"What do you mean you lost him?" I narrow my eyes.

Myles pushes his lips together before running a hand across his blood and dust covered face. "He saw Lucas on the ground and… he left" Myles explains with a sad tone.

"We don't need him" Kane shrugs.

"This way" Ben continues to pull people from the dinner hall, helping them into the hallway if hurt or weak. "One foot at a time, please" he urges.

My worry is Elijah.

I cannot lose him too.

One after the other, our people fight their way through the fire as Ben helps them. They are covered in anything and everything. Food, blood, sweat, tears. The white clothes we were all forced to wear, now painted red with the blood of their friends and the blood of their enemies.

A little girl, around the age of seven or eight, appears through the fire. She looks far too young to be caught up in this. Far too young to be fighting for her life. Her tiny body is shaking. She is a lot smaller than the rest of us, making her easier to hide and slip through the cracks of the fight.

"Careful" Ben pushes me out of the way as a knife comes barrelling towards me.

My body hits a wall, bashing my head against the harsh steel surround us. I groan from the sudden shock of the fall, the impact of my body colliding with the wall sending a sharp pain to my lip and ear. Blood slips down my lip, the clear taste of warm metal spilling onto my tongue.

One gunshot.

Four gunshots.

Seven gunshots.

The hallway is filled with soldiers, fighting one another, and charging towards us. Hunter's soldiers consume most of the hallway, defending each other against the enemy soldiers trying to reach us.

A handful of bodies scatter along the hallway. Some of the bodies belong to our own people. Teenagers who tried to escape the fighting, who tried to run away from the smoke and fire. It is clear they didn't know what was coming for them when they entered the hallway.

"Stick together" I exclaim to the boys as I steady myself.

Their eyes glance my way, their heads nodding as they understand the importance of my words.

Kane spreads his hands out beside him, the claws getting sharper and pointier as he does. They shine in the smoky light, revealing how much strength is held within his fingers. The frown plastering across his lips gives the deadly look in his eyes a real scare to anyone who catches a glimpse.

As my head spins around to get an understanding of my surroundings, a soldiers takes their opportunity to attack.

A soldier, who must have snuck up on me from behind, grabs onto my arm. He spins me around and around until my back hits his chest and my head is met with the tip of a gun. A large handgun. The soldier's hold on my body is anything but gentle and the wicked laugh is only cruel. He grips me tight enough to keep me in my place.

With or without the gun to my head, I can't move.

"Get them out" I shout to Ben and Kane, gesturing with my eyes to the lost teenagers. "Get them all out"

"Move, and she gets it" the soldier warns them.

Nobody knows what to do. Nobody knows if they should stay or go. If they move, he shoots me. If they stay, he may still shoot

259

me. It is a risk they should not take. They should leave while they still can. Get out of here before it is too late.

As I part my lips to tell them to run, a flash of bright blue light blinds my eyes. Electricity flies across the hallway, hitting the soldier in the forehead, electrocuting the man on the spot. A blue spark hits my arm where the man's hand once held, causing me to jump slightly.

Ow.

Myles takes a step forward. "Keep your eyes open. We can't risk losing you too" he offers me a small smile.

I try to smile back at him, but I fail.

My hand rises and my gun fires, hitting the soldier behind Myles. The soldier falls and Myles jumps. He turns his head to look down at the man, holding one of his hands on the back of his head.

"That was close" he nervously lets out a breath.

"Keep moving" Ben encourages some of the teenagers to continue to follow him. They all defend one another as they stick close to the wall on the right.

Ben holds his hands out in front of him, making small gestures with his fingers to move soldiers or guns or bodies out of their way as they swiftly move through the hallway. He is keeping everyone safe as Kane cuts through soldiers with his claws like they are his next meal.

I kick one of the soldiers in the leg, causing the man to stumble forward.

Myles places a force field around the pair of us. We are the only two left out of the Soltrix group. Lucas is dead. Elijah has disappeared. Hunter and West are nowhere to be seen. It is just me and Myles now.

"Use your ability to stop the guns" he yells. I immediately shake my head. "Why not? It could help—"

"I'm not doing it. It won't help" I protest against his idea.

His eyes look from my eyes to the gun in my hands. "You are going to run out of bullets eventually" he warns me.

I want him to be wrong. My eyes look down at the heavy gun in my hands. Two bullets. That is all I have left. I lost the packet of bullets I picked up earlier. I need to search a soldiers body for more. If I can't get more bullets, I have only my fists for protection.

Using my ability may bring the place down quicker.

It isn't worth it.

"Take these" Elijah opens his hand out in front of me revealing a hand full of bullets.

Elijah.

He is standing in the centre of Myles' small force field. I watch Myles look over his shoulder, spotting Elijah. He parts his lips to talk, but I beat him to it.

I push Elijah's chest, causing him to stumble back a little as he closes his fist. "You left us!" I shout at him with anger fuelling me. "You left us here to die"

He stares at my eyes.

"We needed you, Elijah" I continue. "How could you just abandon us like that!"

He stares at my lips.

"You haven't changed. You are the same asshole who found enjoyment in ruining people's lives" I let out all my built-up anger at once.

He only stares at me.

I become quiet and stare back at him.

"Are you done?" he calmly asks.

I push his chest one more time.

"Now I'm done" I say before turning around to search for a soldier's body. I need to focus on finding more bullets for the gun. I can't get distracted by Elijah.

Elijah grips the top of my arm, spinning me back around to face him. "I told you to take these" he repeats, holding out the bullets in the palm of his hand. He waits and waits for me to take them from him, but I don't. I cross my arms and look up into his light blue eyes.

"I don't want anything from you" I spit.

"This is not the time to argue" Myles states. "He left, but he is here now. We are going to work together. I refuse to die because you two couldn't look past your differences for more than five minutes"

He is right.

261

But I don't want to admit it. I glance at Elijah and then sigh, knowing Myles will wait for one of us to agree.

"Fine" I mumble.

"Sure" Elijah mutters.

I watch as soldiers fire all sorts of weapons our way. Each bullet, arrow, fist penetrates the force field, but nothing gets through. Myles has gotten stronger. He can hold the force field for longer. It is lucky. Without the training Hunter has put us all through, this could be a very different situation.

"I can only teleport us to the floor above" Elijah offers us a get away from the hallway. I don't look at him as he talks, letting him continue to talk to my back. If we weren't fighting to get out of here right now, I probably would have shot him myself. "That is as far as my ability allows me to go. Something is stopping me from getting any further"

Something is stopping him using his ability past the next floor. That grabs my attention. "What?" I spin around and narrow my eyes onto his tensed features. I want him to repeat what he just said. "What do you mean?"

"Watch out!" Myles shouts.

The force field breaks, quickly shattering. Millions and trillions of bright blue sparks fall through the air around us, disappearing as soon as they hit the ground.

I duck down, shielding myself from any and every soldier who may try to attack. A fist makes contact with my back, and the side of my stomach. I hold back a gasp that threatens to reveal the pain the person just caused me. I turn around and fire the gun, one last time. One last bullet.

The soldier goes down.

Right beside Myles.

I look from the soldier to Myles. Myles is down. Two of the bullets from the force field have hit him. One bullet in the leg, and one in the heart. Blood spills over his clothes, and the bullets leave holes as a reminder of where they struck.

"MYLES" I scream, loud and clear.

My legs give up on me before I have a chance to stay standing. I fall, tears streaming down my face quicker than ever before. Strong arms wrap around me, pulling me close to their

262

body as I cry. The person keeps me standing, holding me up from the floor.

Myles is dead.

"No no no no" I crumble into pieces as I stare down at Myles lifeless body. Unmoving. Unbreathing. "He can't be... he can't die—"

"We can't stay here, Grace" Elijah talks behind me. "Shit, shit— Grace, we need to keep going" the sound of Elijah's voice sounds like a blurred background noise.

"Myles is gone—"

Elijah's arms tighten around me as my body continues to try and crumble to the floor.

He sighs. "Do you want to end up like him?" Elijah gives me the honest truth.

I shut my eyes as bullets continue to fly our way. Nobody stops for death. The soldiers don't care if I am hurting or if I am grieving. They won't stop until we are dead. Until we are all dead. That is there job.

My tears dry up on my face from the heat still lingering from the fires flames.

Everything feels like a blur.

A hazed blur.

The kind of blur that consumes a person with only their thoughts and emotions.

The ground begins to shake beneath my feet. I feel the walls being pulled in like a magnet, fighting against gravity. The world starts to turn faster. I can't feel my body anymore, only the pain of all those who have been lost to the war, to the long fighting, the attacks.

I feel everything for everyone.

My entire body aches for the pain to leave.

The ceiling begins to cave in, crushing one or two people at the furthest end of the hallway behind us. Lights fall from the ceiling as they detach, hanging low as electric sparks fly out into the air. The sparks are big and loud.

Water surrounds the sparks, creating an electric waves, killing anyone who gets caught inside. The wave swiftly washes through the hallway, stopping before me. It extinguishing the last of Lucas's fire.

263

The large wave of water evaporates behind me, leaving only the soldiers ahead of me.

Nothing is going to stop me.

Nothing can stop me.

The soldiers begin to run the other way, trying to escape the walls crushing them. Everything in sight falls apart. As I feel Elijah's arms leave my body, the world crumbles. He was the only thing holding me together, and now that is gone. Instead, the feeling is replaced with something darker. Something with vengeance and greed.

I want them all to suffer the same way Lucas suffered, the same way Myles suffered. I want the soldiers to feel every ounce of grief and loss I am feeling.

"That's enough" Elijah clears his throat.

I don't stop.

I can't stop.

My lips tremble until a scream breaks free.

Elijah rushes in front of me, coming into my blurred eye-line as his hands find my shoulders. He shakes my body back and forth. "Grace, that's enough" he repeats, trying to pull me from my trance.

Reality flashes across my eyes, snapping me out of my emotions. The truth behind my actions come to light as I look around at the damage I have caused. I lost control. I lost the ability to think straight.

But the soldiers got what was coming to them.

I look around until all I see is Elijah's light blue eyes staring at me. Even after all the chaos of my rage, he is still only looking at me. His entire attention is still on me. One, two, three, four minutes pass before either of us say a word to one another.

It feels like the world stops.

Everything stops.

"Little red, we need to catch up with the others" Elijah encourages me to keep moving.

I ignore the nickname.

We can't stay down here. It is too dangerous. The place sounds like it is about to collapse, crushing anything trapped inside. Leaving is the only hope we have of escaping the brutal end to the PPW.

264

"Hold onto my hand—"

"No" I refuse.

Elijah looks at me with a bored expression. "I am your ride out of here" he reminds me.

I glance from his face to his hand. I feel stupid. "Yeah… get us out of here" I say, looking away from him as heat rises to my cheeks. Embarrassed is too weak of a word to describe how I am feeling.

His hand grabs onto mine, holding it tightly as he closes his eyes. He pictures the place he wants to go, the floor above us, and then in the short blink of an eye, we've vanished from the smoky hallway.

CHAPTER FOURTY-THREE
GRACE

The stairs are covered.

Blood, bodies, guns, bullet cases. Even the smoke has managed to travel into the stairwell, seeping through the open doors and broken walls. The only living things left in this place are the soldiers.

My head spins in every direction.

It only just clicks that we are in the stairwell. We were meant to appear on the second or third floor, not in the stairwell. "This is the stairwell" I state the obvious.

"I know" he agrees.

"I thought we were going up to the next floor" I say, letting go of his hand and taking a step back.

Before he can get the explanation out, someone clears their throat from above us. My head tilts slightly, allowing my eyes to lift up the stairwell. "Grace, Elijah" Ben says our names out loud, grabbing the attention of Elijah. His head lifts up the same as mine, looking into the eyes of Ben.

"We were wondering when you would show up" Kane smiles down at us from the stairs banister. "Where's Myles..."

The realisation hits Kane as soon as the question leaves his lips. His head lowers, followed by Ben's. They both know the truth behind our silent response.

"You made it out" I sigh with relief, trying to bring light back to the stairwell.

A weight lifts off their shoulders as they stare down at us, hope filling the eyes of those surrounding along the railing of the spiralling stairs. I am so happy to see them all alive.

They don't look too badly hurt. I notice Kane still has the fabric wrapped around the top of his bicep. Blood is spilled on their shirts, but it doesn't appear to be theirs.

"Is everyone okay?" I ask, trying to look past them for any sign of the other surviving teenagers.

"Some died on the way into the stairwell, but all in all, most got out" Kane gives us the honest answer.

Ben looks away from us, staring at the wall beside him as a flicker of pain flashing across his features. I can imagine how he is feeling. We have all lost someone today. People we love and care for have died in front of us, murdered in cold blood by the people we have feared all our lives.

I understand exactly how he feels.

"What now?" I ask Elijah.

The sound of the soldiers fighting one another comes from the door. It gets louder and louder by the second. There is more shouts and groans and gunshots. The sound is getting closer and closer with every heartbeat.

"Keep moving" Elijah orders.

"Where?" Ben questions his demand, turning his head to look down at us again. "We don't know where we are going"

They are clueless. "They have never been this far out of the hallway" I whisper, reminding Elijah what kind of a life they have been living. They have no idea what is waiting for them above ground. They don't know there is a whole other way of life waiting for them at the top of this stairwell.

He takes a moment before nodding his head and looking back up to the others. "Go up. There will be a door which will lead to the outside—"

"The outside!" someone gasps, and then another and another until there is more chaos. "We can't go outside"

Elijah sighs to himself. "Trust me. Going up there, it is the only way you will survive" he assures them.

They look confused.

They all do.

"You should lead them out" I suggest to him, knowing they won't go up the stairs without some sort of guidance or instructions to do so. "I'll stay behind you"

His eyes look from my right eye to my left. He can't seem to decide what the best option could be. He nearly protests the idea of leading these people up to the outside, but then I see a slight change in his features. He takes a deep breath with a hand running through his silky hair.

Elijah doesn't disagree.

We begin to make our way up the stairs until we are side by side with the others. Ben looks at Kane while Kane looks at

Elijah. We know what we need to do. We need to stop wasting time and get out. The soldiers can't stay down there forever.

"Stay behind me" Elijah directs his words at me.

"I will" I look up at him.

His eyes linger on mine, not wanting to look away. He is worried. I can see it inside him. No one knows what is waiting for us above ground. Todo Poderoso could be standing by the door himself, waiting for us to walk into his trap. It is a risk we just have to take.

Elijah turns his back to me.

Slowly, very slowly, we walk. We take steps in pairs up the stairs. Two by two, we follow Elijah up the stairwell.

Everyone has so many questions, I can hear them mutter to each other their exact thoughts about being this far away from the hallway. They think we are crazy. Some think we are trying to kill them. They don't trust us. They don't believe we are trying to help them escape.

I wouldn't trust us either.

"Stay close" Elijah shouts to everyone below him.

And we listen.

Seeing Elijah take charge, being in control, it is something I never thought I would like to see.

But God, I find it attractive.

On the last floor, where Hunter's office is located, the door has been left open. Wide open. Maybe in a rush, maybe just forgotten. But the door has been left open.

I stare intensely at the door, hoping to catch a glimpse of Hunter or West. I have no idea where they are. I wonder if Hunter is still in the building. And West, where is West? They could be far away by now, trying to get away from the building before it collapses.

For a moment, I think I see movement in the doorway. I think I see West, but my mind likes to play tricks on me. It could be a lie. The movement could easily be an enemy soldier, waiting to attack us from the shadows.

The movement makes me wonder if Hunter and West are fighting against the soldiers, still trapped on this floor while the rest of us escape. They could be dead. Maybe they didn't stand a chance against the soldiers.

Either way, I need to know for sure.

If they are alive, we can't leave them behind.

Without thinking, I make a sharp decision to separate from the group, running towards the open door. Nobody will notice I am gone until they are outside.

My hands grab hold of the doorframe as my eyes search the open area for Hunter or West.

Bodies upon bodies. Soldiers upon soldiers. I stare death in the face and hold a steady gaze on the blood of its victims. I refuse to move. I refuse to breathe. I refuse to do anything but find Hunter and West. They need to be here somewhere. They need to have survived the attack. I won't believe anything until I see them for myself.

As I continue to stare, looking and looking through the mass of bodies to find the boys, I see movement again. A head lifts, looking at me. "Grace" West calls out my name.

He is sitting in the centre of the open area, surrounded by the men he once fought alongside. He holds a thick black gun in his hands, worried to let it go. His hands could look purple from the tightness of his grip. He is shaking, his body slowly giving up on him. I have never seen him so fragile and scared.

"West!" I almost scream, running as fast as I can to reach him. He stands from the floor, his arms outstretching ready for my embrace. My arms quickly wrap around his neck as my body crashes into his.

"You're alive" I breathe out.

He breathes in my scent, his nose pressing against my hair as my cheek leans against his shoulder. A sad smile forms onto my face, feeling West's arms snaking around my body as he pulls me as close to him as humanly possible. There isn't a word to describe how happy I am he is still alive, how his heart is still beating.

"Hunter went looking for you" he rushes to the point.

His statement makes me pull back from the hug. A hand rises as I almost cover my mouth. "What" I don't hold back the horror I see flash before me at the thought of Hunter going back into the fight to find me. "He would die down there"

West's gaze falls. "He wouldn't listen to me" he shakes his head. "I told him you would get out. He didn't listen"

Hunter cannot be that stupid.

"Where is he now?" I question.

"Not sure. We got ambushed, he had to fight his way to the stairs and by the time I turned around to stop him, he told me to wait here encase you showed up" West reveals.

"We need to go after him—"

"No" he disagrees. "I am going to wait here like I told him I would"

"I will go then—"

"No" he repeats.

"Why not?" I huff.

"I will try to reach him with this" he says, holding up a walkie-talkie from his pocket.

I look at the object in his hand, my eyes narrowing on the speaker. The soldiers used to carry walkie-talkies in the back pockets of their trousers. I can only vaguely remember seeing one or two soldiers use the object in front of me throughout my life.

I never understood what they were used for.

West holds down on one of the buttons. "Soldier eight nine three, radio check" he talks into the walkie-talkie.

There is a long silence between us. Neither of us take our eyes off the black boxy object in his hands. Standing around while we wait for someone to answer is quickly making me realise how much time we are giving the left-over enemy soldiers to burst through the door and shoot us in the back.

"Does anyone copy?" West continues to talk into the walkie-talkie.

Another long silence.

We are both becoming impatient.

"DOES ANYONE COPY" West shouts this time.

Another long silence.

No matter how long we seem to wait, nothing is said on the other side of the line. The silence is growing painful. This doesn't appear to be working, we need to go down and find him. I don't want to lose anyone else.

"Loud... and clear... over" a voice finally talks back through the walkie-talkie.

I don't recognise the voice.

The muscles in West's body relax slightly as relief washes over him. "What's your twenty?" he questions the person on the other side of the walkie-talkie. "Over"

The long pauses between sentences is creating anxiety in my stomach. The knots are tying down the butterflies in my chest, stopping my lungs from catching a moment to let out a breath or two.

"Trapped" they cough out the word. "The ceiling— fall in the— the stairwell" the male voice breaks, either due to their coughing or the walkie-talkie itself. "Over"

"Is Hunter with you, soldier?" West gets straight to the point, ignoring the part about the ceiling and gripping onto the walkie-talkie like his life depended on it. "Over"

"Negative, over" the soldier sounds out of breath.

Whatever all that meant, it doesn't seem good.

West lowers the walkie-talkie, his head tilting down with his hand. He looks defeated. Disappointed. This was not part of their plan. None of this was part of the plan.

"I am going to get him—"

"That won't be necessary" Carter's voice startles me.

My body spins around as West's head lifts from looking at the ground. Carter is standing opposite us, a girl to his right and a man to his left. Neither of them are smiling, but Carter has a smug smile tugging at his lips.

His blonde hair has been slicked back with gel, bringing out the green in his eyes. His sharp jaw looks tensed as he stares between me and West. He is trying to give off a smug and confident expression, but the tension in his jaw and arm muscles tells a different story.

"Hunter is a big boy; he can handle himself" he smirks as he steps forward.

"What are you doing here? What is all this?" I ask, hinting to the attack. "Why are you—"

"Shh now, you can ask all the questions you want later. At this point in time, I need you to stay quiet" he cuts me off, his steps gradually slowing down the smaller the gap between us grows. "West, do yourself a favour, and move to the side" Carter is acting as if he is in control over the situation.

He can't be serious.

"You must be joking" West's bored tone only makes the smirk on Carter's lips spread further across his face.

The response seems to entertain Carter.

One swish of Carter's right hand, and West is flying backwards, his body colliding with the closest wall. The sound of air escaping West's mouth from the sudden impact makes me turn my head. I look from West to Carter.

"Why are you doing this?" I ask.

"Todo Poderoso wanted to gather everyone up while also taking down the PPW. It was a win win in his eyes" he shrugs, taking another step forward.

"People have died—"

"That is the point, Grace" he chuckles. "People die all the time. Nobody lives forever"

He is sick.

Sick and twisted.

"This is wrong" I say to myself.

"Maybe" he chuckles.

"Carter… you don't have to do this; you can put a stop to all of this" I encourage him.

"You and I both know; this is much bigger. I cannot put a stop to this. We are too far past that" he shakes his head. "There is no point fighting the inevitable"

"Please—"

Carter sighs as his eyes linger behind me. He is looking directly over my shoulder. I assume he is fixated on West, his attention remaining on him in an attempt to keep him pushed up against the wall.

"Zara" Carter says another girls name. I narrow my eyes onto him, confused by the name. It is familiar. His eyes land on mine once again. "This may hurt a little" he warns me.

And then I feel it.

A needle pierces my neck, pinching my skin.

The person behind me is quick, stabbing me with the needle and injecting the liquid inside of me before I get the chance to jump away from them.

I snap away from the person, causing their hands to fall from my neck. My hand wraps around the needle still attached to my

272

neck and I rip it out from my skin. I carelessly drop the needle on the floor.

My head slowly turns to the side, coming face to face with the girl Carter had disappeared into thin air with from my room in Soltrix. Her thick black hair, dark brown eyes, and fair skin. She has an ability. She can teleport like Elijah.

"Grace" West tries to call out my name. "Run"

Black dots slowly cloud my vision.

The room doesn't spin, I don't feel sick. Whatever they injected into me, it is only making me tired.

It reminds me of the first time I stepped foot in Soltrix, and Hunter had his men inject the boys. It was as soon as we stepped off the plane. The boys laid on the ground unconscious while I was escorted off the plan.

I grow tired.

Is this the same stuff Hunter has used that day?

Sleep takes over and before I can part my lips to say anything, my body gives up on me. My eyes slowly close as I feel my body fall to the ground, the darkness completely taking over.

CHAPTER FORTY-FOUR
HUNTER

I am almost out of bullets.

My soldiers are down. Some are dead, some have run, and some are dying in front of me.

Grace is nowhere to be found.

She must have escaped, or...

She must have escaped; it is the only explanation for why I can't find her. There is no other option. She made it out with the others, she stayed with the boys and got to the top of the main stairwell alive.

Maybe West found her. He could have found her making her way out of here. But he hasn't made an effort to call me on the radio. I haven't heard from him.

I use one of the dead soldiers' bodies as a shield as one of the enemy soldiers tries to shoot my way.

There isn't many of us left. Maybe ten or thirty. There was no way of surviving this attack, not with the low number of soldiers we already had due to the last attack on Soltrix.

My father knew that.

"What's your twenty? Over" a radio goes off not far from me, almost as if it was beside me.

The voice sounds familiar to me.

West.

"Trapped. The ceiling is about to fall in the stairwell" a soldier coughs out from below me. "Over..."

I turn my head around as I try to avoid the bullets flying my way. I need to find where the sound if coming from. Which soldier is talking?

Nobody seems to be moving, how could they be—

I see him.

"Is Hunter with you, soldier? Over" the radio cuts in and out, making it hard to understand the exact words.

Throwing the body at the soldier firing at me, I shoot the man in the heart. He drops over the balustrade, falling down the stairwell as his heart stops beating.

274

As his body collides with the ground, I make a run for the soldier slumped up against the wall. I need to get to the soldier before he says anything.

I am sprinting.

The man is trapped under six bodies. One of his arms are broken and his right foot has been amputated. Sadly, he has no chance of getting out of here, but I think he knows already.

"Negative, over" the soldier beats me to it.

Shit.

I climb my way through the bodies, managing to slip past the enemy soldiers shooting at my soldiers. I rush back down the stairs, trying to reach the soldier. When I get down to the soldier, I begin pushing the soldier bodies off him.

"No. Give me the radio" I demand.

The soldier looks up at me. "Sir—"

"Give me the radio" I repeat.

He struggles but manages to hand over the walkie-talkie to me. It is almost completely broken. I don't know how he managed to get it to work.

I hold down on the button, holding the speaker against my lips. "Do you copy?" I rush my words.

Nothing comes through.

"It's Hunter. Do you copy?" I announce myself this time.

Why won't they answer?

This stupid radio refuses to cooperate with me. Whoever was trying to find me has just lost their chance.

"Help me" the man pleads with me. "Please" I look from the radio to his eyes. "I have a family. A daughter. She is going to grow up without her father" He is playing with my guilt in hopes that I will save him for his family.

It won't work.

He will only slow me down.

I can't risk it.

"Please" he is looking at me like I am his only hope.

I take a deep breath and continue pulling the bodies off of the man. "Okay, I will help you" I cave, knowing I cannot leave him here to die if I have a chance to save him.

The bodies are light, allowing me to move them to the side without much of a problem. I don't take my time; I need to get a move on. Wasting time is not in the card for me. While I am down here, Grace and the others could be faced with a bigger issue up there.

As the man becomes free of the bodies, he uses his good arm to push his body off the stair.

The soldier tries his best to help me lift him up. I hurl him over my shoulder, using everything in me to carry his body weight. He has muscles, he has heavy guns on the waist band of his trousers.

This is not going to be easy.

"If there is someone behind me, you are to use your gun to shoot them. Understood?" I give him instructions as I begin marching my way back up the stairs.

As I climb back through, there are soldiers in all sorts of directions. The lights are out, the walls are crumbling. There is a thin line between us and the top of the stairs. Soldiers are doing their best to block our way out.

But I have too much at stake to let them win.

They shoot at us, trying their best to hit us where it hurts the most.

I take a gun from one of the bodies and use it to shoot down anyone in my way. The man on my shoulder uses his gun a couple of times, firing at anyone who may be behind us. We are both fighting at our best.

Neither of us want to end up like the rest of my army.

One foot after the other, I march up another set of stairs.

I use all my bullets. I don't look back; I don't bother to turn my head. The stairwell is recklessly destroyed, ruined by our enemies, and filled with my men.

The bodies of women, children, and soldiers will forever haunt me.

"You holding up?" I ask the soldier on my shoulder.

"Yes, sir. Just about" he answers.

I push my way up another set of stairs.

"What's your name, soldier?" I ask another question.

"Hank, Sir" he coughs.

Hank fires another shot. He takes deep breaths and tries his best to stay still due to the sudden jerky movement from my body trying to walk causing him slight pain.

Step after step.

Floor after floor.

We make our way up the stairwell until the only thing left is the door to the outside. I hold my gun up high as I push the door open and walk outside, revealing myself to the harsh sunlight.

Everyone's eyes turn to look my way.

The teenagers cheer, happiness filling their eyes at the sheer sight of my being. They think it's over. They think they are safe again.

They are wrong.

"Hunter" West takes me by surprise.

He frowns at the sight of me.

My eyes are too busy scanning the crowd of people to pay much attention to West.

Grace is nowhere to be seen.

I can't see her.

She should be here.

"Can you put me down?" Hank asks, wanting to get off my shoulder.

I walk down the steps, walking over to a small group of my soldiers who managed to get out before they were killed. I drop Hank on the sand, gently, and lift my head up to meet the other soldiers. "Look after him" I order them. They nod their heads and kneels down to his level.

Slowly, I turn around.

"You" I begin walking over to Elijah and West. Neither of them take their eyes off me. "Where is she? Where is Grace?" I question with worry and anger and sadness.

Why isn't she standing beside them?

She is not dead.

"Carter has her" West answers me. My worst fear comes to life. "She was going to come and find you. I was trying to stop her but she was determined to go after you, and then Carter showed up"

"Don't lie to me" I say in denial.

If the enemy has Grace, my city, my people, are in great trouble. We don't stand a chance of winning without her. She is my strongest weapon against Todo Poderoso. She was my safety blanket in the war.

277

Without her, there is no hope.

No chance of beating my enemies.

"I tried to stop him. He has abilities, I didn't stand a chance against him" he continues.

I drop my gun into the hot sand, my body tensing at the thought of what they will do to her.

Carter has taken Grace to the Supreme, to my father.

Even worse…

Carter has taken Grace to Todo Poderoso.

CHAPTER FORTY-FIVE
GRACE

The darkness has become my best friend.

It comforts and scares me all at the same time. The dark creates a weird sort of safety from the real world, hiding all the true horrors waiting for me in the light. But it also stops me from seeing anything ahead of me, preventing me from being able to defend myself against any danger heading my way.

Gradually, I can feel the liquid they injected into my body wearing off, or I think it is.

A part of me can feel my fingers, and I can move my toes a little. It is getting easier to life my head, but not easy enough for me to sit up. I continue to move my toes until my feet start to work again.

But I can't see anything.

My eyes are open, wide open, but all I can manage to see is the darkness. My eyelashes flutter as I try to push through the dark cloud covering my vision.

Whoever ordered Carter to bring me here, they are making sure I have no idea where I am.

They are attempting to drive me insane.

A cold gust of wind causes my body to shake. I carefully lift my head off the floor, trying my best to turn my head to look around the darkness. I still see nothing. The floor feels like icicles have taken home in the room, spreading ice across the space around it.

I have never experienced cold like this.

My mind goes to a frozen lake, the water turned to ice as the fish freeze from the cold forced upon them. I imagine the floor feels the same. It is colder than anything I know. I feel like the frozen fish in my mind, I picture them feeling the same as how I do right now.

I need to get off this floor.

My head lowers again, the left side of my face colliding with the harsh floor. It is cold on my cheek. My body is laying down face first on the ground. Pain and grief consume me. I can't build the strength to turn my body over.

Soltrix is surrounded by desert. RoseShire is a place surrounded by desert. There is nothing but little villages for miles. The PPW is... was also surrounded by only desert. There was nothing around it.

A cold gust was rare, unless it was night.

This place feels different.

It is too cold to be in the centre of a desert.

"Welcome back to us, Ms Silver" someone talks in the darkness.

A dim light turns on.

Everything around me quickly reveals itself.

A boxlike enclosure with bars wrapping around the dark rusted prison surrounds me. I carefully lift my body off the cold floor as my weak arms shake from the applied pressure. I try my best to look around, my eyes scanning over the rusted bars imprisoning me.

The cage protects the Supreme from me.

"Ms Silver, may I introduce you to Alvaro Villar" the Supreme gestures to the man beside him.

The man is tall, but not as tall as the Supreme, and he looks a little younger. Maybe in his mid-forties. I am not good with guessing age. But the many wrinkles on his forehead tell a story not even he could tell.

His light brown hair and eyes match his tanned skin. Dark hairs are growing along the top of his lips and under his chin, growing all the way from his sideburns.

As much as I would like to learn as much as possible from the Supreme to help Hunter track down his father... I need to focus on getting out of this cage. I don't know how long I have been unconscious for, and I don't know where in the world I could be.

Hunter and West are probably worried.

I wonder what Elijah is thinking.

"Where am I?" I ask them.

My eyes are frantically scanning every inch of the space around me. There is nothing around that could tell me where I am being held. This place is nothing but bars and darkness. I have no hope of finding a way out from my current position, I am going to have to get out of this cage.

I make a move to stand up, only to be pulled back to the ground by heavy metal chains.

A thick chain is firmly attached to my left ankle, another attached to my right wrist. The chains are built into the wall behind me, and they are made short enough to keep me close to the ground.

They are not taking any chances with me.

The Supreme clears his throat, grabbing my attention as Alvaro clasps his hands together in front of his crouch. "Todo Poderoso wants to meet you" the Supreme doesn't look thrilled by the words that come from Alvaro.

My eyes widen.

Todo Poderoso wants to meet me...

"Why would he want to do that?" I ask, already having an idea in my head.

It is the same idea I have had for a while.

After all the conversations between Carter and I, the one sentence would always stick inside my head. He mentioned countless times before about Todo Poderoso being my father, and himself being my brother. Carter told me over and over again the same thing, but I refused to believe it—

I still refuse to believe it.

But that is the only explanation I can come up with to explain why someone as powerful as Todo Poderoso would want to meet someone like me.

Maybe he was telling the truth.

Or maybe he was lying about everything.

I can never tell when it comes to Carter, he is someone I will never trust.

Anything and everything he says may be a lie.

"Put this on" the Supreme throws a silk black dress into the cage, the small piece of smooth fabric passing through the bars and landing on the floor in front of me. "Villar will be back in five minutes to take you to the dining room"

I stare at the silky black fabric in front of me.

281

They want me to dress up for Todo Poderoso, clean myself up slightly and go along with this dinner. They are expecting me to simply accept their demands.

My eyes wander away from the dress.

"We will leave the light on for you in order to allow you to see what you are doing" Alvaro informs me, a thick accent lacing his words.

How considerate of them.

The Supreme doesn't waste time standing around. He makes his way back into the darkness, disappearing before I can get the chance to watch him leave.

Neither of them stand around for too long.

I don't get the chance to ask a lot. My scratchy throat and tired mind won't allow me to say anything important, nothing that helps me.

Alvaro nods his head and begins walking in the same direction as the Supreme.

Neither of them look back.

I am left alone, cold and confused.

CHAPTER FORTY-SIX
GRACE

My wrist has a red mark wrapping around the skin from the chain. I trace one of my fingers along the mark as my feet move one in front of the other.

The mark hurts.

Seeing the outline of the chain, I think back to the bracelet that once clung to my wrist.

Once the chains were removed from my skin, I was able to adjust the silk dress to fit me correctly. I don't think Alvaro or the Supreme had thought about how hard it was going to be for me to try and get a dress on over the chains and in the dim lighting.

Or maybe they wanted me to struggle.

When I was released from the cage, I was handed a pair of black stiletto heels.

They were easy to slip on but now they are hugging to my feet, causing my skin to rub. The heels are making me feel ten times taller than the usual heels would. I feel like I can see over most people, my eyes looking over their heads.

I miss wearing trainers.

I would wear trainers all day every day if I could.

As we walk, we don't talk to one another. No words have been exchanged between me and Alvaro since we left the long hall of cages. He hasn't even looked at me.

He doesn't seem like much of a talker.

We had to walk through the long hall of cages, some of the cages were empty, and some had people trapped inside. I heard them crying out for help, but instead, I looked the other way and kept walking.

It was awful.

I feel terrible for them all, that is a life no longer worth living if they are trapped in those cages forever.

There was a small staircase at the end of the dark hall of cages, the staircase leading up to the hallway we are currently walking through.

This whole place gives me chills.

I am taking every opportunity I can to look around. I look for exits and entrances, security cameras and guards, soldiers and workers. I carefully lay out a map of every door I pass inside my mind. The hallway is now a constant record on loop in my head.

This place, this building, is a labyrinth.

As I try my best to see the outside world through any way possible, I wait for a window to pass me by.

There is very little natural light. Most of the hallways have zero windows. Nothing that reveals where I am. I wonder why? Why wouldn't they have windows? To hide from the outside. To emphasise the point of this place being a prison to many.

Only Todo Poderoso knows.

I keep adjusting the bottom of the dress. It is long, with a slit down the right, starting at my knee and finishing at the bottom of the dress.

The cold is hugging my body, gripping me tight enough to turn my flesh blue. A continuous breeze runs through the long hallway, claiming its place among us. The bitter cold lets everyone know it is here to stay. No matter how much heating they pump through the countless rooms. No matter how many candles they light.

The cold isn't going anywhere.

"Why does Todo Poderoso want to meet me?" I try to spark a conversation out of Alvaro.

As much as I want nothing to do with these people, my curiosity is taking control over everything. I want the silence to break, letting me ask all the questions I have before coming face to face with a man who may kill me by the end of dinner.

He is too unpredictable to me.

The sheer thought of his power over the world scares me to my core.

Nerves are getting the best of me.

There is no telling what I am about to walk into. All the possible scenarios are playing out in my mind, scaring me little by little until the nerves take over my hands and they begin to shake at my sides.

We walk and walk until it seems like we have been walking forever.

"Do you know where we are? What part of the world—"

"FrostMount" he cuts me off, his patience wearing thin.

My eyes widen.

I am in utter disbelief. "We are on his grounds…" I mutter under my breath. This is where Todo Poderoso lives. I am in the city fighting to take down the world. The same city we have been trying to destroy.

I shouldn't be here.

We stop walking in front of two large brown doors. The doors are tall and wooden with golden specs running down the doorframe. They look expensive. At the centre of the doors, there is a pattern carved into the wood. Flowers? Vines? No. I look closer to see they are thorns. Rose thorns. The kind of thorns that hurt to touch.

Alvaro pushes the doors open, both doors swinging to the sides, revealing me to whoever or whatever is waiting for me inside the room.

There are candles everywhere, lit by a match to make the room look brighter than it is. Windows are covered by the long fabrics pulled down from the ceiling. A long dining table stands in the centre of the room, chairs placed underneath.

"Grace" Carter smiles over to me from the furthest end of the long dining table.

Carter is the only person in the room.

He looks clean, a lot neater than he did when we were in Soltrix together. He has cut his hair shorter, allowing the sides a chance to grow new strands. His clothes are brand new, like they have never been worn before.

The only similarity are his eyes.

They haven't changed at all.

I can't decide whether him being in here alone makes me more relaxed or more on-edge.

While I take a deep breath, Alvaro takes the opportunity to nudge me into the large dining room. The sudden movement is a shock to me, but I don't stumble, I walk with my back straight and my head held high. The shoes make it difficult, but I push through the best I can. Carter stands up from his chair, watching me walk through the room.

"You are a traitor" I practically spit at him.

"I've been called worse" he simply smiles.

Carter makes his way over to me as I walk further into the room.

One breath.

Two breaths.

I punch him in the centre of his face.

The punch is fast and hard. All my anger is thrown into my fist. Carter deserves more than a blow to the face. He deserves to be trapped in a cage for eternity.

Like the others I just passed.

He stumbles back until he is leaning against the end of the long dinner table as his hand holds his nose. "What the hell" he groans.

I hope it hurts for a while.

"Was that necessary?" a new voice speaks up.

My entire body freezes at the sound of someone else. I don't turn around. I don't want to turn around. I am too afraid of the truth behind me to turn around and face it.

I don't know what to do.

"Grace, turn around" the voice demands.

The voice has an accent. Something I don't think I have ever heard before. I can't tell where the accent is from. He could be from anywhere. It is the same accent as Alvaro but Carter doesn't seem to have it. From the way they talk, I find the words sound like a melody compared to if they were said by someone else.

I hesitate, but eventually, very slowly, I turn around to face the man I fear the most.

"Isn't that better" the man smiles. "Now, I can have a good look at you"

His bright green eyes stare at me, looking from my face to my hands. I am completely frozen. He runs a hand through his thick black hair, his smile trying to stay up as his lips twitch back to a thin line.

The atmosphere is cold, yet his skin is slightly tanned, like he has been walking in the desert for the last week.

Carter and Todo Poderoso have a similar bone structure, the same jaw and the sharp collars, the emerald green eyes and the slight gap between their lips when they smile. They style their hair in the same way, but Carter is blonde, very blonde. Todo Poderoso has jet black hair.

"Todo Poderoso…" I hold back the gasp getting caught in my throat.

"It is nice to finally meet you, Grace Silver" he steps closer to me.

A thick lump is lodged between my throat, stopping me from breathing.

The breath gets caught in my chest, building a tight knot in my lungs. I curl my hands into fists and hold my arms by my sides. "Don't come any closer" I warn him, forcing the words out of my mouth.

I hope I scare him.

But I am nothing compared to him.

Todo Poderoso moves his arms slightly, almost like he is about to uncross his arms from his chest. A long black coat runs down his body, stopping just before his kneecaps. His suit is white and black, matching the coat. I find my eyes running down to take a short glimpse at his pointed toe shoes, the shiny black leather material has been used on his shoes and on his belt to match one another.

Like a matching set.

"You do not need to fear me" he uncrosses his arms.

"I don't" I lie.

When I first heard about Todo Poderoso, I pictured a tall, scary man with a frown of steel. I did not picture him to be all smiley and… nice. He is calm and collected, put together by the Gods themselves. The way he portrays himself, it is as if he could never be a part of something so vicious as a war.

He shakes his head with… disappointment?

"Please, have a seat" he gestures to the chair opposite where Carter was once seated. "I want to talk to you"

My confusion only grows stronger. He wants to talk to me, but there is nothing I could offer him. "What information could you want out of me?" I ask, wanting him to get straight to the point.

Todo smiles to himself. "Just sit down" he demands this time, trying to keep the smile on his lips.

He can smile as much as he wants, I know what kind of a person he really is. He is a killer, a monster, a psychotic power-hungry man that will stop at nothing to get what he wants. He would ruin the world if it meant he got a taste of something he could only dream about.

I don't protest against his demand.

I need to pick my battles.

Moving across the room, I quickly find myself standing in front of the chair Todo Poderoso had previously gestured towards. I pull the chair out and sit down, watching Carter as he does the same.

Carter resumes his position opposite me.

Nobody speaks. Silence grows between us all as Todo Poderoso sits down at the head of the table. There are three, maybe four chairs between us and Todo.

One of the two clear their throat. I look from one to the other until I see Todo shift slightly in his seat. "Tell me," Todo Poderoso starts, looking from Carter's eyes to mine. "What do you think you know about me?" his question throws me off.

"I know you like power" I answer, honestly. "You will burn the world down until you get exactly what you want"

"Yes" he nods his head. "Anything else?" he is smiling, with wrinkles pulling at his eyes.

Anything else?

I don't understand what he is trying to get out of me.

"What game are you trying to play?" I question him with narrow eyes.

His eyes switch, the thrill is turning into patience. He has to keep himself from attempting to speed up the conversation to suit himself. "I want to know your views on me. I want to know what you have heard. I want to know it all" he explains.

"I know nothing good" I shut down.

I don't want to give him anything.

"How about you tell me about yourself" he changes his question.

Again, I have no idea what to say. "What do you want to know?" I don't know how to respond to his questions. It is like an interview I never prepared for.

I know nothing.

I say nothing.

"Tell me something that is not part of your file" he leans forward a little, resting his clasped hands on the table in front of him, his wrists resting on the edge.

"I…" I take a moment to think about my response. "I saw RoseShire. I was able to live among people, real people, for a couple months" I think of something more recent, something Hunter would not have included in my file.

"Yes" he nods his head again. "I know all about it"

My eyes shoot open.

"How do you know about—"

"A woman, she goes by the name Asha March" he speaks a name I hoped to forget. "She was sending me information on your stay with her"

"She slept with Myles…" I mutter under my breath.

"Your welcome for that, by the way" Carter says through a smirk and chuckle.

My head turns to face Carter. "What?" I purse my lips together. "I am not thanking you"

"It was my idea for her to… you know. He was bad for you, you deserved better than that fool. He was quick to jump into bed with Asha too, must have been desperate" Carter informs me proudly.

I want to climb over this table and strangle him.

"You sonofa—"

"Language" Todo Poderoso cuts me off before I can get the last part out.

I become silent.

Seven, eight, nine…

Eleven people walk into the room, some men and some female, carrying plates of food and two carrying glasses filled with some sort of liquid. They place everything onto the table with forced smiles. They are putting it on for Todo Poderoso, in fear of him.

Once they all leave the room empty handed, I feel as if this is my chance to ask my questions.

Todo Poderoso and Carter begin digging into their food while I lean forward on the table, preparing myself for the next set of words to leave my lips. "Why are you so interested in me? Isn't it Hunter you should be kidnapping for information? He knows far more than I ever will" I push my question.

"Hunter has nothing to offer me. Right now, I want to spend time with my children" I flinch at the last word.

I deny everything in my head.

"No" I shake my head. "I am not—" I cut myself off.

"Carter should have told you—"

"Carter is a liar" I snap.

Carter's eyebrows raise, almost touching the top of his forehead. "Hey, I am right here" he puts his hands up beside his head as his mouth gapes.

He looks offended.

Why does he look offended?

"Any word from his mouth is a blatant lie" I continue, trying to ignore Carter's words.

"For this, he was telling the truth. I am your father, and he is your brother... and Sarah was your mother. She was always too close. I had Sarah killed for it. She was getting far too close to you for my liking" Todo Poderoso explains.

At the mention of Sarah, I want to break down and cry.

He had Sarah killed.

For years, I believed I was the reason she was murdered. I believed she was murdered for speaking to me without a soldier present, sitting with me while I was supposed to be asleep. I thought for so long that I was the reason, the cause of her sad, cruel death.

I blamed myself.

And all this time, it was Todo Poderoso.

"You really are a monster" I hold back my tears.

If Sarah was my mother, and Todo claims to be my father, I would assume that means they... dated?

But I cannot picture the two of them together.

Sarah was so kind, so warm and gentle. Todo Poderoso is all the opposite. He is nothing like her. There is no universe that will ever exist where the two of them end up happy together.

He doesn't back down from my statement. "I do what is necessary" he tries to justify himself.

My hand rises, covering my lips as I close my eyes. I can see the image of Sarah's lifeless body on the ground. The blood pouring over the floor, creating a pool beside my feet. The smell of death flooding the small space. I can still see the two large men carrying her body away from me, dragging her away from me like she was nothing.

After all this time, Sarah was my mother.

"She stepped out of line" he continues, trying to comfort my mind in his own strange way.

She was always a mother figure to me, in my mind, but I never imagined she was truly my mother. Although, thinking on it now, It makes sense why she treated me differently compared to the rest of the people in the PPW.

"Grace—"

He can see the panic and horror and anger and sadness and realisation in my eyes. I feel everything, all at once, like a shock wave to the heart.

"No" I frantically shake my head. I refuse to listen to any more of his explanations, at least for today. "Do not say my name. Do not try to talk to me. I don't want to hear anything from you"

I am emotional.

I am no longer thinking straight.

I am consumed by everything evil.

"Sit down" Todo Poderoso orders me, and it is only then I realise I am standing up.

My head lowers to glance down at the table, and then I look over to Todo Poderoso. "I want to leave" I cry out, feeling the weight of the world grow heavier on my shoulders.

"That is not an option for you, so sit down, and eat your dinner" he sounds demanding.

I don't sit down.

Sitting down would show my weakness, it would reveal exactly how much power he has over me. I won't give him the satisfaction of winning. My feet stay firmly planted on the floor as my arms cross over one another.

"You are going to stay here, with us… with me, and learn our ways. You will grow to like FrostMount, and with time, you will learn that we are not the enemies. You will help us finish what we started. With time, you'll see that family is more important than anything" he keeps his eyes on me, watching for my reaction to each claim he makes.

He is truly delusional.

I will never stay here and help him.

"My *family* are back in Soltrix" I stand my ground, making the word family emphasised.

Hunter, West, Elijah…

They are my family.

No matter how badly Todo Poderoso wants me to be part of his world, I will never join him. Blood may be binding, but it will never be a match to my true family.

His facial features alter.

The mask of smiles and patience falls and replaces itself with a frown of frustration and disappointment. I see his true self for a moment. A moment too long. I saw through him, only for a split second, but I saw him. I know this façade of smiles and kindness is an act.

"You will learn, one way or another" Todo Poderoso stands up from his chair, copying my position. "You will stand beside me as I take down Soltrix, and any other city that wishes to create an enemy out of me"

No.

"Never" I protest. "I will never willingly stand by your side while I watch you turn the world upside down"

Never.

Not in my lifetime at least.

Todo looks from me to Carter. He holds back all the anger shaking inside his curled-up fists. "Take her to her new room, make sure to lock the door before you head to my office" he make his demand clear to Carter.

As quick as the meal began, it ends.

"I am not done—"

"I am sorry, but I am done" he interrupts me. "We will have to talk again when you are calm and settled. Until you can listen to me, I will keep you locked up in your room"

My room?

I don't have a room here. I have a cage. A cage that could fit ten men. An empty cage, filled with thin cold air and heavy chains to weigh me down. There is nothing about the cage that gives me relief when the words locked up escapes his mouth.

The last thing I want to do is return to the cage.

But I don't want to stay in this room either, not with Todo or Carter staring me down.

Carter rises from his chair, moving around the table until he is standing beside me. My lips remain sealed together. I don't turn to look his way, nor do I look at Todo Poderoso. My eyes stare at the full plate of food placed in front of me on the table. Neither of them are worth a glance.

Moving my legs, I walk out from in front of the chair and follow beside Carter as he leads me towards the large doors. I hear Todo Poderoso clear his throat, and then his loud, sharp words erupt in the air around us. He raises his voice, making sure his words reach me.

Loud and clear.

As if he is standing beside me.

"Whether you like it or not, Grace, you are my daughter, and it is about time I started acting like a father" his words are as clear as day.

I wish I didn't hear him.

CHAPTER FORTY-SEVEN
GRACE

We don't speak.

I don't want to talk to him.

I don't want to talk to anyone.

All I can think about right now is leaving. I can only think about going back to Soltrix… going home.

After all the fighting, I want to see Hunter, and West, and… I want to see Elijah. I want to make sure Ben and Kane made it out alive. I need to know everyone is safe.

But I know Myles and Lucas are… they're gone. They were taken from me in the fighting, the attack against the PPW.

They were killed because of Todo Poderoso.

Because of the war.

It was his fault all those people were killed, murdered for nothing but his power-hungry fantasy.

After I blacked out, I only remember waking up here. I have no idea what happened to everyone. They could all have been killed for all I know.

There are too many what ifs and maybes.

I want a definite.

"How do you like the place?" Carter breaks my thoughts, glancing over to me in the corner of his eye as he tries to start a casual conversation.

This feels strange.

We are walking through the middle of the hallway, our bodies as far apart as possible. The last thing I want to do is be close to him. He is a traitor, a liar, a killer, and worst…

He is my brother.

My mind plays over an image of my hands around his throat, strangling him to death.

"I don't want to talk" I make my feelings clear.

"The silence is boring" he frowns.

"Okay. Then go find someone to talk to" I hold back the urge to roll my eyes.

There is nothing I would like more than to watch him try to struggle his way out of death right now. He deserves more than a punch to the face. A bullet or two may work better than my fists or words.

"Tell me, how did it feel to lose?" he smirks to himself.

My blood boils at his words. "We haven't lost" I deny his accusation.

His smirk grows. "Where are your friends right now?" he asks me the question dreading me the most.

Not a single idea of what happened to my friends has crossed my mind. I don't want to think the worst. I want them to be back in Soltrix trying to concoct a plan to get me back. I have hope for them. In my mind, they are together, safe and out of danger.

But hope has always been a very dangerous thing.

"Tell me" I demand.

"They are all dead" he chuckles. "Every last one of them was killed off. Thankfully, it didn't take too long. One or two bombs and a couple bullets, they were out like a light" he is laughing at their deaths.

My entire body stops.

I don't move, I don't breathe, I don't blink.

I can't.

"What's wrong? Has the real world finally caught up to you?" Carter continues to hold his smug smirk as he steps into my eye-line.

Using little energy, I throw Carter up against the closest wall in the hallway. My hand stays in the air in front of me, the palm of my hand facing Carter. He has no way to move. I make sure to force as much pressure on his body as I can, making sure he can't move to get out of my hold over him.

He stops laughing.

He struggles to breathe.

"No. Don't stop laughing. Explain to me exactly what you are finding so funny" I say, calmly.

My tone is steady, as if holding a grown ass guy up against a wall was light work to me. Which it is. I am not strained, or tired, or weak. For once, I feel powerful. I feel as though I can stand here for hours and watch the strength in his eyes turn to dust.

Carter deserves to suffer for everything he has done.

295

I stare up at him, anger fuelling my surge of power.

There is only red. The colour of blood covers my eyes like a blanket of false truths. A mask of deception. My judgment becomes tampered, causing me to act upon emotion rather than rationality.

"You've gotten stronger" he coughs through a chuckle.

His cocky smile only angers me more. He isn't struggling or fighting against me. "I want an apology" I demand.

I want him to admit and confess to everything he has done wrong. The lying, the murder. I want him to completely break down from the guilt of all he has done. He chose to work with Todo Poderoso, he chose to betray us all by fighting against us in the attacks. I will never forgive him for the deaths he has caused.

"You'll be waiting a while" he retorts.

I push him further into the wall, but nothing cracks. The wall doesn't break under the pressure. It stands as a shield, preventing him from escaping my grasp. He has nowhere to run and hide. He is stuck between me and the wall.

"Alright, I get what— what your trying to do. Let… relax would you" he chokes out as the pressure builds on his chest.

His face turns red, his cheeks a sort of rose colour. I want to see him turn purple and blue and…

I let him fall.

His body drops to the ground, a loud thump bouncing from wall to wall until a soldier dressed in red hears it. In the corner of my eye, I see the soldier making his way over to us with his hand holding the end of a gun.

He is ready to shoot if I try anything.

The soldier is by my side in a blink.

"Ms Silver" the soldier acknowledges me. His hand grabs onto the top of my arm. "I will escort you to your room"

"Thank you, Neil" Carter coughs out, attempting to stand up as his arm snakes around his stomach.

I hope the fall hurt.

"This isn't over, Carter" I warn him.

My threat is far from empty.

The soldier begins dragging me away from Carter, his hand gripping my skin enough to stop the blood flow. I don't struggle against the soldier. I need to save my energy for when I try to break out of this place.

Once I have a plan, I need all my energy. If I need to fight my way out of here, I will need to be prepared for anything. I have no idea what is held within this building, this place, there could be anything waiting for me at the exit.

Until I know exactly how and where to escape, I will bide my time here.

"Grace" Carter stops the soldier and I in our tracks. I turn my head to face him, locking eyes with his green orbs as he picks himself up off the floor. He brushes himself off and holds his lips in a thin straight line, masking the obvious smirk that tries to break free. "Just so you know, I'm not sorry. I'm not sorry for any of it" he doesn't break eye-contact.

And then the soldier drags me away.

CHAPTER FORTY-EIGHT
GRACE

The soldier throws me into a dark room.

My body collides with the ground, allowing the soldier time to close and lock the door.

Nothing but quiet darkness. These people seem to like taking away my ability to see. I have been left in the dark twice while being here, but this time, I have not been chained to the wall. I just need to find a light switch.

Slowly, I pick myself up off the floor, trying my best to feel around for some sort of light switch.

My hand runs along any and every wall I come across, eventually feeling a switch close to the locked door. I flick the switch down, turning on the lights.

The room is revealed to me.

The room is a bedroom, much like the one I would sleep in while being in Soltrix, but it is smaller. A lot smaller. The same as Elijah and Myles' room.

At least it is not a cage.

Anything is better than a cage.

It consists of a bed, desk, wardrobe, and a wall of glass. I notice a book placed on the desk with a black inked pen beside it. Someone must have left it in here for me. I walk over to the small book, flicking through the pages to find nothing.

It is an empty notebook.

While looking at the notebook, I notice a bookshelf.

The shelf is filled with books. All shapes and sizes. The last time I saw this amount of books, I was snooping through the Supremes' room. He owned books I had never heard of. Some of the thick books looked like they were old, while some of the thinner books seemed to be brand-new.

How did they know I liked books?

My eyes scan over the titles written down the spine of some of the books. Romeo and Juliet. Wuthering Heights. Jane Eyre. Pride and Prejudice. There are so many books to look at and read, but I want to continue looking around.

I will have to come back to the books.

White pained walls, black covered bedding. The room is a contrast of dark and light, soft and harsh. It is the difference between night and day.

The windows are large enough to let in natural light but directed away from the moons rays.

The moonlight can't touch me.

It could fight and claw its way inside the room, but it will never reach me. The mountains, the tall buildings, it is all preventing the moonlight from reaching over. Instead, they block out everything, isolating the city from the bright light of the world itself.

Slowly, I make my way across the room.

On the left side of the room is where the large square windows stand. The windows reveal FrostMount to me. One foot after the other. My steps grow bigger and bigger until I find myself pressing a hand against the glass.

Snow covers the city like a blanket. The blue sky has been shielded by an army of dark grey clouds. They hold all the built-up snow that hasn't yet been able to fall, sitting and waiting for its chance to break free.

The city is surrounded by tall mountains. At the centre of the city, there are even taller skyscrapers. Looking down, the people of FrostMount look like ants, small and slow, walking among the concrete jungle. The people of FrostMount don't stand a chance of leaving. They wouldn't get past the icy pathway over to the mountains. Even the tall mountains and large infrastructure make sure to trap everyone inside the city.

Todo Poderoso has chosen the perfect prison.

Watching from the glass windows, the whole city stands before me, staring at me through the glass.

A wintery paradise.

A snow palace built for a king.

Snowflakes dance past the window, falling gradually towards the padded ground. The flakes land on a bed of snow, a crash mat of soft protection created by itself.

The desert is a distant memory in a place like this.

If it was up to me, I would burn this place to the ground and watch as Todo Poderoso suffered, tortured by his own creation. I would make him watch his city become undone right in front of his eyes.

One way or another, I will make that a reality.

It will take time, which means I may have to stay here longer than I would like to.

But the weak girl who cried herself to sleep is long gone, she grew up, learnt the way of the world. The true world. She saw the truth and changed.

Now, there is only me.

I will gain knowledge of everything around here. I will learn FrostMount's strengths and its weaknesses. By the time I am ready to strike against Todo Poderoso, I will have all the knowledge I need to take him down for good.

I will do it all under his nose, right in front of him.

He won't know what hit him.

Todo Poderoso has no idea what is coming for him.

Milton Keynes UK
Ingram Content Group UK Ltd.
UKHW021055200324
439767UK00015B/488